PRAISE FOR HATING THE BEST MAN

"Wowza. What a fabulous and riveting take on a second chance romance."

JULIETTE CROSS, AUTHOR, *BRIGHT LIKE WILDFIRE*

"Sizzling and delightful, this second chance romance is perfect for fans of Christina Lauren."

ALICE DUKE, AUTHOR, *STUPID PRIZES*

"All the stars! Hating the Best Man had me in a choke-hold from the first page."

NJ GRAY, AUTHOR, *THE PIECE THAT FITS*

"A glorious novel overflowing with heat, heart, and humor!"

LYNDSEY GALLAGHER, AUTHOR, *LOVE AND OTHER MUSHY STUFF*

I0593313

Hating THE Best Man

JENNY FYFE   NATALIE MURRAY

JN
ROMANCE

Publisher's Note: This is a work of fiction. Names, characters, places, and incidents are a product of the author's imagination. Locales and public names are sometimes used for atmospheric purposes. Any resemblances to actual people, living or dead, or to businesses, companies, events, institutions, or locales is completely coincidental.

Hating the Best Man / Jenny Fyfe & Natalie Murray- 1st ed.

Paperback ISBN: 978-0-6458830-0-8

Cover design by Ink and Laurel

CONTENT WARNING

For some readers, content warnings can hinder the reading experience as they often reveal key plot points in the story. Because of this, we have included a we address that will bring you to the content warning for this book. Should you wish to know what potential triggers this story may contain, follow the link below.

(Please Note: This warning contains spoilers)

www.jennyhickman.com/htbmcontentwarning

FOR EVERYONE WHO HELPED US DECIDE BETWEEN
JERK AND JACK

CHAPTER ONE

RUBY

PRETEND YOU LOVE IT.

That's all I can think as I stare at the neon green shot glass in my fiancé's hand, irritation chasing the sweat dripping down my spine.

"It's a shot glass," Blake says, stating the obvious and twisting the tiny cup around so I can see the etching on the front.

> *Blake & Ruby tied the knot.*
> *Time for a shot!*

"I ordered a truckload of these from our supplier. Got them at an awesome discount too." The blond hair peeking from beneath his baseball cap is dangerously close to the mullet stage.

Part of me dies inside when he forces the cheap plastic cup into my hand. "It looks great," I say through a tight smile. "But I thought we decided on personalized jams as wedding favors."

"No offense, babe, but jams are kinda lame. These are going to be epic. Trust me."

He's gone through all the trouble of ordering these things

and spent heaven knows how much on them. Is there really a point in arguing now? Although I can't help wincing, I say, "I trust you."

He squeezes my shoulder, giving me an exuberant shake. "Can you believe it? One more week."

"I know." As excited as I am that we're finally getting married, I can't wait until the wedding is over, and we're sitting on a beach in Mexico, sipping ice-cold pina coladas instead of sweating in this alley behind my family's store.

"You want these now, or will I drop the boxes at your place?" Blake asks.

"My place is fine. Thanks."

He presses a soft kiss to my lips. "Later, babe."

"I'll see you tonight."

He jogs to the back entrance of his parents' restaurant two doors down. Swiping my hand across my brow, I open our delivery door and step into the stream of cold air pumping through the ancient air conditioner.

My sister Jade falls through the storeroom door at the same time, one hand clutching her chest, her golden ponytail swinging at her back. "It's settled. I'm destined to end up with a man in uniform."

I stuff the tacky shot glass on a shelf between a box of hand sanitizer and a sleeve of Styrofoam cups. Thankfully, she's too busy peering back into the store to notice. "Don't let Officer Williams hear you say that." The handsome deputy has been hounding Jade for a date for as long as I can remember.

Her nose wrinkles like I suggested boiled cat for dinner. "Gross. I'm not going out with Nate the Nark."

Jade grabs my hand, pulling me from the storage room into the main store, where an '80s hair-band ballad crackles through the tinny speakers. She stops behind the register and not-so-subtly points to a guy wearing a pair of fitted black dress pants and a short-sleeved white shirt with gold stripes displayed across his broad shoulders. "Husband material. Aisle three."

Tall. Short, dark hair that sits up messily on top. So far, so good. Although it's impossible to tell how attractive he is without seeing his face, I have to admit that the view from the back is pretty darn good.

Not that it matters to me. Even if he turns around and has the face of an angel, my heart has belonged to the same man for ten years.

"Well?" Jade pokes me in the ribs. "What do you think? Will we make beautiful babies together?"

"Jury's still out. I didn't get a good look."

"Unacceptable." Jade grabs a box from under the counter and shoves it into my arms. "Restock, aisle four. Stat." She nudges between my shoulder blades, and I find my feet carrying me past the shelves of pine-scented floor cleaner and mops that blend into a wall of personal products.

Our small convenience store doesn't stock as wide a variety as the chain store twenty minutes down the road, but our dad insists on carrying a few staples so that customers don't need to trek across county lines for a bottle of shampoo or a bar of soap.

I continue around the fragrant laundry detergent, past stacks of toilet paper and paper towels, reaching aisle three. The uniformed man's still there, whistling along to the radio.

Suddenly, I'm seventeen again, climbing into the back of a crimson-red hatchback with Blake. A car belonging to none other than Flynn Hudson.

Captain of the soccer team. Co-valedictorian. Homecoming King. Prom King. The most popular guy in school.

And a certified asshole.

I retreat at the exact moment he rounds the corner and accidentally rams into me. The box in my hands goes flying, spilling its contents all over the linoleum floor.

"Shit. I'm so sorry," he bursts out. "I didn't see you there."

If there was any doubt before, there certainly isn't now that I hear the all-too-familiar deep voice that used to terrify and excite me in equal measure.

"It's fine," I rush, kneeling to collect the box, wishing there was some way to hide my face. But with my hair pulled back into a ponytail, there's no hope of concealing my ferocious blush, or my identity, unless I bury my head in the box of—

No. Please, please, no.

Tell me I'm not on my knees in front of this jerk, cleaning up a bunch of freaking condoms.

"Here, let me help, Ruby," Flynn offers tightly, kneeling beside me.

Of course, he recognizes me. I've barely changed in the eight years since we graduated. Yeah, my black hair is a lot longer because apparently the mermaid style is a requirement for brides, but that's about it. I still have the same blue eyes. The same freckled nose. The same skin that sees way too much sun.

What the hell is he even doing here? Blake said he wasn't coming in until Saturday. I can't bring myself to look at his face as he scoops up a handful of small, square boxes, leaning in way too close when he drops them into the open box.

If only there was some way that I could pretend he's not here—the way I used to all those years ago, when I'd sweep right past him in the halls or ignore him completely at our shared lunch table while he gave me weird stares like there was food all over my face.

Unfortunately, that's not possible now that I'm so close to him I can see my reflection in the aviator sunglasses hanging from the pocket of his tailored white shirt.

I lift my stiffened chin to look straight at him and bat my lashes to seem unphased.

The dark eyes I expected to see blink back, framed by the

same dark lashes that made all the girls swoon. He's flushed all over. Odd. And he still smells like spearmint gum. The stubble on his sharp jaw—that's new. The smirk on his lips, however, is not.

Why couldn't he have turned into a slob or gone bald or something? Instead, he seems fitter than he did all those years ago—if that's even possible. Because as much as I pretended not to notice him, Flynn Hudson has always been pretty hard to miss.

I sit back on my heels, desperate to put some distance between us. "Oh, Flynn. Sorry. Didn't recognize you." I definitely missed my calling as an actress.

His eyes narrow, and he drops all but one box. "I see you're still as clumsy as ever, Quinn."

"I see you're still an ass, Hotshot."

A second of shock springs to his eyes. But then the corners of Flynn's lips purse into a tight smile that's as fake as my grandma's dentures.

The only times I've ever been anything close to clumsy have been because of him. Like the time he let the door swing shut behind him when I was only a few steps back, making me drop my books everywhere. Or when he jumped in front of me in the lunchroom, sending my tray of tacos spilling all over myself. I'd ruined my favorite T-shirt. I'd wasted tacos. *Tacos.*

I can't believe I used to have a crush on this guy way back when. That was before he slipped a packet of condoms into my shopping basket when I was with my mom. Instead of getting to go to the baseball game with my friends that night, I had to endure yet another in-depth talk with my parents about sex. All because of *him.*

Flynn flips over the box of condoms as if reading the description, and for some reason, my brain thinks it's a good idea for me to say, "Don't worry. We stock the itty-bitty ones on the top shelf."

He huffs a laugh and tosses the packet back into the larger box. Then he stands, grabs a box of XXL magnum condoms from the shelf, smirks, and strolls away whistling along to Paul Simon's "You Can Call Me Al."

Really, Ruby?

You haven't seen the guy in eight years and the first thing you do is make a dick joke?

You're twenty-six years old. Get it together.

I scoop up the mess as quickly as I can before beelining for my sister to break it to her that she's been swooning over the devil himself. Then I find the traitor laughing with him over the register. She rings up his bottle of water, a pack of spearmint gum, and those freaking condoms with a smile on her face.

"Looks like someone's having fun tonight," Jade says, dropping his purchases into a paper bag with *Quinn Brothers* stamped on the front.

Flynn leans his hip against the counter, retrieving the gum and withdrawing a stick. "Not much else to do in this town, is there?"

Is he seriously suggesting that the only thing worth doing in Still Springs is an epic session of screwing? Our little town, nestled in the hills of western Maryland, is a slice of heaven. That's probably why Satan Hudson hates it.

Flynn pays in cash, thanks my sister, and turns pointedly away from me, striding out the door without so much as a glance in my direction. Jade makes no attempt to hide the fact that she's totally checking out his ass until the bell over the door chimes.

I snap my fingers in her face. Eventually, she tears her gaze from the door. The glance she gives me would've been innocent if she wasn't standing in a puddle of her own drool. "Do you have any idea who that was?" I ask.

She sighs. "A god among men?"

"No, Jade. That was Flynn Hudson."

Her mouth falls open, and her head swings back toward the exit. "Hold on. That was...oh. No. No, no, no. He got—" She blows out a breath, fluttering the bits of blonde hair escaping her ponytail. "You know what? I'm not gonna say it." She reaches under the counter for the spoon she'd used in her yogurt at lunch, holding it out to me. "Quick. Gouge my eyes out. It's the least I deserve for making moon eyes over Hotshot Hudson."

"It's fine."

"Yeah, he is."

"I said *it's* fine. *It is* fine."

She blinks up at me, batting her thick, dark lashes. "Can I blame my sad, single state and the lack of eligible men in town?"

"Only this once. But if it happens again, you're dead to me."

My sister gives my shoulder a reassuring squeeze. "Maybe you can avoid him until the wedding?"

We both know there is no hope of me avoiding Flynn.

Not when he's my fiancé's best man.

CHAPTER TWO

FLYNN

The closer I get to The Rocking Horse bar on the corner of Main and Summercrest, the more air leaves my lungs. I brush my clammy fingers up and down my jeans and suck in a breath as I push through the glass door.

I'd hoped for a stealthy arrival so that I could scope out who's here, giving my heart a second to prepare. But apparently, it's a small-town prerequisite to have an adorable little bell hanging off every door that jangles so loudly you can hear it from space.

It's just past midday, and the dingy bar overdecorated with sports memorabilia is mostly empty, save for a huddle of familiar faces that glance up at me from a high table beside the jukebox.

"Flynn high-flying fucking Hudson!" cries a raspy voice I'd know anywhere.

Blake Harrington, my best friend since little league, charges toward me like a linebacker, slamming his firm arms around me while I assess the beaming faces that remain.

She's not here. Good. Maybe she's not coming. Perhaps this little pre-wedding get-together is for the groom's side of the fence. Yesterday, I'd taken the opposite approach and stopped at the Quinn Brothers store to grab a few supplies I could have picked up for half the price at the superstore on the way into town. The idea was that I'd run into Ruby and find that the tightness that used to invade my stomach every time I was around her had long since passed. But it hadn't exactly played out that way.

I lift my chin in an awkward greeting at a few members of Blake's family who I haven't seen in years, before Blake slides into my view, his gray eyes dancing.

"How the hell are you, Top Gun?" He claps a hand on my shoulder.

"You know I don't fly for the military, right?" I try to match the happiness in his smile, but being back here is throwing me for a loop. I haven't been around these people... walked down the street outside...properly seen her face...in eight years.

"Whatever, Maverick," he says with a laugh.

Before I can even say hi to anyone else, he's dragging me over to the bar and ordering me a beer.

I watch the glasses fill and fill, not quite sure drinking is a good idea since I haven't had lunch. Blake shoves a foamy glass into my hand and clinks it against his. "It's been too long between drinks, bro."

I smile at him. "You've had other things on your mind. Congrats again. You finally got down on one knee for Ruby Quinn." My voice slips on the name.

"Ruby *Harrington*, this time next week," he corrects with a proud-as-hell smirk. I guess one thing hasn't changed in this old-school town: getting married is still a badge of honor. I lock the same forced smile on my face that I gave Ruby at the store yesterday.

Beneath the golden glow of the overhanging lights, Blake's a little fuller in the face than when I last saw him and undeniably happy. There's also something off about him that I can't put my finger on.

My brows furrow as my gaze trails over his features. "What's different about you?"

"Dude, I haven't seen you in half a year. There's a lot that's different about me."

I figure it out when he gives me another shit-eating grin.

What the fuck has he done to his teeth? Has he swallowed a whole packet of mint Chiclets? Stuffed his mouth full of snow? Holy shit, they're whiter than white.

"Come over and see the 'rents," he says happily, and we pace over to where Blake's mom stands to wrap me in a tight hug that makes me wish I had more time to spend with my parents this week. But I'm officially on best man duties, starting with today.

I shake his dad's hand, pat his uncle on the shoulder, then fight off a strange swell of nerves to say hi to Frank and Carl from school. I figure out pretty quickly that they both want to talk more about my life as a corporate pilot than their jobs as municipal workers.

"You basically fly famous people around all day, right?" Blake says with an unsure grin, like he still has no idea what I actually do for a living.

"That pretty much covers it," I admit through a light laugh. "Five years of training and junior jobs to become a glorified taxi driver for the rich and famous."

"Who've you flown?" Carl asks.

I rattle off the names of a few movie stars and recording artists that make Carl and Frank smile broadly at each other while Blake sits back and watches me with a strange expression on his face.

"Tell me what *you've* been up to since your last visit," I say to him, giving his knee a light pat. "What's this business merger you mentioned in your texts?"

Before he can answer, the megaphone bell from the door jingles behind my shoulder.

I twist around, and my stomach bottoms out as Ruby Quinn steps into the room, trailed by her younger sister, Jade.

Spinning away from them, my heart thumps stupidly in my chest as I suck on my beer, keeping my back pointed at Ruby while she greets Blake's family with a voice sweet enough to farm into syrup.

Ruby Adeline Quinn.

High school dream girl. Professional heart thief. Leading star of my most well-worn, hottest fantasy.

And the future wife of my best friend.

A future that has suddenly drawn a little too close for my nerves.

From the day Blake called me while I was on a job in Saint Lucia, announcing he was getting married and asking me to come back to town and be his best man, I've been preparing for this moment. But when I ran into Ruby at the store yesterday, I realized that nothing could have prepared me for what it would be like to tangle my eyes with hers again.

I truly thought I was over her.

I convinced myself I was okay with Blake marrying her. Possibly even happy for them both.

Until she fucking bent over right in front of me to pick up those ridiculous condoms, with her face all flustered and beautiful, and her body like a torment to my own, and I'd been sucker-punched in the heart all over again. Like all the years she'd sauntered through our high school hallways under Blake's arm, not even awarding me a single glance.

I school my features as I pin my gaze to the bar, but on the inside, I'm searching for breath.

"Hi, Flynn." A delicate hand lands on my shoulder, and I force myself to turn around, bracing for impact.

Jade Quinn's clear, green eyes blink at me, an unsure smile painted on her face.

"Hey, Jade." I stand up to hug her, even though she'd been a few grades below mine at school and we hardly ever crossed paths.

"Oh, don't you smell good," she says warmly as she pulls back, and I blush and nod my thanks.

My eyes drift past her shoulder, catching Ruby's stare before she quickly turns away, locked in conversation with Blake's mom.

Look back at me again.

Look at me.

Catching myself in thoughts I don't need to be having, I angle my stool toward Blake's old man and lure him into a conversation about the Premier League. I probably hear only half of what he says, my attention firmly fixed on how Ruby flits around our little group, talking to everyone except me.

Because, despite our little interaction at the store yesterday, pretending like I don't exist is evidently still a Ruby Quinn hallmark.

Like I'm back in high school, a childish urge to capture her attention in any way I can sweeps through me.

I chug another gulp of beer while she settles onto a stool with her back to me, sharing muted giggles with Jade as they nurse glasses of white wine.

Ruby never liked me whistling, even though I won talent comps for it when I was a kid. But, for as long as I've known her, she's physically recoiled every time I've whistled like a songbird —including at the store yesterday.

As I watch her absently run her fingers through her dark waves, imagining what it'd be like to rough that hair up even further, I begin to blow gently through my lips, whistling a perfectly in-tune rendition of "Be My Baby," one of my folks' favorites.

I watch her shoulders freeze, a smile pulling at my lips that I have to force away so that I can finish. I draw out the final note for as long as I can hold it, and the moment I cut to silence, Ruby twists around, her deep-blue eyes meeting mine and setting off a firework in my chest.

"Do you mind not doing that?" she asks in a low voice. "It sounds like you're murdering a cat."

I stare at her. "Hi, Ruby," I say in as smooth a voice as I can manage. "It's nice to see you too. And congratulations on your wedding." I lift what's left of my beer in a cheers gesture.

Her cheeks stain red as she quickly clinks her glass against mine. "I thought we already said hello yesterday."

"Mmm, I don't remember those exact words. I think you were too busy counting those Female Pleasure Sensations condoms. When you weren't calling me an ass." My lips quirk up, but, fuck, it hadn't felt good when she'd said that.

"You called me clumsy," she retorts with a hard frown while Jade's wary eyes dart back and forth between us.

"*Clumsy*?" My hand hits my chest over my white T-shirt. "Holy shit. Are you going to be okay?"

Ruby makes a sound of irritation and turns her back, leaving me to simmer with a clenched jaw while Blake sidles up with more reminiscing that I only half hear.

Fuck, why did I say that?

If today is any indication of how this whole thing is going to play out, I probably shouldn't have come.

Carl plonks another beer in front of me as he passes by, and I thank him before taking a grateful swig.

Maybe Ruby is right. Maybe I am an ass. Until yesterday, I hadn't stepped foot in Still Springs since the summer after graduation. Since then, I've been pretty caught up in my career, which has me on the road for two-thirds of every year, indulging in the all-expenses-paid travel, the comfortable salary, the constant variation. I'm rarely in one city for more than a few days at a time—even where I keep my apartment in DC—which has kept things simple.

And yet, Blake Harrington still hand-selected me as his best man. He's the reason we've stayed close since school, going out of his way to visit me in DC and constantly texting. A pang of regret that I haven't been back here to see him slices through me, and I angle my body to his, ready to put my energy into being everything he needs from me this week. Blake is why I'm here.

"Hey, babe!" Blake reaches over my lap to give Ruby's elbow a tug. "Come and sit with us. It's awesome that Hudson's here, huh?"

My heart hammers into my throat as she follows Blake's order like a Stepford wife and shifts her stool to face us. We're now a little triad, and I'm free to let my gaze linger on her face while she brushes her hands over Blake's blond mop of hair. "Did you skip your haircut?" she asks him, leaning forward to comb her fingers through again. The movement exposes a strip of bronzed thigh beneath her white shorts.

Damn, Ruby. You grew up.

Blake rolls his eyes, nudging her hand away. "I decided that I like it like this. A lot of people at work do too. I get compliments all the time."

When she twists toward me, the line in her brow deepens, and that smooth streak of thigh lengthens.

"So, you're a pilot now," she says while I try not to imagine what her legs would feel like wrapped around my neck. "Was that your uniform I saw you in yesterday?"

"Yes, ma'am," I reply dumbly. But being this close to her

makes my brain malfunction. "I finished a job over in Pittsburgh and came straight here. It worked out well."

"So you didn't wear it to impress everyone when you showed up after all this time?" she asks, lifting her glass to her lips.

Blake breathes an unsure chuckle beside me.

"Sorry, what?" I say, holding Ruby's gaze.

She just stares at me like she has a secret pass right into my soul, but I don't turn away.

"I don't know; with what you bought yesterday, I thought you had some pretty obvious plans."

"What I bought yesterday?"

Her eyes move to Blake, her cheeks pinking. While she's clearly not going to say it aloud, we both know she's talking about the condoms. Which I'd purchased purely to be a smart-ass. I can't believe she's even bringing this up.

"Oh, you mean *this* thing that I can't wait to tear open." I dig inside my pocket, and Ruby's brows flash high. I produce the spearmint gum pack I bought with the condoms, pull out a stick, and slide it between my smirking lips. But as I bite into the gum and watch her exchange a long moment of eye contact with Blake in which I could recite the Complete Works of William Shakespeare, I realize I'm an absolute fucking idiot.

"Well, the pilot uniform is a good trick," she says, pulling me back into the warmth of her attention. "Some girls love a man in uniform."

Some girls.

Does that include the one sitting across from me?

"It's a shame you can't wear it to the wedding because there'll be plenty of single women there," she adds like she's my dating coach.

My lips curl up, but I can't feel anything except for the knife that Ruby just shoved into my heart. "I'm actually seeing some-one," I say, and her eyes flash at mine.

Blake jabs my arm. "You are? You kept that quiet. You should've brought her along, man."

"Ah, it's okay. She's a flight attendant for our company and is in Ibiza this week with one of our hedge fund clients."

It's not a complete lie. Bianca is a flight attendant on our roster, and we've hooked up a couple of times on the road, but I've never quite reached the point where I want to take things further, even though she's made it clear that I'm the only one holding back.

"A girl in every port, right?" Ruby says under her breath, but I catch every word.

"What's that supposed to mean?" I ask, frowning.

"Well, pilots *do* have a reputation." She shrugs like it's a perfectly acceptable explanation for her rude assumption that I'm some kind of player because I wear a pretty uniform with stripes.

"Babe." Blake's hand curls around Ruby's thigh. "You're being a little harsh."

She stares back at him, and something in her face makes me feel like she's not enjoying this interaction any more than I am. "You mean to the guy who was a complete bastard to me in high school?"

Blake's mouth falls open, and she turns away with a jaw that could cut glass.

My mind is racing at a million miles an hour in time with my heart. I shouldn't be surprised that Ruby clearly fucking hates me. I was a total dick to her in school because she always treated me like I wasn't even there, so I had to remind her that I was. That I was worthy of at least a fraction of her attention. It was immature, idiotic behavior that turns my stomach to think about, and I'd never treat anyone that way now, least of all her.

Before I've had a second to think, my hand presses against her bare knee, the soft warmth of her skin sending a rush of sparks through me. "I'm sorry, Quinn. I didn't mean—"

She lurches up off her stool, my hand falling away and colliding with my beer, tipping it over my lap. The blast of cold, wet liquid sends me rocking back, but it's too late. Beer soaks through my jeans, from my crotch down to my thighs, like I've freaking pissed myself.

Ruby claps a hand over her mouth, the flash of shock in her eyes quickly morphing into a snort-laugh. Like I deserve to look stupid. Jade arrives behind her shoulder, her brows flying up.

"Dude, *fuck*." Blake stands up, a little sloppy on his feet after the three beers he's sunk.

The rest of the wedding party gather around us like this is the most exciting event to happen in Still Springs all year, which it quite possibly is. Blake's uncle hands me a wad of napkins.

Carl wraps an arm around Blake, his eyes lit with amusement. "Jeez, Ruby, you trying to get the best man to strip or something? Save it for the bachelorette party."

My eyes snap to hers, and she's staring right at me, a little current of electricity firing between us before she blinks away. My throat closes up as I begin papering tiny napkins all over my thighs like I'm a papier-mache sculpture, focusing my gaze there as my mind runs rampant.

Was that a moment?

Did Ruby and I just have a moment?

Blake barks a laugh beside me, a response to something Frank said to him, dragging me back down to reality.

I'm not allowed to have moments with my best friend's fiancée. Whether they're imagined or not.

When I glance back up at Ruby, I find her eyes already on mine. But then she narrows her gaze and turns her back to me.

CHAPTER THREE

RUBY

I DIG THROUGH MY MAKEUP DRAWER, HUNTING FOR A TUBE of mascara.

The thrill of victory still lingers after last night's get-together at The Rocking Horse. Yeah, spilling the drink on Flynn had been an accident—a *happy* accident—but part of me feels like it was karma. Seeing his face afterward... I smile at myself in the mirror. I'll never forget it. And the white chunks of napkin sticking to his jeans all night were icing on the cake.

I unscrew the lid on the purple tube and swipe the wand over my lashes. Putting on makeup is kinda pointless when I'm bound to sweat it off by noon. But on the days I go without, someone usually ends up commenting on how tired I look.

I am tired. Thanks for noticing.

Who wouldn't be after planning a wedding for two hundred people in under four months while working overtime, cooking for the family twice a week, and visiting my grandma every other weekend?

I toss the mascara back into the drawer and traipse across the hall to my room.

"What time is it?" Blake groans from the bed, the covers still made beneath him, and his plaid shirt tucked into his *Unleash the Kraken* boxers that I've tried to throw away several times. There could've been a tornado last night, and he would've snored right through it.

"Six-thirty."

"Why are you up so early? Come back to bed."

"Can't. I have to swing by the store before visiting Grandma." Ever since her fall three years ago, I've been living in her house and helping take care of her. A few months back, the doctor recommended we move her into a nursing home so she could receive full-time care. I feel guilty for not seeing her more often.

Blake rolls off the bed with another moan, his shirt stained from the final round of shots he bought before last call. He slipped one in my hand, too, like he didn't notice I stopped drinking hours earlier. I poured it into the potted plant next to the jukebox.

Blake collects his jeans and shoes from the floor and sits on the edge of the mattress to pull them on. "Can I get a ride to my truck?"

"If you hurry."

When he kisses me on the way to the bathroom, I try not to gag, but he smells like he rolled on the bar's sticky floor before sleeping in an ashtray. *Party-Blake strikes again.*

In the kitchen, I hop on the step stool to retrieve two travel mugs from an upper cabinet, along with the bottle of painkillers my fiancé will definitely need. He'll probably be dying for water as well, so I grab a bottle from the fridge.

I start the first cup of coffee, closing my eyes and relaxing as the delicious aroma swirls around me. I swap out Blake's mug for the second one, add two packets of sweetener, and give the coffee a quick stir in time for him to emerge from the bathroom. He groans with pleasure when he takes a sip. "Thanks for this. I'm dying."

Is it any wonder? Party-Blake has no limits. Something he announced at the top of his lungs at least ten times last night.

"Remember that you need to pick up everyone's shoes today," I say, giving him a poke in the ribs. Blake has one job this week. Two, if you count showing up for the wedding.

He picks up the bottle of painkillers, the pills inside shaking like a maraca as he struggles with the lid.

I gesture for the pills, push down on the lid, and turn. The thing pops right off. "Please don't forget," I add. "The store closes at five, and Latisha's going on vacation tomorrow."

Blake is the best, but sometimes he doesn't listen, and he has a habit of forgetting things. I've planned everything from the groomsmen's custom navy suits to the four-tiered amaretto wedding cake, the flowers for the centerpieces, and the three-course menu. All he has to do is—

"Shoes," he mumbles, his mouth full of pills and coffee. "I will get the shoes."

"Thank you." I snag my mug, grab my keys off the counter, and slip into my flip-flops. Blake trails behind me, sipping coffee and flicking his thumb across his phone. "You have to use the back door, remember?"

He tears his gaze away from the screen long enough to grimace. *The teeth.* How am I not used to them yet? They give me a migraine. Maybe he should go on an all-coffee diet between now and the wedding so they don't blow out the photos like a camera flash in reverse.

"We're getting married on Saturday," he says. "I think the old bat will forgive the sleepover."

I know it's the twenty-first century, and we're both adults.

But my neighbor, Mrs. Felton, is friends with my grandma, who will definitely have something to say about it if she hears that Blake spent the night, and I already have enough on my plate without having to deal with this.

I shouldn't care what anyone thinks. But I do. We can pretend a little longer that Blake doesn't stay over. "Back door. Please."

"Fine. But I'm not going through the bushes."

"You will if you want a ride."

He stomps through the kitchen and grabs the bottle of water on his way outside, grumbling the entire time. I turn the back door lock behind him then run to the front. Mrs. Felton is loitering on her front porch, watching me like she always does.

By the time I reach my car, beads of sweat are clinging to the back of my neck. Before I can slip inside, I catch a glimpse of golden fur beneath the bushes at the front of the house.

"Come here, Bandit," I call.

The Wilson's golden retriever comes bounding toward me. I catch him by the collar and return him to his family's yard, making sure to close and latch the gate that the Wilson kids always leave ajar.

My car's leather seats scald the backs of my thighs when I finally climb in.

I shove my travel mug into the cupholder and turn the key in the ignition. Techno music blares through the speakers, courtesy of Party-Blake. I flick it off before it wakes everyone within a two-mile radius, twist the dial on the air con to max, and back out of the drive.

I make a left at the intersection and then another left into the alley that runs behind the house. Blake scowls from the gravel road, leaves and grass stuck in his hair and a fresh brown stain down the front of his shirt.

I do my best not to laugh when he climbs inside. "What happened?"

"Fucking bushes," is all he says.

He's still in a mood when I drop him off at his truck.

It's a beautiful morning, so I decide to leave my car at The Rocking Horse and walk to work. A few extra steps won't hurt, and I do have a dress to fit into. By the time I reach the crosswalk, my head is already aching.

I need food before my blood sugar drops too low.

Thankfully, it's only another two blocks before the Quinn Brothers' brick storefront comes into view. The building wedged between Quinn Brothers and Harringtons, Blake's family's restaurant, used to be an ice cream parlor until the owner built a new one closer to the school. By this time next year, it'll be opened up, combining the store and restaurant into an all-in-one location selling everything from Mrs. Harrington's famous baked goods to homemade jams, jellies, and ice cream, and artisanal offerings from local artists to attract more tourists and hikers to Main Street.

I'm proud of what my father's family has built, even if business has been down for months now, and sometimes I can't even collect a paycheck. Hopefully, the merger with the Harringtons will turn things around for us, and then Dad can finally retire this year the way he planned without having to worry about helping keep the store afloat.

I pull out my keys and unlock our store's faded red door. Inside smells like old wooden floors, a touch of musty air that'll clear out once I turn on the AC, and a whole lot of home. Jade and I used to walk to the store every day after school. Mom would work the register while Dad stocked the shelves. We'd do our homework in the office and wait for a dollar for each of us to appear beneath the door, which we usually spent on candy.

Dollars that stopped appearing after Mom got sick.

I tug on the cord to lift the roller blinds, allowing the early-morning sunlight creeping across the sidewalk to brighten the shelves and turquoise walls, falling into the familiar routine.

The front door flies open, making me jump when Jade blows in like a whirlwind, blonde ponytail askew, holding an umbrella up like a baseball bat.

When she sees me, the umbrella drops. "You scared me half to death, Ruby. I thought someone was robbing the place."

"And you were, what? Going to stab them with your umbrella?"

"Obviously."

"If you thought there was a thief, you should've called the police."

She waves me off, continuing to the counter to throw her purse and "weapon" on the other side. "What are you doing here?"

"I need to do payroll." Hopefully, she and I will be able to take a wage this week.

"I told you I'd handle everything, didn't I?"

"You don't need to." She already does so much that she barely has time for a social life. Once the merger with Harringtons happens and we start the renovations, both Jade and I will be even busier—especially after Dad retires. We'll do whatever it takes to keep our family business alive with the King family opening a new superstore or convenience store or chain restaurant every other month. You name any business in the area and the Kings probably own it.

We're going to make this work. We have to. Otherwise, Dad says we'll be out of business by Christmas. We've already asked the bank for so many extensions I'm not sure what else we can do.

I didn't give up my dreams only to have Jade do the same.

Keeping our family store alive and thriving means everything to her.

My sister braces her hands on either side of the register, fixing me with a glare that reminds me so much of our mom that it makes my chest ache.

"Did it ever cross your mind that I might *want* to do it?" Even the exasperation in her voice reminds me of Mom.

"I want you to have a life, Jade." She's twenty-three and single. She should be out living instead of being stuck here with us.

"I do have a life. A great one, in fact. So, you can stop taking care of me and take care of yourself. You're getting married in six days. Go home. Relax. We'll be fine. Now, get out." She steals my keys right out of my hand, unhooking the one to the front door as she escorts me to the sidewalk. "We've got this, Ruby. I don't want to see you back here until after the wedding." She slaps my keys into my palm and disappears inside the store.

Great. It's seven-thirty in the morning and I don't have anything to do until noon. Harringtons' doorbell chimes, and the mailman steps out carrying a breakfast sandwich. He gives me a nod hello on his way to the town parking lot, and the smell of bacon leaves my mouth watering.

The moment I step inside the restaurant, Blake's mom appears out of nowhere and wraps me in a hug. "What're you doing here so early, honey?" she asks, her blonde, Aquanet-scented curls tickling my cheek.

"I had a few things to finish up at the store."

She lets me go long enough to grasp both sides of my face. "I hope you don't plan on working so hard when my grandbabies arrive."

I do want children someday—emphasis on *someday*—but if it were up to Mrs. Harrington, Blake and I would've been married the day after graduation and have five kids by now.

"We'll see," is all I say, pulling away and snagging a table by the window so I can watch our sleepy town wake up.

She drags a small notepad from her back pocket, along with a pen. "You want the usual?"

"That'd be great, thanks." My stomach grumbles impatiently, but she doesn't seem to notice. Traffic begins to pick up as people head to work. By traffic, I mean the five cars lined up at Still Springs' lone stoplight. Mrs. Harrington returns with a glass of water then saunters back into the kitchen.

Outside, I spot Frank in his truck—I assume on his way to his shift repairing potholes after last month's heavy rains—and Carl is right behind him in his scuffed-up Chevrolet Impala. Mr. Chen is walking his schnauzer, Biddy, to the town park.

Same as every other morning.

Nothing ever changes.

Except the guy jogging across the road, heading this way.

I hold my breath as a super-sweaty Flynn strolls in, wearing a pair of black athletic shorts and a Still Springs Soccer T-shirt that barely contains his biceps. Thankfully, he doesn't see my mouth fall open when he uses the hem of his shirt to wipe the dampness from his forehead. I try to glance away, but all I can do is stare and think: *How?* Just... *How?*

He pops his headphones out of his ears and smiles at Blake's mom when she heads out of the kitchen carrying a stack of pancakes and a side of crispy bacon. "Morning, Mrs. Harrington. Any chance I could get a glass of water?"

"Flynn Hudson," she says with a smile. "It's so good to see you back where you belong, son."

Does anyone else around here care to say the name Flynn Hudson like it was forged in heaven?

Seriously. Last night, it was like every single person who walked into the bar tripped over themselves to talk to the guy. I still can't figure out why.

Yeah, his job is cool.

Yeah, his uniform is cute.

Yeah, he's handsome as hell.

You know what else he is? A dick.

Blake's mom smiles over at me. "Why don't you have a seat right there next to my daughter-in-law, and I'll grab you that drink."

He turns, and I manage not to slink down in my chair as his deep-brown eyes land on me. His cheeks immediately flush pink, and I have this overwhelming urge to punch him in his annoyingly-pretty face. After hanging there for a moment, the way he stalks over and drops onto the seat across from me makes me think I'm doing a pretty good job of hiding it.

Mrs. Harrington sets the stack of pancakes in front of me, grabs a bottle of syrup from an empty table, and sticks it between us. "You need anything else, Ruby?"

"No, thanks." Unless she wants to kick Flynn out of here. Because that'd be fantastic.

She turns to my unwelcome guest. "Would you like some breakfast too, Flynn? Or just the water?"

C'mon, this guy clearly doesn't eat pancakes. He probably survives on protein shakes and raw eggs. I give him a glare that says, "Don't even think about it," and his smirk expands, even though his fingers are tapping on the table like he's uncomfortable. Good. That makes two of us.

"That sounds wonderful," he says to Blake's mom. "I'll have what Quinn's having."

She turns to go but is still within earshot, so I can't tell him to go back to the ninth circle of hell where he belongs.

I pick up my fork and give my pancake a hard stab. For some reason, Flynn finds that funny and chuckles. The laugh quickly fades when I drag my knife across the pancake and slice it into small pieces.

"I'm surprised Blake isn't here with you," he says in that voice that still does strange things to my stomach.

"He has some last-minute errands to run for the wedding." I douse the stack in syrup and shove a bite into my mouth. Sugar and buttermilk magic bursts on my tongue, and normally I'd try to savor every morsel. But not today. The sooner I finish, the sooner I can leave.

"Like?" Flynn asks.

Like none of your business. "He needs to pick up everyone's shoes."

For some reason, that makes him laugh. "And that's going to take all morning? Most places in this town aren't even open yet."

The way he says "this town" sets me on edge. He may have left, but that doesn't make him any better than us. I stab another bite, pretending it's his eye. I'm not a violent person by any means, but being around this guy has always made me a little unhinged.

Mrs. Harrington drops off Flynn's water and says it'll be a few more minutes for the pancakes.

The eight-year-old Burner triplets burst through the door, clambering for a table near the back. A moment later, Mrs. Burner steps inside, her hair askew and her blue shirt stained with what I hope is ketchup and not blood.

Flynn's throat bobs as he sips from his glass. When he sets it down, he runs his fingertips back and forth through the condensation. "So, you're still working at your dad's store."

What's with the idle chit-chat? I'm perfectly happy sitting here listening to the triplets scream.

"Don't say it like that," I clip.

"Like what?"

"Like you pity me."

"I don't pity you, Quinn. I think it's great."

Yeah, right. Then why is he making that face? "You think it's great, *but*...?"

"There's no 'but'."

I give him a sardonic frown. With that sort of tone, there's always a "but."

He huffs a laugh, returning that smile to his face that broke too many hearts at our school. "Okay, there's a 'but'."

"Ha! See! I knew it." Damn, I love being right with this guy. A second thought chases the first. Why can Flynn and I never seem to interact normally? Even back in high school, on the rare occasions I did talk to him, it always ended weird. Always.

Our freshman year, I asked what he got on a math quiz, and he went bright red, stood up, and walked out the door in the middle of class. This other time, Blake and I ran into him at the old ice cream parlor, and I'd remarked that Flynn and I had ordered the same thing: half chocolate, half strawberry milkshakes. I swear, for an entire month, he showed up to the store every other day to slink around the aisles with a milkshake in his hand, slurping at the straw just to irritate me.

Mrs. Harrington returns with Flynn's breakfast, dragging me out of the unpleasant memories.

He thanks her and unwraps a pad of butter to stick between each pancake while I take a few more bites of mine. "*But* I thought you were going to college to become a vet or something," he says, resuming our conversation.

Does he remember that after all these years? No, that's silly. Blake probably said something. Why does it make me feel uneasy thinking of the two of them talking about me?

I had wanted to be a vet. I wanted to do a lot of things. Spend a year abroad traveling through Europe. Hike the Grand Canyon. Go to a concert at Red Rocks. But then my mom died, and I couldn't let my dad handle all this on his own. Jade had been starting her senior year of high school, Grandma hadn't been doing well, the store was barely covering the mortgage, and Dad was working *all* the time. So, I did what any good daughter would do and moved back home, despite my dad's protestations.

"Plans change," is all I say.

One of the Burner triplets launches a piece of cutlery at the wall. Mrs. Burner closes her eyes and lets her head fall onto the table with a quiet groan. The closest child decides to season his mother's messy bun with salt.

"That's a shame. You would've been great at it," Flynn says.

Hold on. Was that a compliment? Before I can get my head around the fact that Hotshot Hudson actually said something nice to me, he starts talking again. "So, how's the store? Blake says there's some merger happening between your two family businesses?"

"Can we not do this?"

Flynn's gaze locks with mine, his dark eyebrows flicking toward his sweat-dampened hair. "Do what?"

"Act like we're friends who chat over breakfast together." He's Blake's friend, not mine. Besides, it's not like we'll see each other after the wedding. Flynn will go back to his high-flying life, and I'll still be here living mine. There's no need to pretend with him.

"You'd rather sit here in silence?" he asks.

It won't be silent with the triplets blowing bubbles in their cups of chocolate milk. "Kinda. Yeah."

He squeezes syrup onto the corner of his plate, his knuckles turning white. "Sounds good to me."

I stuff a bite into my mouth at the same time he does, both of us chewing with matching scowls. We finish at the same time too, and Mrs. Harrington refuses to let us pay. Although we both thank her, neither of us appears very happy as we make our way to the exit. Flynn pops his headphones back into his ears and shoves through the front door. I expect him to let the door fall closed behind him like he used to in high school, but he catches the handle at the last second, holding it open for me.

I step out into the heat and watch him take off down the road, trying to figure out why there's a lump growing in my throat.

CHAPTER FOUR

FLYNN

I KICK THE SHED DOOR SHUT BEHIND ME AFTER DEPOSITING the lawnmower and jog up to the house, rubbing the back of my neck. I'm running out of time before I have to head off to the park for today's picnic that's part of the wedding celebrations. So much for handing out the rings and giving a speech at the reception; this is turning out to be a week-long extravaganza that has Blake Harrington written all over it.

I planned to hang with Dad for a bit before I left, but while I was on my run this morning, I caught a proper look at my parents' back lawn and decided I couldn't leave it like that.

I keep my hand pressed to the twinge in my neck and push through the back door with a wince.

Dad twists around from where he's standing with a remote aimed at the TV, his brow furrowing. "You okay there?"

"I think I threw my neck out of alignment trying to get your lawnmower started," I reply as we head into the kitchen. "Remind me to buy you a new one before I head back."

A sympathetic chuckle leaves Dad's lips as he carefully wraps a solid arm around me. "You don't need to do that, bud. But thanks for mowing. I'd planned to get to it today."

"I'm buying you the lawnmower," I say, grabbing two mugs.

He stands beside me and watches as I pour two cups of dark roast coffee, both of us slipping into our usual routine in the painfully short spells of time we have together these days. I do things to help him and Mom—which mostly involves buying stuff to cover my guilt over being away so much—and he hovers as physically near to me as he can.

I hand him a steaming cup and rest against the counter, still in my running gear. After yesterday's encounter with Ruby that turned into breakfast together like a form of self-torment, I changed my route this morning to the quieter road skirting the edge of town. "Mom leaves early for work these days. She was already gone when I got up."

Dad's smile is laced with an apology. "You know how ticked off she is that she can't get time off. Even if her boy's home for the first time in eight years, inventory week still goes on."

"Yeah. Tell her I'll be home from this picnic as soon as I can, okay?" I can already visualize Blake trying to drag me to the bar for shots afterward, but as much as I'm here for his wedding, I need some face time with my mom. Their monthly visits to DC, and our hurried holiday dinners at my apartment, thanks to my busiest times of year, never seem to be enough.

Dad lifts his chin at the back deck, and we carry our coffees outside, settling into the outdoor chairs. "Now that's one good-looking lawn," he says with a smirk.

I smile and glance at my watch. I still have a few more minutes until I need to shower and change.

"So, you've had a busy few months, huh?" Dad asks like he doesn't want me to scatter yet.

I sigh, stretching out my legs. "That's one way of putting it. I flew to six countries last month and was only home for four days. But it's not usually quite that bad. I think I burned myself out."

He hmpfs. "Bit of a shame you don't earn frequent flyer miles."

I chuckle into the rim of my cup. "Believe me, whenever I get time off, the last thing I want to do is get on a plane." I settle my gaze on the rolling hills and gnarled old oak trees, inhaling deeply. I can't believe it's been so long since I've been back here. "All I feel like doing lately is *stopping*. In one place."

"That I can understand. No better place for me than right here with your mother." Dad places his hand over mine, giving it a couple of pats. "You know we miss you and want you here too, but it sure warms our hearts to see you out doing what you love."

I angle my body toward the best man I've ever known, but today, his words hit more bitterly than usual. I loved every minute of flight school and battled through some shitty junior jobs after that—like taking up skydivers—but the corporate role I landed last year made all the hard work and endless door-knocking worth it. I could've applied to one of the airlines, and the job security is better, but I did my research and set my mind on corporate early on. While I love flying, I pretty much despise commercial airports, and the corporate pilots I crossed paths with raved about the variety and spontaneity, which were awesome at the start. But lately, I've spent more time staring at hotel room furniture than anyone should have to, and when I *am* home, my apartment feels so empty.

"Where'd you go, bud?" Dad asks, bringing me back. "You were a million miles away."

My throat tightens. "I don't know. Lately, I've felt a bit off. Like something's missing." I lift a shoulder.

"Well, we all get like that sometimes. Nothing to be too worried about unless you start to feel like you're more down than up."

"I don't," I assure him. "Work's great, most of the time, and it keeps me out of trouble. But, sometimes, I have this weird feeling like I'm flying in one big circle. Whereas everyone else is moving in a forward direction. Building businesses. Getting married."

He lifts a brow. "That's the first time I've ever heard you talk about marriage."

"Don't get too excited," I reply with a chuckle. "I'm scarily single. But when I see what you and Mom have, I think it's something I could want. With the right person."

While I've never had trouble attracting date options, finding a woman who'd be cool with my insane schedule is a different story. Finding a woman I'm genuinely interested in has proven to be an even harder task to get my head around.

Like it's on autopilot, my mind flies to one face, one name, one woman.

Why? Why her? Why still?

In the past year alone, I've traveled to more countries than most people will ever see in their lifetime. But I haven't met a single woman, in a single city, who's knocked the air out of my lungs like Ruby Quinn.

I ache to say it aloud, to tell my dad I've never gotten over my high school crush and hear what he has to say about it. But that same crush is about to get married to my best friend—with me as the *best man*—and I can't imagine giving those words airtime, even to my dad.

Instead, I heave a sigh and push off the chair, giving his shoulder a squeeze before I head upstairs with a decision forming in my head.

Today, I'm going to keep as far away from Ruby as possible. Being around her so closely the past couple of days has done nothing to heal these old wounds. I'll say hello at the picnic— even though I know she's going to give me that gorgeous glare like she wants to slap me—and then I'll be everywhere she isn't.

There'll be plenty of people there; surely, it won't be too hard to keep away from her.

When Blake mentioned a picnic, I'd expected some stale sandwiches, a couple of tartan blankets, and a scuffed soccer ball—especially when he asked me to dress in athletic wear. But when I step out of my car at the local park, a mini fair greets me, complete with "Mr & Mrs" helium balloons, folding tables scattered with food platters, bunting, hanging lights, a DJ —what the fuck? Is this the wedding reception?

Blake pushes through a cluster of mingling guests—only some of whom I recognize—and hands me a beer before we've even said hello.

"Did I miss the ceremony?" I joke, and he cackles, making little impressed nods as his gaze sweeps over the party.

"You should know by now: Blake Harrington does nothing by halves." With a mischievous grin, he drags me closer to the gathering crowd. For the next ten minutes, I make eyes with every ghost of my past, saying literally nothing other than, "Yes, it's me, Flynn Hudson," and "I live over in DC now," and "Oh, I'm a pilot," and "You're looking really well too."

I keep a safe distance from Ruby, but every time I catch a glimpse of her from behind in a white tank top and a pair of blue yoga pants, I have to force my eyes away. Athletic shorts will do nothing to hide a semi, which is something I'm determined *not* to get for my best friend's fiancée.

Instead, I keep my attention fixed on the guys from school and end up swapping numbers with Carl. Not that I'm on the hunt for more friends; it's hard enough trying to keep up with the ones I have given my schedule.

"Shrimp tostada?" a silky voice says behind me. I spin to meet the dark eyes of an overly suntanned bleached-blonde in neon pink leggings and a matching crop top.

"Thank you." I scoop a canape off her tray, subtly studying her features while she serves the other guys. She doesn't seem familiar.

"You're not from around here," she says, twisting back to face me. Her gaze makes a quick slide down and up my body.

I smile. "I was just thinking the same thing about you."

"Oh, you were?" Her smile widens, revealing a row of perfectly straight teeth the same blinding shade as Blake's. Is this a Still Springs thing now? Chiclet-teeth?

"I grew up here, but I moved away after high school," I reply between chews.

"College?"

"Flight school."

Her lips twist up.

"You?" I ask politely.

She tinkles a laugh. "I'm from Baltimore. I moved here six months ago when the Harringtons hired me to manage the restaurant and the merger with the Quinn Brothers store."

My brows lift. "Wow, okay."

My sightline shifts past her shoulder, where some locals I don't know are craning their necks to stare at her food platter. But the woman's eyes haven't left me.

"So, are you here for the bride or groom?" she asks.

"Groom. I'm Blake's best man."

"Damn straight he is," Blake says, gliding between us and lightly punching my arm. "I see you've met Tammy. Best food-and-beverage expert in the biz." They share smiles and Tammy blushes.

"Do you want me to help you hand those out?" I offer, pointing at her tray. I don't mind playing waiter—I do it at work sometimes when we don't have a flight attendant on board—but that's not really my point.

Tammy waves a manicured hand at me. "Don't be silly. I'll see you boys later." Her smokey-brown eyes flicker between Blake and me before she slips away, switching places with Ruby, who rounds on us out of nowhere.

"Flynn," she mutters in greeting, and my throat instantly locks.

"Quinn." Saying her name is enough to loosen it. Her name always tasted sweet on my tongue. "You look nice today," I add like a halfwit.

Her brows pinch. "Thanks?" she replies, giving her casual activewear a confused glance.

You have no fucking idea how good you look. You would look good in anything.

I remember that time you came to school on costume day dressed as an inflatable praying mantis, and all I could think about was how the females bite the males' heads off during sex, which sounds like something you would totally do, and yes, it would probably be worth it.

I'd promised myself I wouldn't stare at her, but I'm utterly helpless around this woman. Ruby turns her back to say something to Jade, and I flip my aviators over my eyes and let my gaze cling where it wants to: right on her tight little ass, thinking how perfectly it'd fit in my lap.

"Should we start the games?" Ruby asks Blake, snapping me out of the thoughts I don't want but can't help. "The party's meant to end at four, so I'm a bit worried about time."

"Babe, the party's over when Blake *says* it's over." He wraps his arm around her and kisses her temple. "Did anyone hear me say 'last drinks'? Shit no. But if you think it's game o'clock, let's do it."

"Games?" I parrot, preferring the thought of sipping beer in the shade.

Blake cups his hand to the side of his mouth. "It's game tiiiii-iiime!" Everyone jumps at the sudden call to arms, while he launches into an announcement of the first party game: tug-of-war.

I toss back the last inch of my beer and subtly edge away from Ruby, returning to my pledge to stay away from her, which feels even more vital after being in her company for two minutes. Except I can't fucking stop staring at her. She's smiling warmly at those around us, making sure everyone's having a good time, handing out water bottles and finding a tissue for someone's kid who sneezed. Always so damn sweet.

Tug-of-war kicks off, and I silently question whether it's age-appropriate for our mixed crowd, but the smile on Ruby's face when the girls line up evaporates my hesitation. She clutches the rope and pulls it so firmly that her jaw clenches. Half falling into her sister Jade behind her, they force away their laughter and tug hard until the opposite team, led by Tammy, collapses into hysterics.

The girls have barely gotten up when Blake shoves forward, grabbing the rope with a gleeful grin and calling for the guys to gather. A couple of elderly men hang back, but the rest of us form two random teams, and I end up second in line behind Carl, with Blake facing us in front on the opposite side.

"One-two-three-go!" Blake spits out before we're ready, and my team makes a hard lurch forward.

"Pull like it's the last jerk off you'll ever get!" Carl shout-whispers in front of me, quietly enough that the older ladies can't hear him over the music. I crack up, gripping the rope like it's a lifeline and pulling until every muscle in my chest tightens.

Our sides feel even, and we quickly reach a deadlock, my tennis shoes making small slides toward Blake's team before we give them a good haul back our way. My gaze rubs against Blake's, finding him looking at me with a hard-as-fuck expression on his face like a charging bull. He's staring at me so unnervingly that I glance away and right into Ruby's gaze. It may be wishful thinking, but I'm almost positive I catch her eyes grazing over my straining bicep as I pull hard. The unexpected distraction eases my grip on the rope for half a second, which is enough to send our team plummeting to our asses.

The pain in my neck spasms, and I press my hand to it, hearing Blake's victory cheer and knowing without even glancing his way that he's dancing on the spot. I should've just told him I have a sore neck, but somehow, I don't think he'd have taken it as an excuse.

Perked up by his win, he excitedly introduces the next game, which he calls "Find Your Mate." While Ruby and Jade hand out brown paper bags, he instructs everyone to scatter in different directions. I stroll toward the piñata tree, giving myself a quick neck rub.

"Everyone, stop where you are, and put the paper bag over your head!" Blake calls out, and with my face caught somewhere between a smirk and an eye roll, I do as I'm told like a good little best man.

"The object of the game is to wander around and find your partner without saying a word!" Blake says after telling the DJ to turn off the music. "If you don't have a partner, you don't need to go searching, but you do need to walk around to make it harder for everyone else. Ruby, I'm coming for you, babe! There's nowhere I can't find you; we got this!"

I inhale a hot breath inside my mask and take a few steps forward, bumping into a burly shoulder. One of the guys makes a gruff laugh as we separate. I continue shifting around, wondering if anyone would notice if I slipped over to the drinks table and started carrying a beer around with me.

Two hands suddenly land on my forearms, and I jerk backward.

"I knew that was you," teases a sing-song voice. "It's Flynn, am I right?"

"Tammy?" I say, and she laughs musically, her palm sliding around to cup my elbow.

"Am I keeping you from your mate?" she asks.

I subtly edge my arm away from her. "No, I'm here on my own."

"Me too. Maybe this is a good way to meet someone." She laughs again, but something about her tone makes me think she isn't entirely joking.

"I think we're supposed to keep moving around," I say with an awkward chuckle, taking a step sideways to avoid a tree I know is there. Did Blake really think this game through with trees and tables and shit scattered around? At least the park is fenced, lest someone accidentally roam onto the road.

Two voices cry out happily a few feet away. The croaky grumble that follows is clearly Blake's, and I snicker lightly under my mask. The guy is competitive as fuck. It would do him well to lose a game or two.

A few more couples connect, but the game keeps going, and I do my bit, drifting around in a defined circle. Most pilots have a heightened sense of situational awareness, so I know exactly where I am at all times. The problem is that no one else seems to, so people keep reaching for me, mistaking me as their mate, and stepping on my feet at every turn.

I move to the right this time, and something in my equilibrium shifts as the scent of vanilla finds my nose. I freeze on the spot, heat prickling over my skin.

I know instantly that it's her. The tips of her shoes brush mine as she faces me, and even through my mask, I can hear her breathing—the sweetest, simplest sound that has my own breaths quickening.

Does she think I'm Blake?

I wait for her to move, or to at least speak, but nothing happens. We stand quietly together, the heat coming off her body mingling with mine. Because she can't see me, I close my eyes behind the wall of my mask and tilt a little closer to her like I'm falling into a dream, my heart drumming in my chest.

What the hell am I doing?

People are moving and murmuring around us, yet Ruby and I haven't shifted. I'm about to say something—make a dumb joke—when her chest slams against my own.

A gasp flees her throat, and my arms catch hers on instinct, her soft skin burning into my fingers. Her head flies up, and our masks crumple as they rub together, my lips brushing over something soft, like our mouths just touched through the paper.

"Get off me!" she cries, wriggling out of my grip.

"Sorry," I blurt out, whipping off my mask.

She's staring at me with her mask in her fingers, her lips parted and her eyes wide.

"I'm sorry," I say again, holding my free hand out. Around us, the guests that haven't found each other are still roving around with paper bags on their heads and their arms stretched out like fucked-up zombies.

"You fell into me," I explain to Ruby, who's frowning.

"I didn't mean to," she says forcefully. "Someone knocked me."

"I know. This game's weird as hell."

A breath of a chuckle tumbles off her lips before her face resets to that hard place reserved only for me.

Then she whirls around and stalks off like she can't get away from me fast enough.

CHAPTER FIVE

RUBY

AFTER THE FIND YOUR MATE DISASTER, WE HOLD EGG-AND-spoon races like a bunch of kids at summer camp. It comes as no surprise that Blake wins both rounds. I overhear his mom say he's been practicing in their backyard for the last month and that she had to buy double the number of eggs so she had something to make his dad for breakfast.

Next comes a game where you stand facing your partner and toss water balloons to each other. Every time you make a catch, you take a step back. Blake's shitty throw loses that one for us, but of course he blames me, and now I have to stand around in a soaked tank top. Which sucks even harder when I catch Flynn's fancy-pants sunglasses aimed in my direction.

"Ruby, for god's sake!" Blake rakes his fingers through his sweaty hair. "You're not even trying."

"Yes, I am." It's not my fault he threw the balloon too low.

Tammy and Flynn win, high-fiving each other like they're best friends.

After that, Blake insists on making the teams "fair" by putting everyone's name inside Carl's hat on bits of paper and letting us pick out partners at random. It's pretty freaking obvious that his decision has nothing to do with fairness. Blake doesn't want to be paired with me and is trying to save face. I want to sit out for cornhole, but Jade announces that if she has to play, so do I. She then shoves an ice-cold beer in my hand, cracks open the one she's holding, and tells me to drink up.

The alcohol soothes some of my irritation. I don't like losing either, but I'm not going to throw a fit about it like a five-year-old. Meanwhile, Blake curses and kicks one of the trees when Carl misses the cornhole board entirely.

Flynn and Tammy win again. Isn't that great? They really seem to be hitting it off today.

I'm close enough to overhear her ask Flynn about his job, her whole body angled to his. I step away to grab another drink so I don't have to listen. What would his flight attendant girl-friend think if she caught him flirting with someone else? Are they serious or casual? Not that it matters. I bet she's gorgeous, though, like a model or movie star. Someone tall and exotic from somewhere exciting, like Paris or Japan.

Thank goodness he didn't bring her. I don't need everyone at my wedding staring at Flynn's supermodel girlfriend.

Tammy could be a supermodel, with her tanned legs that seem to go on forever and her stunning smile, even though her teeth are as staggeringly white as Blake's. Plus, she's confident as hell. That woman could get anyone she wants with a bat of her fake lashes and a crook of her manicured finger. She's quite a few years older than us, but I haven't heard of her dating anyone since she arrived in Still Springs.

What if Flynn ditches his supermodel and starts dating Tammy?

That would suck.

Not that I care who Hotshot Hudson dates. But if he and Tammy got together, he'd probably start making the trek back and forth from DC when he's not flying around the world like a

superstar. I'll have to see him all the time, and Blake will probably suggest something stupid like going out on double dates
together like he did for our junior prom.

I can't think of anything worse.

"One more game," Blake demands, dragging me out of my
spiraling mental tangent when he nudges me aside to snag a
beer from the red-and-white cooler.

Everyone but Tammy grimaces at the announcement.

"That's the last one on the list," I remind him. "Why don't
we take a break and eat?" After a few drinks, he'll forget all
about the games. At least I hope he does. Otherwise, he'll end
up in a mood for the rest of the day.

"Sorry, babe. We need a tie-breaker."

"For what? No one is keeping score."

He eyes Flynn still chatting with Tammy and says, "We
need one more."

When Frank suggests a three-legged race, Blake whoops and
claps him on the back so hard that the poor guy stumbles into Carl.

"We don't have anything to tie us together," I point out,
casting a longing glance toward the grill as my hollow stomach
whines. I can almost taste the burgers now.

"I've got cable ties in my truck," Frank offers.

"That seems a bit dangerous, don't you think?" I counter.

Blake knocks his hip against mine. "Lighten up, babe. It'll be
fun. Grab the ties, Frank."

It won't be fun. Not for me. But apparently, my fiancé
doesn't care. I tell myself this is one of those small things to let
slide. It certainly isn't worth fighting over. One three-legged
race, and Blake will be happy...*if* he wins.

Frank takes off toward the parking lot, and Carl grabs his
hat off the picnic table. Tammy and Flynn are locked in quiet
conversation. When she winks at him, redness creeps over his

stubbled jaw. I roll my eyes and drink some more. Hotshot Hudson always did blush like a schoolgirl. Like that time he wasn't paying attention and accidentally walked into the girls' bathroom at school. Or when he was crowned Prom King.

A few minutes later, Frank returns with a bag full of giant cable ties.

"Why the hell do you even have these?" Blake asks him, withdrawing a handful. "You into some kinky shit or what?"

Frank's flush deepens while the others snigger. Jade gives the bits of paper one last stir before holding the hat out to me. "Bride first."

I stick my hand inside and pull out a name.

Flynn

My stomach clenches. I try to drop it back inside, but Jade jerks the hat away and the paper drifts onto the grass, landing beside Flynn's shoes. He picks up the scrap and pales as he reads it, like being paired with me is a fate worse than death. Not that I expect anything less from him.

"Let me choose again," I insist. Being the bride should have some perks.

Jade snatches the paper from Flynn, snorting when her eyes scan the name. "Sorry, sis. Rules are rules."

Tammy must've seen the name, too, because she says, "I don't mind pairing with Flynn."

"Jade's right," Blake cuts in. "Rules are rules." He takes the hat from Jade and shakes it in Tammy's face.

Tammy ends up pulling out Blake's name, and he gives her a one-armed hug that makes her laugh. The two of them, with their equally long legs, are going to be impossible to beat. Jade ends up with Frank, and Trish gets stuck with Carl, who's probably the most gangly person I've ever met.

I press a hand to my forehead, where a headache is building from the heat, alcohol, and lack of food. "Hey, Blake? I'm feeling a bit dizzy. I may sit this one out."

"Babe, you have to play. One last game. Please. For me?"

"You should probably let her get some food before she passes out," Flynn murmurs before taking a quick sip of his beer.

I blink up at him, shocked he'd spoken up for me instead of making some smart-ass comment like he used to. Then again, maybe he's hoping I'll be gone so long that he won't have to run the race with me.

"I'll grab you something to tide you over," Blake offers. Before I can stop him, he's already halfway to the snack table. When he gets back, he hands me a sprig of grapes and a chocolate chip cookie.

By the time I finish eating, everyone has been attached to their partners except for Jade and Flynn. I sidle up next to him, holding my breath as Jade fastens a tie above our ankles. Everyone else is laughing and practicing while Hotshot and I don't even look at each other.

"You're going to have to get closer," Jade says from where she kneels. "Closer. Cloooser."

The length of his firm side presses into me, heating my skin through his T-shirt.

"Good, now hold still," Jade says.

It's an entirely unnecessary command considering Flynn and I have become statues. I'm not even sure he's breathing while I, on the other hand, sound like I've run a mile already.

Jade pulls the tie, cinching it right above our knees. "It's too tight," I tell her. "Cut it off and put on another one. It's cutting into my leg, Jade. Jade!"

Does she listen? Nope. She stands back, says, "Try not to kill each other," and heads over to where Frank is waiting.

"Calm down. It's not that tight," Flynn mumbles, but his thick, soccer-player calf is rubbing against my leg. Does he still play? I shove the unwelcome thought away.

Up close, he smells like spearmint and soap and traces of sweat. The combination should be gross, but it isn't.

He shifts, and his muscular arm slips around my shoulder.

My entire body recoils. "What do you think you're doing?"

He doesn't let go. If anything, it feels like he holds me tighter. "I'm not really in the habit of losing, and if we're going to beat the other teams, we need to work together."

It's just one more game. I don't have to win, I only have to survive. "You're sweating on me."

"You're not exactly Ms. Dry-and-Fresh either," he shoots back.

The others practice in the green, hobbling toward the starting line closest to the playground. I try to take a step but can't because Flynn is made of rocks. "Are we doing this or what?"

"We don't really have much of a choice, do we?" He gestures toward my arms pinned to my sides. "Put your arm around my back."

"Ugh. Fine."

His shirt is damp but not dripping. His toned thigh brushes against mine, and I feel self-conscious about how sweaty I am. I put on deodorant this morning, didn't I?

We do this sort of hobble-hop thing to get to the starting line, neither of us finding a rhythm. His legs are too long, and mine are too short, and—

"Stop fighting me, Quinn. We need to move together. This one first." Flynn pats his leg attached to mine then settles his warm arm back in place.

Blake grins at us from the other end of the line, appearing way too smug. "On your marks—"

"It's not fair for you to start the race," Flynn counters. "We should choose a neutral party."

Exactly, I think.

Blake twists around to Mr. Harrington. "Hey, Dad! Can you start us off so Flynn can't accuse me of cheating when I beat his ass?" he asks with a laugh.

Mr. Harrington strolls over to where we're all waiting and raises a hand in the air. "On your marks..."

Flynn's head tilts toward me until I meet my reflection in the lenses of his sunglasses. "This leg first, remember?" he says.

"Got it."

He's still gazing at me, making my cheeks burn a little.

"Get set..."

My arm tightens around Flynn's waist until I can feel the cut in his hip beneath my fingers. My heart pounds a bit harder at that.

"Go!"

Everyone lurches at the same time.

Right away, we're in last place, but I focus on Flynn's movements, doing my best to find a rhythm. *Swing-hop. Swing-hop.* I can't believe it when we catch up to Carl and Trish and then bypass Jade and Frank. Blake and Tammy still have a slight lead, but if we keep this going, we could reach the finish line first. *Swing-hop. Swing-hop.* It's almost like skipping.

I may not have been very athletic as a kid, but I was one hell of a skipper. And Flynn's always been a skilled sportsman.

I can't believe it. We're pulling ahead.

I laugh when Blake curses as we pass by him. Jade and Frank are on our heels. Everyone is cheering us on.

Holy crap.

We're going to win.

I never win anything.

Somehow, my hand ends up laced with the one Flynn has draped around me, and he's holding my other wrist in place against his hip. Everyone else has adopted similar positions and no one seems to be paying us any attention, but this feels too close. Too warm. Too intimate.

When Flynn's fingers graze slightly over mine, I lose my timing and stumble forward. He catches me by my waist, stopping me from ending up face-down in the grass. Blake and Tammy surge ahead, and my hopes of winning the race fade with each uneven step.

"I'm sorry," I choke, my lungs on fire. "I'm trying my best. I got distracted and—"

Flynn stops, and the other couples blow past us. He stares down at me, his chest rising and falling heavily. I wish I could see his eyes to know what he's thinking, but he's still wearing those damn glasses, so all I can see is my own sweaty, beet-red face.

"We're going to lose," I say.

"I really couldn't care less," he replies softly. "If you're not having fun, then what's the point? This week is supposed to be about you. The *two* of you," he amends with a pinch of color in his cheeks.

Blake comes hobbling over, still attached to Tammy, and slaps Flynn on the back. "Sorry, man. Should've warned you that this one isn't very fast."

I feel my brow tighten, and I know that Flynn is watching me without having to raise my head.

"Nah, she did great," Flynn says to Blake, sending a little tingle to my stomach.

Jade swears from where she's kneeling beside Carl and Trish. "Does anyone have a spare pair of scissors lying around?" she shouts with a nervous laugh. She holds up the scissors that just broke into two halves. Everyone at the entire party shakes their head.

I need a minute alone to sit in the shade and breathe, but I can't do that if I'm attached to Flynn. I tug on the cable tie biting into my thigh, ignoring the way he flinches. His leg is so much thicker than mine; this has to be hurting him even worse.

"Let me try to slide it off," he grumbles.

"That's what I'm already trying to do."

"*Ouch*. Careful. You're gonna cut yourself—"

Oh, please. I'm not going to cut anyone. "I know what I'm doing."

"Just leave it."

More determined than ever to get the stupid thing off, I wedge my finger beneath the stiff band, twist and wiggle, managing to get the tie down far enough to slip over our knees and fall around our still-bound ankles.

"Shit, Quinn." Flynn kneels beside me, and his finger scours the inside of my thigh. Everyone is watching us.

"Stop," I try to say, but no sound emerges.

"Your leg must be cut."

Sure enough, there's a deep-red stain where the cable tie had been wrapped around my leg. *Dammit*. I'd told Jade it was too tight. "It's fine."

"Do you have a change of clothes? You should probably put something on the cut so it doesn't ruin your—"

"I said it's fine." I smack his hand away and pull off my shoe, finding a similar mark on my ankle.

Flynn sits back on the grass, the movement tugging me forward. "Unless you plan on chopping off your own foot, you may as well sit down."

Some of my frustration subsides when I sink down next to him. It's not like we're going to be stuck together forever. "Maybe I'll cut off yours instead."

Although he chuckles, there's no mirth to the sound. "I bet that would make your day." He doesn't say any more, just stares in the direction of the gigantic Mr. & Mrs. helium balloons that Blake special-ordered for today.

While Flynn's gaze is locked elsewhere, I do something I used to avoid at all costs: I let myself really look at him.

Was he always this tall? Objectively, I can admit he's gorgeous, but that's nothing new. The first time I saw him, I was so mesmerized that I nearly walked straight into one of the door dividers in the school hallway.

Flynn winces up at the puffy white clouds. A moment later, he begins massaging his neck.

"Was I that bad in the race that I screwed up your neck?" I ask.

One corner of his mouth pulls up, his gaze still fixed straight ahead. "More like my parents' lawnmower gave me whiplash when I started it this morning."

It's sweet that he took the time to mow his parents' lawn. Then again, he hasn't been home in eight years, so it's the least he can do.

Stop it, Ruby. You promised Blake that you'd be nice.

I can be nice to Flynn. He's been nice to me today, even though I lost the race for us, hasn't he?

"I guess I could rub it for you if you want," I offer grudgingly, realizing too late how suggestive that sounds. "My dad suffers from neck and back pain, and I help him out all the time," I quickly add. When I was little, Dad used to pay me in cookies for a "world-famous" Ruby massage.

"Absolutely not," Flynn chokes out, almost tilting away from me.

Whatever. I didn't want to do it anyway. His neck is probably all sweaty and disgusting.

Flynn's head twists left and right, scanning the crowd.

"Where's Jade? It can't be that hard to find someone in Still Springs with a pocketknife."

I know better than to be offended, but every time he makes a remark like that, it feels like he looks down on this town. Like he looks down on me.

"You really hate it here, don't you?" I mutter.

His jaw kicks back. "No, I don't. Why would you even think that?"

"Doesn't matter. Forget I said anything."

"You can't say shit like that without an explanation."

He wants an explanation? Fine. "The moment you graduated, you ran right out of town and never looked back."

Blake told me that he and Flynn had their final summer together all planned out: a road trip to the beach...camping by the falls...fishing at the lake. Then Flynn ditched Blake to go chase his high-flying pilot dream. I can admit that part of me is just jealous. What must it be like to put yourself first all the time, to go for what you want, consequences be damned? But mostly, I can't fathom how someone could be so incredibly selfish.

Flynn doesn't so much as glance at me when he says, "I have my reasons for leaving." Quieter, he adds, "But that doesn't mean I never looked back."

I almost shake my head as I turn away, wondering why I even care. "Was it worth it, leaving everyone behind? Even your family—"

"Hold on a minute. I see my parents all the time."

"Oh, really?"

"Yes, *really*. They come down to my place at least once a month."

That's something at least, I suppose. "Why haven't you been back to see Blake then? In eight years, not once have you made an effort to visit your 'best friend.' He's always the one driving down to you or flying off to meet you in Vegas for *his* birthday."

Flynn glances away. "I've been busy."

"Yeah. I'm sure you have." We've all been busy. That doesn't change the fact that you're supposed to make time for the important people in your life.

His mouth opens and closes like he can't find his words before Jade appears out of nowhere, brandishing a knife. "Well, what do you know?" She waves the blade between us, a coy smile hinting at her lips. "The two of you *can* get along."

Flynn's mouth snaps shut, and he gestures toward the weapon. When Jade hands it over, he saws at the cable tie until it snaps, then launches to his feet and bolts away. I roll my eyes. High school all over again.

Jade frowns down at the cut tie and back at where Flynn has disappeared through the crowd of guests lining up at the picnic tables for lunch. "What the heck did you do to him?"

Why does she assume this is my fault? "All I did was tell him the truth."

And sometimes, the truth hurts.

CHAPTER SIX

FLYNN

There's nothing quite as humbling as nailing your dream career, only to come home after nearly a decade and be basically told you're a selfish dick.

Ruby's little lecture rings in my ears all the way to my old hatchback, which I fling open and escape inside like a safe space, the vinyl seat sticking to my sweaty thighs. Blake's gonna give me hell for skipping out of his picnic early, but there's only so much of all this I can take.

My leg's still buzzing where Ruby's soft calf was pressed to mine, and I frantically wind down the window before shoving the car into gear and taking off toward Mom and Dad's. Slowing up at Still Spring's only stoplight reminds me how absurdly small and insular this place is; how hard it is to change people's impressions of you in a town that feels trapped in time.

My unofficial introduction to society was as a little league soccer star—the kid who scored ninety percent of the goals and was the subject of in-fighting between clubs in our county for years. Not that it mattered; I started out with Still Springs Soccer Club when I still had a mouth full of baby teeth, and even though we only took the championship once, I was always loyal to my team.

By the time I took my first nervous step into the halls of Still Springs High School, I was known as the best center forward in the state, with Blake Harrington as my trusted second striker. Blake and I had been zoned for different elementary and middle schools, but we'd played soccer together for the same club since we were seven. We'd been so excited to finally be at the same school that we spent the first week taping dumb signs on each other's lockers like "For a good time, call this number" (mine) and "You're going to die in ten days" (Blake's, which kind of freaked me out).

As I continue to drive, the memories shift to freshman year, when Blake was chasing after every bit of skirt within a two-mile radius. My interest in girls didn't really spark until the fall of our junior year, when a quiet girl named Ruby Quinn sat beside me in science class on the unfortunate day we had to dissect a rat. I knew who Ruby was, but I'd never really given her a second thought. Until my gaze caught the side of her face when she wrinkled her nose up at the ice-cold rodent splayed out on its back, a first impression rolling through my head that I haven't been able to shake off since.

You're beautiful.

It wasn't only her face...her ocean-blue eyes, her cute-as-hell freckled nose, her black waves of hair that she pinned back, inviting the world into her prettiness. It was her manner; her delicacy and care as she handled the little animal that wasn't even alive, making slow and gentle cuts with her scalpel while everyone else hacked in. It was the way she couldn't look at me flush in the face without blushing. The strange rush of longing that tightened my throat when our legs accidentally brushed beneath the table.

She barely even spoke to me, and after I accepted that I was developing a hopeless crush on her, I couldn't be around her without wanting to puke, but in a weirdly good way. For the next eight months, I circled around her like a pussy, too scared to talk to her but stealing glances in her direction. The few times we said more than two words to each other outside the classroom were in the short spells she was around Blake, who she knew through her parents. To be honest, I thought I'd forget about her quickly and move on to one of the other blossoming girls in our year. But by spring, I was seventeen years old and fucking desperate for Ruby Quinn. When junior prom rolled around, I hadn't yet given it much thought until Martina from my social studies class gave me a whispered heads-up that some of the girls were taking bets on who I was going to ask. The shortest odds were for Wendy Moore—a gorgeous, red-headed cheerleader who was constantly dropping books around me and bending over to pick them up. But there was only one person I wanted wrapped around my arm at prom, and Ruby wasn't even listed on the poll.

Still, the whole thing lit a fire under me. I had to grow some fucking balls, walk right up to Ruby, and say these words: "I think I love you. Will you go to the prom with me?" Or at least the second part.

But after Josh Murphy invited Lara Reyes by ordering a box of her favorite donuts with *"PROM?"* spelled out in pink icing, I decided I'd have a better shot with Ruby if I did something romantic. The problem was, I had no clue what Ruby liked. I started questioning why I was into her so much when we'd barely shared a conversation, but the answer was always the same, and it had nothing to do with words. It was a feeling...a deep pull in my gut that had me constantly imagining what it would be like to touch her lips with mine, to thread my fingers through hers, to ask her all the questions about herself I didn't know the answers to. I hadn't asked for this feeling, I didn't know where it came from; it was just *there*. A constant knowing in my head and my heart.

So, that week at school, I told Blake I'd walk home the long way with him and pressed him for tips on what made Ruby smile so I could ask her to go to the prom with me. I may as well have asked him how often he jacked off to porn or what was in his internet search history. A storm descended on his face, and he turned beet-red and told me he'd already asked Ruby to prom and that she'd said yes.

My chest had crushed inward, and a wall shot up between Blake and me that didn't recede for months. It was just a prom—just a girl—but I noticed him back off from me for a while, and I sure as hell wasn't keen on being around him either. It made me feel like an asshole that I couldn't be happy for Blake, but every time his lips curled over Ruby's name like she belonged to him, my insides twisted up. I ended up asking Wendy to the prom, and she screamed and did a high kick that nearly knocked me out.

As I make a right off Summercrest, I remember how I spent that entire dance fighting to keep my eyes off Ruby in her scarlet-red prom dress with a long slit up the side. But every time I stole a glance, I caught a moment between her and Blake...an exchange of prolonged eye contact, a deliberate brush of their knuckles like they couldn't help but touch each other, his fingers grazing the curves of her backside while they were slow-dancing. It was fucking torture. I tried everything to stop wanting my best friend's girl, but like I was on the butt of a sick joke, I ended up craving her more with every day that passed by.

The more I liked her, the less she spoke to me or even looked at me. So, I started doing stupid shit to get her attention. Rather than buck up and talk to her, I'd tip over her paint palette in art class or slide into her favorite seat right before she did. If she voiced an idea during a class discussion, I'd stick my hand up and pick apart her argument until her whole face turned red. It was lame and mean, but I was seventeen and heartsick for someone who wouldn't give me the time of day. I haven't stopped regretting it. If I could, I'd reach back in time right now and give my teenage self a smack in the head.

When senior year hit, I drilled my focus into studying so I could get into college and get the hell out of Still Springs. But after a few career counseling sessions and a joy flight in a Cessna that my parents bought for my eighteenth birthday, I applied to flight school instead. When I got my acceptance letter, I rushed up to Blake at school the next day to tell him, finding his arm draped around Ruby. So, I showed them both the letter, and Ruby looked at me and said, "Bon voyage!" with a weird sort of sarcastic look on her face.

Hiding how much that hurt, I'd tossed her my best smile that always made girls' eyes light up and allowed myself one last, long look at her. Because that was the moment I decided this infatuation with a girl who didn't even like me was officially over. I was going to become a pilot, and I was going to fly out of Ruby's life and never look back.

Two goals I went on to achieve, so why the fuck do I feel so empty right now?

The memories finally fade away as I make a left turn onto my parents' gravel driveway, my fingers tightly gripping the steering wheel.

If there was any doubt left after that excruciating pancake breakfast at Harringtons, today rammed home that Ruby still hates me as much as she did back in high school.

It's not like I can't make sense of that. We haven't seen each other in eight years; she has no idea who I am now. She only knows me as that jackass from school.

What I can't get my head around is *why*—after all this time —I'm still running from Ruby Quinn.

"Okay, so you wanna be Mario or Luigi?"

Blake slurps an oyster out of its shell and pushes the plate toward me, but I wave a hand at him.

"Thanks, but I better save some room for my burger." The truth is that I once heard a disgusting story involving food poisoning from seafood at Harringtons that's never left me, even though I'd never bring it up with Blake. "And it's your wedding; I'll be Luigi," I add in response to his question about our matching costumes for tomorrow's bachelor party.

"Screw you! I'll be Luigi. Mario's bland and boring as fuck. You owe me for bailing out on the picnic."

"Okay," I reply, a little confused as to why he even asked. "Works for me. Bland and boring sound perfect at the moment." In the middle of the night last night, I woke up startled, thinking I was sitting on the flight deck with no clue where I was flying.

"Well, you're shit out of luck there. You're the talk of the town at the moment. Which I will allow, even though you're kinda stealing my wedding thunder." He winks at me and brushes a napkin over his lips.

"What do you mean I'm the talk of the town?"

"The prodigal son finally returns," he explains in a dramatic tone. "And as a pilot, no less. Come on, you know as well as I do that's tabloid gold around here."

I laugh. I guess I don't mind being gossiped about if it's harmless stuff.

Blake lifts his beer to his lips. "How's that all going, anyway? Every time I text you these days, I never know which city you're gonna be in."

"Work's good. You know I had to bust a gut to get the job I

have, so I don't really like complaining about it, but I've told you before: all the traveling is pretty much the best part *and* the worst part. Even though I'm getting paid to see the world, I'm always doing it alone. Apart from the other crew, there's no one to go for dinner with or see the sights with. And it's a shitload of packing and unpacking suitcases."

"It does sound tiring," he says, which is of little surprise. Blake's always been a small-town guy intent on staying put in Still Springs, and I respect that. My parents are the same and have created a beautiful life together here that seems to make them both happy. While I can't imagine ever moving back, or giving up flying, the thought of having more of what they have has become a key theme in my head lately.

Blake scoops up another oyster. "I suppose all the traveling is hard on your relationship, huh?"

My brow pinches. "What do you mean?"

"The girl you're seeing. The flight attendant who's in Ibiza this week. Or do you guys travel everywhere together?"

Shit. I'd already forgotten my little white lie to save face when Ruby assumed I was desperate for a date—right after she accused me of being a cheating Lothario because of my profession.

"We're rarely scheduled together. And Bianca isn't technically my girlfriend," I admit. "She's someone I hook up with now and then." *Now I sound exactly like a playboy.*

Blake's eyes dance. "Betcha there's no shortage of hook-ups in your phone. Good-looking guy in a pilot's hat. Only in town for a day or two. No risk of girls becoming clingy and shit. Lucky bastard."

I make a face at him. "Corporate pilots don't wear hats. And what are you talking about, man? You've been with the same girl since you were *seventeen*."

"Exactly!" He throws back a swig of beer as my mind fights

to catch up. Why does a guy who's about to get married seem so excited about the idea of no-strings-attached booty calls?

"Beef burger with the lot; hold the cheese?" tinkles a vaguely familiar voice. I glance up into Tammy's smirking face, her dark eyes pinned to mine. She's in skin-tight navy jeans and a lacy black top that catches my eye for half a second.

"Hey," I say, my mouth kicking up into a smile. "That's my bad boy you've got there."

She bends so close when she slides the plate in front of me that I catch a whiff of musky perfume. "Well, who doesn't love a bad boy?" she murmurs, looking into my eyes before she pulls back.

I shoot Blake a subtle look, finding his features pulled tight as he stares up at Tammy. She deposits a plate of fish tacos in front of him before her palm lands on his shoulder.

"You two enjoy." She gives him a light squeeze through his shirt. "It's on the house." She glances at Blake—the part-owner—and laughs. Even though it's really not that funny, his whole face lights up as he cackles with her.

After Tammy saunters away, I lean across the table to him, lowering my voice. "What's her deal?"

A line appears on his brow. "What do you mean?"

"She seems friendly." I smirk at him and raise a brow as I hook my burger in my fingers. "Is she single?"

Blake blinks at me. "Yeah, but she's like a decade older than you, man. And she has a kid."

"I'm not interested. But I get the feeling that, if I was, or even if *you* were, she'd be up for it."

"Bro, don't talk about her like that. She's an employee," he says, giving me the same look that he used to when we'd argue over a bad soccer pass that cost us the game.

"I didn't mean it that way. I only meant that she seems a little lonely, and someone nice should take her out on a date."

I'm actually not sure what I'm saying. Blake's reaction to this is throwing me.

"If you want to take Tammy out on a date, take her out on a fucking date," he mutters like he doesn't give a shit either way, his gaze falling to the fish taco in his fingers.

"I don't want to take Tammy out on a date," I clarify, wanting to laugh or at least get out of this stupid conversation. "But what I *do* want is some more intel on the bachelor party tomorrow. I still feel bad that you planned the whole thing without me. You know I wanted to do it."

He waves a greasy hand at me. "All the links you sent me were a bit spendy. You know money's never an issue, but I'm not about to line the pockets of some tight-ass whitewater rafting company or overpriced vineyard serving cat's piss wine. Plus, The Rocking Horse said they'd slash their prices if I could get over thirty people."

I chuckle. "*Thirty?* Who'll be there?"

He covers his mouth as he chews. "Frank and Carl, of course. My dad, my cousins, my uncle, a few buddies of mine you haven't met yet...Chris and Paul from the restaurant, and from school, Luca, Shawn, and Jeff. Oh, and Ruby and Jade, of course. We've got the numbers."

I cough up a small chunk of tomato. "Ruby's going? But it's your bachelor party."

"It's a Jack and Jill party," he replies like I should know what that means. "Bachelor and bachelorette. Stag and hen. Don't get me wrong, I'm fucking pissed that we can't do strippers if the Mrs. is there, but we needed to combine parties to get the thirty guests, so I'm taking this one for the team. But strippers are item one on the agenda next time we hit Vegas," he adds, holding his fist out at me.

Ground beef rolls in my stomach as I accept his fist bump. I'm ready to beg my fucking insides not to have this childish reaction every time I'm faced with the prospect of being in the same room as Ruby.

Flynn Hudson, get your shit together.

"Does that mean Tammy's going?" I brave, unsure if I should venture back to this topic. But I'm at least sixty percent sure that Tammy's vaguely interested in me, and if I'm going to be locked in a bar with Ruby for hours on end—with copious amounts of alcohol—a distraction wouldn't hurt. Even though I'd have to be careful not to lead Tammy on or give her the wrong impression. I'm not a complete ass, despite what Ruby thinks.

Blake nods, and I take another bite of my burger, settling this in my brain. Tammy certainly is pretty, and smart to have the role she does, and it's kind of nice that she has a kid. It also doesn't hurt that she seems like the type who'd go to a costume party dressed as Wonder Woman or Jessica Rabbit. I can't pretend to myself or anyone else that I'm looking to start up with someone from Still Springs, but if she wants to point those seductive eyes in my direction and share some decent conversation with me, I could get on board with that. Especially if it helps keep my mind away from places it shouldn't go.

While I'd be kidding myself if I believed my attraction to Ruby was purely physical, the last time I saw her in a costume, she was dressed as a giant praying mantis. She's not the type to flaunt her body in something sexy, so my dick should behave tomorrow night too. I clink my beer against Blake's and ask him which team he thinks is gonna take out this year's UEFA Champions League, finally able to take a breath.

CHAPTER SEVEN

RUBY

THE DARK-HAIRED GIRL IN THE PHOTOGRAPH ON MY DAD'S living room wall smiles out at me, one of her front teeth twice the size of the other. Unlike most kids, I didn't lose my two front teeth in quick succession. After the first one fell out, the second didn't get loose until the adult tooth beside it had grown in almost completely. Needless to say, second grade was not a good year for me.

My mom used to cut my hair. Which was—

No, I can't say it was fine because anyone who saw these school photos from kindergarten through eighth grade would agree it absolutely wasn't. My grandma had cut my mom's hair, and my grandma's mom had cut my grandma's hair, and so on and so on—probably all the way back to the Dark Ages. Because that's where the thick, uneven bangs I had up until I turned fourteen belonged.

In middle school, the boys flocked to the popular girls with trendy haircuts they'd found online. No one noticed me sitting in the back, hiding behind my wall of bangs. Back then, I hadn't cared. Who wanted to date a middle-school boy anyway? They smelled funny and their voices were squeaky.

But by the end of eighth grade, I found myself wanting to be seen.

On my last day of middle school, I finally got up the nerve to tell my mom that I didn't want her to cut my bangs anymore. For the entire summer, I wore those things pinned back on either side of my forehead like two curtains. They looked really stupid and got crazy sweaty. Then, the week before high school started, I took out the pins.

I looked like a totally different person. *Felt* like a totally different person. Then I tried to take my transformation one step further by going blonde from a box. Would *not* recommend. Vera, the owner of Still Springs' only hair salon, came to the rescue, not only correcting my terrible dye job but giving me my first proper haircut.

If only I could tell the awkward girl in the photo that boys would begin to notice her from the day she started high school. That so many of the kids she'd had classes with for years would ask if she'd just moved to town.

I take a few steps to the right to study the "new" girl, her teeth straightened by braces and her bangs tucked behind her ears. Instead of the generic picture with a blue-gray background from my junior year, Mom had framed the photo from my first prom with Blake. It wasn't your typical prom picture. There were four of us in this one: Blake and Flynn with their arms around each other's shoulders, me tucked under Blake's free arm, and Flynn's date, Wendy, leaning into him.

Sometimes I wonder if Blake only asked me because he felt bad that I didn't have a date. Not that it mattered in the end. Being with Blake has always been easy, and it was just as effortless to slip into something more. He was my first everything. Boyfriend. Kiss. Love.

My eyes slowly drift across to Flynn, and his hair that should've been curling around his ears. Instead, he'd worn it slicked back with gel. He'd never done his hair like that before and never did again.

I shake my head. What a silly thing to remember.

The front door flies open. Jade plows into the entryway, lugging a brown paper sack and two black garment bags on hangers. "So sorry I'm late. We had tourists come in right before closing, and they wanted to *browse*." She says the last word through her teeth, tossing the brown bag onto the kitchen table.

"It's fine. I've only been waiting for ten minutes."

"Good. Here." She shoves one of the garment bags at me. "This one's yours. Hurry and change so we can get to the bar."

She carries her own bag upstairs to her bedroom while I head into the powder room off the kitchen. Blake put Jade in charge of picking out our costumes for the final event in *Weddingpalooza*, and she's refused to give me any hints.

When I unzip the bag, my lungs stall in my chest.

Inside, I find a maroon sports bra, a white button-down top —err...*half* a button-down top that ties at the waist, a tiny black pleated skirt, a gray cardigan, knee-high socks, black Mary Janes, and two fuzzy pink scrunchies.

"Jade!" *No answer.* "Jade! I'm not wearing this!"

It's one thing to wear a costume on Halloween. Slutty nun? Go for it. Sexy nurse? Perfectly acceptable. Sleazy clown? Highly encouraged.

But it's June, not October, and we will be the only people in town dressed up.

I could strangle Blake for insisting on making such a big deal out of this week.

The picnic? Fine. Great. A totally normal summer event. Bachelor party? Also normal. Combined with my bachelorette party? I've heard of people doing that before.

But a costume party on top of it all?

I pinch the bridge of my nose, attempting to ward off the brewing headache.

"You have to wear it!" Jade shouts from upstairs.

No amount of swearing will make this any better, but I swear anyway as I shed my shorts and T-shirt for the ensemble. There's only a small mirror above the sink, but I don't need to see myself to know my entire body is on display. The last thing I need is the whole town seeing me walking around with half my ass hanging out.

Mom used to keep everything. There's probably an old costume up in the attic somewhere.

I jump at Jade's knock on the door. "Come on, Ruby. Open up and let me see."

I fix my face into a glare and unlock the door. Jade grins from the other side in a skin-tight orange catsuit, her long, blonde hair pulled into a tight ponytail on the top of her head.

Even though I'm not thrilled about her little plan, I find my lips lifting into a smile. We used to dress up like Britney Spears and put on concerts in our bedrooms, although our outfits were never as accurate as these.

"We can swap if you're not happy?" she offers. "But I think you look amazing."

I tug on the bottom of my "shirt." I think I'd feel even more exposed in that catsuit. Plus, Jade is super-hot in it. "No. This is fine."

One more night, I remind myself. Tomorrow, the wedding party will be moving into the renovated farmhouse beside the giant barn a few miles outside town where we're holding the ceremony and reception. Getting married in a barn wasn't my first choice, but Blake had begged me to consider the venue owned by the King family—who basically own half the county—because of the huge "locals discount." With its linen-white exterior and cathedral ceilings, it's way prettier than I'd imagined, and once I saw it, I was happy enough to make the reservation.

Friday is decorating day, followed by a wedding rehearsal and dinner, then it's the big day on Saturday. Thinking about everything that still needs to be done makes my stomach churn. All these extra events Blake's come up with have only added to the stress.

Jade pushes past me to grab the fuzzy hair ties I'd left on the sink.

I throw my hands up. "I draw the line at pigtails."

"You have to! They're the best part."

I groan and give in to make my sister happy. My hair is so long it looks ridiculous, but Jade assures me I'm a fox.

"Well, this fox is going to have one drink and leave before everyone in town sees me in this," I mutter, following her out of the powder room.

"False. You are going to have way too many drinks and have this thing other people call *fun*." On our way to the front door, Jade swings by the island to grab that suspicious paper bag.

I catch a flash of neon pink inside and my stomach drops. "No penises."

She clutches the bag to her chest, avoiding my gaze.

"I mean it, Jade. You promised." I refuse to wear one of those disgusting headbands with penises on springs that wiggle every time you move, or eat penis-shaped candy. Blake's dad is coming tonight, and the last thing I need is for him to see me sipping beer from a penis straw dressed like this.

"Ugh. Fine." Jade digs into the bag and produces a neon pink bachelorette sash. "You have to wear this, though. No complaints."

"Isn't the costume bad enough?"

She shakes the thing in my face. "Choose. This, or the penis headband."

JADE INSISTS I WAIT OUTSIDE ON THE STREET WHILE SHE pops inside The Rocking Horse first. A random guy in a blue car wolf-whistles through the window on his way past. *God*. I cross my arms over my exposed cleavage.

A moment later, Jade reappears and grabs my hand, dragging me into the bar. When I hear "Baby One More Time" blaring through the speakers, I find myself fighting another smile. As much as I don't want to do this, I have to admit it is kind of funny.

"Oh," a male voice chokes out behind me. "Holy shit."

I spin to find Flynn clutching his beer to his chest, gawking at me like he's been slapped. Instead of wearing the Mario costume Blake bought him, he's in his pilot uniform from the other day. The only difference is his neon pink pilot's hat.

"Is there a problem?" I ask, propping a hand on my hip.

Flynn shakes his head, a muscle in his jaw ticking as his gaze slips down my half-bare torso before he suddenly turns away from me.

"Oh, yeah! There she is!" Blake tackles me for a beer-flavored kiss and squeezes my ass with his massive white Luigi gloves. "You look shit hot, babe," he says against my lips, kissing me once more before letting go. His green cap with a white "L" sits slightly askew on his head, and his wallet peeks from the front pocket of his stretchy blue overalls.

I mutter a thank you, tugging on my skirt so Blake's uncle behind me doesn't get a good view of my backside.

"Aren't you supposed to be Mario?" Jade asks Flynn.

The only reason Blake wanted to do a fancy dress theme

was to have a couple's costume with Flynn, the way they used to back in school.

"Don't get me started," Blake groans. "Flynn claims it 'didn't fit him.'" He's probably trying to make air quotes, but it's hard to tell with the gloves.

Flynn rolls his eyes. "I've already told you that the pants didn't even reach my ankles, and the shirt looked like it was painted on."

"I wouldn't have minded that one bit," Tammy says with a laugh as she glides in, her toned stomach peeking from beneath her leopard-print two-piece. All she's missing is a big yellow snake around her shoulders. The way she sidles up close to Flynn makes me wonder if they're here together. If they'll be leaving together. Not that it's any of my business. That's his girl-friend's problem, not mine.

Blake shakes his head. "I'm sure it wasn't that bad. Mine's fine."

"Yeah, but you're shorter than me."

"Am not."

Sighing, Flynn presses his beer to his lips.

I warned Blake about ordering from that cheap-as-hell discount site, but he refused to listen. "It doesn't matter," I say before this can become a thing. "I love your costume, Blake. Who needs Mario anyway?"

"Yeah, who needs him? Fuck Mario." Blake pulls me in for another kiss. "You want a drink, babe?" he murmurs against my lips.

"Sure." A beer is exactly what I need to help me relax. He stamps a final kiss on my cheek before making his way to the bar. A few people I know from town offer their congratulations as they pass by on their way to a booth in the corner. For the first time since I put it on, I'm thankful for the sash because it lets people know this isn't my typical Thursday night in Still

Springs.

Flynn withdraws a folded sheet of paper from his back pocket and shouts, "Number three," right when Blake arrives back with a foamy beer.

Blake pulls out a similar page from the front pocket of his overalls and laughs before scanning the crowd.

"What's that?" I ask.

Flynn hands me the paper. "According to Google, the best man is supposed to organize the games at a bachelor party."

I scan the list.

1. *Start a conga*
2. *Drink 3 shots in 20 seconds*
3. *Kiss a bald man's head*

I glance up and find Blake hugging Mr. Drew, our former high school principal who's been bald for as long as I can remember. Then Blake lifts onto his toes and plants a kiss right on the old man's head.

All the groomsmen and the rest of Blake's friends burst out laughing. Flynn has his phone out, recording the whole thing.

"Blake has to do all of these?"

Jade peers over my shoulder. "That's genius. Ruby, you should do it too."

"This is Blake and Flynn's thing." I learned a long time ago not to try and get in the middle of a Blake-and-Flynn thing. Besides, I'm sure after what I said at the picnic, Flynn probably wants nothing to do with me.

"Come on." She tugs my arm, giving me a shake. "Please! You already turned down the penises."

Flynn's bottle pauses halfway to his mouth.

We are *not* discussing penises within earshot of Hotshot

Hudson. I double-check the list to see if there's anything I wouldn't do.

4. *Do 15 push-ups every time the best man whistles*
5. *Teach someone to line dance*

I glance up to catch Flynn smiling at me. "Blake can't dance," I say.

His grin widens. "I know."

6. *Speak with a British accent for 10 minutes*
7. *Serenade a girl*
8. *Wear someone else's clothing*
9. *The floor is lava*
10. *Talk non-stop for 3 minutes*

Nothing *too* bad. Am I really considering this? How stupid am I willing to act in front of all these people? "What does number nine mean?"

Instead of answering, Flynn sets his beer on one of the high-top tables, cups his hands around his mouth, and shouts, "Lava!"

All the groomsmen leap around, climbing onto stools and tables—Blake ends up on Tammy's lap. Carl jumps onto a bench beside a young couple who seem like they're on a date. Frank's stuck halfway to the bar, his head whipping from side to side before he swears.

"Drink up, Frank!" Flynn says, and the smirking bartender sets a shot of dark liquor on the bar. Frank stalks over and downs the shot, slamming the glass onto the bar when he finishes.

"What do you say, Quinn?" Flynn's still smiling at me. "You wanna play?"

I can't tell if it's an invitation or a challenge, but he clearly expects me to say no. Everyone always expects me to say no. But

Jade was right. This is going to be my only bachelorette party, and I deserve to have fun.

"Why not?"

I find Mr. Drew, walk right up to him, and kiss his smooth, shiny head.

That's the way the night goes—Flynn and Jade taking turns shouting numbers from the list of dares while Blake and I perform them. When number two hits (*Drink 3 shots in 20 seconds*), I think I might die and definitely puke a little in my mouth. Blake doesn't seem to fare any better. I can't remember ever laughing this much.

"Number six!" Flynn shouts.

6. *Speak with a British accent for 10 minutes*

My British accent isn't too bad, thanks to my Jane Austen movie obsession. Blake goes for a sort of cockney-esque accent, using words like *blimey*, *bloody*, and *bloke* to refer to everything and everyone except his dad, who is *old chap*. The muscles in my stomach ache from laughter.

I sink onto the stool beside Flynn, struggling to catch my breath. "I was dreading tonight," I confess when I finally do. "But this has been fun."

He returns my smile. "I'm glad."

Jade swings by to steal the paper sitting beside Flynn's beer. "Number eight!" she calls out.

8. *Wear someone else's clothing*

I snatch Flynn's pink pilot hat right off his head and plant it on mine. Across the room, Blake is stuffing his arms inside Tammy's blue jean jacket that hangs on the back of a chair.

I expect Flynn to seize his hat back, but his hand doesn't

move from his beer. When his gaze flickers back to mine, an apology bursts from my throat. "I'm sorry for what I said at the picnic. What you do with your life is none of my business. I was wrong to bring it up."

Flynn runs a hand through his dark hair, which is all ruffled up from the hat. "Wow. Ruby Quinn admits to being wrong."

At this point, I don't think anything can ruin my buzz, not even his mocking tone. "You should write it down in your calendar. It doesn't happen very often."

"Please. I remember you being wrong a lot back in high school."

I slam my beer down in mock offense. "Like when?"

"Like when you wore a white dress on our field trip to the state park."

"Oh my gosh, I totally forgot about that." At the end of every high school year, all the students spent a day at the park where we'd had our picnic a few days ago. I'd worn the new white sundress my mom had bought me for church. It ended up pouring before we got back to the bus, and our teacher had to give me his jacket so that no one could see through my dress. My next thought hits without warning: *Is that why Flynn remembers the dress?*

He tilts his bottle toward me. "Then there was senior skip day."

Half a laugh bursts from my lips. "That wasn't my fault. Latisha told me it was on Thursday."

"Senior skip day is always on a Friday. Everyone knows that."

I hadn't known that. *Obviously.* "You've been wrong too, you know."

"Me? Never."

"Eleventh grade, I told you that the answer to that question on our lab report was mitochondria, but you insisted it wasn't. I got my first *B* because of you."

Flynn snorts. "Okay, once."

I'm trying not to smile, but my lips have a mind of their own. "Junior year, you let Blake convince you to get frosted tips with him." With Blake's blond hair lightened by the sun and the chlorine from his parents' pool, his tips had blended in. Flynn's hair was too dark, and he resembled a '90s Justin Timberlake. He'd gotten his hair buzzed short a week later—which admittedly looked good—and it had taken until Christmastime to grow back to its normal length.

"Yeah, the tips were pretty bad," he says.

"So bad. I feel like they should be counted twice."

His carefree laughter does something strange to my stomach. I can't recall one time Flynn genuinely laughed with me instead of *at* me.

Blake, Frank, and Carl smack their hands against the bar in tandem, counting down like it's New Year's Eve. The shot glasses in front of them shudder with each *bang*.

"Oh! I know another one!" I nearly fall off my stool but manage to hook my foot beneath the rung at the last second. "Junior prom. You put a bunch of gel in your hair and wore it slicked back. Your 'mafia' hair single-handedly ruined our photos."

Flynn holds up a finger. "That was strategic. Wendy wouldn't stop touching my hair all week, and it drove me crazy. So, I put a bunch of shit in it to keep her hands off."

Teenage boys. So dumb. "You could've told her to stop."

His lips press against the rim of his bottle, curling into a smile. "I didn't want to embarrass her."

"Why not? You embarrassed me all the time."

Flynn's smile slips off his face.

I'm drunk enough not to care that I just made this one-hundred percent awkward. But his comment had stung. Why had Wendy's feelings been worth protecting and not mine?

My words come out softer than I feel in my chest. "I never did anything to you."

Flynn drops his bottle without taking a sip and starts picking at the corner of the label. He takes a few seconds to answer. "You pretended like I didn't exist."

"Only because I was with Blake, and…" I bite my tongue to keep the rest from spilling out. Now really isn't the time or place for pointless confessions.

Flynn nudges my knee with his, sending sparks shooting up my thigh. "And what?"

"Nothing. It doesn't matter."

What good would it do to confess that I used to have a crush on him? I swallow that bitter secret, chasing it with a sip of warm beer.

Flynn's shoulders lift as he inhales a deep breath. It's got to be the alcohol swimming in my mind, but when he chuckles, he sounds almost nervous. "Want to know something funny?" he asks.

"Sure." I could use something to make me laugh right about now.

"I didn't really want to ask Wendy to the prom. I wanted to ask you."

His reply nearly knocks me off my stool.

For a few long breaths, we sit there, and neither of us is laughing.

Ruby, you have to say something.

"Why didn't you?" It's a pointless question, and it doesn't matter now at all, but for some reason, I need to know the answer. Flynn had a million chances. We had almost every class together, shared the same lunch table, hung around with the same group of friends. If he'd wanted to take me, why didn't he just ask?

"Baaaabe." Blake slings an arm around my shoulders, leaning in hard enough to make me sway. He's missing his green hat and one glove; the other one looks like he tried to clean the sticky floor with it. "Let's karaoke."

"One sec. I'm talking to Flynn." My head is spinning, and it's not just from alcohol. I need to know his answer.

"*Babe...*"

Flynn doesn't look away from me when he says, "Number seven."

Blake lets me go to check his own list.

7. *Serenade a girl*

He takes off jogging toward the corner of the bar, where the karaoke machine's been sitting unused for the entire night, and snaps up the microphone. After punching a few buttons, Blake straightens and says, "This one goes out to my one and only, Ruby Quinn." He does ridiculous finger guns at me. The first notes for "Wannabe" chime through the too-small speakers, muffled and crackling.

"Blake asked you first," Flynn says so quietly that I almost don't hear him over Blake's screeching. He's not a bad singer, but for some reason, he thinks it's funny to imitate the original artists instead of doing his own rendition. And Blake Harrington is no Spice Girl.

"No, he didn't," I say in a lowered voice. "Blake asked me on our walk home from school on the same day you asked Wendy."

Flynn's brows gather, the intensity in his molten-brown eyes stealing the air from my lungs. "He didn't ask you until *after* I asked Wendy? You're sure?"

I nod.

His eyes narrow on where Blake is swaying out of time to the music. There's something urgent in Flynn's tone. "If I'd asked, what would your answer have been?"

It doesn't matter.

Still, the alcohol pumping through my veins makes me brave enough to admit the truth.

"I would have said yes."

CHAPTER EIGHT

FLYNN

My heart is pounding in my chest like a jackhammer.

I would have said yes.

Ruby's eyes flicker back and forth between mine for an endless moment before she blinks away and returns her gaze to Blake as he belts out an off-key song *for her.*

Flynn Hudson, what are you doing?

I glance around in a mild panic, my eyes hunting for Tammy in her barely-there Jane-from-Tarzan costume. But when I spot her near the bar with a couple I don't know, my inclination to leave Ruby and go talk to her is about minus fifty billion. Especially after Ruby just told me she'd have gone to the prom with me if I'd asked. My chest tightens with the possibility that Blake lied to me about having already asked Ruby when I told him that I wanted to. Would he really do that? It was so long ago; maybe we've all got our timing mixed up. Why should it even matter to me now?

"So, what's with the pink hat?" Ruby chews her straw at me, still wearing the hat in question. I try to ignore what the sight of it on her head does to my insides.

I also decide not to read anything into the fact that Blake's still serenading her with 'Wannabe'—a pretty fucking unromantic song, if you ask me—and Ruby seems more interested in asking me questions.

"It was a graduation present from the guys from school. Orchestrated by your dearest betrothed, of course."

She nods, her eyes making a sweep from my shirt and tie down to my dress slacks. "Your Mario costume didn't fit, huh?" She lifts her brows like she's onto me about something.

"Couldn't even get it on, it was so small," I reply honestly, sipping my beer.

"Here I was thinking you sneaked in the uniform because it's cuter."

She turns back to the karaoke show, and I stare at her profile. "You think my uniform's cute?"

She shrugs. "If you want to look like a male stripper."

A half-laugh leaves my lips, unsure what to make of that comment.

"Maybe I should've put a strip tease on the list then," I murmur, instantly regretting the words.

Flynn, behave.

"I'm kidding," I add quickly, but the truth is that Ruby wouldn't need to remove a single article of clothing to get me heated up. Especially when she's dressed as schoolgirl Britney. When she first walked in, I nearly had to leave the room to adjust myself. So much for praying mantis costumes.

"Bet your girlfriend likes the uniform," she mumbles into her straw, and a little thrill washes through me.

"I don't have a girlfriend," I admit. "Or a girl in every port. I was seeing someone, but it's not serious."

"The flight attendant?"

The fact that she even wants to know throws me for a loop.

"That's the one," I reply, her direct gaze making my cheeks catch fire.

The Spice Girls song ending steals our focus, and Blake tosses the microphone at Jeff from school, who's hovering nearby in an Austin Powers costume. Jeff's hands jerk up on instinct to catch it, and his beer bottle smashes to the floor. Instead of helping the poor guy clean it up, Blake snatches back the microphone like he's thought of something.

"Ladies and gents, we have a musical superstar in our midst!" he rasps into the microphone. "Flynn Hudson!" He aims the microphone in my direction then mimes a pulling rope action like he's dragging me toward him.

Musical superstar, what the hell?

I groan into the lip of my beer and consider an escape route, but I'm the best man, so I'm shit out of luck. I steal a glance at Ruby, whose eyes flash past mine, before I head toward the karaoke spot, wondering what song will embarrass me the least. But Blake's already selected "I Heard It Through The Grapevine," which crackles through the cheap-ass speakers as he tosses me the mic.

This song's long intro buys me a few seconds to hum out the pitch in the back of my throat before an idea slams into my head. Because tonight I was given a taste of Ruby's full attention on me, and I'm not ready to let it go.

"No cats will be murdered in the making of this song," I say obscurely into the microphone.

Blake grunts out a "Huh?" while my eyes flicker over to the cutest set of pigtails I've ever seen. One side of her lip quirks up.

I then angle the microphone several inches from my mouth, so I don't destroy anyone's hearing or cause glasses to shatter with the shrill sound, and begin whistling out the song into the microphone. The room erupts like I'm some sort of pop star, and by the time I'm done, everyone's laughing, cheering, clapping a hand on my shoulder—even Ruby's smiling at me—everyone seems impressed except Blake, who shakes his head at me like I've lost it.

I don't want to steal his thunder or anything, so I snatch my list out of my pocket, give it a quick scan, then call out, "One!"

Blake checks his list then shoves it into his pocket, grabbing Tammy's waist, who's standing a few feet away, and pushing her into a conga. She's good fun and wiggles her hips, swinging her butt at Blake while those around them join up behind him, forming a giant snake. I toss back my last sip of beer and head toward the back of the line, and somehow, Ruby arrives half a second ahead of me, and my hands land on her bare waist.

Blood rushes into my cheeks and makes its way south as I clutch onto her, the heat of her bare skin beneath her knotted-up shirt burning into my palms.

I have no idea whether she knows it's me behind her, but I have to focus to stop my brain from melting when my fingers slide up and down her skin as we move, accidentally brushing her lower ribs a few times.

When the song finishes, I let go right away, not wanting to make her uncomfortable, and I sure as hell don't need the torture. She turns around and passes me a shy smile that's so damn cute, I have to stop myself from reaching out and pinching her cheek. After I catch sight of Blake cheering in the background, I take a step back and do what feels completely unnatural. Yet I've learned to do it so well.

I turn my back on Ruby Quinn and walk away.

It's nearly midnight, and poor Blake's trying to teach his cousins to line dance, except Blake can't dance for shit, even when it's something simple. When he trips over his own leg and flies sideways, I catch him with a "whoa there, buddy," and rescue him by leading him over to the bar.

My intention isn't for him to order another drink—he's so glassy-eyed that I'm surprised he can see who he's talking to—but instead of just hanging out with me, he sidles up to the bartender and orders us two more beers.

"Man, your outfit is awesome," the young bartender says to Blake. "Love the mustache, but the teeth are the best bit." He chuckles as he pops the caps off our beers.

Blake's brows pull together. "Dude, these are my real teeth."

I clamp a hand over my mouth, making a solid effort not to crack up before I guide Blake over to two empty stools. Deciding that I need to keep a close eye on him in case he wipes out, I hit him up with some small talk, but he keeps pushing the conversation toward the wedding.

"Do you think you'll ever get married?" he asks in a slurry voice.

With a will of their own, my eyes land on Ruby.

I look back at Blake and lift a shoulder. "I hope so. Although I always seem to say that when I spend time around my parents. Once I've gone back to DC...who knows. It'd be good if I found a date first."

Blake's staring at me through squinted eyes like he has to concentrate really hard to understand what I'm saying. "You're not short on dates," he says like it's not even a question.

"No," I admit, picking at my beer bottle label, "but short on genuine connections."

A gruff laugh spurts from his lips. "*Genuine connections?* What's this new-age shit?"

I smirk at him, caught somewhere between enjoying the familiarity I have with this person I have so much history with and feeling like Blake and I have fallen into totally different stratospheres. Which I blame myself for after skipping town for so long.

"Hey man, I'm really sorry I haven't been back here more often. That's gonna change from now on." I give his beer bottle a light tap with mine. The slight movement almost sends Blake tumbling off his chair, and I decide not to do it again.

"Why haven't you been back? Ruby thinks it's because you think you're too good for this town."

My gaze drops to the floor, and the very stupid boy in me clings to the fact that Ruby even talks about me. "I don't think that. At all."

"I know, man; you're busy," he says supportively.

"My schedule's so insane that whenever I get home, I just want to park my ass on the couch and not move."

Blake nods.

"I've got nothing against this town; I love this place. What you're doing with your family restaurant and turning it into a hybrid business with the Quinns' store is awesome. You're building something solid for the future that you can leave to your own family one day." While my mouth keeps talking, my head's saying: *You're rambling, Flynn. You're rambling to cover up the real reason you left Still Springs and couldn't bring yourself to come back.*

Over Blake's shoulder, my eyes drift to that reason before I wrench my gaze off her and back onto my friend.

"I'm excited about the merger," Blake says, now looking like he can only see out of one eye. "Tammy's ideas have been..." He gestures the act of a bomb going off. "And it was all my idea in the first place. I fucking *love* that. It wasn't something my parents told me to do. This one's all mine."

I smile, knowing what this must mean to Blake, whose mom and dad are nice enough but can be controlling at times. "You should be super proud. The business, the wedding. Next, I'm sure it'll be a beautiful home somewhere with some mini-Blakes running around the yard."

And mini-Rubys. Warmth seeps into my chest, filling it up.

Blake doesn't even try to hide his eye roll. "I guess."

For a moment, I just stare at him. "You *guess*?"

He chugs back a third of his beer then shifts his stool closer to mine, wobbling while he does it. When he lifts his face, there's a fear in his eyes that I haven't seen since I took him up in my skydiving plane when he first visited me in DC.

"How do you know if you're doing the right thing?" he mumbles, his cheeks staining pink. "I mean, I know you don't know—you've never gotten married—but how should I know if *I'm* doing the right thing?"

A flash of alarm ripples through my stomach. "Are you having second thoughts?" I ask under my breath so that no one will hear.

I expect Blake to scoff right away, but he doesn't. He simply blinks at me with that panicked expression slapped on his face.

"It's all right," I reassure, giving his knee a light pat over his costume overalls. "Everyone feels like this before their wedding." I wouldn't have a clue if that's true, but it's what I've heard.

"I love Ruby," he affirms, and a ridiculous moment of jealousy passes through me. "But sometimes I think we're getting married because it's what everyone expects of us. Because we've been together so long, and our families have been friends for so long, and then there's the merger, and my parents say that if it goes well, they're gonna give me the restaurant when they retire soon, and..." His voice trails off as he stares up at nothing like he's gotten lost somewhere.

I have no fucking idea what to do with this information. Are these standard doubts before a life-changing event? Is this drunk talk? Or is Blake genuinely questioning his decision to get married? And what the hell does his business merger have to do with it?

Across the room, Ruby and Jade squeal and jump onto a table, playing the lava game, even though I haven't called out the number. A trace of a smile pulls at my lips.

For all my secret, shameful dreams about Ruby, the sight of her being such a good sport about this bride thing—while her fiancé sits in front of me and tells me he's not sure whether he wants to marry her—makes my gut feel hollow.

I force a smile at Blake. "You've got an amazing woman, you know. And from where I'm sitting, you might be the luckiest man on the whole planet. I'd give anything to have what you have."

His eyes warm up, and he raises his bottle in a cheers, even though it's empty. I clink my beer against his, glad that he's too drunk to have read between the lines. But *fuck,* it felt good to get it out.

CHAPTER NINE

RUBY

FOR ALL MY COMPLAINING, LAST NIGHT HAD BEEN FUN. I smile as Jade flicks the blinker and turns off the main road onto a curving driveway lined with evergreen trees. *Really* fun. The hangover this morning? Not so much. But my sister waking me up with scrambled eggs on toast in bed made up for it, especially when she's not usually a morning person. She's done so much for me this week.

"My quads are so sore from jumping on tables," Jade says with a laugh.

"At least your arms don't feel like jello." I don't think I've ever done that many push-ups before. Turns out, Flynn's kind of a sadist. We must've done at least fifteen rounds. I'll be lucky if I can lift my bouquet tomorrow. That image summons another whip of pre-wedding jitters, and I inhale a deep breath.

Jade snaps up her sun visor, peering through the windshield at the rolling green fields and beautiful, sprawling white barn overlooking a blue-green pond. "I forgot how pretty this place is."

Next to the barn sits an old stable that's been converted into a bar. On the other side of the gravel parking lot is a two-story white farmhouse with blue shutters—our home for the next two nights.

Blake pulls in behind us, his black truck kicking up a cloud of dust. The bass from whatever music he's listening to thuds so loudly I swear the ground shakes. Behind him, Flynn is driving the same red hatchback that he used back in high school. But the man who steps out of it isn't the same jerk I remember.

He's changed so much.

Of course, he has. It's been eight years.

I really don't know him anymore. Last night's conversation comes flooding back, bringing a rush of heat to my cheeks.

"You pretended like I didn't exist."

Had all those infuriating things he'd done *really* been poor attempts to get my attention? That sounds so stupid; it can't be true. If Flynn had liked me, he would've just talked to me like he did all the other girls in school.

"I wanted to ask you."

The confession shouldn't make my heart flutter, but it does. He'd seemed genuine when he'd said that, but I had been fairly tipsy, so maybe I'm wrong. What would have happened if I'd gone to prom with him instead of Blake?

Flynn tugs off the hooded Still Springs Soccer sweatshirt he's wearing, and the white T-shirt beneath lifts with it.

My breath hitches. Flynn may have changed, but his abs sure as hell haven't.

I tear my gaze away before anyone catches me staring.

Freshman year, a few of my girlfriends and I attended one of the soccer games at school. Afterward, we went down to wait outside the dressing room to congratulate our team on their win. I can still remember the moment the door opened, and I caught a glimpse of Flynn with only a towel around his trim waist, those very same abs on glorious display.

That was the day my secret crush began.

Junior year, we sat next to each other in science class, but he barely spoke to me unless he had to. I used to tell my friends I was going to games to watch my friend Blake play, but that had been a lie.

No one knew, not even Jade.

Just me and the pillow I used to cry in when Flynn started being mean to me at school.

That was before I realized that if a man likes you, he'll treat you with respect. If he doesn't, then he's only a boy, and no one wants to be stuck with a boy for the rest of her life.

Blake hops out of his truck, his black tennis shoes crunching against the gravel. "I can't believe it's almost time to do this thing," he says with his too-white smile.

I shove all thoughts of Flynn out of my mind, focusing on my husband-to-be. "Yeah, I know." The last four months since Blake proposed have flown by.

Jade hauls the first box of decorations out of the back seat of her car, and Flynn paces over to help. I keep my head down as I step past them and pop the trunk. My wedding dress is stretched across the top of our suitcases and boxes with the centerpieces, hidden from view inside a white garment bag.

"You have the suits, right?" I throw over my shoulder at Blake, draping the dress over my arm to keep the bag from dragging.

"'Course, babe." He unhooks a bunch of black garment bags hanging in the back of his truck and swings them toward me. I count to make sure there are four, just in case.

Some of the tension in my shoulders loosens. "And the shoes?"

He winces and begins rifling through his back seat like they should be there when I have a sinking feeling they're not. "Tell me you didn't forget to pick up the shoes."

He doesn't respond.

"Come on, Blake. I told you Latisha was leaving for vacation. You were supposed to pick them up days ago!"

In any other town, a store would remain open during business hours, no matter what. That's the professional thing to do, after all. Not in Still Springs. Some days you could go to the bookstore and find a sign saying they're closed for lunch. Once, the ice cream parlor was shut because the owner took his staff on a whitewater rafting trip. I've seen actual "gone fishin'" signs, a few "wife just had a baby," and one "sick day" sign, where someone had taken a black marker and crossed out "sick" and written "hungover."

Not even Quinn Brothers is immune to this flaw. Come tomorrow morning, there will be a sign taped to the door saying "Ruby's getting married," and any potential customers will have to travel to the Kings' superstore twenty minutes away. Terrible for business, but it's a quirk the locals have all grown accustomed to.

Blake rakes his fingers through his sandy-blond hair, leaping back to the ground with a grimace. "I didn't forget. I just didn't get around to it. Between work and the picnic and bachelor party, I've been a little busy."

"That's why I told you not to jam so much into this week." Why is it that all this other stuff has taken priority, and the one thing I asked him to do is the one thing he lets slide? It's like he cares more about the party than the actual ceremony. Doesn't he realize that without the wedding, there wouldn't *be* a party?

"Come on, it's not my fault. Flynn couldn't get time off, so I had to wait until we could all be together. I couldn't do this without my best man. Don't be mad." He catches my wrist and pulls me in for a hug. "I'll run to Morgantown and get some shoes in a bit."

"You're supposed to help decorate. And you have to build the arbor."

"That's not going to take all day. I'll be gone for two hours, tops."

I'm too warm and sticky and annoyed to have him all over me. I unhook his hands from around my shoulders and stomp toward the house. I've organized everything for this wedding. *Every single detail.* I wanted him to help me a little bit. Was that too much to ask? Apparently so.

Gravel sticks in my flip-flop. I kick it free with a curse.

"Everything okay, Quinn?"

In my anger, I hadn't seen Flynn come up beside me, his hoodie abandoned on top of the box he's carrying.

"Blake forgot the shoes."

Being mad at Blake is pointless. He'll apologize a few times like he always does, then act like everything is fine until I get over it. And if he decides that I'm taking too long, he'll get mad at me, and I'll end up apologizing.

"I picked them up," Flynn says.

I halt at the base of the stairs, catching my annoyed reflection in his aviators. "Picked what up?"

"The shoes for the ceremony. Blake mentioned them the other day along with a bunch of other stuff, and I didn't want him to forget—"

I throw my arms around his neck, catching a chest-full of cardboard box. My garment bag slips to the ground, and I don't even care. "Thank you."

It takes a second for me to realize Flynn's turned as stiff as a corpse. Another second to register how firm the muscles in his shoulders feel. My face burns when I let him go, which has nothing to do with the sun beating down on us. He's Blake's best friend, not mine. After last night, though, it kinda feels like we're becoming friends. But we aren't. Are we?

"Sorry." I collect my dress from the gravel. "I just...thank you."

Flynn's neck flushes against his white T-shirt. "It's no big deal."

It's a very big deal to me.

"So, um..." I'm desperate for something to say that won't make things awkward. My gaze snags on his car. "Nice wheels, Hotshot."

"Yeah. Not really a glorious return to town, is it?" He laughs. "I finished a job over in Pittsburgh before coming here, so I didn't have my car. My dad picked me up in this old flame."

"Move it or lose it!" Jade hurries past, one box balanced on top of the other.

If she's not careful, she's going to drop them both. "Jade, give me one of those."

"I've got it." She makes it up the three steps to the wrap-around front porch without stumbling. But then the door swings open, and she jumps back, ramming into me. A tall guy steps through, a pair of black sunglasses pushing dirty-blond hair off his forehead.

The box in Jade's hands tilts, and a jumble of fairy lights almost spills onto the porch. The guy takes the box from her in his tattooed fingers, an easy smile warming his face. "Well, if it isn't little Jade Quinn. It's been a while."

Jade blinks at him like she's never seen a hot guy before. *Earth to Jade.* "H-hey. Yeah. It has."

How the heck do they know each other?

The guy shifts his blue-eyed gaze to me. "You must be Ruby. I hear congratulations are in order."

I push my way around my gawking sister. "Thanks."

"The house is all ready," he says, nudging the door open with his black leather boot. He sets the box inside, next to an umbrella stand. The guy runs his hand up the back of his neck. "Ah, the sheets are fresh, and there are extra towels in the upstairs hall closet. This place runs on well water, so if you're planning a whole bunch of showers, try to space them out. Or I suppose you could team up in the shower if you're so inclined," he quips, his playful eyes finding Jade's. He breathes a light laugh and turns back to me. "There's wood down by the pond if you want a bonfire; be sure to use the sand bucket to put it out when you're done. I think that's it. Here ya go." He drops a set of keys into my hand. "If you need anything, call Wilson. His number's on the fridge. Check-out is at noon on Sunday."

I don't think Jade blinked once the entire time the guy was talking. Her eyes were too glued to the ink decorating his forearms.

"Thanks." I slip the keys inside my jean shorts pocket.

"No problem. Have fun. Don't do anything I wouldn't do. But if you do, take photos." He winks then mutters an "excuse me" to the guys, angling himself between Flynn and Blake before heading up to a gleaming vintage motorcycle parked in front of the barn. He climbs it like it's a second skin, kick starts it with his boot, and an almost animalistic rumble fills the air.

Jade is still staring long after he's ridden away.

I give her shoulder a nudge to make sure she's still alive. "You okay there, sis?"

"That was Dylan King," she murmurs.

"Hayley's older brother?" Hayley's been Jade's best friend since third grade. Her family owns this property, but I hadn't expected one of them to be onsite. Especially not *that* King. While I know Hayley somewhat, her brother Dylan graduated the year before I got to high school, so I'd never met him until now. Although, I've heard plenty.

I scowl at Jade. "Don't even think about it."

"Think about what?" She blinks at me, but I'm not buying the innocent crap.

"You know what. He's way too old for you." If she really

wants to get into what I've heard about Dylan King, I'll tell her in private.

My sister's brow pinches.

"Not to mention he's a total dick," Blake adds on his way past, the screen door slamming behind him. "You'd think with all their money, they'd have staff out here getting the place ready. Hah, maybe business isn't booming after all."

"Or maybe he was staying here while it was empty," Jade returns immediately. "He had a big duffel bag attached to his bike."

Blake grunts as two more cars tear up the drive. I recognize Frank's old blue truck and Tammy's black sports car. Frank and Carl jump out in unison, wave, and head around to heave a cooler out of the back of the truck. Blake and I had initially discussed that only the best man and maid of honor should stay at the farmhouse. But then he'd gone ahead and invited Frank and Carl anyway. Just like he invited the two of them to be groomsmen without asking me first, even though I'd already decided to have only Jade as my bridesmaid.

Jade joins me back on the porch a moment later. "Who invited Tammy?"

"Me, I guess?" At the bachelorette party, I'd been in the bathroom fixing my pigtails when Tammy had come in. We'd bonded over lipstick—as you do at midnight with a few drinks on board—and I'd mentioned that, since she was going to be at the barn all day getting the tables and kitchen ready for the reception, she should stay with us. I honestly hadn't expected her to take me up on the offer.

Frank and Carl lug the cooler up the stairs, sweat already rolling down their temples.

"Hey, guys." I hold the door open, doing my best to maintain a smile.

"Hell yes!" Blake flips open the lid before the guys have time to set it down and snatches out a beer.

"It's eleven-thirty in the morning," I point out, hoping he gets the hint.

"Relax. I'm only having one." He twists open the cap and takes a deep gulp.

Carl and Frank glance between Blake and me before reaching for the cooler in slow motion while Blake sniggers over his beer.

If Party-Blake comes out to play today, I swear I'm going to call this whole thing off. I refuse to walk down the aisle if my husband-to-be is hungover.

The door slams and Tammy appears in tight white pants, rolling a red suitcase across the kitchen floorboards. "Hey, girl," she says to me. "Thanks for the invite. Staying here really makes prepping for tomorrow a helluva lot easier."

"It's no problem," I reply. We have plenty of food, and another pair of hands helping out can't hurt. "Was it hard to get a sitter on such short notice?" That had been her only concern last night.

"Not at all. My neighbor usually watches him when I work late, and she didn't mind."

Jade claps her hands, drawing everyone's attention to the staircase. "All right, listen up. Ruby, you're upstairs in the master suite. Tammy and I get the other two rooms up there. Blake, you're with Flynn tonight." Blake punches Flynn's shoulder. Flynn shakes his head and laughs.

Jade frowns at Carl and Frank quietly sipping beer. "And you two, you're stuck in the bunk beds. Now, put those beers down and help us carry everything inside."

By the time I reach the barn, the box in my arms feels like it weighs a thousand pounds, and there are still four more that need to be lugged up here. I set the box down on the gravel and fish out the keys Dylan gave me before unlocking the oversized padlock on the door.

The muscles in my arms scream in protest when I give the massive rolling door a hard shove to the side. Cool air shoots out, fighting against the outdoor heat, which is a relief considering tomorrow is supposed to be another scorcher.

Round tables are already scattered around the cavernous room, with space left in the center for a dance floor. In twenty-four hours, I'll be standing here in my wedding gown with a second ring on my left hand and a new last name.

Ruby Harrington.

I've been doodling that name on my notebooks since I turned eighteen, and now it's going to become a reality.

My heart should be bursting with excitement. Instead, all I can think about is Blake not picking up those damned shoes.

If I'm being honest, it's not really about the shoes.

It's the week-long party. The money his parents spent on renting this venue, the catering, the open bar. The two hundred guests we've invited—half of whom I don't even know. All things Blake insisted on.

For what?

It's like all of this has become some sort of elaborate performance—a play I've been rehearsing for my whole life, with everyone who watched Blake and I grow up together as the spectators. What happens when the curtains close, and the venue clears out, and it's just the two of us again?

The thought leaves me with a strange, empty feeling.

I set the box on a table and sink to the cold floor, lying on my back and staring up at the iron chandeliers dangling from the thick white beams.

I love Blake. I've always loved him.

But somewhere between our junior prom and this moment, I can't help but feel like we've lost something. Something important. Vital, even.

Sometimes it feels like he doesn't even want to get married. I shove the thought away as quickly as it comes. If he didn't want to marry me, he wouldn't have proposed.

A caramel-brown shape flitters in my vision, and my eyes land on what appears to be a wren sitting on one of the rafters. "Hey you," I murmur.

Footsteps sound from outside the barn. By the time I sit up, Flynn is standing in the doorway, clutching two more boxes. "Hey. Jade told me to bring these up."

"Thanks. You can put them over there." I gesture to the table where I'd abandoned the other box. "Where's Blake?" He really should be the one helping, not Flynn.

"Prepping the bonfire for tonight. Jade's making sure he doesn't accidentally burn off his eyebrows before the big day."

A laugh slips out of me, but the sad thing is that Flynn's not joking. Our senior year, Blake ended up doing just that right before graduation, when he was attempting to light his parents' new grill at his end-of-school party. I drop my head into my hands, not sure whether I want to laugh or cry.

I then point up at the tiny, feathered shape. "There's a bird up there. Who knows how long it's been stuck in here; I only just opened the barn doors." I whistle to encourage the bird to fly outside, but then I catch myself and glance at Flynn. "I should know better than to whistle in front of a pro."

He breathes a chuckle and takes a few steps closer to the

bird. He curves his hands around his mouth and whistles a perfectly beautiful note. *God, he's good.* For a moment, the bird doesn't budge, but then it suddenly launches into flight and swoops out the door.

"Oh, thank goodness." My eyes scan the wooden floorboards for bird poop. Although, that's not my first worry. I would've hated to see something happen to the poor thing.

I catch Flynn gazing at me before he quickly glances around the room. "You ready?" he asks.

"I kind of have to be, don't I?" It's not like I can back out now. Or that I want to. Because I don't. I definitely don't. What would I even do if I wasn't with Blake? Jade's always complaining about how shallow the dating pool is. I've never even been on a date with anyone but him. I wouldn't know how to act.

Why am I thinking about this? I'm getting married *tomorrow*. Of all the things to worry about, this doesn't need to be on the list.

Flynn clears his throat. "I mean to go back to the house."

My cheeks catch fire. "Oh, yeah. Right. Of course." I shake the thoughts from my head. Getting married is a huge deal. I'm allowed to be a little nervous. "Sorry. Yeah, I'm ready." I get back up and straighten my shorts.

Flynn's head tilts ever so slightly as he watches me. "You okay, Quinn?"

I give him my best smile. "Why wouldn't I be?"

His eyes search mine. "You tell me."

This isn't the time or the place or the person to confide in. That's what pillows are for. "I'm fine."

I give the barn a final once over. The linens will be dropped off soon, then we can get the candles in place. The flowers are set to arrive at six-thirty this evening, most of them going down to the arbor that Blake should be building by the pond.

I tell myself again it's all going to be perfect, but what I really need is to hear someone else say it. I glance up at Flynn. "This place is great, right?"

He pushes his sunglasses up onto his forehead and glances around. "Sure. I guess."

"You guess?"

He plucks a bud vase from the center of the closest table, peers through the glass, and sets it back down. I'd wanted a destination wedding. Just me and Blake, his parents, Dad, and Jade. But Blake hated the idea of not celebrating with *everyone*.

"Not posh enough for a city guy like you?" I ask Flynn, only half teasing. I want him to like it. I'm not sure why. Maybe we are becoming friends after all.

"It's not that. I like the idea of something more intimate. My mom and dad snuck off to the shore and eloped." His face warms at the thought.

"Hotshot Hudson." I clutch some nonexistent pearls at my throat. "Are you a closet romantic?"

His deep-voiced laugh echoes through the empty space. "Maybe I don't like the idea of a bunch of people staring at me."

"Oh, please. You probably love being stared at."

He picks up a votive, turning it over in his long fingers. "Depends on who's looking."

The muttered comment makes my knees a little weak.

Light streams through the barn's paneled windows, casting the sharp angles of his face in a soft golden glow. I let my eyes linger, just for a moment.

He's even quieter than I remember. More introspective. Still cocky, but not as obnoxious about it.

Have you lost your mind?

You shouldn't be looking.

Especially not at him.

Flynn returns the votive to the table and turns to me,

tucking his hands inside the pockets of his dark jeans. "All this is great if you're into it, but it's not supposed to be about the wedding, is it? It's supposed to be about the marriage. At least that's what my mom says."

"She sounds like a smart woman."

That sounds like something my mom would've said too. She'd loved Blake. He'd been so good with her when she got sick, swinging by my parents' place on weekends when he'd come home from college to help out his folks at the restaurant.

I feel the smile melt from my face.

I didn't visit her nearly as much as I should have. I'd been convinced the treatment was going to work and that she would get better.

"I'd give anything to have my mom with me this weekend," I say softly.

Maybe that's what has me feeling so off-kilter. Mom will never get to see me in my dress. We won't get to sit on the couch and flip through the wedding album. She won't pick out her favorite picture and hang it in an ugly oak frame on the living room wall.

I'll never get to ask her if she thinks I'm making a huge mistake.

I don't even realize I'm crying until the compassion in Flynn's face turns blurry. After a few moments, his warm arms slip around my shoulders, drawing me into a spearmint-scented cocoon.

I know I should pull away, but my feet remain firmly planted, and my arms clutch onto him. "Sorry," I manage through my tears.

Flynn's sigh flutters the hair at my temples. "Nothing to be sorry about, Quinn."

His arms tighten around me, his breaths unsteady near my ear, and I wait for the sting of embarrassment to come.

It never does.

Flynn is the first to step away, drawing back and returning his hands to his pockets. His eyes are soft and warm as he gazes down at me. "I remember your mom from junior prom. She must've taken at least a thousand pictures of all of us on your porch."

Hearing him bring up prom tickles the inside of my stomach. I want to ask him more questions about what had happened back then, but I decide those questions are better left unsaid. Instead, I huff a laugh and wipe the tears from my eyes, leaving my fingers smudged with black mascara. "She loved pictures." And she insisted on printing *all* of them. The albums back home take up half the attic.

Flynn smiles. "At graduation, I overheard her bragging to a bunch of other women about how her girl was going to be a veterinarian."

A lump forms in my throat, and I can't seem to swallow. If I'd known what was going to happen to Mom, I never would have left Still Springs. Part of me thinks she knew that, and that's why she never told me how far the cancer had spread until it was too late. "She loved telling people that." Everyone who came into the store knew *Ruby Quinn is going to be a vet.* "I feel like she'd be disappointed that I never went back to college."

My face immediately heats. I can't believe I said that out loud. I've never told anyone that.

"Why didn't you?" Flynn asks.

I shrug. "Because Dad and Jade still need help." Maybe after the merger, we'll be able to afford to employ a few more people to cover my shifts, but right now, we don't have the money for outside hires. Plus, there's the cost of education to consider. Back when I was in college the first time, I had scholarships.

Flynn's head tilts, sending a lock of hair across his forehead. Each passing second in his company leaves me a little more nervous. "I'm sure your mom would be happy as long as you're happy," he finally says.

Would she, though? My mom had been the one encouraging me to study hard, apply to college, and really go for what I wanted. Sometimes remaining in Still Springs feels like I've let her down. Like I let myself down.

But that's a conversation for never.

I give my cheeks another swipe with the back of my hand and force a smile, more than ready for a change of topic. "I bet your mom is thrilled with everything you've done with your life." Her pilot son, flying fancy planes to fancy places.

For some reason, my comment makes Flynn frown. "Most of the time, yes. But she still worries about me living out of a suit-case so much. Sometimes it's... I don't know." His frown deepens. "I'm on my own a lot."

How am I supposed to respond to that? From the outside, Flynn appears to have everything. Is he secretly unhappy?

It's none of my business, so I don't ask.

What surprises me most is that I really want to.

CHAPTER TEN

FLYNN

I WIPE SWEAT OFF MY FOREHEAD, TURNING THE DIAGRAM instructions for the arbor upside down, but they make even less sense that way. I try to tell myself it's my bachelor party hangover that's making building this thing for Blake feel more brainbreaking than calculus, but my heart knows that's a load of crap.

I haven't been able to concentrate on anything since that hug with Ruby this morning.

When I let my mind travel back there—to the feeling of her being tucked up inside my arms—my chest thuds hard and butterflies crowd my stomach. I can still smell the vanilla in her hair and feel the rise and fall of her soft breath against my T-shirt. My entire body is stained with Ruby Quinn, and right now, I don't know how to get her out.

My mind also keeps replaying our conversation from last night at the bar, making my insides melt into something way hotter than the sun beating down on my shoulders.

"I would have said yes."

Those words make me want to fly through fucking time and go back to that school hallway and walk right up to that sweet, shy girl and ask her to the prom the way I should have. Everything would have changed—at least in my dream version of how that night would have gone. It would've been me turning up on her doorstep with a corsage and hearts in my eyes. Me winding my fingers through hers as I led her to the dance floor just to have an excuse to hold her. Me gently pushing her hair back so I could stare into her eyes, seeking permission, before I lowered my lips to hers.

It could've been me.

It should've been me.

A rush of anger grinds my jaw when I think about Ruby's revelation that Blake asked her to the prom at the last minute. If that's true, he'd flat-out lied to me weeks before that. Their two versions fit together about as much as fire and ice, and it doesn't take a genius to figure out who's been telling stories. Ruby has no reason to lie, and while Blake may have always been a doting friend, he's the most competitive person I know—especially when it comes to me.

Every time I try to give him the benefit of the doubt on this, a voice inside my head laughs. *You're not stupid, Flynn. He did this. He wanted Ruby for himself, so he tricked you into believing they already had a thing going when they didn't. He deliberately snuffed out the spark of hope that you'd had for her and lit the flame for himself.*

And what did I do? I backed off immediately like a best friend should, so Blake could be free to pursue the girl he didn't even deserve. Because if this is true, he didn't just lie to me; he lied to Ruby, cheating us both out of what could have become the beginning of something beautiful. Sure, she obviously liked him enough for things to have worked out between them, but what if she'd been curled up under my arm that night instead of his? Would she have still chosen him? Or would it be me standing beneath that arbor tomorrow?

All I'd wanted was one chance to find out, and Blake stole it from me.

I suck in a get-your-shit-together breath and remind myself that I'm as much to blame for how things turned out as him. I should've told Ruby how I felt about her long before prom. I shouldn't have begun teasing her and pushing her away like a dick the moment she started getting close to Blake and ignoring me. That epic fuck-up is entirely on me.

A hand snatches the arbor instructions page from me, and I spin to find Blake looking like he's been run over. "Are you all right?" I ask.

"I can't be around Ruby right now," he grunts. "She's still going on about the fucking shoes, and my head can't take it today."

My brow furrows as I pin my gaze to the wooden planks. "You should go easy on the beers tonight. You're getting married tomorrow."

"Yeah, yeah." He waves a hand like I just said he's got to get his teeth drilled or attend his own bail hearing, then grabs my water bottle and chugs the whole damn thing. I gladly turn my focus to the arbor, and we get it built quickly, but the mental effort alone is enough to make our headaches spike. We flop down onto a wooden bench, and I make a silent pledge not to drink anything alcoholic today. I'm also determined to feel better tomorrow, considering what I'm going to have to face.

A speech, Flynn. That's what you have to face. And the handing out of the rings. Probably some dancing. That's all.

Not watching the only girl you've ever lost your breath over getting married to your best friend.

Last night didn't change anything.

Blake grips his knees and sighs beside me. "Hey, thanks for dealing with the shoes; you saved my ass. I can't believe Ruby made such a thing out of it. I thought they didn't become nags until after you get married."

My gut tightens, and I force away the urge to shoot Blake a glower. "The shoes are a pretty key factor," is all I say in defense of Ruby.

"They're just shoes. We'd go barefoot if we had to," he scoffs, like dancing in a barn with bare feet isn't a fast track to splinter hell. "On the plus side, I think being the shoe savior redeemed you with her," he adds with a sidelong glance. "She sure didn't like you in high school, but she spoke well of you this morning. Her eyes were all lit up and shit."

Warmth spills into my chest, chased by a sharp twist at his mention of high school. While asking this question to a sober, hungover Blake could be considered the worst timing in history, the words fly past my lips before I can stop them. "I've been meaning to ask you something. Do you remember when I told you I was going to ask Ruby to the prom, and you said you'd already asked her?"

His brows bunch together. "Yeah, why?"

I swallow the boulder in my throat. "Was that true? Or had you actually not asked her yet?"

Blake blinks at me with his mouth slightly open, the air between us turning so silent that the cry of a bird passing overhead makes us both jump.

"Why would you ask me that?" he says.

I can feel my skin turning hot. As pissed off as I am, I probably shouldn't be bringing this up when he's marrying her tomorrow. But still, the words are out, and there's no putting them back in. At least I've already planned how to frame it without it sounding like I'm crushing on his girl.

"No reason other than Ruby and I were chatting last night about high school and how keen I was on Wendy. She mentioned that she didn't think she'd get a date to the prom because no one asked her until the last minute. Then I remembered our conversation that happened weeks before the prom. Which doesn't mean anything to me now, but I was just curious."

His eyes fall away from mine. "Of course, I didn't make it up, bro. Why would I? Ruby's obviously gotten mixed up. She's all over the place these days." He runs his palm up the back of his neck and sucks his bottom lip between his teeth, repeating the exact gestures he made throughout our Vegas weekend, when his shit poker face cost me six hundred bucks.

I stare at him, letting the ugly truth worm through me like a parasite.

Motherfucker. He did lie about it.

It's not a word I'd ever thought I'd attach to Blake, but it rings in my head with a deafening cry. Ruby and Blake's whole relationship can be traced back to that prom. His lie led to me giving up my entire life in Still Springs so that he could have his girl without my feelings for her getting in the way. What's worse, he's still lying to my face about it.

The burning pressure inside me boils over, and I lurch to my feet and tell Blake that I need to lie down for half an hour to reset my sore head.

Because right now, I can't look at him without wanting to do something really fucking stupid.

My attempt at a nap turns into an hour of staring at the ceiling, fighting off the brewing storm in my mind. I sit on the edge of the bed and scrub my hand down my face.

It's time to get over this high school shit, Flynn. No matter how you feel about the past, Blake and Ruby are getting married tomorrow. Try to be happy for them. At the very least, it's what Ruby wants, and she's done nothing wrong. Don't be a selfish fucker.

I inhale a calming breath and wander over to the barn, finding it empty aside from the tables and a mound of folding white chairs. I continue past it in the direction of the shed, peeking inside to meet a mess of table clothes and stacked plates.

Tammy lurches up from behind a small tractor, where she'd been crouching over a box of what I think are napkins.

"Oh, Flynn, hi."

"Hey. Do you need help with anything? I'm looking to be put to use."

A smile breaks out across her face as she steps toward me, a stylishly knotted napkin hanging from her fingers. "Well, aren't you a helpful boy? Your parents should be proud. Helpful *and* handsome."

I'm not quite sure what those two things have to do with each other, but I thank her and cast my gaze around the makeshift storage space. "Want me to tie up those napkins for you?" I offer, even though I'm not sure I'd be any good at it.

"You know, you didn't talk to me nearly enough at the bachelor party," she says, ignoring my question. "I waited for you all night."

I sink my hands into my pockets and smile. "Sorry about that; I was taking care of the groom. Keeping the man of the hour suitably entertained."

When she closes what's left of the space between us with a gleam in her eyes, I catch on to what's happening here.

There are worse things than a pretty girl's attention on me, especially when I'm consumed with someone I can never have, so I purposefully don't shift back when Tammy steps so close to me that the tips of our shoes brush.

"You're an incredible whistler, you know that?" she says, gazing up at me.

I don't know why that still embarrasses me. "I've been told once or twice. Thank you."

"It's quite a skill. Imagine what else you could do with that mouth."

She breathes the words so lightly that I'm not even sure I heard them right. But her eyes are hovering over my lips, and an urge to shut this down right away overcomes me.

"Tammy, I—"

"I think you're one of the most beautiful men I've ever seen in my life." Her palm lands on my forearm, her voice turning low and husky. "I know this sounds forward, but tomorrow's going to be such a busy day, and I might not see you afterward, so I had to say something." She lightly strokes her fingertips up and down my arm. "Everyone's gone down to the house," she adds, a suggestion in her eyes. "No one has to know, and in fact, I'd prefer it if no one did. It would make my situation easier." An almost guilty look crosses her face, but I'm having a hard time making sense of anything right now. I don't want to hurt her feelings, so I let her continue rubbing my arm, even though I'd really prefer she didn't.

"This is really flattering, Tammy," I say carefully, "but you know I'm leaving town right after the wedding."

Half a laugh flees her glossy-pink lips. "I'm not asking for a relationship, Flynn. Even though a man like you sure isn't made to be enjoyed only once."

Her brow dips like she's ready to eat me alive, which is my cue to back the hell up. She loses her grip on my arm when I take a step away.

"I'm sorry. I'm not really looking for something casual." I offer her a smile that I'm sure lands somewhere between apologetic and a touch freaked out.

When I tell her that I should probably go and turn to leave, she blurts out my name.

"Please don't mention this to anyone," she says. "Especially Blake. You know we have a professional relationship, and I don't want him to think any less of me."

"No, of course not," I reply, frowning at her belief that she's done something wrong. "I won't say a word."

Her eyes cloud with something that looks like loneliness.

"It's not you," I reassure her.

She tries to smile. "I know. It's you, right?"

I nod and return her smile before turning my back on her, the truth showering down on me.

No. It's *her*.

BLAKE AND I DON'T SAY MUCH TO EACH OTHER AT THE short wedding rehearsal or at the dinner afterward. The prom lie still feels bigger in my head than it should, given it happened a decade ago, but I'm not sure what Ruby's reason is for being so quiet. She sits and silently picks at her food beside Jade. The atmosphere's so fucking somber that I worry Blake's going to do something stupid like start lining up shots or suggest a game of beer pong, so I remind him that we still haven't lit the bonfire.

"Perfect call, dude," he says before chugging the rest of his water. "I feel like getting lost in a fire trance tonight and hitting the sack early."

Relieved to hear that, I get up and begin stacking plates while we all do our bit to clear up after dinner. Tammy hasn't met my eye since the shed and opts out of the bonfire night, muttering something about needing to call her little boy. I shoot her a smile as she passes by, our gazes connecting in a way that makes me concerned she thinks I've had a change of heart, when I'm only trying to make sure she's not feeling like shit about earlier.

When she slips into the kitchen, my gaze falls on Ruby's stare before her eyes quickly flicker away. I watch her gaze shift to the door that Tammy went through before it returns to me, and I have to push away a ridiculous urge to go up and tell her I'm not interested in Tammy.

When Jade steals Ruby's attention by saying something in her ear that makes her smile, I shake off my messed-up thoughts.

After the house is cleaned up, we all traipse down to the pile of wood beside the pond that Blake's been working on since we got here. Except it seems to have doubled in size since the last time I saw it.

"Dude, are you trying to set the place on fire so that you don't have to get married?" I say, genuinely kidding. I'm trying to get rid of this slimy feeling of being pissed off with him, and he just laughs.

I pull out the lighter I'd grabbed from the house and hold it against the tinder in several places. The kindling ignites easily, but the bigger logs need some encouragement. I check around for some leftover newspaper that we rolled up to add to the pyre when Blake grunts behind me.

"Why don't I go get the gasoline can and—"

"No!" the rest of us shout, and he flings his hands up.

"Jeez, just kidding," he mutters, his red ears making me wonder if that's true.

A few of us fold up some large sheets of newspaper and fan the flames until the logs catch and the fire kicks up into a healthy twist.

I plonk myself down on a flat piece of earth beside the guys while Ruby and Jade settle across from us on the opposite side of the fire. At first, the intense heat and the dancing flames act like a sedative, and we sit and murmur quietly to each other while Ruby tosses bits of sticks in, occasionally laughing with Jade.

"We should make s'mores," Ruby eventually suggests loudly enough for us all to hear.

Blake hmpfs. "Yeah, where's Tammy when you need her?"

"You can't make a fucking s'more, man?" Carl says to him, and a laugh rolls out of Blake.

"Not as good as she can, I bet. That woman is sent from food heaven."

I catch Ruby's eyes on Blake and give his lower leg a nudge with mine. "You got crackers, marshmallows, and chocolate? Your girl wants s'mores."

He yawns into his fist. "Sorry, babe, but I think we're going to have to save the s'mores for our first camping trip," he calls out to Ruby. "I'm beat, and I know there's a reason I should be getting an early night, but I can't think of what it is."

She gives him an amused smile as he clambers up like his legs are filled with lead and walks over to kiss her goodnight. Now all I can think about is Blake and Ruby going camping and being bundled up together in one blanket in front of a fire, and I have to curl my fingers into a fist to give the painful jealousy inside me an outlet.

Reality hits me like a slap in the face. This thing I have for Ruby is getting worse, not better. I'd thought that being around her and Blake for a few days—seeing them together—would shock me into the understanding that Ruby Quinn is *not an option*. Regardless of what went down in high school.

And I know she's not. I know it, but it's like I don't under- stand it. I feel like my soul is fighting against it or something. I'm beginning to hate myself for it. I hate watching Blake bend down to take her lips with his and ruffle his fingers through her hair, feeling like I want to pull him off her and shove him away with both hands.

I cross my arms over my chest, giving myself a silent shove instead of Blake.

One more day, Flynn. One more day, then you can go back to the life you worked so hard to build. You can go back to pretending Ruby doesn't exist. It's what you have to do, and you're going to do it.

I sink so deeply into my thoughts that when I lift my head again, I notice that Frank, Carl, and Jade have also stepped away from the bonfire, presumably to go to bed.

The second thing I register is that Ruby is looking right at me. Her eyes pull mine into hers like magnets, and our gazes fuse tightly together, tangling up. An electrical current shoots between us before running down the back of my spine.

I know I should look away, but I don't. And neither does she.

My whole body heats up with equal parts desire and shame, the two emotions mingling in my throat as I sit back and stare at Ruby while her eyes burn a trail into mine. Even from here, I can see her chest rising and falling as much as my own.

This feels more dangerous than any flirtatious banter we've exchanged, and yet I can't tear my eyes away from hers. And when her gaze makes a quick but unmissable slide down and up my body, a hot feeling leaks into my bones that feels a lot like hope.

While I know nothing can ever happen with her—and I'm ashamed for even wanting it—I feel like something just became real that I'd believed was reserved only for my dreams.

So, I do the smallest thing that I'm half hoping won't even be noticed because it sends guilt rushing to my cheeks.

I fill up my face with the affection that I work so fucking

hard to hide and let it travel through the flames, from my eyes to hers.

I'm sure that'll be what it takes to scare her away, but instead, her eyes soften and burrow a little deeper into mine. And when my lips pull up into the smallest, most nervous of smiles, so do hers.

CHAPTER ELEVEN

RUBY

THERE'S LOOKING AT SOMEONE, AND THERE'S *LOOKING* AT someone.

Then there's whatever Flynn is doing right now that's making my heart hammer in my chest and my body feel like I dove headfirst into the bonfire.

Everyone's gone. It's just me and Flynn and the fire. I should go inside, but I don't.

There's something different about him tonight. I can't put my finger on it, but whatever it is makes me feel like a deer stuck in a speeding car's headlights.

Stop looking at him.

I can't.

You're getting married tomorrow, a voice in my mind shouts. A voice I can barely hear over the blood pounding in my ears.

There's something in the depths of his dark eyes that I've never seen before. Something dangerous. It feels like, if I look too closely, I'll find myself at the edge of a cliff, falling into nothing.

Or everything.

Flynn is the first to glance away, picking up a stick and

tossing it into the fire. "I can't stop thinking about what you said last night."

I toy with the hem of my pale blue dress, needing to give my fingers something to do. "Oh, yeah?"

He nods. "And I can't help wondering how different things would be if…if I hadn't been such an ass."

All through dinner, my mind had been consumed by the same exact thought. If Flynn had asked me to the prom, maybe he and I would've gotten together instead of me and Blake. But then again, maybe not. There's no way of knowing if my life would've completely changed course because of one date or if I would've found my way to Blake despite it all.

My mom used to say, "What's for you won't pass you by." I can't remember where she got the saying, but it was one we heard a lot growing up. If I wasn't meant to be with Blake, I wouldn't be marrying him. Besides, Flynn had wanted to be a pilot more than anything. Flying was all he talked about during our final semester of high school. Would he really have given up his dream to stay here with me? And if he had, would he have resented me for it?

I could go down this rabbit hole forever, but the fact of the matter is Blake and I aren't together just because of prom. We have ten years of history, of firsts, of onlys. Our lives fit like two puzzle pieces.

"It's nice of you to finally admit that you were an ass," I say in a poor attempt to lighten the mood.

"It's hard to argue with the truth." Flynn doesn't so much as crack a smile as he drapes his arms over his knees, still watching me through the flames.

Now I should go inside.

I don't.

"Do you ever wish you'd left Still Springs?" he asks, catching me a little off guard with the sudden subject change.

I smooth my clammy palms down my dress. I love being near my family, but part of me—a part that's bigger than it probably should be—wonders what would've happened if I'd finished college, become a vet, and discovered what life is like beyond the unchanging hills of Still Springs.

But I don't say any of that because what's the point in wondering what could've been when it's too late to change course? So instead, I ask a question of my own. "Do you ever wish you'd stayed?"

Silence stretches between us, accentuated by the occasional *pop* from the graying logs.

"That depends," he finally says, his eyes locked to the bonfire. "Would it have made a difference?"

I find a twig on the ground, turning it over and over in my hand. If I could have met *this* Flynn—the one who had made me feel like I wasn't a burden at the picnic, the one who had me laughing so hard last night that I almost fell off my stool, the one who had wrapped me in his strong arms and let me cry against his T-shirt. If I could have met the man that he's become instead of the boy I once knew, I think it *could* have made a huge difference.

"I guess we'll never know," I whisper. "Because you didn't stay. You left and never came back." I snap the twig in my fingers and throw it into the fire.

When I glance up, there's a look on Flynn's face that's going to be seared in my memory forever. I feel every single emotion flickering in his liquid eyes as if they're my own.

Pain.

Frustration.

Regret.

Heat paints my cheeks, but it has nothing to do with the bonfire and everything to do with the guy sitting across from me, still staring with the intensity of an inferno.

Put out the fire, Ruby.

Flynn opens his mouth, but before he can say anything, I jolt to my feet, grab the bucket of sand, and dump it over the flames. A plume of smoke lifts in the cool night. Flynn curses and coughs, scrambling away from the gray cloud billowing toward him.

The fire is only half out, but there's no more sand, so I turn and run for the pond.

"Quinn, wait."

I don't.

I can't.

There needs to be distance between us. I kick off my flip-flops and sprint toward the shore, the bucket swinging and dewy grass tickling my toes as I go. The moment I reach the glassy sheet of water, I jump in, not caring about the hem of my sundress getting soaked. Cold water surges over my legs, but I'm still too hot. Mud squishes between my toes, and I wade through reeds until I hit a clearer patch and dunk the bucket.

Flynn comes to a halt on the shore. He's a little breathless when he says, "There's something I need to tell you."

My chest begins to burn. *Put out the fire.* "No, there isn't."

"Ruby—"

Hearing him say my first name hits me right in the heart. *I can't have this.* I catch the lip of the bucket with both hands and launch the water at Flynn, hitting him square in the face.

"What the hell, Quinn?" he sputters, wiping his eyes. His wet T-shirt clings to the ridges of his chest and abdomen.

It takes everything in me to force my gaze from the trail of dark hair disappearing beneath his jeans.

Put out the fire.

I dunk the bucket again, not sure whether I need to dump it on him or myself. "Whatever you need to tell me can wait until tomorrow night." When the vows have been spoken, and the rings exchanged. When the dinner is over and the dancing is done.

When it won't matter.

Then he can tell me.

Flynn shakes his head. "It can't wait." Water laps against my knees when he drops in and walks toward me.

"Then it shouldn't be said at all." I wish he still had on those stupid sunglasses so I couldn't see the devastation in his eyes. "Don't look at me like that."

He steps closer. I step back.

"Like what?" he says.

"Like you—" I cut myself off, unable to say it aloud because once it's been said, it can't be unsaid.

When he takes another step, I adjust my hold on the bucket. Before I can dump it on him, he catches the thing and tosses it toward the shore. I bolt toward deeper water, running from him —from whatever this is.

Guilt churns in my stomach, thicker than the icy sludge at my feet. I make it two steps when something slimy and *definitely* alive slides against my calf. I yelp and launch myself away from it, clinging to the closest solid object, which happens to be Flynn's toned torso. My legs wrap around his hips as I struggle to escape the water. My nails dig into his sculpted shoulders as I climb him like a freaking tree.

He curses. One large hand slides to cup my backside, keeping me steady and drawing me closer until our heaving chests meet. Moonlit ripples reflect in his endless eyes; drops of water cling to his lips. When water from his shirt seeps into my dress, I start to push him away, knowing how wrong this is. And yet my fingers have a mind of their own, threading into his damp hair. His free hand catches the back of my neck, drawing our foreheads together, sliding down until his thumb presses against the seam of my lips, and the rest of his long, cool fingers curl around my chin, holding my head firmly in place.

Our mouths never touch, as if that makes any of this excusable.

"You're the reason," Flynn whispers. "The reason I left and never came back. The reason I can't fucking breathe, my chest is so tight. It's you. It's always been you."

His confession burns me from the inside out.

Why now? I want to scream. If it hadn't taken him eight years to show me who he really is, maybe...

I shove that thought down as far as it'll go, finally summoning the strength to untangle myself from him, but his hold only tightens. "Let me go."

He doesn't fight me. His hands fall to his sides, and I'm back in the water for only a moment when he says, "I've tried."

"Yeah, well, you should've tried harder."

I don't mean about letting go, and from the pain in his eyes, I think he knows it. He should've tried being nice to me. Being my friend. Being someone I wanted to run to instead of run from. Being someone easy to love instead of someone easy to hate.

I drag down the hem of my dress where it sticks to my thighs, realizing too late that the water has made the thin material completely transparent. I fold my arms over my chest as I stomp toward the shore.

Blake has put in the work. Yeah, sometimes he's immature and drives me nuts, but he's been there for me through thick and thin. Like my first year of college, when I was so homesick it made me cry. When my mom took a turn for the worst. When she died. When I gave up college. When I made the decision to stay in Still Springs.

Blake is steady. Constant.

He's exactly what I need.

Marrying him isn't a mistake.

This—the stolen looks, the lingering stares, the troubling doubt.

This is the mistake.

If Flynn hadn't come back to town, this would never have happened.

I whirl around to find him dragging both hands through his hair. My voice hardens. "You haven't earned the right to say shit like that to me."

Droplets of water slip down his forearms corded with muscle. "I know. *Fuck*. I'm so sorry, Quinn. So fucking sorry."

He can keep his apologies...and his moonlit confessions.

I don't want them.

I continue to the bank, catching my flip-flops and running for the house, my thoughts whirling at a million miles an hour.

Nothing happened. Our lips never touched. I never said anything that crossed the line. I've never been anything but loyal to Blake.

All that may be true, but I still can't help feeling like I'm going to puke.

I don't stop running until I'm inside, standing at Blake's bedroom door, needing to see him before Flynn gets back. I know I've been irritated with Blake all day, but that doesn't justify what just happened. He deserves the truth.

I make a hurried knock, but he doesn't answer.

"Blake?" A puddle of water pools at my feet; bits of grass and mud still cling to my toes. "Blake, please. I need to talk to you." My hand twists the cold brass handle.

I find him tucked beneath a patchwork quilt, snoring away.

"Blake?" I shake his shoulder until he groans. "I need you to wake up."

He rolls over, propping himself up on his elbows and

blinking up at me. "Everything okay, babe?" he asks, his voice thick with sleep.

Shame clogs my throat. Thankfully, it's too dark in here for him to see the horrified expression on my face. "No."

He sits up straighter. "What's up? What's the matter?" His brow furrows as he squints at me. "Wait...are you *wet*?"

Where do I even begin? "I was getting water to put out the fire and got wet and...I hugged Flynn. It was a...a long hug."

"Good," he says through a yawn.

Hold on. Did he just say *good*? "Why is that good?" Why isn't he pissed? Obviously, I need to explain myself better.

Before I can, Blake catches both my hands, squeezing my cold fingers. "Because it's about time you got over what happened in high school. I don't want my two favorite people at each other's throats every time we're together."

We won't be together after this, though. Flynn is going back to DC, isn't he?

"I still shouldn't have hugged him." And I definitely shouldn't have lingered. "I should've gone to bed when everyone else did."

Blake's free hand makes a dismissive shake. "It's fine, babe. Seriously. Calm down."

I search his face for anger or irritation—even disappointment—but all I find is a soft, sleepy smile. "You're not mad?"

"Why would I be? Are you marrying Flynn tomorrow? Because I could probably use a heads-up."

"Of course not," I choke out, my face igniting for the hundredth time tonight. But Blake's unfazed reaction allows me to catch my breath.

"Exactly." He flops down onto the mattress. "Let Hudson keep his consolation hug. It's about time that guy was runner-up for something. I scored the real prize."

I don't know how I feel about being referred to as a prize,

like this is some sort of trophy competition. But I'm really in no position to point that out to him, and I guess it's his way of telling me I'm special.

"I'll see you in the morning, okay?" he says, his eyes sinking shut.

I start for the door, praying I don't run into Flynn on my way upstairs. When I finally reach my bedroom, I stop and take a breath. After tomorrow, all of this will be behind me.

The memory of Flynn's emotional face flickers through my mind.

No matter how hard I try, I can't get it out.

CHAPTER TWELVE

FLYNN

I WAKE UP HARD. AND NOT THE "I NEED TO GO PEE" KIND of morning wood. I mean the "last night, Ruby's legs were wrapped around my thighs while I gripped her ass" kind of hard.

I squeeze my eyes shut and roll onto my stomach, fighting flashbacks that keep charging into my head. But the friction of my erection against the mattress escalates those mental images into ones of Ruby lying beneath me, and I flip onto my back, draping an arm across my face.

Fuck, fuck, fuuuuck.

How did I let things get that far last night? One minute, Ruby and I were staring at each other across a bonfire; the next, our foreheads were pressed together, her lips so close to mine that we were sharing the same breath.

It had taken all the willpower I had not to kiss her. Not to kiss the life out of my best friend's fiancée, who he's marrying *today*.

Flynn, you're officially a shit best man.

Landing the latest Challenger jet in the Swiss mountains while a bunch of rich assholes are playing drinking games in the cabin? Easy. Having Ruby Quinn look directly at me for more than ten seconds? I lose all my damn sanity. The only reprieve I have right now is that Blake left early this morning to talk to Tammy about the food, so he doesn't have to look at my fucked-up face.

My god, the things I said to Ruby last night. Without even a drop of alcohol in my system.

Blake may have fed me a lie in high school that I don't think I'll ever get over, but he was a kid back then—just like I was when I started teasing the hell out of Ruby to get her to acknowledge my existence. There's no fucking excuse for a grown man doing what I did last night.

I kick out of the bed like it's coated in slime and head straight for the shower. I need to wash away the burning imprint of Ruby's bare skin pressed to mine, her stupidly intoxicating smell, the torturous sight of her sopping-wet dress glued to her chest, the dark circles of her nipples showing through it.

Fuck. Me.

I yank off my boxer briefs, shove the shower door open and spin the taps on, blasting cold water over my head until I gasp. My dick is still so hard I can't stand it, and I clench my jaw and focus on the task at hand. I lather soap over every inch of my body before pouring shampoo over my hair and scrubbing my fingers through it.

I'm clean as a freaking whistle, and yet I've never felt dirtier.

I rest an arm against the glass door and shut my eyes, making a silent plea for last night to have never happened. It's not only the guilt of what Blake would think if he'd seen Ruby straddling me while I whispered in her ear, but it's the absolute mess it's made of my heart. It was a glimpse through the window of what it would be like to have her. The most epic torment I could imagine.

If only I hadn't been such a pussy in high school. If I'd

struck up a conversation with Ruby instead of going all tongue-tied and treating her like shit as the worst kind of coping mechanism for her lack of interest in me. Because of that mistake, Blake's about to put a ring on her finger, and I'm standing here with a guilty conscience and a throbbing dick.

I give in and wrap my hand around myself, aching for a release that's not going to come from any imagined scenarios or porn fantasies. Not this time.

It's not like I haven't jerked off before to the idea of Ruby doing all sorts of shit with me. It's what got me through my hormone-filled senior year. But this is different. This time, when I tighten my grip and slide it up and down my full length, nothing in my head is made up as a light moan rumbles out of me. The images are vivid and real.

I can still see the rivulets of water running down Ruby's neck and into the valley beneath her wet dress that I wanted so badly to peel down, setting my mouth free.

The way her breath seized up when I clasped her chin and held her still so I could stare into her fucking gorgeous eyes and show her how I feel about her.

I can feel her silky thighs tightening around my backside when my foot slipped a little and our hips pressed together.

I imagine how she'd feel wrapped around me like that, but stripped naked, the softest parts of her body rubbing against the hardest part of mine.

My dick thickens further, and I bury my face in my forearm and kick up speed, seeing nothing except Ruby's eyes burning hot across that fire, making me ache for her. Then I see it all in quick flashes: smooth breasts, hard nipples, her legs spread open for me, her pussy wet and glistening. Warm liquid fills my hand, and I pant into my arm, letting the intense pleasure spill through my bloodstream and numb me all over.

Then I punch the shower door almost hard enough to break it, imagining it's my face.

After changing into a pair of shorts and a black T-shirt, I pace the room like a restless animal, working up the courage to go outside and show my face. At this point, I'm not even sure who I'm more nervous to see, Blake or Ruby.

What if she told him what happened last night? Will he call off the wedding, kick the door down, and introduce his shoe to my jaw? I doubt Blake could take me in a fight, but if he wanted to shove his knuckles into my eye, I don't think I'd stop him right now.

My stomach twists into knots as I reach for my tablet, swiping open my emails. The only thing that's ever saved me from spiraling into self-destructive mode when I've been this upset about something is work. If there was a jet sitting outside this room right now, I'd be hard-pressed not to slip inside it and fly the fuck out of here.

I've been getting heaps of emails lately from other companies offering me contract work to cover their pilots stuck in training or on vacation. As long as the shifts don't clash with my employer's schedule or exceed regulations on how much I can fly, I'm free to take them.

I type out an email to the guy who contacted me last, giving him all the dates I'm available. I bite away the nagging feeling that I'm pushing myself further away from my promise to wind down work and shoot for more balance in my life. Because right now, the thought of going back to my empty apartment in DC, while Ruby and Blake jet off to Mexico and lock themselves inside their hotel suite, turns my blood to ice.

The email sends, and a shred of tension leaves my body. With any luck, my calendar will fill with shifts, and I'll soon start to forget this week ever happened.

I let that depressing truth wash over me as I lay out the pieces of my suit on the bed. While I'll always appreciate Blake choosing me as his best man, and I'll probably never look at him the same way after finding out about his lie, I've proven beyond a reasonable doubt that I don't deserve to be here. I shouldn't have even come back to Still Springs. I'd severely underestimated the hold Ruby still has over my heart. And as pathetic as that is, I can't seem to change it, no matter how much I want to.

I'm sitting on the edge of the bed with my head in my hands when Blake pushes through the door. After his early night, he looks fresher than I've seen him in years, and my affection for him flares in my chest. I don't want any more lies to come between us. An urge to man-up and tell him about last night surges into my throat, but I swallow it back down.

"Hey, man," I say, getting up. "How are you feeling? Nervous?"

"Strangely not." He parks his butt on his bed and sits with his hands braced against the mattress. "I feel weirdly normal. Like it's just any other day."

"That's a good thing, I suppose," I offer, even though I'm not quite sure that's true. But he and Ruby have been together for so long now that I guess they're already as good as married.

It's a moment of clarity that yanks me back down to earth.

This is right. Blake is meant to marry Ruby today, and just because the very thought of her makes my heart melt into a puddle, that doesn't mean I have any claim on her. I don't. What happened in high school is ancient history, Ruby ended up with Blake, and now they're happy together.

So, I'm going to do what I came here for. I'm going to stand at my best friend's side when he marries the girl he loves. I'll smile, congratulate them both, spend my last few days with my parents, then quietly slip away. Except, after last night, an unsettling feeling keeps nagging at my brain, telling me that leaving Still Springs isn't going to be enough this time. Not after I've held her soft body against mine and looked into her eyes—beyond the wall she keeps there—and felt her looking back.

"You okay, dude?" Blake asks, his brow crinkling up. "You've got a face like someone kicked your dog then ran over it."

A bewildered laugh bursts out of me. If only he knew that the reality is almost worse.

"Yeah, I'm fine. So, what's the plan?" I ram an enthusiastic smile on my face, needing to get through today. "The ceremony's at two, right? I assume you don't want to run into Ruby before then. Do you want to go for a run? Kick a soccer ball? Take the fishing rods out? You're the boss."

"To be honest, I want to get the ceremony over with so we can get to the party." His brows wriggle up and down, and I have to laugh. Blake leans back on his elbows. "You better have written a kick-ass speech for me."

I chuckle at the thought of the speech I've written, which is basically a thousand words of roasting the groom. If there's one guy who oozes material to poke fun at, it's Blake Harrington.

"You know you've got no chance in hell of hearing my speech before the reception, but do you want to practice your speech on me?"

He shrugs. "Sure, why not."

He leans down to dig through his duffel bag, pulling out a crumpled piece of paper. I can see from where I'm standing that it's only half a page of handwritten scrawl, which he begins reading out.

"Firstly, I want to thank everyone for coming here today. I was really excited to see you all and give this speech, but now that I'm married, I should probably get used to never being listened to."

Blake grunts a laugh while my brows raise.

"Everyone here knows that Ruby is a wonderful and caring person," he continues. "I've definitely married Mrs. Right. I just had no idea that her first name was 'Always'." He snorts into his fist. "But on a serious note, I'm grateful you all came here today to support Ruby and me, especially those who have traveled, like my best man, Flynn Hudson." My lips quirk up as he shoots me a glance. "I will be handing the mic over to Flynn soon for his best man speech, which he has assured me will be full of sexual innuendo."

What the fuck? Blake!

"Today is the happiest day of my life," he adds, reading, "and will continue to be with every year that passes. Just don't expect me to remember any of it because, tonight, we are going to paaar-tay!"

He smacks the speech down on his thigh and smirks up at me.

The words of support he's probably waiting to hear die in my throat. Where is the mention of Ruby's mom, who passed away, or something about her dad or Jade? Where are the thanks to all the people who helped put the wedding together? Where is the part where he says something genuine and heartfelt about his amazing wife?

"So, what do you think?" Blake asks.

I can't let him give this speech. The guy isn't stupid; he runs a highly successful restaurant, is halfway through a merger, can play soccer like a pro, and has the best taste in women of anyone I've ever met. But he tries so hard to be funny and the life of the party that I feel like he's lost sight of what today is about.

I suck in a breath and sit beside him. "There was some funny shit in there, man, but it doesn't quite fill out the time in Ruby's schedule, right? Your speech is meant to go for five minutes. Let me help you figure out what else you can put in."

He shoots me an appreciative nod. "Sure, bro, that'd be awesome." He reaches for a pen from his bag and taps it against the page, his face turning blank. "What else do you think I should say? Oh, wait. There's a joke I heard once that I was going to include but didn't. It goes: Marriage is like going to a restaurant. You order what you want, but when you see what the *other* person has, you wish you'd ordered that."

"No!" I resist the urge to face-palm. "Start with what you love about Ruby. Something that isn't a joke."

He chews his bottom lip and stares at the page. "Well, she's kind, and caring, and makes me laugh. She's always been there for me, and I guess her cooking is a bit better than it used to be."

I swallow a laugh. "Good. Start with that. Maybe not the cooking part. Stick to the positives."

Blake begins scribbling, and when he writes out the words, "Her kisses are soft and warm," I have to turn away.

When he dots his final sentence and gives me a thankful smile, my guilt over last night overwhelms me, sending my words tumbling out in a throttled rush. "Blake, there's something I need to tell you about last night."

He blinks at me, and my mouth dries up. I stand and put a few paces between us. "Ruby and I were at the bonfire and..."

"I know," he says. I gape at him, a little dumbstruck. Why is he getting up and clapping a hand on my shoulder rather than punching me in the dick?

"Ruby already told me last night," he adds. "You guys hugged or some shit. It's fine. I'm actually glad about it. It's time you two put all that high school crap behind you and start getting along."

Wow, okay.

"What else did she say?" I can't help but ask, even though I should really drop this topic before my luck runs out.

"Just that she should have come inside with everyone else instead of staying out with you."

A spike of pain pierces my chest, but I work to keep my face impassive.

"It's all right, dude," he says, giving my arm a playful whack. "Don't look so freaked out. I know you'd never be interested in Ruby."

Heat sears my cheeks like I'm standing too close to a fire. "What makes you say that?"

He drops his speech inside his duffel bag. "A high-flying pilot who travels the world for free and looks the way you do?" He blows a raspberry through his lips. "Why would you be interested in *Ruby*?"

My lips pop open as he gives his suit a pat where it's hanging on the door before disappearing inside the bathroom, humming a Spice Girls song.

I can't help but wonder why Blake wasn't more concerned about my prolonged hug with his fiancée. Because if Ruby was my girl, and she told me that happened with another guy, I sure as shit wouldn't be humming. And I definitely wouldn't be telling the guy that she wasn't good enough for him.

CHAPTER THIRTEEN

RUBY

THERE'S HEAT.

So much heat.

From the fire. From his body. His hands. His mouth. I'm powerless to fight it, begging the flames to consume me. I clutch tighter, wrapping myself in him. Letting down my walls, feeling him rush inside like a rising tide.

"*Ruby...*" My name falls from lips I've never tasted, a forbidden song. He clings to me, a world of starlight reflecting in his dark eyes.

"Don't let me go," I whisper.

"Ruby..." His voice fades.

His heat is gone.

I'm cold. Shivering. Alone.

"Ruby!"

I jolt upright. Jade is standing at the foot of my bed in a silky pink robe, the words "Maid of Honor" embroidered across the breast and a towel twisted into a turban on her head. "Wake up, sleepyhead. Your alarm has been going off for the last fifteen minutes." She tosses my phone onto the bed beside me.

"Sorry," I mutter, scrubbing a hand down my face before

checking the screen. No new messages. No missed calls. A few notifications on my socials, but I don't bother with those since it's already a quarter to ten. I never sleep this late.

Holy shit, it's my wedding day.

I need to shower right now if I'm going to be ready for my hair appointment at ten-thirty. I kick the covers aside and smile as if I didn't just wake up from a dream about my fiancé's best man. As if what happened last night won't stay with me for the rest of my days.

The garment bag hiding my dress hangs from the curtain rod in the window. I can't even look at it without feeling sick to my stomach.

It doesn't matter, I tell myself.

It doesn't matter because it's never going to happen again. Today, I'm marrying my best friend, and I'm going to spend the rest of my life loving him the way he deserves to be loved.

"You want breakfast?" Jade asks, uncoiling the cord from around the hairdryer and plugging it into the socket. The towel from her hair lands on the floor.

"No time. I'll get something in a bit." I grab my body wash and hurry into the bathroom for the fastest shower I've ever taken, glad for the time crunch. Rushing gives me less time to think about last night.

About where it could've led.

Nothing happened.

Maybe if I say it enough, I'll believe it.

I tuck a shower cap over my hair to keep it dry and step into the stream of hot water, letting it scald me until I feel clean, which takes longer than it should.

By the time I finish, there's a knot embedded in my stomach.

It'll be fine.

Another lie I tell myself as I slip into the lacy underwear I bought for beneath my dress. I barely recognize the woman staring at me from inside the foggy mirror. The frown. The dark circles under my eyes that hold too many secrets.

Secrets I bury deep down where my discontentment lives, knowing I have no right to be discontent.

My life is amazing. This is only a hiccup.

We can't help who we're attracted to. What matters is how we handle that attraction.

I'm choosing to pretend it doesn't exist.

It was a hug.

I hug people all the time.

It sounds like Jade is talking to someone in my room. My mind immediately conjures a vision of Flynn, and the knot in my stomach doubles. I throw on the silky white robe with "Bride" written in sequins across the back that Jade bought me and hold my breath as I reach for the knob.

When I emerge from the ensuite and find Jade alone, the stomach knot shrinks.

"You didn't wash your hair?" she asks.

It takes a second for her question to register.

Get your act together.

"No. Um. Vera told me it'll curl better if it's not squeaky clean." Which is a relief because there's so much of it and it takes forever to dry. I don't have forever. I have fifteen minutes before Vera arrives, and the makeup artist is scheduled for twelve-thirty. Then it's the dress and final touches and the aisle at two.

I catch Jade's wince before she turns away. There's a phone in her hand. *My* phone. "Did someone call?" I ask.

She sets the handset down on the dresser beside my makeup bag. "Yes, but don't freak out."

Doesn't she know that telling someone not to freak out always has the exact opposite effect?

"We have a little problem," she says.

A flash of last night rips through my mind. "Blake's calling off the wedding, isn't he?" I sink to the end of the bed and clutch my forehead with both hands, my lungs seizing up.

He said it wasn't a big deal.

What am I going to do?

Everyone's going to be here, and I'm going to look like a complete idiot.

I give myself a mental shake.

Really, Ruby? You're losing Blake, and your first thought is about what the town is going to think? What the hell is wrong with you!

"Geez, Ruby." Jade sits beside me, nudging my shoulder with hers. "When you doom-and-gloom, you go dark."

She sounds way too calm for this to be a jilting emergency. "So, it wasn't Blake who called?"

"No, it was Vera. She's been throwing up all night and is still sick this morning. Felicia is coming in her place. She'll be here in fifteen minutes."

A rush of breath leaves my lungs. Not Felicia. She has a thing for hairspray and tight curls. If she does my hair, I'm going to end up looking like Shirley freaking Temple.

Jade nudges me again. "What's going on with you? Why on earth would you think Blake was calling off the wedding?"

Her question reminds me that I have bigger problems than a possible bad hair day. Should I tell my sister this shameful secret? Would getting it off my chest make me feel better, or would the confession stir up all the emotions I'm doing my best to forget?

I open my mouth, but shame wins, and I stay silent.

I'm her big sister. It's my responsibility to take care of her, not the other way around. This is my burden to bear. "I'm just nervous."

It's not a complete lie. I'm nervous about seeing Blake.

About seeing Flynn. About having two hundred people watch me walk down the aisle. My heart beats hard against my ribs, and I have to clutch the mattress to keep from falling over. "Maybe I need to eat something."

"Let me run down to the—"

"You finish getting ready. I'll go."

"Ruby, let me help—"

I'm already out the door and heading for the stairs, needing to move, to stop the torrent of thoughts in my head. Mercifully, I find both the living room and the kitchen empty. I grab a chocolate protein bar from a box Jade left on the counter, tear open the wrapper, and shove it into my mouth like it's the last meal I'll ever have.

I'm mid-chew when Blake strolls in wearing a pair of shorts and an old Still Springs High T-shirt. He freezes in the doorway, his hands flying over his eyes. "What are you doing down here, babe? You know I can't see you before the wedding. It's bad luck."

Between Blake forgetting those damned shoes, the hug, and Vera, he may as well add it to the list of bad luck plaguing this week. I bite off another chunk of the bar, chewing until my jaw aches. That's when I notice a big glob of chocolate staining the front of my robe. I run to the sink, grab a cloth, wet it, and scrub.

And scrub.

And scrub.

It's only making the mark worse.

I can't do this.

Call it a sign from the universe or karma—whatever you want.

Before I realize what's happening, my cheeks are wet.

Blake peeks at me through his fingers. "Woah. Are you crying?"

Once the tears start, I can't seem to get them to stop. "Blake, I... I..."

His hand drops, and he's in front of me, holding me by the shoulders, rubbing reassuring circles with his thumbs. "Look at me. Tell me what's wrong."

I blurt out the first thing that comes to mind. "Vera's not coming."

His brow furrows. "Your hairdresser?"

I nod.

"So?"

"*So*, I don't want to go out in front of all those people covered in chocolate and looking like trash."

"First, you're not going to be covered in chocolate because this is your robe, not your dress, okay?" He nudges my chin until I'm staring into his gray eyes. "Okay?"

I nod.

"Second, I have never seen you look anything but perfect. You could swap out that robe for your dress right now, and I'd still marry you. Actually, wait." He drags his thumb down the corner of my lip. I spot a tiny smear of chocolate on his finger before he pops it inside his mouth. "Now, you're perfect. This is you and me, babe. It's always been you and me. We've got this."

The door flies open, banging against the wall. "I'm here! I'm here!" Felicia stomps in, a curling iron in one hand and a bag swollen with combs, brushes, and cans of hairspray in the other. "Let's get you ready for your wedding."

"See?" Blake's smile returns some of the warmth to my bones. "It's all gonna work out."

I'T'S NOT GOING TO WORK OUT.

That's all I can think as I sit on the stool in the master bedroom, staring at myself in the mirror in Jade's pink *Maid of Honor* robe, my stained white one discarded on the bed.

Felicia claps her hands, bouncing up and down on her toes behind me. "Oh my gosh, I love it! Do you love it?"

My smile feels so brittle that all I can do is nod, making the curls swing back and forth. When it's wet, my hair nearly reaches my waist. Right now, it's struggling to touch my shoulders. It's like the 1980s vomited on my head.

"Now, don't you worry; these are gonna fall just right." Felicia drags on the end of a curl, but it springs back into place as tight as ever. "Perfect! Just perfect. I can't wait to see it with the dress!"

"Yeah. It's going to be great."

It's not. It's so not.

She takes her tools and slips out of the room.

I run my fingers through my hair. And make it worse.

Oh no. No, no, no.

This is it. Every bride's nightmare come true.

I look like shit on my wedding day.

I'll have to see myself in these pictures forever. FOREVER. My kids are going to look at them and ask me why I stuck my fingers in an electric socket. Blake's mom already said she wants to hang a photo on the restaurant wall. My hairdo is going to be plastered all over social media, and I'm probably going to become a freaking meme, and—

A knock at the door freezes my panic spiral.

"Ruby? Are you all done? I'm dying to see!"

I can't bring myself to answer Jade.

"You're killing me! You know what? I'm coming in." The door opens, and Jade sweeps inside, looking like a magazine model with her floor-length, dusty-rose chiffon dress swaying and her blonde hair curled loosely, framing her pretty face.

When her gaze connects with mine, her hands fly up, covering her mouth. "Oh... Oh no."

Tears cling to my lashes, waiting to fall.

"We can fix it." Jade steps forward, her hands splayed out like I'm a wild animal backed into a corner.

"How? There's so much hairspray, it may never move again." Not to mention, the makeup artist will be here in ten minutes. There isn't time to fix it.

This is exactly what they mean when they say karma is a bitch. This is punishment for last night.

Jade disappears into the bathroom. A moment later, she's pulling me off the stool, dragging me into the ensuite, and shoving me toward the shower. "Get in."

"It's fine."

"It's not."

Steam fills the room, fogging up the mirror.

"Jade, there isn't time. The makeup artist will be here in—"

"This is your day, Ruby. Everyone else can wait."

"But... Felicia will know I washed my hair."

"You'd really put a hairdresser's feelings over your own on your wedding day? Ruby, that's so freaking *you*!" Jade grabs my arms and gives me a firm shake. "If there is ever a time for you to be selfish, now is that time."

I reach for the tie at my waist but hesitate.

"If she says a word, tell her I hated it," Jade persists. "Seriously. Blame me. Better yet, I'll tell her straight out that she made you look like one of those girls on the child pageant circuit."

A laugh bubbles out of me. "I love you, sis."

"I love you too. Now, get your butt in that shower and wash your damn hair. Your future husband is out there waiting for you."

CHAPTER FOURTEEN

FLYNN

A JITTERY EXHALE BLOWS THROUGH MY LIPS, MY FINGERS trembling as I rub them against my navy-blue suit pants. Why the hell do I seem more nervous than the groom?

Blake's standing beneath the arbor beside me, laughing with Carl in hushed tones, while I'm sweating bullets inside my three-piece suit—which has nothing to do with the weather.

You can do this, Flynn. This is exactly what your eyes need to see so your heart can move on.

So why do I feel like I'm about to watch my fucking funeral unfold?

Blake's gentle shake of my arm snaps me out of my screwed-up thoughts. "It's been nearly an hour," he hisses. "Where's Ruby?"

I cast my gaze over the guests sitting patiently on white folding chairs, most quietly chatting, some glancing at their watches. "Brides are always late," I whisper.

"Do you think you can go look for her?"

I nod right away. "Sure, man. Of course." I swallow the shameful secret that a part of me is so quick to dash away in the hope that Ruby will turn up while I'm gone and I'll miss the wedding entirely.

You're truly a spectacular best man, Flynn. A gold star for you.

I slide my hands inside my pockets and head toward the house, spying a flash of Jade's blonde hair through Ruby's bedroom window. My stomach flips as I head up the stairs and give the door a few taps with my knuckles. It swings open, and Jade gives me an apologetic grimace.

"I promise you she's coming," she says, fiddling with the strap of her pale-pink dress. "Wow, you look handsome," she adds as Ruby steps forward, her deep-blue eyes finding mine.

Oh, fuck.

For a moment, I turn completely numb before a sudden rush of emotion streams through my body, gripping my lungs. "Ruby, you look..." My throat locks at the sight of her in her ivory dress, all lacy and tight at the waist, while flowing out past her feet.

You're so gorgeous it hurts.

"I'll be one sec; I need to pin this strap," Jade says with a sound of irritation before disappearing inside the bathroom.

"Did Blake send you to come and get me?" Ruby asks, her gaze making a quick sweep over the tailored suit hugging my body.

What I would give to have you.

"He did." I jam a smile on my face. "You're not going to send me back with bad news, are you?" I'm clearly joking, but the question rouses a pathetic glimmer of hope that I ignore.

"I'm so sorry." A flash of insecurity eclipses Ruby's face. "We had a bit of a hair issue." She fingers one of her loose waves then drops it like she hates it.

"You look...absolutely incredible." I hold back a thousand

more compliments and go for something light instead. "But I've gotta say, I kind of miss the Britney Spears costume."

Her smile hits me in the chest. "And I kind of miss the pilot uniform."

I smirk and gesture with my head. "I have it in my room." Her eyes expand, and my smile vanishes. "I didn't mean that the way it came out."

Our cheeks heat in unison as we stare at each other, the memory of last night sliding between us, pushing its way back in.

All the things I'm desperate to say to her gather in the back of my throat.

I haven't stopped thinking about last night.

"As soon as Jade's done, I'll be ready," Ruby says in a trembling voice.

"Okay. I'll wait here and come with you."

Please don't marry him.

Her lips pull up in a wary smile. "Is Blake freaking out?"

"No, he's fine. Trust me, when he sees you, he's going to be knocked out."

Her gaze drops, but the smile holds.

I don't know why I can't let you go, Quinn.

The words float past my lips in a whisper before I can stop them. "About last night. I need you to know—"

Jade springs through the bathroom door with a grin. "Are you ready?" she asks her sister.

Ruby presses a hand to her stomach like she's nervous and sucks in a deep inhale. "I'm ready."

I'M SURE THERE ARE THINGS THAT WOULD HURT MORE than watching Ruby Quinn get married to someone else. Like simultaneous gunshot wounds. Being buried alive. Having all my fingernails ripped out, one by one.

I don't want to feel this way. I do everything in my power to think only about what Blake and Ruby have found together. There is a part of me that can watch them say their vows and feel truly happy for them. If I step out of my own body, like it's not really me sweating beside that arbor, I can get there.

But every time I meet Ruby's eyes, I'm right back where I started. When she made a slow walk up the aisle with her arm hooked through her dad's, her gaze found mine and held on for a few breathless heartbeats, and a lifetime of what-ifs flashed through me, burning me up inside.

It's not about you, Flynn, I think for the millionth time as I pass the polished rings that glint in the sunlight to Blake. But while I stand and watch Blake and Ruby gripping each other's hands while the preacher declares them husband and wife, my heart just about dies in my chest.

Be happy for them, you dick. Think of this as the best day of their lives rather than the worst day of yours. Two high school sweethearts just tied the knot. This is a good day.

They kiss, I smile and clap, then Blake leads Ruby back down the makeshift aisle to cheers and confetti.

I spin around and share the expected looks of pride with Frank and Carl before my parents worm their way through to me and hug me hello. I lean into my mom like a kid, letting her soothing energy find its way into my chest, bandaging my broken heart. I want to stay with them, but Carl lifts his chin at me, and I reluctantly part with their company to go take wedding photos. Because apparently, my veins need another torture injection. But I need to buck the hell up and remember how to be a good friend.

As I head across the grass with Frank and Carl, spotting the rest of the wedding party ahead of us, my mind travels to the email I received while we were waiting for Ruby. It was a schedule filled with work shifts. In a couple of days, I'll be meeting a jet in DC and flying some corporate CEO around Europe for the next month. I don't even know what I've been thinking lately, craving something that resembles my parents' life. Airports, cockpits, and hotel rooms—that's my world now.

I almost have to laugh when I clue in that the photos are being taken right beside the pond. *Of course.* I deserve the punishment after what went through my head at that ceremony. Ruby's dad arrives with Blake's parents, and the lot of us line up and pose for so many photographs that my cheeks hurt from smiling, especially when I just can't put my heart into this, no matter how much I wish I could.

I constantly notice Ruby playing with her loose curls like she's unhappy with them. So when her gaze falls on mine over Blake's shoulder, I mouth the words, "You're beautiful."

I'm not trying to be an asshole—I just want her to know she's perfect—but when her eyes turn soft, my cheeks heat up, and I glance away, struck with guilt.

That's the moment the ache in my chest returns, and this time it doesn't let up, no matter how much I try to fight it. The heartache builds and doubles then quadruples as I stand back and watch Blake wrap his arms around Ruby from behind while the camera clicks and whirrs.

Out of nowhere, it hits me.

She's gone. Forever.

My eyes begin to burn.

Oh my god, I'm actually going to fucking cry.

There's a sharp pressure inside me that needs to be let out, so I murmur in Carl's ear that I'm going to find a bathroom. Before he can reply, I stride away in an aimless direction, needing to be alone and cursing myself when I round on a huddle of wedding guests toasting and laughing.

I'm seconds from breaking down, so I frantically push past them, searching for somewhere to hide, when a strong hand takes hold of my arm.

"You okay there, bud?" My dad blinks at me through concerned eyes, his fingers clutching a champagne flute.

I nod, too choked to speak, and his lined face blurs in my vision as my eyes fill up.

"Come here." He gently guides me away from the people and around to the back of the stable. "What is it?" he asks, his face paling.

I brush the heels of my hands over my eyes, catching the tears that won't stop spilling.

"Son?" Dad presses, a little breathless.

"It's fine," I say quickly before he can think the worst. "Everything's okay."

"It sure doesn't look like it." He bends to set his glass down on the ground then stands back up and eyeballs me, sending me right back to being a kid. "Talk to me, Flynn."

A sigh laced with lead drags through my lips. I don't even know how to put this. If I say these words to him, it'll be the first time in my life I've admitted them aloud.

I steady myself in Dad's deep-brown eyes. "I'm in love with someone," I say in a pained voice.

The line between his brows doesn't soften. "And why isn't that happy news?"

My gaze shifts to the stable wall because I can't look at him when I say this next part. "She's...married."

I brace myself for judgment and wrath, but when I brave a glance back at Dad, all I find swimming in his eyes is shock and sympathy.

"And she's here today?" he guesses slowly, his eyes clouding over like he's wondering which of the married wedding guests it might be.

"She's here, yes."

For several tense breaths, we stand and stare at each other. While Dad doesn't push me to tell him who the girl is, a piercing need to get this whole thing off my chest overwhelms me. "It's Ruby, Dad."

His eyes flash wide. "Ruby Quinn?"

I nod before the truth catches up with me. "She's not Ruby Quinn anymore," I mutter, studying my caramel-brown shoes. "Ruby Harrington."

The name rolls through my head before I can stop it. *Ruby Hudson.*

Dad cups his hand on my shoulder, drawing me back into myself. "Oh, Flynn." His lips press tightly together.

"I know." My voice wobbles. "It's far from ideal."

He brushes his thumb back and forth over my shoulder as he continues to hold onto me. "Has something happened between you two?"

My mind shoots straight to the pond, and Dad's mouth falls open at the expression on my face.

"No," I say quickly. "Not like that. But I don't know, we might have had a *moment,* I guess." I lift a shoulder, the seeds of doubt growing in my head, telling me I imagined the whole thing.

He puffs a wearied exhale. "Of all the girls..."

"I know. Believe me, I'd change it if I could. I'd give anything not to feel this way, but I can't help it."

His lips twist down. "How long have you felt like this about her?"

I swallow the razor in the back of my throat. "Ten years."

Dad's face falls. For a moment, he says nothing, then his

brow tightens up. "Is that why you haven't been back home until now?"

Fresh tears rise in my eyes, and I nod, my forehead falling into Dad's shoulder as he wraps his arms around me. I hide in his neck, feeling everything crush up—my face, my hands, my heart—as I cry silent tears until my shoulders shake. His palm runs up and down my back, and I let the tears fall until his suit is stained wet.

"I'm sorry," I eventually mumble, collecting myself enough to pull back and wipe my eyes.

"You don't need to be sorry." The way his face creases with concern makes me feel worse. It's been a long time since my parents have had to worry about me.

I inhale deeply, trying to fill my lungs with air, but they're clenched too tight. "I think I need to leave," I admit under my breath, hating myself. I could not have been a worse best man.

He nods sadly. "I think that's probably a good idea, bud. You'll feel better if you go back to the house in Still Springs and put some distance between you and Ruby. Your mom and I can join you."

"No, no. You guys should stay and enjoy the wedding. And I can't leave yet anyway. I need to do my speech first."

"Are you sure you want to do that?"

"I have to. It's the absolute least I can do for Blake."

He sighs. "Okay."

I scrub my hands up and down my face, giving myself a silent pep talk to pull myself together. "I'll come and see you and Mom before I go. Thanks so much, Dad. For everything."

Emotion fills his eyes before he drags me into another bear hug. "Listen to me, Flynn," he says in my ear, his deep voice a calming presence. "I *promise* you. One day, you are going to tell a girl you love her—and mean it—and she's going to say those words back to you. Okay? I promise you that."

I clutch onto him, willing those words to be true.

Right now, they feel impossible to imagine.

I walk Dad back toward the low hum of conversation, leaving him to find Mom in the muddle of guests and no doubt explain to her my fucked-up situation.

After slipping into the bathroom to make sure I don't look like I've been crying my eyes out, I splash cold water on my face and wander back to the pond, but the photos have finished up. A low cloud rumbles overhead, and I up my pace and begin heading back to the barn. On the way, I dig inside my suit pocket, but my fingers come up empty.

Shit, where's my speech?

I must've left it in the room this afternoon when I gave it a final read-through.

Low-level music blends with rumbles of laughter as I pass by the barn, poking my head inside. I spot Ruby standing near the head table with Jade, but there's no sign of Blake.

We're still a ways off speech time, so I continue down to the main house, pulling out my room key. I twist it in the slot and push the door open.

At first, I don't believe what I'm seeing, like I've landed in an alternate universe. But when the impossible image doesn't change, my stomach hits the floor, and the world around me comes to a grinding halt.

Blake is staring at me, open-mouthed, with his slacks pooled around his ankles. In front of him lays Tammy, half-naked and stretched out on the bed, her legs locked around his bare ass.

CHAPTER FIFTEEN

RUBY

I smile and greet each and every guest, thanking them for coming and apologizing over and over for being late to my own wedding. They all reassure me that it was worth the wait for such a beautiful ceremony.

I didn't trip and fall. I didn't falter. I stayed the course. After the dinner, drinking, and dancing, all of this will be behind me.

The barn belongs in a fairytale, with twinkle lights strung up in the eaves and bud vases in the center of each table, surrounded by flickering candles. I really couldn't have done any of this without Jade and her Pinterest board. I always knew I was going to marry Blake, but for some reason, actually getting to this moment felt like such a monumental task.

Everything is running a little behind schedule, but since the drinks are free, no one seems to mind. The only person who seems flustered is me.

The ceremony is over, so why do I still feel so nervous?

I nod to a few cousins I haven't seen in years on my way to where Jade has strung up a bunch of old photos between the barn's lofty windows. Some are from Blake's parents' wedding, and a couple are from Mom and Dad's. Seeing Mom's smile makes me misty-eyed, and I have to fan my face. Jade even found a photo from the day our grandparents got married. In the center of the display hangs the picture from junior prom of Blake and me with Flynn and Wendy.

Blake looks so young, his face rounder than it is now. But his smile is the same—minus the pearly whites. Down at the photo-shoot by the pond, I'd surreptitiously asked our photographer if there's anything she can do to fix them. She'd winked and assured me that her Photoshop skills are excellent.

Without effort, my eyes drift to the other guy in the photo.

"I still remember you coming down the stairs that evening."

I whirl around, finding my dad smiling at the prom photo, clutching two full drinks. He hands me a mojito, tears welling in his eyes. It's a wonder he has any left after blubbering for most of the ceremony. "You were so pretty in that red dress. Then you showed me those ugly flip-flops you insisted on wearing beneath."

"Hey, they were comfy," I laugh, taking a sip. If I drink too much before eating, I'm bound to be tipsy by the first dance. Although the citrusy cocktail tastes so refreshing and is doing wonders to settle my nerves, so it's hard to pace myself.

Dad scans the rest of the photos, stopping on the one of him and Mom holding a knife together behind their wedding cake. "She was watching you today," he says. "I can feel it in my bones."

I blink back tears. "I hope so."

He collects me for yet another hug. Over his shoulder, I can see a bunch of phones pointed at us and hear the clicks of cameras. I turn my face into Dad, wishing I could have this one private moment without feeling like the whole world is watching.

"I love you, pumpkin."

"Love you too, Dad."

He returns to the table where my grandma sits in her wheelchair beside Blake's aunts and uncles. I slowly sip my drink, scanning the barn for the one face I haven't caught sight of since our photo shoot down by the pond. Where is Flynn?

Part of me is glad he's not milling around with the rest of the guests. At one point, when I was walking down the aisle, our gazes had locked, and it had taken everything I had to glance away. I know Blake loves me. And I love him. But I can't remember there ever being a time when Blake looked at me like *that*.

So, I'm glad Flynn isn't here, because now that I'm married, I won't be looking back.

Felicia appears out of nowhere, giving me a slightly awkward one-arm hug. "I told you those curls would fall just right, didn't I?"

Guilt pinches my chest, and I hide my grimace behind my drink. "You sure did."

"You're so dang pretty all done up, but I knew you would be." She tugs on the ends of my hair and makes a face. "Should I run out and get a bit more hairspray to keep it from going flat? All this humidity is a killer on curls."

"I really appreciate it, but I think I'm good."

"If you change your mind, you just holler."

"Thanks, Felicia."

Jade gives me a subtle wink from over her glass of pink gin and tonic, and I stifle a laugh.

My sister says something to the woman she's talking to—who must be one of Blake's relatives because I've never seen her before—then slowly makes her way over to me.

"I told you those curls would fall just right, didn't I?" she whispers in my ear.

The sip I just took of my drink nearly comes out of my nose. "Shut up," I choke, my nose and throat burning.

The strawberries floating in her glass slosh around when she laughs. "I really thought you were going to lose it when she offered you more hairspray."

"How does she not know? My hair is completely different."

"Well, she has been drinking since the ceremony, soooo..." Jade chases her straw around her glass before catching it between her fingers.

"No way."

She nods and gives me a conspiratorial smile. "I saw her pull a flask from her purse during the vows."

"Do you think she was drunk when she did my hair?"

"Who knows? Maybe."

That would explain so much. Although, if Felicia had been drunk, I would've smelled it, right? We share a laugh until the preacher comes over to us and we sober right up.

"Ladies."

"Pastor Remley," we say in unison.

He opens his suit jacket and fishes out a white envelope from the inside pocket. "Which one of you wants to take care of this?"

I expect it to be a card, but it's a letter addressed to the courthouse.

Jade motions at the envelope. "Give it to me."

He goes to hand it to her, then pulls back at the last second. "It's very important that this marriage certificate gets filed, so don't you go losing it. First thing Monday morning, I want you to pop it right in the mail. Think you can handle that?"

"I'll do my best," she says, smirking.

"Good." He finally hands it over. "Now, time to get another one of those yummy little crab cakes floating around here." He rubs his hands together and heads toward one of the catering staff balancing a silver platter.

Tammy really outdid herself with the menu. Harringtons

has always had good food, but since she arrived, it's gotten even better.

"Here." Jade hands me her glass. "You hold that while I run to the house and put this certificate where I won't lose it."

"Thanks. If you see Blake, can you tell him to hurry up? They'll be serving dinner soon." He said he'd be right back, but that was twenty minutes ago. It's not like him to miss an opportunity to be the center of attention.

CHAPTER SIXTEEN

FLYNN

I WANT TO THROW UP. EITHER THAT OR SLAM MY FIST INTO Blake's face.

Before I can get my head around what I just walked in on, Tammy flings off the bed and yanks down her dress, mumbling something vaguely apologetic before escaping through the door.

I don't know who'd win the prize for looking the most dumbstruck right now—Blake or me.

He frantically tugs up his suit pants and tucks in his shirt while I fight to locate my breath. My chest is so tight that I can't speak.

"You didn't see anything in here," Blake says. "This didn't happen, you hear me?"

Rage flashes through my body like a lightning storm, and I lurch forward and grab him by the collar, fisting it until he gasps.

"What the actual *fuck?*" I say through my teeth. "How could you do this? How could you do this to Ruby? Don't you even know how fucking lucky you are!"

A sharp pain throbs in my chest as I give him a hard shove backward.

"I cannot believe this," I continue breathlessly. "I cannot believe you would screw someone else on your fucking wedding day!" I lunge at him again, and Blake stumbles backward, driving me to take a breath to cool myself down. Just because I want to beat the shit out of him right now doesn't mean I should.

Blake's cheeks turn ashen, his gaze pinned to the floor. "I didn't mean for it to happen."

A mirthless laugh bursts out of me. "No? You mean she accidentally wandered in here and fell on your dick?"

His eyes narrow. "Don't fucking judge me. You haven't been here in years. You don't know shit about what's really been going on in my life."

My lips press tightly together because he's got me there.

But when I think about Ruby over in that barn, looking like heaven, with a ring on her finger and a smile that's all sweet innocence, I want to punch this guy. There is no part of me that takes any joy out of this, despite my feelings for Ruby. I'm devastated for her.

I drop onto the edge of the bed and clutch my forehead with both hands.

"How long?" I ask Blake in a voice thick with disgust. "How long has this been going on?"

He takes a moment to mumble a reply. "A couple of months. She was after me from the day she arrived in town; kept throwing herself at me." He glances down.

The urge to tell him that Tammy came onto me only yesterday gathers in my throat, but I decide against it. There has to be a better time than now to share that little detail with him, if I do at all.

"I love Ruby," Blake says, and I want to reach down his throat and pull that precious name out of his lying mouth.

Instead, I shake my head grimly. "How can you say that? Honestly, man. You've gotta be real with yourself. You got married two hours ago, and now you're in here fucking someone else."

Tears glaze over his eyes as he looks away. "No, I do," he says, nodding to himself. "I do love Ruby. But Tammy, she's..." His shoulders lift up and down. "She's a *woman*. Ruby's great, but she'll always be that shy girl from high school to me. Tammy's seen the world...got big ideas...knows shit that blows my mind."

Yeah, I'll bet she blows your mind.

An ache stretches my chest at the thought of how Ruby would feel if she heard his confession.

"Please don't tell her," Blake says, his eyes begging. "Let this secret die here."

I rest my chin on my palm and stare at him, my body so consumed with revulsion that I don't know what to do with myself. How could I have so easily believed that this guy has changed since high school? He's still playing us all for fools.

"How could you do this to her?" I ask him again.

"Why the hell do you care about her so much? You're *my* best man. So start acting like it."

I get up on my feet. "What's that supposed to mean?"

"It means that this doesn't even have anything to do with you. What the fuck do you know about relationships?"

"Enough to know that you don't screw someone else when you're in one. Especially on your wedding day." I turn away so that I don't have to look at him.

After a few moments of uncomfortable silence, Blake heaves a sigh. "I need to get back."

I spin to face him. "What?"

He reaches for his jacket and slides his arms into it. "You heard me. I've got a reception full of people out there."

When he takes a step forward, I grab onto his arm. "Blake. You can't go out there and pretend like nothing happened."

He jerks out of my grip. "The hell I can't."

"Blake!"

He shoves past me and pushes through the door, leaving me with my mouth hanging open.

"Fuck!" I throw my fist into the wall—two, three, four times. Pain splinters through my hand, and I shake it vigorously.

What do I do? What the hell do I do?

Do I go out there like Blake and pretend I saw nothing? How can I do that? How can I do that to Ruby?

The feeling of someone's eyes on me makes me twist toward the open door, where I spot Jade hovering in the gap.

"Jade," I gasp, running my fingers through my hair. *My god, what did she hear?*

She steps into the room, her eyes darting around like she's searching for someone.

"Are you okay?" I say in the most normal voice I can muster.

"Has something happened?" Her eyes are wide.

"What do you mean?"

"A few minutes ago, I saw Tammy running out of this room looking really weird and disheveled. Then, as I was coming back downstairs, Blake came out looking furious as hell." She steps toward me. "What's going on?"

My head goes berserk trying to come up with possible scenarios.

Blake didn't like the food Tammy chose for the reception, and they had an argument about it.

Blake and Tammy aren't agreeing on the direction of the merger.

Tammy wants time off to spend with her son, but Blake won't give it to her.

"Flynn!" Jade snaps a finger in my face. "You look like you've seen a ghost, so I need you to tell me right now what's going on."

She crosses her arms in a "give it to me straight" stance, but her skin has turned the color of milk.

My throat locks up, and my palms sweat at my sides.

Fuck, Flynn, just lie! This will break Ruby's heart.

No, don't lie. That will make you as bad as Blake.

Jade's hand clutches her lower stomach. "Oh my god," she breathes. "Tell me something isn't going on between Blake and Tammy. I know that sounds crazy, but lately, I've noticed they spend *a lot* of time together. And she's constantly touching him. Have you noticed that?"

When my cheeks catch fire, Jade's hand flies to her mouth. "Oh no. No, no, no, Flynn, *please,* no. Tell me I'm wrong about this."

My eyes begin to burn, and she grasps my wrist tightly. "Tell me I'm wrong," she says like she already knows what's coming, her voice trembling.

A question rings in my head, obliterating every other thought.

Whose side are you on, Flynn? The guy you've known since you were a kid who's turned out to be a lying prick, or the girl you've been in love with for ten years?

How can you let him do this to her?

My voice comes out so weak that it's barely audible. "I just caught Blake having sex with Tammy."

Jade nearly collapses forward. I lunge, steadying her in case she falls.

"I'm so sorry," I continue. "I know, it's fucking terrible. I can't believe it either."

Jade looks like I did about twenty minutes ago: like she's lost the ability to speak.

"I don't know what you want to do with that information," I add with a weary sigh. "Because I know it's not my place to tell Ruby. And I'm sure Blake's going to kill me when he finds out I told you. I was planning on leaving anyway, so I think it's better if I go."

Jade nods, tears welling in her eyes.

"I'm so sorry," I say, wrapping my arms around her because if there's something I can't handle, it's a Quinn sister crying.

She hugs me tightly like she's grateful before stepping back. "It's okay. I'll figure out what to do. I'll look after Ruby."

I give her a look of support, repressing an urge to stay here. It hurts to leave when I have no idea if Jade will tell Ruby or how Ruby will react. I don't have their phone numbers or email addresses. Maybe I should reactivate my social media accounts.

I watch her through the doorway as she drags her feet back toward the wedding, not envying her predicament one bit. Jade seems the type who won't let Blake get away with this, but I can't be sure.

Bile rises in my throat at the thought of Blake getting to keep this dirty little secret. He told me he'd been screwing Tammy for months. *Fuck him.*

As I shove my clothes into my bag, I swallow urge after urge to bound over to that barn and tell the whole reception that Blake Harrington is a lying, cheating asshole who doesn't deserve to put his hands anywhere near Ruby.

I tug at my tie, about to get changed, when my eyes snag on a piece of paper on the floor beside my bed. I grab it and unfold my best man speech, making a face at the words that sound like they were written by another man.

Because Blake and I are not the same people we were half an hour ago.

That guy is a snake in the grass, no matter how much he pretends otherwise. And while I'm not exactly innocent, and I've probably let myself stare at Ruby a little too much—even fantasized about her—I would never have made a play for her as long as she was with Blake, despite what happened at the pond. I would never even dream of hurting her this way.

My speech still hangs from my fingers, and I go to rip it up before a thought steamrolls into my head.

Just because Blake Harrington can't admit his truth doesn't mean I have to hide and keep secrets. I'm officially done playing by this guy's rules. Before I drive out of Still Springs and never look back, there's one thing I need to do.

My heart leaps as I sit down and flip the speech over to the blank side, reaching for a pen.

CHAPTER SEVENTEEN

RUBY

I'VE HEARD PEOPLE SAY THEIR FACES HURT FROM SMILING, but I never understood that sentiment until this moment. Every time I try to give my mouth a break, someone else sweeps in and starts complimenting and congratulating me, and I'm right back to it like a toothpaste commercial.

Not only does my face hurt, but the mojitos are starting to go to my head. That protein bar I had before the ceremony is long gone, and as good as the hors d'oeuvres are, I really need to eat something that's not the size of a thimble.

Speaking of thimbles, I still hate those damn shot glasses sitting at the place settings. Talk about tacky. Why couldn't Blake have forgotten about those instead of the shoes?

My gaze snags on the cake table. Would anyone notice if I sneaked a sliver from the back part? It's going to get chopped up anyway. I steal a spoon from the closest place setting right when Jade appears in the barn doorway.

She snatches a flute of champagne from a tray and slips between guests, heading straight for me. I stuff the spoon inside my pocket like it's some sort of contraband. Before I can ask why she's so flushed, she downs her entire drink and discards the glass onto the closest table. "Hey." She doesn't smile. "I was trying to think of the right time for this, but..." Her eyes shift to Blake, who's hunched over the DJ, clicking buttons on his computer. "We need to talk."

Right then, the catering staff begin lining up at the door, presumably to bring us food. Tammy flits between them, her face flushed. My stomach growls, but it's so loud in here no one notices. "Does it have to be right now?"

"It's really important. Please. Just two minutes."

Blake sidles over to us, running his fingers up and down my dress as if he's tracing the lace. "Hey, babe. You ready to eat? I'm starving."

"Yeah, just a sec. Jade needs me."

His gaze flickers to my sister, and he frowns at her. "Can it wait until after dinner?"

"No, Blake. It can't wait." She grabs me by the wrist and drags me through a gap in the guests, straight out the door and around to the back of the barn. The wind kicks up, shaking the leaves on the trees and rippling over the pond down the hill. It's a miracle it hasn't started raining yet.

Jade lets me go abruptly, wiping her hands up and down her skirt.

"Geez, Jade." I rub my red wrist. "Where's the fire?"

She doesn't laugh or smile. She just stares at me, her green eyes wide and her face pale. My stomach hits the floor. I've only seen Jade look this way one other time—the night our mom died. "What's wrong?"

Her eyes pool with tears. "I don't know how to tell you this, so I'm just going to say it. Blake's cheating on you."

The accusation is so ridiculous, I want to laugh, but my sister is crying, and she never cries and—"With *who*?" I shriek. Blake is always at work, or with me, or with Carl and Frank, or his parents. This isn't right. When would he even have time to—

"Tammy."

"No way, Jade. *No*; they're just really good friends." I mean, yes, they've been spending a lot of time together lately, but that's because of the merger. Isn't it?

Jade watches me, her eyes wary like I'm about to have a meltdown.

My entire body stiffens. Am I wrong? The many nights Blake left work late...the time he "forgot" date night...that trip he and Tammy had to take to Baltimore to meet with the restaurant architects, and he talked me out of coming with them. *Oh my god.*

All those times, had he really been with *her*?

My heart thrashes in my ears until it's all I can hear. "You're sure?"

She nods. "We just caught them together in the house."

My jaw hits the ground. "He slept with her *today*?" I clutch onto the barn wall for support, my legs threatening to give out.

Blake is cheating on me.

My brain refuses to process the words.

He's supposed to be my one and only. He's my *husband*!

How long has this been going on? Is it only Tammy, or is he sleeping with other women too? Blood rushes to my head and my vision swims. I think I might pass out.

Why would Blake do this? Why did he let me walk down that aisle in front of all those people, smiling like a complete idiot, vowing to love and honor and cherish him when he is *cheating on me*?!

My stomach twists up so tight that I gasp; bile burns the back of my throat.

Does Tammy make him happier than I do? Does he love me at all? *Oh god*...does he love *her*?

I manage a few ragged breaths, my head spinning. Tears threaten my eyes, but there will be plenty of time to break down later. Right now has to be about minimizing the damage. "Does anyone else know?" I gasp at Jade.

"Just me and Flynn."

Those words twist the dagger in my bleeding heart.

I bury my face in my hands, fighting back another surge of tears.

You're not enough.

Blake knows it, Tammy knows it, Jade knows it, and now Flynn knows it.

Jade's cool fingers slip around my wrist. "What do you need from me? Want me to kill him? Because I will. I'll drown him in the freaking pond."

What *do* I need? To run and hide, but that's not a freaking option considering it's my *wedding day*. Do I want her to kill him? No. I want to do it myself.

Like some sort of sick joke, Blake suddenly jogs into view from around the corner and smiles at us, gesturing for me to come back inside. To where our family and friends are buzzing with excitement.

I swear I can hear the rumors now.

Did you hear about poor Ruby Quinn?

Divorced before the ink on the marriage certificate was dry.

That asshole is going to make me the talk of the town for the next decade. I know I need to deal with him, but right now, I can't even wrap my head around this. I need some time to figure out what the hell I'm supposed to do.

Thunder rumbles in the distance as I straighten my shoulders and smooth a hand down my dress. "Nothing," I tell Jade. "Do absolutely nothing."

She reaches for me, but I step away. "Ruby—"

"Don't say a word to anyone. Okay? All of these people came out of their way to be here. You know nothing, this day is amazing, and we're going to smile and laugh and have a good time so that everybody else can still enjoy their night."

She nods and runs her thumbs under her eyes, clearing all evidence of her tears. "Whatever you want, Ruby, I'll do it."

After she hugs me tightly and whispers that it's going to be okay, I paste on a smile and return to the reception, my chest caving in. My grandma pulls me down for a hug from her wheelchair, the blue veins in her hands visible through her paper-thin skin. My dad kisses me on the cheek and tells me for the hundredth time that he loves me.

At least someone does.

Because the man smiling at me from the other side of the head table sure as hell doesn't. Two empty chairs wait for Jade and me. The seat on the other side of Blake is suspiciously empty. I don't have it in me to search the room for my husband's best man, who now knows that Blake cheated on me a few hours after we tied the knot. I've never been so humiliated. Carl and Frank laugh unknowingly over their beers.

When I sit down, Blake attempts to lace his fingers with mine, but I pull my hand away. I can sit next to him. I can keep this fake smile pinned to my lips and pretend I don't know about Tammy. But if he touches me, I will lose my shit.

How am I going to survive our first dance? Maybe I should drink myself into a stupor then tell everyone I'm sick.

Did you hear Ruby Quinn got sloshed at the wedding and had to leave?

Divorced already? I always knew they'd never work out.

Blake probably left her because she's boring and bland.

I shove the wine glass back from my plate.

It's been a while since my last drink, and I know what will happen if I have any more alcohol. I'll start getting emotional and end up saying or doing something I'll regret.

When the servers bring the first course, Carl leans across Flynn's empty chair to smack Blake's arm. "Where's Flynn?"

It's impossible to miss the way Blake's shoulders tense. "I dunno, man." He reaches for his beer with shaking fingers.

"He better get here quick, or I'm gonna eat his portion. This shit is good." Carl cuts off a hunk of sea scallop ravioli and stuffs it into his mouth.

I slice into a piece but can't bring myself to take a bite. Not when I know who made it. Did they talk about me while they were together? Did they laugh at how naïve I was to have suspected nothing? It makes me sick to think that I'm the one who invited Tammy to stay with us at the farmhouse. Did they hook up when I stayed behind at the bonfire? How can Blake sit here, laughing and smiling as if nothing is wrong?

I push the ravioli around with my fork, making it appear as though I've eaten at least some of it.

When Blake asks me if everything is okay, I tell him the truth. "I feel sick."

"Just eat more," he says with a warm smile. "You always feel better when you do."

I want to rip the rings from my left hand and throw them at his face. I want to pick up my plate of ravioli and dump it on his head. I want to scream and shout and ask him *why*.

But I don't do any of those things. I pick up my glass of water and take a sip to hide my grimace. The plates are still being cleared when the main course arrives. One of the servers collects Flynn's untouched entree plate and asks Blake if she should box it up.

The smile drops off his face, and he shakes his head.

I look right at him. "Where's Flynn?"

"How should I know?" Blake mumbles around his bite of beef tenderloin.

Jade glances up long enough to glare daggers at my new

husband. If she doesn't keep it together, I'm definitely going to fall apart.

"He's your best man, isn't he?" I push, waiting for the lies to come.

Blake's mouth flattens into a thin line before he takes a sip of beer.

Does he feel guilty at all? When I finally confront him about the affair, will he confess everything or deny it until his dying breath?

My eyes slip down to the polished gold band circling his left ring finger. Could I find it in my heart to forgive him? Do I *want* to forgive him? How could I ever trust him again?

A tall figure appears in the doorway. My held breath hisses out when Flynn walks into the room. His tie hangs loosely around his neck, and his dark hair is sticking up like he's been raking his hands through it over and over.

He isn't looking at Blake; he's staring straight at me.

My face catches fire, and I clutch my water glass as if it can save me from the depth of emotion in Flynn's eyes. The same emotion I'd glimpsed last night at the pond. Had it only been last night? This feels like the longest, most hellish day of my life.

Flynn moves like a man on a mission. If only I knew what that mission was.

Carl and Frank break into applause, whooping and hollering as Flynn strolls over to the DJ playing background music and tells him something that I can't make out over the roaring in my ears. The young man scrambles to turn knobs and toggle switches until the music fades. Flynn grabs a microphone from the table. When he flicks the switch on the bottom, sound pops through the speakers.

Jade's hand lands on my knee beneath the table. "What's he doing?"

I shake my head, my stomach hollowing. I have no clue.

Flynn drags a piece of paper from his pocket and begins unfolding it.

"Oh, hell yes." Frank laughs, clapping Carl on the shoulder before dragging out his phone. "It's speech time. You shittin' it, man?" he asks Blake.

Blake's fingers clutch his fork so tightly that his knuckles whiten.

Flynn lifts the microphone to his lips; his heavy exhale rattles through the speakers.

"Hi, everyone; I'm Flynn, the best man. Most of you probably know me as Ron and Linda's son, who are, of course, here tonight. I can see that some of you are still eating, so I promise not to take up too much of your time."

Blake lifts in his seat like he's about to jump up, and I hiss at him not to move. His eyes flash at mine until Flynn clears his throat and our attention snaps back to him.

"As the best man, my speech should, I'm told, be a ruthless and funny take-down of the groom. And, trust me, there are plenty of things I know about Blake that would shock you." Flynn's eyes shift to Blake, whose breath seizes up beside me. "But instead of doing that," Flynn adds, "I'd like to talk about someone else for a few minutes if that's okay."

A sharp exhale leaves Blake's throat, and I shoot him a glare that could cut steel. But Flynn's still talking, so I set my gaze back on him.

"While I'm not up here to talk about myself, please just go with me on this for a sec." Flynn clears his throat. "Some of you might already know that I fly planes for a living."

A cat-call sounds from a rowdy table, and Carl whistles with two fingers. Frank bangs his fist on the table a couple of times, vibrating all our glasses.

"When I became a pilot," Flynn continues, "I made a promise to my amazing parents that I would never get into a plane that didn't fly straight. I've done my best to keep that promise, but right now, I've never felt more off course."

He scrubs a hand down his dress slacks before adjusting his grip on the paper. A few silent seconds pass as he scans the words he's written. No matter how many times I swallow, I can't get rid of the lump in my throat.

"Back in my junior year of high school," Flynn says, "a girl walked through the door of my science class and right into my heart. While I won't overload you with details, I could tell you which exact table we sat at, the shade of green she was wearing, the first soft words she ever spoke to me, and how irreversibly she knocked me off my feet.

"I developed such a crush on this girl that I literally couldn't speak to her, I was so tongue-tied. Because of that, we bounced apart rather than drifted together, and the lovesick kid in me started doing something really stupid. To get her attention, rather than just talk to her, I began teasing her. And rightly so, instead of coming near me, this precious girl slipped further away." Deep regret coats his eyes as they flicker to mine. "Believe me, I've paid the price for it because I lost her back then, and the truth is that my heart has been searching for her ever since."

My chest wall is pounding like a bass drum. Because as much as I can't quite believe what I'm hearing, there is no question in my mind who Flynn is talking about.

He takes a deep breath. "That girl still makes my heart race and my cheeks hot and my stomach flip as much today as she did then. Even more so, to tell you the truth. So, in the spirit of tonight, I feel like it's time I put that scared little boy aside and just admit how I feel. Even if I can't walk up to her right now and say it."

Supportive cheers ripple through the guests, and Blake's aunt claps with her hands held high. Blake mutters, "What the hell?" beside me, but—as out of place as this speech is—I can't take my eyes off Flynn.

His liquid chocolate eyes drift back to mine and hold on.

"If I had a drop of sun for every time I've thought about this girl, the world would never know darkness," Flynn says. "Every time I look at her, I catch a glimpse through a window of the life I dream about but can never step into. My work has taken me to more cities than most people can name, but I promise you that the most breathtaking place in the world is wherever she is."

Blake turns slightly, and I can feel his eyes boring into the side of my face. I don't dare look at him or at any of the confused faces in the room—even Jade, who's breathing heavily beside me like she knows the truth too. Right now, there is only Flynn and me. Like through the burning flames of the bonfire.

"There's not a single thing I would change about her," Flynn says, emotion swelling in his eyes. "She is the most selfless person I've ever met. She is what beauty means to me. She shines, everywhere she goes. And she deserves to be the only star in the sky of the lucky man who gets to sit beside her."

Flynn's voice thickens. "So, while it breaks my heart to know that she will never be mine, the truth is that I will always be hers." He inhales deeply and folds his speech back up. "And now the plane feels straight. Thank you, everyone. Enjoy your evening."

Blake releases a long breath as Flynn drops the mic onto a table and weaves his way out of the barn. My mind has stalled somewhere between shock and something that feels a lot like giddiness. Which can't be right. This is the worst day of my life.

I catch Flynn's dad watching me, a strange, wide-eyed expression on his weathered face.

"Holy shit," Blake whispers.

Holy shit is right. Even after Flynn's confession about prom the other night and what happened at the bonfire, I had no idea he felt like *that*.

I finally get up the nerve to turn toward Blake. I'm not sure what he sees on my face, but whatever it is makes his gray eyes widen. Everyone around us is trading whispers and theories of who the mystery girl could be, while I struggle to find my next breath.

"There's not a single thing I would change about her."

Me. Flynn had been talking about *me*.

Suddenly, Blake's mouth drops open. "He was talking about you..." he says under his breath, as if I'd spoken my thoughts aloud.

"We don't know who he was talking about," I counter, even though my voice trembles with the weight of the lie.

He shakes his head, his face turning as white as the barn's walls. "Bullshit. You two sat together in science our junior year. I remember."

Of course, he does. He couldn't remember the wedding shoes, and yet he remembers who I sat next to ten freaking years ago.

"I'm going to kill that fucking traitor," Blake growls, and from the way his face flushes and his eyes narrow to slits, I think he's angry enough to do it.

I catch Blake by the back of the shirt before he can launch himself from the chair and chase after Flynn. My face may feel like it's melting, and I may be surrounded by hushed whispers and a fuming husband, but having Flynn say all those beautiful things about me in front of all these people is the only thing I want to remember about this day.

Blake tries to unlatch my fingers, but I'm still holding on for dear life, keeping him at my side.

"Let go, Ruby."

It's as if his demand dumps a bucket of ice water over my head.

Let go, Ruby.

I can't hold on anymore when there's nothing to hold on to. I can't keep him here when it's clearly not where he wants to be. My grip loosens and my hands fall to my lap as I blink at the face of the man I've loved for ten years, seeing only a stranger staring back.

Blake's face contorts into something ugly. "I knew he had a crush on you back in high school, but I can't believe he pulled that shit at my fucking *wedding*. The fucking nerve of that guy. He's dead to me. If I ever see him again, I'm going to hit him so fucking hard, he'll choke on his teeth."

All I can do is stare at him as he rants.

Suddenly, I know exactly what I need to do.

I just don't know if I have enough courage to do it.

But then I see Tammy's bleached-blonde head at the back of the crowd beside my wedding cake. A spark ignites in my chest, expanding and growing until it becomes a fiery inferno. I gave this guy *ten years*. Ten years I can never get back. He stole my twenties from me.

"You selfish asshole," I say under my breath so no one else can hear.

Blake blinks at me like he can't understand the words coming out of my mouth. I say them again, slower so he can keep up. "The only reason Flynn said all that in front of everyone is because he caught you screwing someone else."

Blake's face turns as white as his teeth. He tries to catch my hand, but I smack him away. "Babe, please. Let's go somewhere so we can talk, just you and me."

"You think I want to go anywhere with you?"

Jade's hand slips to my knee. She murmurs my name, but I

can't tear my gaze from the man who promised me the world but ripped out my heart instead.

Blake drags his hands through his hair, his gray eyes welling with tears. "I'm so fucking sorry. I started getting cold feet a few months ago, and—"

Hold on. He's been sleeping with her for *months*?

"I don't know..." He drops his head, pressing his palms to his eyes. "Everyone kept hounding me about when I was going to propose, and it was the next logical step, so..." He shrugs.

Fucking shrugs.

That's when it hits me: Blake never wanted to get married in the first place.

"I'm such an idiot." I can see the pathetic image of myself, sitting in my white dress with two rings on my left hand, surrounded by everyone we know, married to a man who doesn't even want to be with me. Who married me because it was the *next logical step*. Who's been screwing someone else behind my back for months. On our wedding day.

"Babe, please."

Tears spill from Blake's eyes, yet I feel not even a hint of sadness for him as I twist the rings from my fingers and set them on the table. "I'm not going to file the marriage certificate."

"Ruby—"

Let go, Ruby.

"You and I are done."

He grabs the rings. "Put these back on. Please. I love you. I swear I do. Give me a chance to explain!"

I don't even have it in me to knock his hand away when he tries to grab me again. It's like someone injected me with anesthetic, leaving me completely numb.

His head shakes, and his voice wobbles. "We'll figure this out like we always do. Please, Ruby. It's supposed to be you and me, remember?"

"I remember." Blake was the one who forgot. "It was supposed to be you and me, but then you decided you'd rather it be you and *her*." I turn to Jade, ignoring the whispers and murmurs. "I can't be here anymore."

She goes to stand up, her brow lined. "I'll come with you."

"No. Please, I...I need you to handle all this." I wave my hand at the room, but I can't bring myself to look at the sea of faces swimming around me.

She gives my knee a gentle squeeze. "Go. I'll take care of everything."

I slip off my chair and head straight for the door. Blake isn't the only one who calls my name, but I don't stop. I keep moving until icy raindrops splatter my overheated skin, mixing with tears I didn't realize were falling.

Before Blake can come after me, I break into a run.

I don't even know where I'm going. I just know that I need to escape.

I run until my lungs are on fire, and my sopping dress feels like it weighs a million pounds. I run past cars and trees until I catch sight of red lights illuminating the night as a small hatchback reverses away from the farmhouse. My feet pick up speed, slipping down the muddy path.

I run, and I run, waving my arms in the air like a crazy person, but the red car doesn't slow.

"Wait!" I shout, even though there's no way he can hear me over the clap of thunder and pummeling rain.

Then the red taillights ignite as the car lurches to a stop.

By the time I reach Flynn's hatchback, I've lost one shoe and all my dignity. I drag open the passenger door to find him sitting on the driver's side, his eyes red and swollen.

"Flynn," I gasp, my chest burning and my stomach doing somersaults. "Take me with you."

CHAPTER EIGHTEEN

FLYNN

MY EYES ARE TRYING TO FUCK WITH ME.

Either that or Ruby is standing on the road beside my car, her hair slicked with rain, her ivory gown soaked through, and her cheeks wet.

My heart is leaping out of my chest, and I must be gaping at her because she says my name again.

"Get in," I say quickly, like a ghoul might suddenly appear from the shadows and snatch her away. A ghoul that looks a lot like Blake Harrington.

Without hesitating, she climbs in beside me, bringing a whiff of vanilla perfume and heaven. The length of her dress sweeps mud everywhere, but I couldn't care less. Somehow, Ruby's tucked inside a car with me, and I'm turning the wheel toward the exit road.

"Thank you," she says, her voice tight and tear-stained, and a sick feeling washes through me as my brain catches up to what's really happening here.

What's happening is that Ruby and Blake's wedding turned into a shit show, and your little spontaneous sonnet was the closing number. Focus on that, Flynn.

When I spot that her left ring finger is bare, my gut turns hollow.

"I'm so sorry, Quinn," I manage to get out.

While I'm sure it'll hit me later, I'm not even that embarrassed at how I poured my heart out to her through a microphone. What I can't stand is seeing her so broken.

She rests her shoulder against the window, staring at the blur of wind-whipped trees through the rain-coated glass. "It's okay," she says eventually. "I didn't run away because of you. It's...Blake."

She says his name like it's toxic.

"I know." A flashback of him grunting into Tammy makes me tighten my grip on the steering wheel.

Then my mind locks on to what else she just said. "*I didn't run away because of you.*" Is she talking about my speech? I know I made it pretty obvious to her who those words were about, but I sure hope the rest of the reception didn't catch on. The last thing Ruby needs is everyone thinking I'm the reason for her sudden wedding escape.

She presses her hand to her head, squeezing her eyes shut as if she's fighting tears. "You don't have anything to eat in here, do you?"

I don't even have to think. I lean across the center console, my arm brushing her knee as I unlatch the glove box. From inside, I pull out the chocolate bar I bought as a lame peace offering after she told me off at the picnic, but never gave to her. The thing has melted and reformed more times than I can count, but it feels semi-solid inside the wrapper when I hand it to her.

"Thanks." She laughs, but there's no humor to the sound. "This one's my favorite."

"Yeah. I know." She used to pull one out of her backpack every day between our third and fourth period classes.

I can feel her eyes on me, but by the time I navigate around the next bend, she's back to staring out the window.

"Thanks again for letting me come with you," Ruby says around a bite of chocolate.

"Of course." My voice comes out soft and a little needy. I clear my throat. "Where do you want me to take you?"

That's me: Flynn, the taxi driver. Usually, we're in the sky, but whatever.

She sucks in a deep breath, then holds it for a second. "To my grandma's place in Still Springs. I've been staying there. I can show you where it is when we get closer. If that's okay." Her glance at me is lightning-fast.

"Sure."

No, Flynn. She wasn't going to say, "Take me anywhere you're going," or "Take me to a hotel and stay with me a while." Fuck, my mind is spinning off its axis right now.

She makes a jerky shift in her seat like she's uncomfortable in that water-logged dress, and I check I'm driving as fast as I legally can so that she can soon change into something dry.

For a few minutes, silence chews up the air as we cut down the desolate country road thickly flanked with pine trees. I can feel the wheels turning in that beautiful head of hers, but instead of asking what she's thinking like a pest, I reach for the radio.

"Do you mind if I turn this on?" I ask, and she shakes her head. When I tap on the dashboard, I catch her eyes grazing over my busted-up knuckles from where I'd punched the wall. I flip through music stations until I find a song that doesn't sound like it should be played at a wedding or a funeral, giving myself a mental smackdown.

You are alone with Ruby in your car, and you're reverting to that mute, crushing high school kid. Speak, Flynn!

I swallow the rock in my throat, reaching for the only honest words I can find. "This probably doesn't mean much, but I'm so sorry for how this all turned out. You don't deserve any of it, and I hope you know that none of this is even close to being your fault."

Dumb, insufficient words, but I don't want to say too much and accidentally make her feel worse.

I glance at her, but her eyes stay away from mine.

"I'm also sorry for any part I may have played in it," I add for the record, my voice wavering with regret over that badly timed speech. "This was meant to be the happiest day of your life."

I feel her gaze finally cling to the side of my face. "How do you know it wasn't?" she murmurs, and my stomach dips hard.

I don't know what she meant by that, but before I can even think whether I should ask, she expels a huff and begins fidgeting in her seat again like she's fallen into an ants' nest.

"You okay?" I ask.

She's gripping and tugging at the bodice of her dress like she's trying to pull it off her skin.

"Are you cold?" I tap the heat button a few times, turning it up.

"No, it's not that," she mutters, scraping her hands down her sides while her brow knits up. "I just..." She grits her teeth. "This thing is so tight and wet, and...Blake kept running his hands over it, and..." An irate sound bursts out of her mouth before she frantically reaches behind her back with both hands. A sharp zipping noise cuts through the radio track, and a second later, she's yanking the sleeves off her shoulders like the dress is covered in insects.

Holy fuck.

The back of my neck buzzes like it's caught fire, and I fight like hell to keep my gaze pinned to the road instead of where it wants to go.

In the corner of my eye, I see Ruby lifting her hips and peeling her dress down her thighs and past her ankles, exposing a long strip of bare, tanned leg that wakes up my dick.

Stare at the road, Flynn.

"Are you okay?" I ask with a tremble as she bunches up the huge mass of white lace and shoves it into the back seat behind her.

"Sorry." She heaves a sigh and shakes out her hair. "I had to get that thing off me, or I was going to lose my mind."

My fingers bite into the steering wheel as I wrangle all the willpower I have not to turn my head and look at her. I lose the battle for half a second, glancing in the rearview mirror at enough of an angle to catch a flash of lacy lingerie and sun-kissed skin. I wrench my eyes off her, but I can still see her bare leg near mine, and I beat away the mental image of sliding my hand beneath her thigh and hooking her leg over my own, right here in this car. I shift in my seat, already at half-mast.

Fuck, I'm the one losing my mind.

"God, I'm so sorry. You must think I'm *insane*," Ruby says, crossing her arms over herself.

A protective feeling burns through me, and I lean back to fumble around the seat behind me, but it's tricky while I'm driving. "I should have a sweatshirt back there... It's clean."

Ruby turns to reach for it, her arm sliding against my bicep as I twist back to face the road.

Heat stings my cheeks, and I turn the temperature down a fraction while Ruby slips my blue soccer sweatshirt over her head.

"This smells good," she comments immediately, like her brain's as whacked-out as mine. I steal a glance at her sitting there like my wet dream, my giant soccer hoodie draping to her thighs. *Fuck, could she be any cuter?*

"Thank you," she says, giving me a small smile. It's the first time since we left that our gazes lock together. It's so hard to look away that the car does a tiny swerve, and I apologize and refocus on the road, reminding myself that I have precious cargo on board. I can't help but think how much Blake would lose his shit if he knew where Ruby was, but that can't be my problem. The dude screwed someone else on his wedding day, and if Ruby wants to be anywhere but with him, he only has himself to blame.

Before I know it, I'm making a left onto the road leading to Still Springs. The closer we get, the deeper the hole growing inside my gut gets.

I'm not ready to let her go.

I have to remind myself that she needed a ride, and I was in the right place at the right time. In two days, I'll be in DC, getting ready to fly a plane to Europe. *You're just taking her home, Flynn.* At least I don't have to feel like I wimped out of telling her how I feel about her, even if I couldn't do it the way I wish I could—just the two of us, with me apologizing on my knees for high school.

Ruby gives me a few directions, but when I pull up outside her grandma's brick rancher and kill the engine, she doesn't reach for the door handle. Instead, she shifts to face me, her eyes drifting to my knuckles.

"What happened to your hand?" she asks softly.

My throat tightens up. "After I found Blake with Tammy, I kind of wanted to punch his face, but instead, I took it out on the wall. I should really send it some flowers."

Ruby doesn't smile. Instead, she leans back in her seat and looks at me like she's seeing me for the first time. "Can I ask you something?"

"Sure."

Her breath turns a little shallow. "Your speech..."

Blood rushes to my cheeks as she chickens out of her question, her mouth suddenly closing.

"Was about you." I feel the affection burning in my eyes as they drift over her features.

Her eyes widen a fraction—like she couldn't be one hundred percent sure until now—and when her voice stays silent, I feel the need to keep going.

"I'm not sorry about what I said, but I am sorry about the timing of it. I guess I was so pissed off with Blake for making you feel the way he did. I wanted to tell you—and everyone else—that, to me, you're the most perfect thing in the world."

My face flushes hot, and Ruby swallows tightly. For a few moments, we sit in silence, letting those words—and everything I'd said in that speech—fill the gap between us.

"What did you mean when you said I was the reason you left town?" she eventually asks. "When we were at the pond."

That wasn't what I would have expected her to wonder about. I shift to face her, resting my temple against the seat. "Isn't it obvious? I couldn't handle the fact that you were with Blake."

Her voice thins like she's as nervous as me. "I thought it meant you hated me. Because we didn't really get along in high school."

No, Quinn. I was a fucking dick to you in high school because I was crazy about you, and you wouldn't give me the time of day. None of it was your fault.

"That's not why I left," I say, my eyes holding hers. "And I'm pretty sure that hating you is physically impossible for me."

She flushes pink, and *god*, she's so fucking pretty that I have to look down again. But her soft voice pulls me back.

"Last night at the pond..." she begins, and I do something stupid and cut her off.

"I'm so sorry about that," I say in a rush, desperate for her not to put me in the same box as Blake. "I know we had some... eye contact, but I wasn't trying to push myself on you. I would *never* do that."

We're both breathless now. "It wasn't just you, Flynn; I was there too."

"But I want you to know that I would never have tried to cross that line knowing that you were engaged to Blake." Words spill from my lips that I know I shouldn't say, but it's always so hard to reel myself in with her. "Tell me I imagined it," I add under my breath.

"Imagined what?" Her voice is a whisper, her eyes trailing over my face.

It takes me a moment to work up the courage for the next bit. "That some part of you wanted to kiss me."

An invisible axe crashes down between us, severing a cord of respectable distance that's been between us all week. Blake's face flashes into my mind, and I shove it out.

When Ruby doesn't answer right away, I get cold feet and jump back in. "I shouldn't have said that. Sorry."

Flynn, this girl just found out that her new husband has been cheating on her. Leave her alone.

"Come on, I'll get you inside," I say, pushing open my door. Thankfully, it's finally stopped raining.

I move around the car to open the door for her, my heart wrenching when she steps out in my soccer sweatshirt with the name *HUDSON* printed across the back, looking like my dream girlfriend and personal cheer squad.

"You can keep the shirt," I say, trying to make things easy for her, even though it's an old team one I can never replace. "I'm not saying you'd *want* to," I add with a nervous chuckle as we head up the front path. "I meant that you don't need to worry about the shirt. I'll get it later, or...whatever."

I'm just mumbling shit now, but Ruby jerks to a halt beside

me. "I don't have my keys. My sister's still at the barn, and...*shit*." She presses her hand to her forehead, squeezing her eyes shut. "I'm an idiot."

"No, you've had a lot on your mind," I say softly as she crouches before the doormat and skims her hand beneath it. Her fingers come back empty, and she begins searching everywhere she can think of for a spare key. I start helping her out, even though I don't know this lady's house. When we don't find anything in the front, we go around to the back door. She tries the handle, then curses and starts checking under patio furniture and the flowerpots beside the door, even though it's apparent there's no key.

Ruby scrapes her fingers through her damp hair. "Dammit!"

I'm fumbling for what to suggest. There must be someone in this town she knows who isn't at the wedding, but it's late, and Ruby seems fixed on getting into this house.

"Do you know how to pick a lock?" she asks.

I reluctantly shake my head. I haven't tried that since I was a kid, and I don't want to fuck up her grandma's lock.

"I need to get inside," she huffs like it's important to her. As I consider calling a locksmith, she strides over to a small stone birdbath on the wet grass and hefts it under her arm.

"Whoa. What are you doing?" I pace toward her, but Ruby's already at the back window. "Quinn, no!"

She swings and smashes the glass so hard it breaks, and a neighbor's dog begins barking up a storm.

I rush up to her and gently take hold of her shoulders, turning her to face me.

"Are you okay?" I ask, scanning her skin for blood.

And there it is, dripping from her left pinkie finger.

"Oh no," I say, my brow furrowing.

"Do you have tissues?" she asks, and I shake my head.

"Here." I tug up the hem of my T-shirt and wrap it around her finger, squeezing gently but not enough to sting.

"Your shirt," she protests, but I hold on tight.

"I'll buy another one." I dab at the cut a little and lift the fabric. "It's only small," I say, leaning out of the porchlight so that she can see the cut doesn't need stitches.

I curl my hand around her finger again, the fabric bunching between us, and yet the heat of her skin burns into mine.

Ruby's eyes make a quick slide across my exposed stomach before lifting back to mine. "I'm sorry," she says, looking all sheepish and painfully gorgeous. "If you didn't think I was crazy before, how about now?" She gives me a cute squint, and I feel my face flush.

My voice comes out a little rough. "When I think about you, crazy isn't exactly the first word that comes to mind."

Her eyes darken at that, and I focus on stopping the bleeding in her finger while trying not to eat up her bare thighs with my eyes.

"There," I say finally, releasing my T-shirt from her hand. Without thinking, I reach for Ruby's fingers again to inspect the cut, my heart pounding out of rhythm at the feeling of skin against skin.

"Does it look okay?" she asks in a breath, and I nod, but all my attention has zeroed in to where her fingers are brushing back and forth over mine, sending little zings through me.

I should let go of her hand, but I don't. It feels too soft in mine...too warm. Too at home.

She lifts my hand to bring my injured knuckles to her mouth, pressing her soft lips to the red, inflamed skin and kicking all the air out of my lungs.

"You didn't imagine it," she says in a whisper, her hand gripping mine tightly as it falls back to her side.

At first, I don't know what she's talking about.

But then I remember what I'd said to her in the car.

"You did want to kiss me?" I ask softly, my fingers caressing hers.

She nods slowly, and I inhale a sharp breath as we step forward at the same time and bring our foreheads together.

Ruby lets go of my fingers and clutches the back of my neck with both hands, my palms shifting to grip her waist as we turn together until her back is pressed against the wall. My knees nearly give out as she rubs my forehead with hers, her sweet breath fanning over my lips.

In an instant, we're back in that pond, our foreheads fused together, and her endless eyes staring right into my soul.

"*Fuck,* Ruby..." I breathe, a sharp need gripping me everywhere.

Her lips are parted, her pupils are dilated, and I *know* she wants me to kiss her.

But a voice rings in my head. *She got married today to someone else. She just found out he was cheating on her. She's only trying to feel wanted.*

The thought of being nothing but her rebound sickens my stomach, and I go to pull back, but Ruby doesn't let go.

"*Flynn,*" she begs, her lips torturously close to mine.

I close my eyes and take a deep inhale, breathing in every part of her.

"I don't want to take advantage of you," I say, my breath mingling with hers. "You're upset; this is not how I want this to go."

"I know," is all she says, her voice achy, tugging at my heart. I don't want to be Ruby's rebound, nor do I want to do the wrong thing. But if anyone deserves to know how much they're wanted, it's her.

I clutch her jaw firmly, staring my want into her eyes before I cover her mouth with mine, pressing down hard. A flood of heat bursts through my bloodstream as her arms wrap around my neck, and I slide our lips together, feeling hers open up, inviting me in. Our tongues catch and drag together in a hot, hungry glide, and I grasp her face, angling it so I can taste every part of what I've dreamed about for ten years. My heart is exploding in my chest, and she's grasping at my shirt and pushing herself against me, filling me up with so much heat that I'm starting to believe in spontaneous self-combustion.

She's gasping into my mouth like she can't get enough—like this is the best kiss of her life—and there's no question it's mine. I can feel how much she wants me as I clutch onto her waist, wanting so badly to slide my hands beneath my sweatshirt and feel her everywhere.

Instead, I press her hard against the wall and tangle our tongues, showing her how starved I am for her, how much I need her. I'm waiting for relief, but our kiss is only becoming more frantic, and I'm completely lost in her, which is why my stomach plummets when she suddenly pulls away.

Her lips are all swollen and kissed, her cheeks flamed, her hair messed up, and I'm taking mental snapshots in case this is all I'm ever going to get.

But the confused, startled expression on Ruby's face sends a wave of panic through me as I step back.

"Do you want to stop?" I ask, still breathless, still so hungry for her.

Her eyes travel over my face, and she makes a deep inhale as I wait for her answer.

CHAPTER NINETEEN

RUBY

"Do you want to stop?"

Flynn's words ring through my mind.

I somehow manage to say, "We should." This isn't what either of us needs. Flynn has made his feelings for me as clear as day, and I can't even wrap my head around how I'm feeling from one minute to the next. I'm angry. I'm embarrassed. I'm nervous. I'm...relieved.

I'm also so freaking turned on that my body feels like it's melting, and all I want to do is kiss his beautiful mouth over and over again and feel the bite of his stubble against my chin. The possessiveness of his hands on my body, his desperation matching my own.

Except...he's leaving Still Springs in a few days.

He'll leave and never look back, just like he did before.

It's not fair of me to ask Flynn to keep going—to help me forget anything and everything—but when he draws away, taking all his heat with him, I find myself reaching for his arm. "But what if we don't?"

What if we throw caution to the wind and see where this goes? Let the fire in our veins consume us. Let tomorrow's problems live in the future while the two of us revel in the present together.

He stills his retreat, his warm eyes burning a path to my soul. "I care too much to take advantage of you. I never should've kissed you in the first place."

There's only one person who took advantage of me today, and I left him behind in that barn.

I rise onto my toes; a cool breeze tickles my bare thighs as the hoodie I'm wearing shifts with the movement. I brush my lips against his, loving the soft puff of air that escapes when he sighs. "What if I'm the one kissing you?" I whisper, placing his hands on either side of my waist. His fingers immediately contract as if he can't help but hold me. His erection presses against my stomach. Instead of backing away, I lean into him and shift my hips, smiling when he hisses against my cheek. "What if I'm the one taking advantage of you?"

"Shit, Quinn." He backs me against the house, pinning me to the bricks, his forehead dropping back to mine. His hands sear a path down my hips to my backside, cupping and lifting until my legs wrap around him the way they had at the pond. "Please, take advantage of me," he says. "Take advantage of me all you want."

That's all the encouragement I need to catch him by the back of the neck and drag his mouth to mine. To give in to the madness. I need to know what it's like to be wanted by this man I've hated for so long. I need to know what it's like to make him lose control.

His hips begin to rock against my own, slowly at first, as if testing the waters. Not even thirty seconds later, our breaths are coming out in ragged gasps, and sweat beads on my forehead as we move together and begin to find a rhythm, our clothes the only barrier separating his hard length from my core. My heels dig into his lower back; my nails rake down his soft neck and cut arms. When he hits the right spot, my brain short-circuits and a sound I've never made before rumbles out of me.

This feels so good. *Too good.* The kind of good you only get when you're completely alone and can chase your own pleasure instead of helping someone else find his. And we haven't even taken off our clothes. Somehow, that makes it even better. Like we couldn't stop to save our lives. It feels inevitable. Forbidden.

Flynn grinds harder, pulling another moan from my throat. I should be embarrassed, but I'm so far beyond that nothing else matters. "That feel good, Quinn?" he whispers against the shell of my ear.

I barely rasp out a "Yes" before he drags against me again. Heat pools low in my belly, burning like that bonfire last night. He captures my mouth for another kiss, as slow and deliberate as his thrusts.

"You want me to get you off like this?" he asks.

"I'd love to see you try."

His deep chuckle vibrates against my lips before we're both searching for more.

Every kiss, every touch, every thrust brings me closer and closer to the edge.

My legs begin to tremble, my heels at his back urging him to move quicker as the tight pressure inside me builds until light bursts from behind my eyelids like the grand finale fireworks on the Fourth of July. My head spins as I ride the waves of pleasure pulsing through every nerve in my body.

"Look at you," Flynn says on a breath, his hips stilling when he draws back to stare down at me. "You're so beautiful. Quinn, I—" He bites his lip as if it's the only way to stop himself from whatever it is he's about to say.

My cheeks ignite, but thankfully it's too dark out for him to see. I can still feel him straining against his jeans. "You didn't—?"

"Come in my jeans like a teenager?" He chuckles against my neck. "No." His fingers dig into my ass where he still holds me. "But if you don't stop wiggling, I'm going to."

I want to make him feel as good as he did me and watch his handsome face when he loses himself. He sets my feet back on the cold concrete porch, and I reach for the button on his jeans.

"It's okay, Quinn." His long fingers wrap around my wrist, drawing me into his arms instead. My cheek meets his chest, and I inhale the spearmint and aftershave combination that's so uniquely Flynn it makes my heart clench. "You are so fucking amazing," he says. "I hope you remember that."

I hope you remember that.

His choice of words makes my galloping heart fall still.

It sounds like a wish for the future. A future without him around to remind me.

It sounds like a goodbye.

I open my mouth to respond when I hear pounding on the front door. "Ruby?" a man shouts.

Flynn and I jump apart and drop to our knees.

"Ruby Quinn?" the man calls again.

"Who the hell is that?" Flynn mouths, adjusting himself in his jeans.

"I don't know," I whisper back. The man's voice sounds vaguely familiar. It's not my dad or Blake—thank goodness. Who else would be coming by my house this time of night?

"Ruby, are you in there? It's Officer Williams."

My eyes widen at Flynn. "What do I do?" I hiss because, apparently, my brain no longer functions.

"Go? Maybe he can open your door."

"Good point."

You've got this, Ruby. Go out there and smile like you didn't just dry hump your husband's best man on the back porch.

I stand and drag down the hem of Flynn's sweatshirt to

cover as much of my bare skin as possible. When I round the corner, I ram right into Officer Williams' gigantic flashlight. We both stumble back, and his eyes expand when he realizes it's me. "Hey, Nate. I mean Officer Williams. What brings you over?" I say far too brightly for a woman with no pants on and whose hair is a tangled rat's nest of damp waves.

The deputy sheriff peers down at me through narrowed eyes.

He knows.

You're being paranoid. How could he possibly know? Just don't turn around and reveal the name printed on the back of your sweatshirt.

"Mrs. Felton called. She said she heard glass breaking. Thought it could be some of the neighborhood kids."

My sharp laugh seems to startle us both. "Yeah, sorry about that. I forgot my keys, and um...thought it'd be a good idea to break a window to get in. Probably not the smartest move, but I didn't have my phone to call Jade, and I can't find my spare key anywhere." *Stop rambling. You sound guilty as hell.*

At the mention of my sister, he releases a nervous chuckle and runs his hands through his dark red hair. "I can text her if you want. And I might be able to open the door if you'd like me to take a look."

"Would you mind? That would be amazing." Otherwise, I'd probably have to stay at Flynn's until my dad or Jade get home. *Have you completely lost your mind? You can't stay with him.*

Nate returns his flashlight to his utility belt. "No problem. Let me get a few things from the car."

Reality hits me like a kick in the teeth when I spot Flynn's car parked behind mine. If anyone drives by and realizes whose hatchback it is...

As if I haven't already given Still Springs' rumor mill enough fodder for the next freaking decade.

Did you know Ruby Quinn left her own wedding with the best man?

His car was parked outside her house all night.

I heard she hooked up with him on her back porch.

Nate doesn't seem to notice me spiraling next to him. In no time at all, he has Grandma's front door open and the foyer light on.

I thank him again as he returns his tools to their black case. "Need me to take a look at the window?" he offers.

"No! I mean, no, it's fine. Just a bit of glass. I'll take care of it." The last thing I need is for him to find Flynn hiding on my back porch.

Nate still doesn't leave; he kind of stands there awkwardly, shifting his weight from one foot to the other, staring past me into the house.

Before I can ask if there's anything else he needs, he says, "So I heard you left the wedding in a hurry."

Here I thought my stomach couldn't sink any lower. Bad news travels fast.

"Everything okay?" he asks.

"Everything is fine. Thank you. I think I...I might've got food poisoning."

He gives me a look like he doesn't believe a word coming out of my mouth but mercifully doesn't press the issue. Nate says goodnight and heads back toward his police cruiser.

As my eyes catch on Flynn's car, my little bubble of insanity finally bursts. I just made out with Hotshot Hudson like a horny teenager...*on my wedding day*. I did *more* than make out with him. What had I been thinking? It was incredibly selfish to throw myself at him like that, especially knowing we can't have a future together.

"You get in?" Flynn asks from the shadows, his shoulder

resting against the side of my grandma's house. He looks so perfectly disheveled; I want to eat him alive.

"Yeah, I did. Thanks so much again for bringing me home. I should say goodnight."

The thought of being by myself makes me want to puke, but I need to let Flynn go. There's no point in learning to rely on someone who isn't going to be around.

"Are you sure you're okay to be alone?"

No, I think, but I have to get used to it eventually.

I need to sleep. I need to think. I need to deal with the fact that my entire world has fallen apart. And I can't do any of those things with Flynn here because he makes me want to do anything but think.

"I'll be fine," I say, praying it's the truth.

He cups my face with his busted-up hand, smoothing his thumb along my cheek. His mouth opens, but before he can speak, I cut in. "Thank you, Flynn. Really. I don't know what I would've done today without you."

Actually, that isn't true. Without Flynn, I would still be looking like a fool while my husband screwed another woman.

He smiles softly down at me, his eyes glistening. "Anytime, Quinn."

His hand slowly drops like he's reluctant to let go, and the walls that we've kept between us for so long begin to rebuild, brick by brick.

I retreat into my grandma's house so I don't have to see him reverse out of the driveway. So I'm not tempted to call him back and ask him to do something stupid, like stay. Numbness returns to my veins as I pad through the silent house and try to keep my screaming thoughts at bay.

But when I walk into my bedroom and find rose petals sprinkled over the bed and a strip of unlit candles lining the windowsill, I drop to my knees and cry.

CHAPTER TWENTY

FLYNN

I haven't slept properly in days, yet, this morning, I've never been more awake. It's like someone spiked my blood with every kind of sugary stimulant on the shelf then pushed me off a cliff, but instead of falling, I'm flying. I flop an arm behind my head and stare up at the yellowing ceiling of my old bedroom, my smile impossible to hold back.

I woke up thinking it was a dream, but the way my heart is whipping my chest—the raw feeling of my thoroughly kissed lips—assure me it's not.

Holy shit, I made out with Ruby last night. I tasted that unbelievably sweet mouth that I haven't stopped thinking about for a decade.

And she kissed me back.

She more than kissed me; she devoured me, like it was the last kiss she was ever going to get.

My eyes fall shut as the images take over my mind again, giving it what it wants. Last night, I stroked my hands over her incredible ass, gripped her hard and pressed myself against her, and *fuck*—I even watched her come. Her cheeks had flushed pink, her lips had fallen open, her eyes had turned heavy, and I was spellbound. Lost to her.

I want more.

I want to push my hand up under her dress, drag down her underwear, and touch her everywhere. I want to gaze into her eyes, watching the pleasure take hold when I make her feel so good.

As I lay in bed thinking about it, my hand travels south because I need to relieve the throbbing pressure, the same way I did when I got home last night.

A sound from outside the door makes me snap my hand off myself. The murmuring voices of my parents pass by the door and fade away. They're heading downstairs, and even though their tones are hushed, I hear my name.

Shit. My head fills with the memory of my dad's face in the barn when I'd given my speech. Of course, he'd known exactly who the mystery girl was, but nothing about what had gone down between Ruby and Blake before that. All my parents had seen was their son commandeer the room at his best friend's wedding and declare his feelings for the bride. Dad had turned white, and his fingers had gripped Mom's tightly on the table— just like the time I'd left them standing inside the tiny airport outside Still Springs to take my first solo flight in a Cessna.

The joy that's been swimming through my body since last night evaporates when I think about how easily I'd opened my heart to Ruby in front of the man she'd just married, dumping a truckload of fuel over their burning relationship. Of how *she* might be feeling this morning after we kissed, while I'm lying here with my dick in my hand.

That thought pushes me out of bed. *Fuck, Flynn.* Right now, I need to keep my shit together, and it's not going to help anyone if I keep reliving that speech and beating myself to smithereens over its consequences. That speech was meant to be about only me and Ruby. Except I'd invited half of Still Springs to the show when they hadn't even asked for tickets.

The smell of cooking eggs and bacon wafts up from downstairs, and I duck into the shower and quickly change into a T-shirt and a pair of shorts.

I inch downstairs with my stomach flipping over itself like I'm doing the walk of shame. I tell myself again that I'm lucky to have amazing parents. They've supported every decision I've ever made, so there's no reason to believe this will be any different.

I brave a step into the kitchen, finding Mom's back to me as she circles a wooden spoon over a pan on the stove. *Deep breath.*

"Morning," I mumble, heading straight for the cabinet with the coffee mugs.

"Son," Dad greets from behind his newspaper. He's sitting at the dining table while Mom cooks, completing the predictable image of old-school, small-town parents. So much has changed in my life that I love having this one piece of my childhood preserved. Even though it's been eight years since I've stood in this kitchen, there's nowhere in the world I feel safer.

Mom sets down her spoon and comes at me so fast that, at first, I think she's gonna slap me for my speech. But instead, she reaches up to kiss my cheek. "Morning, sweetheart."

A long, heavy breath leaves my lungs. I give her a hug while darting a glance at Dad over her shoulder, but he's still silent.

Mom returns to the stove as I pour myself a coffee, digging up all the courage I have. "I'm afraid to ask, but what happened after I left last night?"

I'm looking at Dad, but it's Mom who replies while separating the scrambled eggs onto three plates. Her voice wavers when she tells me that Ruby disappeared from the reception not long after me and that Jade had gone around to all the tables, calmly explaining that Ruby wasn't feeling well and had turned in for the night. Mom said Jade was wonderful—fielding nosy questions and apologizing on behalf of the bride. After everyone finished their dinner, they all went home, and the cake was left untouched. I'm sure the town gossipers are having the time of their lives trying to piece together the real reason for Ruby's sudden departure.

Mom and I join Dad at the dining table, my stomach curling into a fist. "And Blake?"

Mom slices into her bacon. "Not sure. He also slipped out soon after Ruby, and I didn't see him for the rest of the night, nor his groomsmen, so maybe they all left together."

I steal a glance at Dad, whose silence is freaking me out as much as anything right now.

He's taking slow bites of his eggs, his brow pulled a little tight.

"I'm really sorry," I blurt out, and Mom and Dad exchange glances. "Something happened before the ceremony, and then the speech...it just came out, it felt right—"

"What do you mean something happened?" Dad cuts in gently, and I'm relieved to hear him speak. "You and Ruby are together?"

"No, no. Nothing like that." *God, I wish.*

I push my fork around my plate, searching for more of an explanation that I can't give. "There's some stuff going on that you guys don't know about. I hate keeping things from you, but this is about Ruby, and I need to ask her first before I can talk to you about it."

"It's okay, son." Dad reaches out to give my forearm a pat. "Your mother and I aren't upset with you." Mom gives me a sad but supportive smile. "We're just worried about how this is all going to turn out for you, Flynn," Dad continues. "It's clear you have very strong feelings for Ruby, but she's married now."

"I know."

His tone stays soft. "I don't know if Ruby quitting the reception halfway through has anything to do with you, but most of the town will be talking about it. If anyone suspects it had something to do with your speech, then it'll be Ruby who'll have to deal with what that implies, given you're heading back to DC tomorrow."

My appetite disappears at the thought of my non-negotiable departure tomorrow. Why did I book all those extra shifts like an idiot?

I couldn't give two shits what people say about me, but I don't want to leave Ruby behind to deal with the fallout of all this, and I don't want to be sitting in a hotel room in some European city while Blake is banging on her door. No matter what that guy did to her, they were together for ten years—nearly half their lives. They've got serious history, and he's got an advantage that I can't compete with.

He's *here.*

I'm WIPING UP THE LAST PAN IN THE SINK, STILL BEATING myself up over my overloaded schedule, when I spot my dad through the kitchen window, peering into the back window of my car. *Oh, shit.*

I toss down the hand towel and dash outside.

"Yes, that's her wedding dress," I say as I walk over to him. Damn, Ruby and I had both forgotten about it last night.

Dad spins around. "I was checking your tires for you, and I guess a mountain of white lace is hard to miss."

"You don't need to check my tires; I'm a big boy," I say with a trace of a smile, trying to lighten the atmosphere, even though it feels like a bomb went off in Still Springs last night. And my tires are clearly not the most interesting topic right now.

"It's not what you think," I say. I know what Dad's imagining now that he's seen Ruby's wedding dress stripped off in the back of my car.

"Son, what you do is your business."

"I did *not* do what you think I did with Ruby on her wedding night." I turn around to make sure Mom's not hearing this then lower my voice. "I drove Ruby home from the reception. I was already leaving, she flagged down my car, and she was upset. So, I took her home. Her dress was wet from the rain, so she changed into a shirt I had in the back. That's what happened."

Then we kissed, she straddled me while I was harder than I've ever been, and she came apart in my arms.

My heart presses against my chest. I miss her. I want to see her...talk to her...see how she is. Before I left last night, that cop had turned up, and—that's when I remember the broken window. Ruby lives alone, and she really smashed that thing up good.

"Hey, do you know how to repair a broken window?" I ask Dad before running him through the events of Ruby trying to break into her grandma's house.

He rubs his brow. "Sure, I think I can fix that. At least good enough until she can get a glass company along to replace it properly."

"That's great. Actually, if you tell me how to fix it, I'm happy to go and do it."

The faintest trace of a smirk finds Dad's mouth, even though he's still frowning. "Oh, you would, would you?"

He's caught me out, and a blush sweeps over my cheeks. If I go to Ruby's house to repair the window, not only will that help her out, but I'll get to see her. A rush of warmth flows through me that almost makes me lightheaded. Man, I've never had this many conflicting feelings. I'm so scared of getting hurt, but I'm so powerless to stop any chance I might have with her.

Up until now, a small part of me couldn't help but wonder whether I wanted Ruby so badly because of how unattainable she was. That once I'd got something out of her, this thing I have for her would disappear. But last night had the opposite effect. My feelings for Ruby are all over me today, crowding my throat, my heart, my lungs. Making me need her, crave her. I've never been so sure about her.

Dad sighs at me. "Let me go and see what tools I've got in the truck, Flynn. Because I think it's important that you get that window fixed as soon as possible, right?"

My small smile feels guilty, but I can't wipe it off my damn face. "Right."

MOM HELPS ME HANG OUT RUBY'S WEDDING DRESS TO DRY, even though I have no idea whether Ruby even wants it back. She sure didn't seem to want to be anywhere near it last night, but it's still hers, and I don't want it to get moldy.

I have to psych myself up before I pull my phone out of my bag. Ruby doesn't have my number, so I don't expect to have heard from her, but I'm bracing myself for a torrent of threats and abuse from Blake. I can't blame him if he wants to kick the shit out of me. Sure, he did something horrific, but I still admitted my feelings for his wife in front of all his wedding guests. While I never said her name, Blake knows that Ruby and I sat together in science class; he knows I used to tease her. Surely, he'll have read between the lines of that speech. I rub the back of my neck, my palms sweating, as I tap my phone to life.

Notifications from work fill my screen, and I scroll through them, finding nothing from Blake. Either he's still stewing, or my speech went totally over his head after all, but I suspect it's the former.

The only way I can think to contact Ruby is through social media, so I swipe through my phone, searching for an Instagram icon, but then I remember I deleted it ages ago. I re-download the app and sit for a good fifteen minutes trying to remember my fucking password. I fail multiple attempts and decide to reset it before finally accessing my account.

I've never posted, and my profile pic is still the default image, so I change it to a picture of one of the jets I fly because screw putting a selfie of me on there.

I've never had enough guts to follow Ruby on Instagram, but that doesn't mean I didn't spend half a night once stalking her profile over a six-pack of beer. I find her profile again, which is still set to public, sending a protective feeling through me. Doesn't she know that any guy can lie back on his bed and scroll through these photos like I'm doing right now?

I don't think she knows how ridiculously gorgeous she is. What her smile does to my insides.

I swipe through image after image—Ruby and Jade eating ice cream cones, Ruby making a face while sipping from a glass of lemonade, Ruby grinning over her shoulder at whoever was taking the picture—stopping only when I reach a photo of her and Blake sitting in two matching kayaks.

My gut twists sharply, and I make quick swipes of my finger until I reach the top of her feed, then click "follow" and open a message window. I type out a few messages with trembling fingers. I keep pressing send and then thinking of something else I want to say, and—*fuck*—I've sent eleven.

I toss my phone onto the mattress like it's diseased. Can I delete some of them? But what if she sees that I've deleted messages I'd written to her—that'll make me look deranged.

While I wait for her reply, I keep busy by wandering back downstairs to help Dad sort out the tools in the back of his truck.

After he runs me through the process of repairing the window, I check my phone, but there's still nothing from Ruby. Doubt crawls into my head, eating away all the hope I've been carrying around since last night. Ruby could so easily have woken up this morning feeling the exact opposite to me. She could be sick with regret that we kissed while I'm standing here like a lovesick fool.

Last night probably had nothing to do with you, Flynn; it was about Blake. Ruby just wanted to feel desired by someone after his betrayal.

A cold feeling of dread ices up my veins, and I check my Instagram again. I don't think Ruby's even read my messages.

That's when it clicks: she didn't have her phone last night. She might not even get my messages today at all. Then I'll be leaving for DC, and she'll still have a broken window, and I can't leave it like that, and...shit, should I turn up there with the tools? I don't want her to think I'm stalking her.

"Oh, son, I haven't seen you this mixed up since high school," Dad says, bringing me back to earth.

I give my head a shake. "Sorry, I'm fine. I just haven't been able to reach Ruby."

"Do you want me to call her father?" he suggests. "I could probably get his number from someone. I think the store will be closed today."

I consider it, but the last thing Ruby needs right now is for word to break out that Flynn Hudson is trying to get a hold of her the day after she bolted from her wedding right after his passionate speech.

Instead, I reopen Instagram and find Jade's account and send her a message. A little speech bubble appears almost immediately as Jade types out a reply. A flurry of anticipation swoops into my stomach. While kissing Ruby was mind-bendingly beautiful, I just need to *talk* to her about last night...to ask her if it meant anything to her, even though the timing of it couldn't have been worse.

When I glance up, Dad's eyes are pinned to my face.

"Goodness me, bud, you've really put me in a tough situation."

"What do you mean?"

He shakes his head. "I'm terrified for you, but I also can't help but be happy for you. Look at you." He cups my chin and gives me that affectionate, slightly marveling expression that parents get. "You've fallen all the way down the rabbit hole, haven't you? Just like I did with your mother."

I don't even try to hide the glow in my eyes, which Dad would spot from behind three concrete walls and a blindfold.

"Just remember, she's married," he warns. "I don't want you to get hurt."

His words knock the blush off my face. "Ruby's marriage to Blake isn't what you think. I wish I could tell you why, but...I can't. It's too personal to Ruby."

"You don't have to tell me. But can you say with all certainty that whatever happened between Ruby and her husband is going to end their relationship for good?"

Her husband.

My creased brow draws Dad closer to me. "I'm not trying to cause you any more pain, bud. I just want you to keep your expectations realistic, okay? I want you to be very careful with that heart of yours." He curves his large hand around my shoulder and squeezes.

I know I need to hear these words, but they're hitting way

too close to home. What Blake did to Ruby is disgusting, yet my mind is screaming at me to get my head out of the clouds.

This is Ruby Quinn. She's the most caring, selfless, forgiving person you've ever met. She's loyal and committed to her family, to Blake's family, and to the merger. She does what she thinks is best for everyone else—always.

If there's anyone I know who has it in them to forgive that cheater for what he did—and with the sweetest of intentions —it's her.

I'm fucking terrified of how I'm going to survive if she chooses Blake over me. *Again.* My heart clenches in my chest, and I press my hand over Dad's as he grips my shoulder.

"Go see her, bud," he says gently. "Go see the woman you're so sweet on. No matter what happens, your mother and I are here for you."

Tears spring to my eyes as I pass him a brave smile that's so lost and lovelorn, he lets out a sound of sympathy and pulls me in for a bear hug.

Something tells me I'm gonna need it.

CHAPTER TWENTY-ONE

RUBY

I WAKE UP WITH A START TO THE SOUND OF SOMEONE beating on my front door. When I go to roll off the bed, my foot cracks off the oak footboard. *Hold on.* My bed doesn't have a footboard. I blink at the blue and white striped wallpaper, taking a moment to remember where I am.

Grandma's house.

Guest bedroom.

I couldn't bring myself to sleep in my own room after I saw the way it had been decorated.

The door-pounding begins anew, and I drag on the pair of sweatpants that I vaguely remember twisting out of in the middle of the night because I got too hot.

When Jade sees me, she waves from the other side of the glass. I quickly unlock the door and slide the chain free. The moment it opens, she drops the duffel bag I left at the farmhouse and collects me in a hug, squeezing me until my back pops.

"How are you?" she asks, pulling back and sliding her sunglasses up over her curled hair.

"I don't know." My brain hasn't been awake long enough to decide. I don't feel like crying at the moment, so that's a win.

Then again, I'd drowned in tears last night, so maybe I'm dehydrated. Only one way to find out. I meander over to the sink and fill one of the glasses in the drying rack with cool water.

"What about you?" I ask.

"Pissed. Angry. Livid."

"So, it's your typical Sunday morning, then?"

"Basically." She smirks, both her brows raised. "Nice shirt."

I don't feel like explaining why I'm still wearing Flynn's sweatshirt or how I got it in the first place. Thankfully, she doesn't ask, even though she must be dying to know.

Jade's smirk fades as she drops down at the kitchen table, unhooking her purse from her shoulder and slinging it over her chair. "Sit. We need to talk."

I ease into the chair beside hers, twisting so that we're facing each other.

"I called my lawyer friend, Miriam," Jade says. "She told me that even if we don't file the license, your marriage is legally binding. You'll need to file for divorce."

My face falls. "You're kidding." *Well, isn't that fantastic?* I can't wait for people to find out that I decided to get a divorce on my wedding day. As if this isn't already humiliating enough.

"That's not all," Jade adds with a grimace. "Blake is going to have to agree to sign the papers."

I try to imagine that. Blake won't want to stay married to me...will he? Sure, he'd been upset when I left last night, but if he really loved me and wanted to be with me, he wouldn't have been with *her*. But then again, this is Blake.

"And if he doesn't?" I ask.

Jade pulls a notebook out of her purse and flips to a page in the middle. She leans an elbow against the table, reading from her notes. "After a year, there's no prevention of divorce. But you'll technically be married for the year if you can't get him on board."

Perfect. A few hours of marriage could end up costing me a year of my life, and who knows how much money for a lawyer.

"What did Dad say?" I ask. "Was he disappointed?"

She furrows her brow. "Why in the world would he be disappointed? You did nothing wrong."

Except for making out with Flynn after the wedding then staying up half the night thinking about it. "Did you tell Dad the truth about Blake?"

She nods. "I'm sorry. I know it's not my story to tell, but he was so confused, and he kept begging me to explain what was happening."

"It's fine. I'm actually glad you did." That means I don't have to. "What about everyone else?"

"I told them that you weren't feeling well. They seemed to buy it. But Blake... I'm pretty sure he saw you leave with Flynn."

Shit. I pick up my glass of water and press it against my burning cheeks.

Jade's hair slips over her shoulder when her head tilts. "He messaged me, you know."

My stomach swoops. "Who?"

"Flynn."

"What'd he say?"

"See for yourself." She drags her phone out of her purse, types in her keycode, and slides the handset across the table. Her Instagram app is already open on the screen.

@FLYNNSTAGRAM

Hey. It's Flynn

I don't have Ruby's # so I messaged her on here

Then I remembered that she doesn't have her phone, so I'm messaging you

Obviously

The window at her place is broken

Do you think it would be okay for me to come fix it?

@JUST_JADE

That'd be great, if u don't mind

Thanks

Reading those few sentences shouldn't make me feel all warm and fuzzy inside. But it does. And he said he messaged me too. My stomach does the same flippy thing it used to do when I rode on the Ferris wheel at the county fair. "Do you have my phone?" I ask.

Jade's lips curl into a mischievous smile as she withdraws my phone from her purse. I can't help the way my cheeks flush hot when I unlock the screen. There are so many notifications, messages, missed calls, and DMs it makes my head ache. I ignore them all and click on Instagram. There are a bunch of messages there as well, but I click through to the *Requests* and find the only one I care about.

His username makes me snort. *Terrible. Just terrible.* His messages, however, leave me grinning like an idiot because, apparently, the good sense I'd lost last night hasn't returned.

@FLYNNSTAGRAM

Hey, it's Flynn

I don't have your number, so I hope this is okay

I can't stop thinking about your broken window

Actually, I can't stop thinking about a lot of things that happened, but I'm trying to focus on the window so I don't make it really awkward with my parents

> I told Dad about it

> The WINDOW

> Get your head out of the gutter, Quinn

> He told me how to fix it

> I hate the idea of leaving you

> With a broken window

> So let me know if you want me to come over

A little while later, he sent more messages.

> I talked to Jade

> I'm coming over

> Let Mrs. Felton know so she doesn't call the cops again 😎

Flynn is coming over?

*Wait...*why am I smiling?

I can't be smiling over some other guy until I've figured out this mess with Blake.

"I can't see him right now," I tell Jade. If I see him, I'm not entirely sure I'll be able to keep my hands to myself.

"Why not?" she asks.

I can't tell her because I don't want her to think less of me for what I've done. But I want to. I really, really want to get this terrible, horrible, beautiful secret off my chest. Maybe if I'd shared with her the way I was feeling before the wedding, things would've ended differently. Maybe I would've had the sense to listen to my gut when I felt like something was wrong and called the whole thing off.

Am I really going to keep this secret forever? If I can't talk to my sister, who can I talk to?

"After Flynn took me home last night, I... I kissed him," I confess. *I kissed him and I liked it*. No. I *loved* it.

Jade's mouth drops open.

"I know, I know. It was so stupid." *Stupid, stupid, stupid.* "It's just...he was so sweet on the drive back, and we started talking about what happened at the pond, and—"

"What happened at the pond?"

Shit. I didn't mean to tell her that part. "He hugged me, and I hugged him back, but that was it."

"This was before the wedding?"

I nod.

"Did anything else happen last night?"

I bring the glass back to my face.

"Holy shit, Ruby! Tell me you didn't sleep with him." She clutches my knee. "Actually, you know what? Tell me you *did* sleep with him. Tell me you slept with him, and he rocked your world, and you don't even remember that asshole you married."

"No! No. Absolutely not. I kissed him. And..." I screw my eyes shut so I can't see the shock on her face when I say, "There may have been some hip action."

She's quiet for so long that I'm not sure she heard me until she says, "How much hip action are we talking about?"

I cover my face with my hands. "He got me off."

"With *just* hip action?"

I peek through my fingers to find her grinning. "Stop sounding so impressed."

"But it *is* impressive. I've never met a guy whose hips were that dedicated."

I know exactly what she means. Blake hadn't touched me in forever. Now that I think about it, I can't even remember the last time we had sex. It must have been at least two, if not three months ago. And when he did touch me, getting me off wasn't exactly at the top of his to-do list.

Last night, it felt like Flynn couldn't get enough of me, and I'd lost myself in that feeling. In him.

"It doesn't matter, though," I say, the memory heating my blood, "because I am literally just out of a ten-year relationship, and Flynn's leaving, and it would never work."

"Do you want it to?" Jade asks, studying me with way too much intensity.

"No. That's crazy. Don't be crazy." *Stop thinking about it, Ruby. You can't. Last night was a one-time thing. You need to keep your head on straight.*

A rapid knock on the door tears me out of my thoughts. When I glimpse a tall figure with dark hair through the glass, my heart kicks into overdrive.

"Looks like it's too late to cancel," Jade murmurs.

Before I realize what's happening, I'm opening the front door, and Flynn is giving me a shy smile in a pair of dark athletic shorts and a faded blue T-shirt, a toolbox in one hand and a notepad in the other.

My stomach whips up into that fluttery mess that's becoming all too familiar. I blurt out the first thing that comes to mind. "Flynnstagram? Really?"

His chuckle makes my chest turn warm. "You're not allowed to make fun of me for something I made when I was eighteen. Statute of limitations and whatnot."

"False. I will absolutely be making fun of you."

A lock of dark hair falls onto his forehead when he shakes his head. The smile slips from his face. "How're you holding up?"

"I'm fine."

His head tilts, and his eyes grow serious. "It's okay if you're not."

I trace the shape of his face with my gaze. His broad shoulders. The ridges of his muscles where they peek from beneath his sleeves.

Even if I wasn't technically married, Hotshot Hudson is off-limits.

"I'll *be* fine," I say. Eventually, it'll be true, right? And if I'm not, it's not his problem, is it? I search the driveway and street for signs of Flynn's hatchback, but all I find is an old blue truck parked in front of Mrs. Felton's house.

"Where's your car?"

"Dad's tools were in his truck, so I borrowed that."

That's probably a good thing. Wouldn't want anyone driving by to recognize his car in my driveway.

On the other side of the stoop, I spot a ball of golden fur peeking from under the hedges. It's just the distraction I need to keep my hands from reaching for Flynn. "Come here, Bandit."

Flynn turns to see what caught my eye, then sets his tools down and whistles. The dog comes bounding out, leaping onto the stoop with a yelp and attacking Flynn with wet, sloppy kisses.

"I have to admit, I'm kinda jealous," I say, my heart swelling way more than it should at the domestic scene playing out in front of me.

He's leaving. He's leaving. *He's. Leaving.*

And when this guy leaves, he tends not to come back.

Flynn glances up at me and smiles, his deep-brown eyes crinkling at the corners. "You're welcome to lick my face anytime you want, Quinn."

"Jealous of *you*," I amend with a laugh, my face flushing as I catch the dog's collar. "Bandit never greets me like that."

I ruffle the curly hair behind the dog's ears and tug him toward the Wilsons' house, telling Flynn I'll be right back.

"I'll head around and check out this window you

destroyed," he says, hopping off the side of the stoop and disappearing around the corner.

Once Bandit is locked up safe in his own yard, I hurry back home. Jade is in the kitchen, staring out the back window at where Flynn has his toolbox open on the back porch. "You want some coffee?" I call out through the cracked window.

"That'd be great. Thanks," he returns with a smile that takes me a second to look away from.

Jade finally moves from where she's been leaning against the counter and collects her purse from the dining room. "I'm going to head out and leave you to it," she says with a not-so-subtle wink.

"He's just fixing the window."

She hums as if she doesn't believe me. "Let me know if he *fixes* anything else while he's here."

I know what she's suggesting, but there's nothing else for Flynn to *fix*. He's leaving town, and I'm staying here. It's up to me to fix my broken life.

I say goodbye to my sister and slip a mug beneath the coffee maker. When it finishes brewing, I start to add the sweetener but stop myself. This coffee isn't for Blake. It's for someone else.

I may never make coffee for Blake again.

Will Tammy make coffee for him? Has she already? Does she know he likes the sweetener in the yellow packets, not the pink or blue ones?

I shake the thoughts away. Blake has already stolen ten years from me, and I refuse to let him take another second.

Outside, I find Flynn securing the cracked window with thick white tape. A few shards of glass glitter on the porch, but it's not as bad as it appeared last night. The glass will need to be replaced, but that shouldn't be too expensive.

"I don't know how you like your coffee," I confess with a nervous smile.

He peers into the mug. "Black is perfect. Thank you." His fingertips brush mine when he takes the drink, sending tiny sparks shooting down my hand.

Same as me. Not that it matters, since this is the only cup of coffee I'll ever be giving him. Steam curls around his face as he raises the mug to his lips. For some reason, the simple sight makes my heart feel like it's trying to burst through my ribcage.

"Thanks for coming by to check on the window," I say, my voice coming out a little husky.

Flynn glances over his shoulder. "I didn't do much. But it should stay put until the glass place opens tomorrow. I'll call them first thing and organize for someone to swing by and fix it properly."

"I can call them myself," I say, although it's nice having someone take care of me for once.

"I know. But I'd like to do it if you'll let me. You have enough on your plate right now."

That's an understatement. Although I don't have to go back to the store until next week, I'm already dreading it. Then there's the whole divorce thing. I should probably go to the clinic, too, just to make sure Blake didn't give me anything. For all I know, he's been screwing other people for the last decade.

Flynn sips his coffee. Over the rim, he says, "About last night..."

"I think it's best if we pretend it didn't happen," I say softly.

We both look down, and Flynn sighs. "That's gonna be hard for me to do, Quinn. After fantasizing about kissing you for a decade, that memory is never leaving." He sets his mug on the windowsill and shifts closer. "As a matter of fact, I was up half the night trying to figure out how to make kissing you a regular occurrence."

The thought of kissing Flynn again brings about a whole

new wave of flutters. Still, a regular occurrence? How's that supposed to happen when he's off flying around the world?

He glances sidelong at me, the sunlight hitting the stubble on his chin just right. "Do you think we could start with you going out on a date with me?"

Is he crazy? We can't go out together.

"Not right now," Flynn rushes. "The timing is shit, I know that. It's just..." He runs his hand through his dark muss of hair, and I find my fingers itching to do the same. "I'd love a chance to redeem myself after being such an ass in high school. When you're ready, of course."

"What makes you think you can redeem yourself?" I ask, delaying the inevitable for a moment longer and basking in the warmth of his gaze.

Flynn's eyes travel over my face, sending my pulse skittering. "I'd say the way you cried out my name last night was a pretty good start."

The memory burns anew, setting fire to my core. We're literally standing in the exact same spot we were last night. It would be so easy to give in to this attraction building between us. To reach out, grab him by the collar, and drag his perfect lips to mine.

But the light of day has brought some clarity.

Even if it weren't for his past relationship with Blake, there's no way Flynn and I could ever work. It's not just the past getting in our way or the shitty timing. It's Flynn's crazy schedule. It's the fact that I live in Still Springs and he doesn't. If I've learned anything from movies, it's that long-distance relationships never work.

You're getting ahead of yourself.

Flynn isn't asking me to be in a relationship. He just wants to go out on a date. That's what guys like Flynn do. They date around and keep things casual. I really don't know if I can do casual. In twenty-six years, I've only dated one person, and my relationship with Blake was anything but. Plus, the thought of casual and Flynn—

Before I can respond, there's a knock at the door. "Ruby?"

My heart stalls in my chest.

Flynn whips toward the raspy voice; his shoulders stiffen. "Is that—?"

"It's Blake."

My unfaithful husband is the last person on earth I want to see right now, but I need to at least talk to him if I'm going to convince him to give me a divorce. Plus, I have no clue how to answer Flynn's question about a date. My head is so muddled that I can't think straight.

There's only one thing I know for sure: if Blake finds out about me and Flynn, he'll *never* sign the divorce papers.

"Blake can't know you're here," I say to Flynn. "Is it okay if you leave out the back before he sees you?"

Flynn's cheeks flush, and pain flashes through his eyes before he blinks away. A muscle in his jaw ticks as he bends down to collect his toolbox.

I don't want to hurt Flynn, but I honestly can't see how this could work out for us. Blake turning up is a sharp reminder that there are too many obstacles in our way. It's better if we stop now before things get even more painful. "I'm sorry. It's just... this is all too messy. It's probably for the best if we stay away from each other. Like old times."

Flynn doesn't respond.

I go to say more, to try to put my thoughts into words, but Blake bangs on the door again. "*Ruby?*"

"I'm sorry," I say to Flynn again, my heart pinching sharply as I sneak into the kitchen and quietly close the door behind me, taking a moment to inhale a deep, fortifying breath. Blake is still in his shirt from the wedding, albeit without his jacket and tie.

When his bloodshot eyes lock with mine through the front window, my stomach sinks even lower.

The moment I open the door, the harsh smell of alcohol hits me square in the face. "What do you want, Blake?"

His eyes well with tears as they drag down my face, but he quickly swipes the wetness away with his stained shirtsleeve. Judging by the bags under his eyes, he likely hasn't slept at all. "I needed to see you, babe. To say I'm so sorry for everything."

When he steps forward, I close the door a bit more, making it clear that he's not welcome inside.

"Tell me how to make it up to you," he begs, his voice hoarse. "I'll do anything."

I don't think there's anything he *can* do. Some couples can move past infidelity, but I don't think I'm that type of person. I could see myself forgiving him someday, but trusting him? No way.

"The damage is done," I say.

"This can't be the end. Ruby, please. We need to talk about this. I'm..." His face suddenly pales; sweat beads on his brow. The moment his eyes bulge, I know exactly what's going to happen. By some miracle, Blake manages to make it to the side of the stoop before he vomits all over the bushes.

Part of me wants to lock the door and leave him to his misery. But knowing I need him to cooperate with me on the divorce makes me push that thought aside and rush back into the kitchen to grab a roll of paper towels and a glass of water. When I get back to the stoop, I find Blake curled up on the concrete pad, groaning.

"Here." I hand him the paper towels, waiting until he wipes his face before giving him the water. "I really hope you didn't drive here." I can't see his truck anywhere, but Flynn's dad's truck is still parked in the same spot. Blake hasn't seemed to notice it yet, but it's only a matter of time.

Blake sips the water slowly, his face still green. "I walked. I had to see you. Had to talk to you. How could you do this to me? How could you leave with *him*?"

Thankfully, he doesn't notice my harsh intake of breath. "We're not having this discussion when you're drunk and smell like puke." After what Blake did, he has no right to question me about Flynn.

Blake groans again.

Can I really send him back home in this sorry state? I could drive him back to his parents', but if he vomits in my car, I'll never get the smell out. And in this heat...

I need to pretend a little longer, at least until he's sober. "Come inside," I say, helping Blake to his feet. "We can talk after you get some sleep."

CHAPTER TWENTY-TWO

RUBY

My palms feel like they're leaking as I stand on Blake's parents' front porch. After he passed out on my couch yesterday morning before we'd had a chance to talk, I'd retreated to my room to wait out his hangover. Then I saw the rose petals and couldn't stay in that house with him a moment longer. So, I drove over to Dad's. By the time I got back later that afternoon, Blake was gone. Typical. The man has the patience of a gnat.

I scrub my hands against my shorts, swallow past the lump in my throat, and knock. Part of me hopes he's not here, even though delaying the inevitable drags out the shit show that has become my life.

The door swings wide, but it's not Blake who answers.

Mrs. Harrington looks as perfect as ever, her blonde hair styled in soft curls and her blue pinstripe shirt tucked into a pair of khaki shorts. The only thing that isn't perfect is the glare she's giving me, like I'm a piece of gum stuck to the bottom of her gold flip-flop. "You're not welcome here," she says.

The venom in her tone makes me flinch. This woman has known me since I was a child. She used to babysit Jade and me when our parents went away for weekends and our grandma wasn't available. How can she hate me for something her son did?

That's when it hits me.

She doesn't know the truth.

She thinks this is all my fault.

I understand why Blake wouldn't tell all the other guests what really happened, but surely he should've told his mom. "I need to speak to Blake," is all I say, my emotions twisting into an ugly thing in my chest.

The staircase behind her creaks, and the man I married appears in a pair of black tracksuit pants and a white T-shirt with a red stain down the front. "It's fine, Mom," Blake says, nudging past her. "You can go back inside."

Mrs. Harrington turns with a huff and stalks down the hallway. Blake reaches back to close the door behind him, then gestures to the porch swing.

The speech I practiced the entire drive over rumbles through my mind. It's one thing to say these things to an empty passenger seat and another thing entirely to say them to the man I've been with for a decade who is standing so close that I can smell his body spray.

The swing's springs whine when we sit, and I have trouble holding his gaze.

Blake scrubs a hand across his eyes, heaving a weary sigh. "I'm so sorry, babe," he says for what feels like the hundredth time, going full puppy dog with his eyes.

Is he sorry for what he did or sorry that he got caught?

I can't say it's fine because it's not. But part of me wants to say those words so he stops giving me that lost look. "Why haven't you told your mom the truth?" I say instead.

"The last thing I need is Mom making me feel shittier than I already do."

I shake my head as I turn away. He deserves to feel shitty.

I feel shitty, and I didn't even do anything wrong. "But you *are* going to tell her."

He leans forward, the swing swaying as he rests his elbows on his knees. "You know my parents. If Mom finds out I fucked up, she and Dad will never give me the restaurant. And they'll definitely fire Tammy. She moved here for this job and has her son to think about."

My chest twists up so tight that I can't breathe.

Blake doesn't want *her* to get blamed, and yet he's perfectly content to let *me* get thrown under the bus. Yes, Tammy has a son, and I'm not trying to be insensitive to that, but she's an adult. She made the choice to sleep with my fiancé. With my husband, only hours after we got married.

Why should I be the only one to face the consequences?

Why didn't anyone want to protect me?

I get off the swing and step away from him, my hands fisted at my sides. "I filed for divorce," I say in a flat tone. "You'll be served some time next week." The meeting with Jade's lawyer friend this morning had been quick and relatively straightforward since Blake and I have no children and no shared assets.

Blake shoots to his feet, the swing banging against the backs of his legs. "So what, you're just done with me? I make one mistake and—"

"How long have you been sleeping with her?" I ask, needing to hear him say it again.

His gaze flashes to the window, then back to me, a flush creeping up his neck.

"How long, Blake?" I press.

He rubs a hand down the back of his hair, his teeth scraping his lower lip. "Two months, okay?"

My stomach rises into my throat. Two months. Half of our engagement. No wonder he didn't have time to help plan the wedding. He was too busy screwing *her*. "So, it's not just one mistake, is it?"

This time, when Blake's eyes fill with tears, I feel nothing. He scrubs angrily at his eyes, his hands tightening into fists. "Fucking Hudson. He's lucky he's gone, otherwise, I'd kill him."

Hearing him speak so terribly about someone who, up until Blake cheated on me, had been a friend to him, makes me want to scream. "This has nothing to do with Flynn," I say, somehow managing to keep my voice level.

Blake's chin jerks back. We glare at each other for an impossibly long moment before his lips curl into a mocking smile. "So it's 'Flynn' now, huh? I bet you two got nice and cozy after you left *our* wedding together. Did he fuck you and leave you the way he does every other girl he's been with? Because that's all you'll ever be to a guy like him. Another fucking landing strip."

"Don't you dare talk about him like that. I'm done with this conversation, and yeah, I'm done with you," I say, throwing his own words back at him. "Just sign the damn papers when they come. And tell your mom what really happened, or I will." The lump in my throat grows when I turn to leave.

Blake laughs, but there's nothing jovial about the sound. "If you do that, there won't be a merger."

My footsteps still.

"If my mom finds out the truth," he goes on, "she'll call the whole thing off. The merger, their plans to give me the restaurant, it'll all be over."

Reality sucks the air out of my lungs. I couldn't care less about Blake getting his damn restaurant, but if the Harringtons call off the merger, my family's business will go under. Our store is failing as it is. Dad says we may not be able to make it to Christmas. We *need* that merger.

Slowly, I turn, icy bitterness replacing my anger. "So, what? I'm supposed to let everyone think this is my fault?"

Blake's eyes are like steel. "Yes."

This isn't fair. I shouldn't have to take the fall for this, but right now, I can't think of any way around it. Blake is right. His parents are notoriously hard on him. If they learn he's the one who ruined us, they'll definitely cancel the merger as punishment since it started as his idea.

There's still a chance they'll do that anyway.

"If I agree to take the fall, you'll make sure the merger goes ahead?"

Blake nods.

My family knows the truth about what happened. That's what matters. What Blake's parents think about me is irrelevant. As soon as those contracts are signed, I'll set the record straight. "Fine."

Blake blows out a relieved breath, his shoulders relaxing as he practically skips back into his parents' house.

I climb into my car, feeling even worse than I did on the way over. Somehow, I manage not to cry the whole way home. But when I get inside and find the window I'd broken has been replaced and my wedding dress hanging from my back door, the tears finally come.

Flynn came through for me despite the way things ended between us.

I fish my phone out of my purse to text him. Seeing the plane in his profile picture makes my heart beat a little faster as my finger hovers over the keypad.

What if texting gives him false hope? Is it better to leave things as they are? The last thing I said to him was that this was too messy. That hasn't changed. If anything, my life has become even more complicated. He's respected my wishes so far to stay away from each other, so I need to do the same with him.

My stomach sinks as I close the app and open my texts to Jade instead.

> Do me a favor? Tell Flynn I said thanks for taking care of the window.

I SHIFT ON THE STOOL BEHIND THE REGISTER, MY THIGHS sticking to the worn pleather seat as I watch familiar faces pass our front door without so much as a wave. Since Tuesday, we've had twelve customers. *Twelve.*

Mrs. Wilson comes up to the register with a pack of diapers, toilet paper, and a jug of bleach.

For some reason, she keeps glancing over her shoulder at the door as I key in the items. "Everything okay, Mrs. Wilson?"

"Everything is...fine," she replies.

"You sure?"

She bobs her head. After paying, she grabs her purchases, clutching them to her chest like I'm going to try and take them back.

"Don't you want a bag?" I ask.

"No, no. I don't want anyone..." She bites her bottom lip as if she's nervous. "Never mind," she mutters. "I need to go."

Back in the office, Jade hunches over a bunch of papers, her head in her hands. Before I can say anything, she glances up and smiles. It's not a real smile, though. Neither of us has had one of those all week.

"Is it just me, or are people acting really weird lately?" I ask, propping a shoulder against the doorframe.

The old chair squeaks when she leans back and stretches her hands toward the ceiling. "I haven't really noticed."

The bell jingles, and although it's my turn to man the front, I don't have it in me to smile and pretend to be pleasant. "Do you mind grabbing that? My feet could use a break."

"Sure. No problem." Jade's out the door before I can say another word.

When I hear my neighbor Mrs. Felton's gravelly greeting, I'm relieved my sister is the one dealing with her and not me.

"Looks like business is down," Mrs. Felton remarks. She's probably buying cat food for her three cats like she does every Thursday.

"Some days are slower than others," Jade says. The register beeps as she rings in the items.

I peek through the gap in the door. Six tins of cat food, just as I suspected.

"It's not right," Mrs. Felton says. "What your sister did to poor Blake Harrington."

My breath hitches.

"What do you mean?" Jade clips.

"Folks around here are awfully upset about the way Ruby left that boy high and dry—and on their wedding day, no less. But to run off with his best man? Just scandalous."

Is that the reason no one is coming into the store? Because of me? How in the world did Mrs. Felton hear about Flynn? Is that what Blake is telling people now?

Jade shoves the bag of cat food across the counter. "What happened wasn't Ruby's—"

I push through the door, hoping my flushed face doesn't give away my eavesdropping. "Hey, Jade, can I talk to you for a second?" I give the elderly woman a wave. "Hi, Mrs. Felton."

Although she doesn't return my greeting, Mrs. Felton looks appropriately chastised when she turns toward the exit, the tins of cat food tucked inside her mammoth black purse.

The moment the door falls shut, Jade unleashes a frustrated groan. "Can you believe that woman? Seriously. You didn't *leave* Blake—"

"Technically, I did."

"Yeah, but it's not your fault!"

"Please don't worry about it."

Her blonde braid swings violently when she shakes her head. "I'm going to go out there and tell the whole damn town what a lying, cheating piece of—"

"Jade!" I take hold of her arms, forcing her to meet my gaze. Her brow furrows as she blinks down at me.

I feel terrible for not telling her about my deal with Blake, but I know exactly what she would've done the moment she learned the truth. She would've said screw him and the merger, and we'd lose everything. None of this would be happening if things with Blake and I hadn't spontaneously combusted. This is something I can do to help my family.

"I love you, and I love that you're so willing to stick up for me," I tell her, "but this isn't your problem. It's mine. People are going to believe whatever they want, no matter what we say." And sometimes, the truth does more damage than good. "Don't worry. It'll all blow over soon."

It doesn't blow over. Three more weeks pass, and the rumors are still as vicious as ever. In some of them, I'm pregnant with Flynn's child. In others, I'm just the bitch who decided to ditch my husband on our wedding day.

Business is slower than ever, and the Harringtons have rescheduled meetings about the merger twice. Blake was served the divorce papers last Friday, but he's obviously been too busy playing the victim to sign them.

It's only seven o'clock, and I'm already in my PJs, but if I go to bed now, I'll end up lying there thinking about everything I've done wrong, and I've spent enough time *thinking*. I sink onto the couch and dig my phone out of my purse to mindlessly flip through Instagram. It's a nice reminder that some people have lives that aren't in shambles. Like Carl. Looks like he bought a new car. My cousin Lance went kayaking with his kids.

And Blake...

My stomach drops.

He's posted a photo of him sitting at his mom's desk in the restaurant's office with a caption that says, "Overcoming."

Overcoming *what?*

How are there over thirty comments? People saying that he needs to stay strong, that he'll get through this rough patch, that he's better off. One woman even offered to help him get over me.

Meanwhile, I haven't received one message after the initial fallout. No one's asked me for my version of events; no one's reached out to see if I'm okay.

Blake is going about his life, reveling in the attention, and I'm here, stuck on a loop, one disappointment after the next, with no end in sight.

I want to scream at the unfairness of it all.

What a selfish asshole, throwing me under the bus every chance he gets so that he can have his parents' restaurant. I may have agreed to bite my tongue because of the merger, but does that mean I'm supposed to sit here and do nothing until Blake decides otherwise?

I rage-scroll past Blake's post, my teeth grinding together.

Phil and Latisha just celebrated their third wedding anniversary. Good for them.

Justine's daughter celebrated her first birthday. Isn't that wonderful?

Oh, look! Elliot and Loren got engaged. I hope he doesn't cheat on her on their wedding day.

When I hit a video posted by Frank, my throat instantly dries up.

Holy shit. He'd recorded Flynn's entire wedding speech and put it *online.*

I watch Flynn fumble as he unfolds the paper, my heart hammering the same way it did that day. When he begins speaking, there's so much emotion in his voice. Anger. Resignation. Longing.

Hearing it all again shreds my heart to ribbons.

I slide my finger down the top of my screen and press record. I want to watch this when I'm feeling sad, to be reminded of what it felt like to be wanted by a man willing to stand in front of two hundred people—and their smartphones—and profess his feelings for a woman he said he hadn't stopped thinking about for ten years.

For me.

I've pulled up Flynn's profile so many times since he left, flipping through the few pictures he's posted, mostly of planes and historical monuments. Have his parents told him about the rumors? How's he holding up after losing his best friend?

I miss him. Is that stupid? I barely even know the guy, and yet he's become the only bright spark in a sea of dark days.

I want to text him. Even more than that, I have this overwhelming urge to see him.

I've reminded myself a thousand times why that's not a good idea, but all the objections I had when he first asked me out don't seem as insurmountable as they did before. Yeah, he lives a few hours away, but why is that bad? If anything, it seems like a good thing considering everyone in Still Springs has turned against me.

He never actually said he was looking for something casual. I assumed that's what he wants because of his lifestyle. Maybe I can do casual. Maybe I'll even like it, considering how my one and only serious relationship turned out. If I start something with Flynn and it's not what I want, then I'm no worse off than I am now. At least I won't have to worry about running into him in town.

Another point for him being in DC.

Then there's Blake.

After what he did, I don't owe him anything, and neither does Flynn.

I'm finished letting Blake and his lies control my life.

I click into Flynn's profile, but this time I don't hesitate to type out a message that I've wanted to send since he left.

CHAPTER TWENTY-THREE

FLYNN

It's well after 1 a.m., yet the rooftop bar in Barcelona is pumping house music while well-dressed locals stand around sipping cocktails and posing for selfies. There's a bed waiting for me in the hotel next door, but with the noise coming out of this place, I'm not sure I could sleep even if I was tired. And it's not like I have anything to get up for tomorrow. After flying in a CEO this morning ahead of his three days of business meetings, I've got nothing to do for the next seventy-two hours except wander around a city that I've been to twice and fight to keep my mind off everything that went down in Still Springs.

And off her.

The sad, dejected feeling that's been living inside me for the past month thickens as I sit at the bar and thumb through the latest flood of abuse from Blake. It hurts to read this stuff from someone I used to be so close to, and every day, I hope it'll stop. But he's as fired up as ever and was probably half tanked when he sent these.

@ITSBLAKEHARRINGTON

> You are the sorriest excuse of a friend to have ever existed

> Never talk to me again, fuckhead

> Good luck with your lonely life

> You think you'd even have a chance with Ruby?

> HAHAHAHAHAHAHAHAHA

> Keep dreaming, asshole

> She hates your guts and wouldn't touch you if you were the last man alive

I resist the urge to reply to that one with a play-by-play of Ruby coming apart in my arms on her grandma's porch.

But then images of the day that followed that night crash into me like a flood. Me heading over to Ruby's house to fix the window and trying to tell her how I felt about our kiss, which abruptly ended when she kicked me out the second Blake showed up. Then she went and invited him inside her fucking house. I'd heard the whole thing play out while I was sneaking away to my dad's truck like a dirty little secret. They're probably back together by now because he's so damn pushy, and she's so damn sweet and forgiving.

And, once again, I'm thousands of miles away, so I can't do jack shit about any of it.

With my gut in my throat, I scroll down to Blake's most recent message.

> You even think about coming anywhere near Ruby, and I'll slice up your airplane tires the next time you're about to fly

I'll video your burning body and watch it go viral

You can't just cut into the tires of a Challenger jet, dumbass. And why would a plane crash if it couldn't take off in the first place? Honestly, Blake, have a fucking think for a change.

I toss my phone onto the bar and throw back a gulp of sangria, my eyes catching the stare of a dark-haired woman leaning across from me. She's model-gorgeous and throws me a flirtatious smile before ordering a drink from the bartender.

I set my gaze back on the replay of an old La Liga match on the flatscreen TV.

A body slides onto the stool beside mine, and I'm hit with an onslaught of woody perfume and bed eyes. It's the woman from the bar, who says something to me in Spanish, and I give my usual apologetic reply.

"Lo siento, no hablo Español."

Her mouth quirks up. "It's okay, Captain America; I speak English." The bartender slides her a fruity cocktail, and an urge collapses over me to get up and leave so I don't waste this woman's time with my sorry-ass mood.

"What is your name?" she asks in a honeyed accent that could make any man get on his knees. Any man except me.

I barely glance at her. "Flynn. You?"

"Gabriella."

I manage to return her smile until her flowing black hair makes me look away, my heart stinging.

"So, what is such a handsome American doing all alone here in Barcelona?"

Just go home, Flynn. Go to your room, pass out, and wake up tomorrow feeling the same way you did today and every other day for weeks now. Like you've held heaven in your hands then had it ripped from your fingers.

I reply with bare-minimum information about being here for work, and that I'm a pilot for a private company, but everything I say only draws her lean body closer to mine.

This isn't a new story. It's the one where I sit alone in bars, cafes, restaurants, and museums in foreign cities for hours on end. Sometimes pretty girls come right up to me like Gabriella, and sometimes I end up taking them back to my room for an entire night or a long afternoon. One time in Rome, it was right after a morning espresso and a cornetti, which sure was one way to start the day.

But nothing about any of that appeals to me now. The thought of taking this elegant, long-legged Spanish girl next door and losing myself in her soft warmth makes me feel cold all over.

Because there's only one girl I want in my bed, and she doesn't want me.

She's married.

She's engaged.

She's got a boyfriend.

She's going to prom with your best friend.

My mind travels further back in time with every wall that's risen between Ruby and me, and I sigh, feeling like I've swapped one unattainable fantasy for another. A month ago, all I wanted was to know what it would be like to hold her and caress her lips with mine. Now, I've been upgraded. I want to *be* with her. To know her. To lace my fingers with hers and call her my girlfriend.

I want everything, and I've got nothing.

"You're here alone?" I mumble, glancing around the space.

Gabriella smiles around her glass like she's been caught out. "No, my girlfriends are over there." She nods her chin at a cluster of women sitting on lounge chairs, a couple of them looking over at us, whispering conspiratorially.

"Will you join us?" she offers.

My chest feels weighed down by bricks, and I wonder if distracting myself with some mindless conversation would be such a bad thing before my phone buzzes from the bar.

Fuck off, Blake. He's easily sent me thirty messages today alone. As pissed off as I am at him for what he did to Ruby—and as guilty as I still feel over what happened after the wedding—losing the guy I thought was my best friend hasn't helped the ache in my heart, even if he and I haven't been as close as we were when I lived in Still Springs. It's the reason I haven't blocked his number yet—a small, pathetic part of me is still holding on to the dregs of that friendship. It all hurts like a fucking bitch.

I try to ignore the message, but Gabriella's looking at me through her lashes like I'm dinner and dessert, so I pick up my phone in an effort to appear busy.

My heart flies into my throat.

> @RUBYQ
>
> You get one chance to make up for high school, Hotshot
>
> Better make it good xx

Holy shit.

I read the message twice...three times.

"Is everything okay?" Gabriella asks, and because she doesn't know me from Adam, I must have enough shock wiped across my face to warrant that question from a stranger.

"Yeah." My stool scrapes as I stand up, my eyes still locked on my phone. "Sorry, I have to go. It was nice to meet you. Have a great night."

She pouts, but all I can think about are the words inside my shaking palm.

I catch the elevator downstairs and head out onto the street that's still bustling at this time of night. I lean against a wall as I type out a reply.

@FLYNNSTAGRAM

> Are you asking me out on a date, Quinn?
> Because I might have to check my calendar

@RUBYQ

> Does your calendar show YOU taking ME out
> on a date, smartass?

Warmth spills through me, chased by a torrent of relief that she's clearly not back with Blake, but before I can reply, she sends another one.

@RUBYQ

> Where in the world are you?

@FLYNNSTAGRAM

> Barcelona, Spain 🇪🇸

@RUBYQ

> It must be close to 2 a.m. there. Hope I didn't
> wake you…

@FLYNNSTAGRAM

> No, bonita. This is Europe. Everyone's still
> having pre-dinner drinks.

@RUBYQ

I don't know if my heart can take much more of this swinging pendulum between hope and doubt that I've been on with Ruby since the pond, but here I am—jumping right back in like a glutton for punishment. The warning bells are already ringing in the back of my mind, but when it comes to this girl, I'll take what I can get.

@FLYNNSTAGRAM

Calendar says yes. When?

@RUBYQ

When will you be home next?

My fingers hover over the keypad, my gut tightening up. At the rate my schedule is going, I don't think I'll be back in Still Springs for months at the very least.

@FLYNNSTAGRAM

I'll check my roster tonight and let you know

@RUBYQ

Ok. Hope to see you soon

Does this woman even know what she does to me?

@FLYNNSTAGRAM

Me too. We should really do it more often.

See each other, I mean!

Your mind's always in the gutter, Quinn.

@RUBYQ

Night, Hotshot

Damn, she's signing off.

@FLYNNSTAGRAM

Night, Quinn. I'll check tonight and set a date for our date.

Ugh, you said that already. Do you want to sound a little more whipped right now, Romeo?

I'm so dazed by this turn of events that I barely see what's in front of me as I walk up the stairs to my room on the third floor. The first thing I do after flicking on the light is grab my tablet and open up my calendar of shifts.

My heart sinks into my stomach.

I don't know what I'd expected to see—I'm aware of how fucking full my dance card is. After my flight back from Barcelona in three days, I'll be in DC for barely twenty-four hours before I fly out to a few cities on the west coast, followed by back-to-back flights to the Bahamas, Costa Rica, then back to the west coast across the next month.

I hiss out a curse and throw my tablet onto the mattress. Even though my schedule's always tight, it's never been this jam-packed. It's because I took on all those extra shifts, wanting to keep busy while Ruby and Blake were exploring their new-found wedded bliss. I'd had no idea that the girl of my dreams would be asking me to take her out—an offer she could as easily withdraw if I take too long, and she gets cold feet.

I reach for my tablet again, my eyes returning to my three-day window in Barcelona. I open up my emails and type out a message to my boss. He's a good guy and seems to like me, so when I ask him if I could fly out of Spain tomorrow on my own dime as long as I'm back before my next shift, I'm pretty confident he'll okay it. I did something similar last year when my parents traveled through England, and I met them in London while I had a few days off in Prague. As long as I'm back when I'm supposed to be, it's usually not a problem—probably because it saves the company money on per diems and hotel rooms.

After I send the message, I hit the shower and switch on the

TV to ESPN, rubbing my eyes. I need to sleep, but the butterfly storm in my stomach has other ideas.

What's there even to do in Still Springs for a date? The staff at Harringtons would probably slam the door in my face if I tried to take Ruby there for lunch. *Shit no.* I need something more discreet, not to mention more impressive. Maybe a hike at the springs with a picnic, or—

My phone buzzes from the bedside. I reach for it, hoping it's Ruby and not Blake, but it's neither. It's a reply from my boss, who's in DC and constantly checking emails.

> Go for it. But be back for that flight. This client already wants my balls as a necklace.

A DAY AND A HALF LATER, I'M PULLING UP OUTSIDE RUBY'S grandma's rancher like a time warp to a month ago, my heart thumping hard in my throat.

Before I've even switched the car off, the front door swings open, and there she is—walking down the front path with her head adorably ducked. *My sweet, shy girl. I've missed you.*

My stomach flips at the sight of her in a summer skirt that barely covers half her thighs, her gorgeous top half swathed in my soccer hoodie that she's bunched up at the waist. *Goddamn, Quinn, now you're torturing me for fun.*

I can feel my stupid doe-eyed look when she sticks her head into the open window on the passenger side.

"I hope you're not planning to return that," is the first thing I say, lifting my chin at the hoodie. "Not the best choice for summer, but damn, it's cute on you."

She smiles, the pale-pink lip gloss she's wearing catching the light.

Are you gonna let me mess up that perfect smear today, Quinn?

"I'd say it'd look pretty cute on you too," she throws back.

My pulse skitters, then she's climbing into the seat beside me, bringing her bare legs and her knock-my-socks-off scent.

Do I kiss her hello?

Before I can answer that in my head, she reaches for me as if on instinct, pulling my cheek to her lips and stealing all the breath in my lungs. She quickly pulls back.

"Nice car," she says, glancing around the leather interior of my BMW X3. "Although not quite as impressive as the old red one. I thought you'd put a little more effort into our date."

I breathe half a laugh. "The hatchback is what does it for you," I say. "Noted."

I'm trying to play it cool and not smile like a giddy idiot, but it takes work. *Don't fuck this up, Flynn. I'll deck you if you do.*

For a few heart-pounding moments, we stare at each other. "How are you?" I ask softly.

A mixture of emotions floods her gaze. "I wish I knew how to answer that. It's been crazy here since you left."

My chest twinges. I'm not sure she'd want me to add my two cents, so I just sit and watch the thoughts untangle in her head.

She covers her eyes. "Where do I even start? I'm not sure if you heard, but I'm pregnant."

"What?" I choke out.

"That's right. And the baby is yours. Surprise!"

"But we haven't even—"

"Oh, Hotshot. You know things like truth and facts are irrelevant when spreading vicious rumors." She rolls her eyes. "I just thought you'd like to know what you're getting into in case you want to back out now. Not only is the town rumor mill in overdrive, but Blake and I are still officially married, even though it's only on paper. There's no option for annulment, and he has yet to sign the divorce papers. I don't even know if he's going to."

A cold feeling crawls inside me, yanking me back down to earth.

Two minutes in Ruby's company, and she's already talking about Blake.

But I'm glad she's telling me this. It's a reality check I clearly need.

This isn't your girlfriend. She's technically married to a guy who you called your best friend for most of your life. You're just the rebound who's here to help heal her wounds. Maybe this is just a way to comfort each other over what you've both lost.

I don't want Ruby to feel worse than she already does, so I cover my insecurities with a smirk. "I can't believe I'm going to be a dad. I better start looking for a real job."

She laughs. "It's really good to see you."

Now, there's nothing fake about my smile. "You too."

"Enough about *him*." She sighs and clicks on her seatbelt. "Where are you taking me in this crappy BMW, Hotshot?"

I let out a laugh and switch on the engine. "It's a surprise. But I hope you like wings and good views." *Keep her smiling today, Flynn. She needs it.*

"Wings?"

I can feel her ticking over those clues in her head as I drive toward the turnoff onto the highway, sensing her steal little glances at me that make me glad I did this. Even though the Blake situation is far from solved, if she wants me to be here with her, I'm helpless to stay away.

I rest one hand on my thigh, too aware of how closely her strip of tanned leg is slanted toward mine. I'm so desperate to touch her—to run my palm up that soft thigh or hold her hand—that I flex my fingers open and shut a few times.

She's watching me again. "Thanks for coming back here so soon after I texted. I didn't expect you to…"

"Get on a plane in Europe and fly here just so I could take you out?" I finish, my eyes finding hers. "Did you expect something different? I've been waiting for this date for ten years."

I have to watch the road, but I don't miss the effect those words have on her face.

"You're a lot more charming than you used to be," she eventually says, and I can't help but laugh, even though I'm guilty as fuck on that count.

She looks out the window, and words that I've wanted to say since high school gather in my throat. *This is your chance.*

"I'm really sorry, Ruby." The shame that edges my voice draws her surprised gaze back to me. "I'm sorry for high school. For treating you so badly because I had such a hopeless crush on you. It's not an excuse, it's…an explanation." My voice deepens with regret. "I wanted you so badly back then, you have no idea."

Even though I can't look at her for long while I'm driving, she barely takes her eyes off me. "Just back then?"

I steal another glance at her, our eye contact buzzing hot. "You really have to ask that?'

She shakes her head, the look in her eyes making me want to stop the car and pull her into me, continuing what we started on her grandma's porch. The way she's breathing makes me think I'm not the only one reliving that moment.

"Okay, I admit, it's too hot to wear this," she says, gripping the neck of my hoodie. She tugs it up over her head, and my gaze zeroes in on the tight white tank top hugging the mounds of her breasts, making my lips part.

She catches me, and her cheeks warm as I return my gaze to the road, spotting the turnoff up ahead. It's been a while since I've been to this place.

As soon as I make a right, Ruby's mouth falls open around her smile. "Oh my god. You're not serious!"

I maintain my coy silence, even though she's totally figured it out because there's not much else down this dirt road.

"Flynn!" She gives my arm a playful whack, and I feign being in pain.

Her smile widens as we turn into the local airfield used mainly for skydivers, rescue operations, and recreational flyers before the smile slips off her face.

"I think that's Vera's husband's car." She points at a black truck in the parking lot.

"Who?"

"My hairdresser." She claps a hand to her forehead. "I think her husband is the caretaker here."

The alarm on her face jabs a needle into my chest. She doesn't want to be seen with me.

Of course, she doesn't, asshole. You're the rebound, remember?

"It's okay," I reassure her, hiding the pit in my stomach. "We don't need to go inside, it's all been organized already. My dad went to school with Steve King, who owns the plane we're taking out. It's already waiting for us." I nod at the Cessna 210 sitting beside the runway. "But we can go if you want. Just say the word, okay?"

"No way. Let's pull around the other side if that's all right."

"Sure."

I park around the back of the tiny terminal building, and Ruby falls into step beside me as I lead her toward the plane, our bodies so close that the backs of my knuckles accidentally brush against hers a few times.

The nervous silence between us makes me ramble. "If you're hungry, I've got something in mind to do afterward for that. But if you need it..." I dig into my back pocket and produce one of those chocolate bars she likes.

Her lips fall open, her eyes warming. "Thank you."

"Anytime. I'd happily buy a lifetime supply of these things if each one earns me that smile I haven't stopped thinking about."

Her steps slow, and anticipation heats the back of my neck because I'm getting that feeling again, like she wants to kiss me as much as I want to kiss her. *Fuck, should we go do that instead, Quinn? Screw the little air show I'm about to give you—take me somewhere private and use me. Let me make you feel good after all the shit Blake put you through.*

Because that's what this is, Flynn. And don't you forget it.

I shove that thought away, and when we approach the white aircraft shining on the taxiway, Ruby's smile expands. "I can't believe we're going up in that." She snaps a couple of pics with her phone, which is damn cute because this little plane ain't got nothing on the usual jets I fly.

"You're not afraid of heights?" I smirk as we pause in front of it.

"Not that I know of. I've flown a few times before, and I've always been fine."

"Cool. Well, if you start to hate it, I'll bring us right back down." I pull the airplane keys out of my pocket and dangle them on one finger. "You ready to see what Still Springs looks like from the sky?"

She presses a hand to her mouth, chuckling. "I don't know why it surprises me that planes have keys like a car."

"Only the smaller planes. Not the big boys."

She seems to be liking everything I'm saying today, and her chest rises and falls a little faster as I step past her to unlock and open the Cessna door, the side of my body grazing hers. She doesn't move an inch and instead watches me do my pre-flight walkaround to check the aircraft, crossing her arms.

"Do you have to be so sexy?" she asks, like she's accusing me of something.

I blurt a laugh. "What?"

"I mean, look at you." She gestures toward me. "And you also happen to be able to fly this thing? Anything else?"

She seems half shocked by her own confidence, but I love that she can be like this with me.

I step closer to her, watching the way her eyes change as my tone roughens. "Is that a challenge, Quinn?"

Before she can reply, I tip my head at the plane, inviting her to get inside.

As she slips past me, her gaze stays locked on mine, flushing heat through my body that tightens my shorts.

And if I said I didn't stare hard at her sweet ass when she climbed up inside the aircraft, I'd be a bigger liar than Blake Harrington.

CHAPTER TWENTY-FOUR

FLYNN

I climb into my seat beside Ruby's, keeping the plane door open for airflow until I can crank up the air con. Her bare shoulder brushes mine as I check over the gauges, making sure everything's where it should be. Even though we're still grounded, Ruby's holding her phone up to the window, snapping photos. An adoring chuckle escapes my lips as I get the latest weather conditions from the ATIS data.

She glances at me, smiling. "What?"

"Nothing. You're just cute, that's all." I unhook the passenger-side headset and hand it to her. "Wear this, and you can hear what's going on."

We both cover our ears with our headsets, making conversation difficult for the time being. I twist the key in the ignition, firing up the engine. Even with her hearing muffled, Ruby's brows fly up at the sound of the plane's roar, excitement dancing in her eyes as I run a check of all the systems.

Okay, she likes planes. Add that to the list of things this girl does to me.

Most Cessnas I've been in have two yokes to steer with, but Steve King's kitted this one out with just one driver's seat, which

I'm happy about because it means extra space for Ruby, although the 210 model is already roomy. She's figured out her seatbelt, but I lean over to check it's tight enough. Her vanilla scent wafts over me, mingling with her gentle breaths against my ear as I give the belt a few tugs. Her soft hand brushes over my forearm, and my eyes flicker to hers, our mouths inches apart. She stares right into my eyes, and for a few moments, I lose myself in those blue depths.

"Ready?" I say, part of me still wishing we could get off this plane right now and do something even more fun.

She nods, and I reluctantly shut the plane door and settle back into my seat, but I let my bare leg lean close to hers, drawing the heat of her skin.

The smile returns to her face as she holds her phone up to take another photo—this one of me. I don't know many guys who enjoy having their picture taken, but I rest back in my seat and try not to look like a douche.

She snaps the pic then lowers the phone to her lap, her eyes glowing as she studies the photo. It makes my heart beat harder, but I force my attention off her and onto getting this Cessna up into the sky. While the engine's warming up, I flick on my microphone and ask the tower for permission to take off. After they grant it, I check that Ruby's okay then begin our short taxi onto the runway, making sure the plane's where I want it and that everything looks good. Once we're nicely lined up, I advance the throttle to max power, and we begin tearing down the runway. Ruby squeals beside me—so fucking cute—and when we reach eighty knots, I gently pull back on the yoke and up we go, that rush of weightlessness surrounding us as we become airborne.

Ruby's peering out the window with a grin, and years of learning how to do this feel worth it—just for this moment. She reaches across to cup her hand over my forearm like she can't resist touching me. We're now high enough for me to release one hand from the yoke, and I take her fingers and thread them through mine, pulling our joined hands down into my lap.

Her breath shallows as she gazes at me, and I can't turn away because she's way more captivating—more beautiful—than the view of Still Springs from fifteen hundred feet.

"You okay?" I mouth, stroking her fingers with mine.

She nods, and another conversation drifting through the headset interrupts us as our plane continues to climb. There's always chat going on between the tower and other flyers, and I'm pretty sure Ruby's surprised at how busy it is in the air. Still holding her hand in my lap, I slip off my headset and gesture for her to do the same. We don't need them now that we're flying out of controlled airspace, and it's quiet enough for us to talk easily over the engine noise. I glance out the window, swallowing tightly every time Ruby brushes her thumb back and forth over my hand.

Still Springs is comically tiny from up here, and we spend a few minutes pointing things out to each other, like Ruby's grandma's house, my parents' place, the high school, and the Quinn Brothers store dotting the main strip. Beyond the town lies blankets of green hills and thin ribbons of rivers that I haven't seen from this height in years. When Ruby tries to film a video with one hand, I let go of her fingers so she can do it properly.

While she does that, I check over the instrument panel, absently whistling out a song I heard on the radio this morning before I catch myself.

"Sorry, I forgot you don't like that," I say with an embarrassed chuckle.

She gives me a look like she's about to make a big admission. "Okay, fine. I like it when you whistle."

My lips kick up, even though I'd already figured that out. "You do, huh?"

"I like when you call me Quinn too. I hated it in high school, but like...*other things*...it's grown on me."

"Yeah?" My voice deepens a little. "What else do I do that you like?"

A blush sweeps over her cheeks, and a swell of heat moves between us.

The plane suddenly dips with a gust of wind, and Ruby's fingers slam onto the seat.

"It's okay," I reassure her. "It's only a bit of wind. We're fine." I glance over the gauges, and there's nothing even remotely alarming.

But the drop seems to have made her nervous, so an idea strikes me.

I jerk my chin at the yoke. "Want to give it a go?"

Her eyes widen.

"Come on. I'll show you. It's easy. You'll probably put me out of a job in five minutes."

A voice in my head tells me I'm getting a little cocky now but fuck it. She wanted a fun date, so why not kick the thrill up a notch? I reach across to unclick her seatbelt then gently fold my fingers around her waist, urging her closer to me.

She laughs nervously. "What are you doing?"

"I've got you." The aircraft cabin is slightly smaller than the inside of a minivan, and there's just enough room for me to guide her up out of her seat and over me until she drops right into my lap, facing the windshield with her back to me.

"Flynn!" she squeals with excitement, and I smile as I guide her fingers around the yoke, trying to ignore how perfect she feels between my legs. I let go only to unclick my seatbelt, which is only needed for take-off and landing.

Her hands are shaking, so I flatten mine over hers until

we're flying the plane together, loving the sounds she makes when I tilt the aircraft left to make a turn.

"You're doing great," I say, my lips dangerously close to her neck. Instead of leaning away from me, she rests her back against my chest, and I wonder if she can feel how hard my heart is beating.

Her soft voice rumbles through me. "I can see why you chose this job. It's so nice up here."

"Well, unfortunately, I can't say all my passengers are as sweet as you. Or as sexy."

She laughs. "I hope not." She grips my fingers possessively. "I love that it's just us up here."

She feels so fucking good cradled in my lap, relaxing against me, and I can't help but brush my nose against her hair. "Me too. I wish I could stay up here forever with you."

"Why can't we? How much fuel we got?" she jokes, making a show of peering at the fuel gauge.

I smile and tighten my arm around her waist, and we sit quietly for a little bit before she says something in a soft voice. "I'm so glad you came back to Still Springs. Obviously, the circumstances aren't ideal, but..." I rest my chin on her trembling shoulder. "You're so different from the Flynn who left town all those years ago. It's like you've come back as the guy I met in junior year. The one who sat next to me in science class. The one who I couldn't stop looking at or thinking about. The one who still gives me butterflies."

My forehead falls into her hair. "Quinn, you're killing me."

Everything around us starts to change. The air becomes thicker. The sound of the plane dies away, even though I keep checking that everything's fine. The current of electricity buzzing between us gets stronger as Ruby gently runs her fingers up and down my arm.

Words drift out of my mouth that I can't keep in anymore.

"You know...ever since I left town the first time, I feel like I've been looking everywhere for you. All over the world. But here you are. Where you've always been."

She melts against me and tilts her face up, staring into my eyes.

I whisper her name, this feeling so intense that it almost hurts. She reaches up to catch my cheek in her palm and drags my mouth down to hers. I gasp a sigh and push into her mouth, wrapping our tongues together. It opens up a hunger in me, and while I keep one hand on the yoke, my other hand pulls her closer against me, deepening our kiss. She moans softly into my mouth, and every so often, I have to open my eyes and glance around to make sure we're safe. But fuck, I don't have a hope of stopping this. Our mouths are wet and hot as they move together, our breaths turning ragged and wild, and I know she can feel my hard-on pressing into her.

I'm half expecting her to shut this down, but instead, she leans harder against my chest, shifting her hips until my dick pushes up between her legs through my shorts, falling into the right spot.

"Fuck," I bite out, wrapping her hair around my fingers and gently pulling her head back against my shoulder as I thrust up against her as much as I can in this confined space.

She breathes out another moan, and I'm already so turned on that it's making me lightheaded. I glance at the gauges, one hand still gripping the yoke. *Still good.*

I tilt my hips up against her again, and her legs fall open wider in the seat.

"You feel what you do to me?" I say into her neck.

"*Flynn,*" she says desperately, arching her back.

"One sec," I manage to whisper, keeping one arm around her while I lean forward and push one of the buttons.

"What are you doing?"

"Switching to autopilot. Because something needs my attention right now more than this plane."

Once the plane's safely flying itself, I reach around to capture her breasts in my hands, savoring the way her breaths hitch when I squeeze them through her tank top. *Fuck, she feels so good. I could come just by doing this.*

I slip my fingers beneath her tank top and bra straps and peel both down together until her breasts pop out, inhaling sharply as I stare down at her from over her shoulder.

"Is this okay?" I ask breathlessly, and she nods.

I wrap my arms around her, hugging her for a moment before my hands go where they want to. I catch her breasts in my palms and knead them until my mouth waters before stroking my fingertips over her nipples.

"Flynn, the plane," she whispers, even though she's pushing herself into my hands.

I drag my tongue over her neck, making her sigh. "The plane's fine."

She's practically gyrating on my dick now, showing me she wants this as much as me, yet she suddenly seems acutely aware of where we are.

I swipe her hair over one shoulder and rest my cheek against hers. "It's okay, I promise."

"But I don't want to crash."

I breathe a laugh into her neck. "We're not going to crash. We're on autopilot. You need to trust me." But she's still tensed up, so I pull back a little to look at her. "Do you have a pilot's license?"

She shakes her head, all flushed skin and kissed lips.

"I've spent more than three thousand hours flying; I know what I'm doing. And I've got *you* on board, which makes this the safest flight in the world." Her eyes move back and forth between mine as she gazes back at me. "But if you want to stop..."

She grabs my neck and crashes her mouth to mine, and we're back to desperate, tangling tongues and breathless moans. My hands return to her breasts, squeezing and kneading harder this time until a sharp need grips me from the inside out.

"Turn around," I murmur urgently.

"What?" she says, even though she's already doing it, lifting up on me and shifting her body around until her thighs part and she's straddling me. Her knees bunch up on either side of my hips, her soft skirt spilling over her bronzed thighs. My heavy-lidded eyes lock to the hard peaks of her nipples that draw my tongue to the front of my mouth.

"That's better," I breathe huskily before she's on me again, kissing me ferociously and grinding against my dick so hard that my eyes almost roll back in my head.

I stroke her nipples then pull one toward my mouth, moaning with relief as I lock my lips around her. My lips suck and my tongue swipes as I work my mouth over both her breasts, taking my sweet time because there's nothing on earth that tastes better than this.

I pull back and gaze up at her, not sure where to look—at the flushed, sexy haze in her eyes, her glistening nipples that I've worked so hard on, or the peek of white cotton panties from beneath her skirt that's ridden up over her parted legs. And that's where my gaze stays.

"Look at you," I say, my voice a little achy as I brush my knuckle up the fabric that's clinging to her soft skin because she's so wet. When a needy whimper rolls out of her, I repeat the movement, pressing a little harder this time, working my knuckles deeper into the groove as I run them up and down over the cotton. She tilts back and breathes a moan that about does me in.

I let my fingertips slip inside the edge of the fabric. Slick wetness coats my fingertips, and now I'm the one making needy sounds.

Ruby begs my name like she's desperate for more, and I push my hand higher up her skirt, finding the waistband of her underwear and dragging it down. She takes over and slips her panties down and off her legs, her body shifting back into place over me, her pussy opening up in my view.

Fuuuuck.

I'm fucking *lost* now. Completely entranced by her. But at no time do I lose focus on where we are and making sure the plane is safe.

I don't miss the sudden wash of shyness over Ruby's face, so I reach up to stroke my fingers through her hair. "You're so fucking beautiful," I whisper. "I've never wanted anyone as much as I want you." I bring my lips to hers. "Can I touch you?"

She nods, and I reach around to run my palms over her mouth-watering ass before I bring a hand to her center and make a tentative stroke against her. I've barely done anything, and yet she almost collapses into me as a contented sound leaves her lips, her wetness seeping onto my fingers. I delve deeper, brushing two fingers up and down her slick folds before finding and gently rubbing her clit. Sexy little moans well up in her throat as I play with her before I circle a finger around her opening then sink my finger deep inside her warmth. Ruby throws her head back, and now it's me making sighs of pleasure as I twist two fingers up inside her. She's so tight and hot, and there's nowhere else I'd rather be than right here.

"Do you need to come, Quinn?" I slide my fingers in as far as they can go, curving them inside, before dragging out and pushing back in.

Ruby bites down on her bottom lip like the pleasure I'm giving her is almost too much, and I need to kiss it better, so I use my free hand to pull her mouth to mine. For what feels like hours, but is probably only minutes, I feel her everywhere, inside and out, coating my fingers in her need for me while we kiss and pant into each other's mouths.

Ruby's hand finds its way to my shorts, cupping my aching dick and palming it up and down over the fabric. Pleasure rolls through me in a heady wave, then her hand dips inside my waistband and clutches me bare. I groan, breathing her name before she pushes down my shorts until I spring out into her gaze.

Ruby's eyes turn dazed, like she likes what she sees, and I can't help but push up into her hand when she wraps her fingers around me. We're both touching each other now, my fingers buried deep inside her while she strokes me up and down, her thumb brushing over my head and making me hiss through my teeth. In my dreams, it was always me touching her...never had I imagined it would be her touching me. *Fuck, where is this even going?*

She wriggles her hips closer to mine until my dick rubs up against her slick skin, almost sinking inside with the force of how hard I am. It feels so good that I can't resist sliding up and down her a few times, my fingers biting into her hips. She grinds against me, making a demand.

"What do you want?" I ask in a husky voice.

Instead of replying, Ruby's teeth sink into her bottom lip again, and she rolls her hips, forcing another groan out of me.

"You want me to fuck you right here?" I pull her harder against me. My dick is so close to her opening that I have to grit my teeth and force some self-control.

"Yes."

My elation dies when she asks if I have a condom. I almost laugh. Of course, I fucking don't because this was not where I thought today was going to go. I shake my head. "I didn't exactly plan this."

"What about the ones you bought at the store?"

"I only did that to piss you off. I don't carry those things around in my pocket."

A half-bemused, half-disappointed look crosses her face before a thought flashes in her eyes. "When's the last time you got...*checked*?"

It takes me a second to figure out what she's asking. "I went to the doctor a couple of months ago. I usually go every year. I'm clean. Haven't been with anyone since."

I could give myself a million high-fives for having done that so recently.

"I got tested a few weeks ago," she says. "After..." She doesn't finish that sentence and doesn't need to. If my partner had been screwing around on me, I'd get checked right away too. "Everything came back fine, and we don't have to worry about pregnancy. I have an IUD."

Anticipation takes hold of me, heat swelling through my body as I blink up at her, nodding. "Okay then."

"As long as it's safe with all this too," she says, making a quick gesture at the cabin.

I gently clutch her jaw and force her to look at me. "You think I can't fly a plane and make you come at the same time, Quinn? Watch me."

Desire fills her eyes as I slide my dick up and down her center again, coating it in her slickness before I take hold of it, lining myself up against her. I watch her face change as I push all the way inside, her eyes turning heavy as she moans deeply—just like in my fantasies.

"That's it," I say, groaning as Ruby slides up and down my full length, the pleasure so intense that I can barely take it. My fingers squeeze her ass as I thrust up and she presses down, our bodies slipping into a perfect rhythm as an overwhelming feeling of connection to her clamps down on every part of my body.

Ruby's lips collide with mine again, and she strokes her tongue inside my mouth, paralyzing me with pleasure.

Her fingers pull at my hair as she rides me harder, and I increase my speed, my fingers finding her waist again and holding her in place so I can drive myself up into her until she cries out.

She then falls against my neck like she's turned boneless, her shallow breaths puffing over my skin. "I want to lie down, but we can't. It's too small in here."

"No, I like you on top," I say roughly, dragging my tongue over her neck. "Then I can worship you." My fingers clutch onto the mounds of her breasts, and I'm tonguing her nipples again, showing her how much I need her.

But the truth is that there are so many things I want to do to her right now but can't. I want to flip her onto her back and hike her legs over my shoulders so I can take her so deep that she'll want me inside her forever. I want to press her up against a wall, wrap her legs around my thighs, and fuck her so hard that she forgets her own name. I want to bend her over on a bed, ass up, so I can devour her with my tongue before burying myself inside her again.

When Ruby falls forward and folds her arms around my neck, crowding me in her warmth and scent, I have to work hard not to come. I slip my fingers between us and find her clit, circling and rubbing it while she moans into my skin. It doesn't take long before she clenches around my dick as I thrust into her, hard and deep, my lips finding her ear as I sense she's close.

"Come on, Quinn. Give it to me."

She cries out, her pussy tightening hard and pulsing. A sudden swell of ecstasy rushes through me, filling me up with so much white-hot pleasure that I collapse back into the seat and stars burst in front of my eyes.

Our arms wrap around each other in a tight embrace as Ruby pants into my neck.

"Flynn," she whispers, squeezing me, and I run my palm up and down her back, checking the plane for the millionth time and silently thanking it for being so well-behaved.

Thank fuck for autopilot.

Ruby turns to rest her head against my shoulder, and we sit like that for what feels like a long time, catching our breaths and gently stroking each other.

I catch sight of the endless stretch of blue sky through the window as our little plane happily whirs along, trying to keep my heart from exploding out of my chest.

I'm in a plane, with Ruby Quinn in my arms. If this isn't heaven, I don't know what is.

CHAPTER TWENTY-FIVE

RUBY

We may be sitting in Flynn's car outside my grandma's house, but I'm still a million miles up in the sky, floating among the cottony clouds. I'm not sure what I'd expected from a date with Hotshot Hudson, but it certainly hadn't been *that*.

Heat creeps up my neck, and I can't stop smiling. Apparently, neither can he.

"That had to be one of the best dates I've ever been on," I say.

He scratches his jaw, his eyebrows flicking up. "One of them, huh?"

"Top five. Easy."

"Oh, really? Top five? Wow." Flynn clutches his shirt over his heart. "Thanks, Quinn. Thanks a lot."

I hope he knows I'm lying. Just in case, I say, "It was incredible. Thank you."

"You're incredible," he says so warmly I want to eat him up.

I toy with the car door's handle, smoothing my fingers up and down the cool metal. I'm not ready to leave, but we've been here for fifteen minutes, so I probably should. "Are you sure you have to go back?"

Flynn's smile fades. He presses himself back against the seat and sighs. "Yeah. I do."

At least he sounds regretful. That has to count for something, right? "I guess I'll see you in eight years?"

"Is that what you want?" he asks, raking a hand through his thick hair.

"No." What I want is for Flynn to take me back up in that plane and fly us away from everything and everyone. I want it to be just the two of us without any drama or responsibilities. Heck, I want to be seventeen again and be the one to ask Flynn to the prom.

But people don't always get what they want.

"You know," he says slowly, twisting to face me and reaching for my hand, "this date doesn't have to end right now. You could always come with me to DC."

My chest expands at the thought. "Be serious."

"I am. You can stay in my apartment, lie by the pool, go shopping, see the city. When I get back from my next job later this week, we could have a bit more time together before my next shift, and you can escape"—he gestures toward the road leading to Main Street—"all of this for a few days."

I can't do that...can I? I mean, Jade *did* suggest that I should take a few days off to see if business picks up. The idea of my very presence hurting the store makes me sick to my stomach.

But the prospect of getting away—and with Flynn—makes me feel like everything is going to be okay. And Dad's there with Jade to help out.

"You really want me to come with you?" I say, needing to be sure Flynn's not just asking because he feels guilty about having sex with me then leaving. I knew exactly what I was getting into when I climbed on top of him.

"I think I've made it pretty clear how I feel about you coming with me, Quinn." A cocky smile plays around his lips that makes it even harder to get out of his car.

Am I going to do this? The moment the question pops into my mind, all I can think is, *I'm totally going to do this.*

"Okay."

Flynn beams. "Really?"

"It's not like I have anything better to do," I add with a wink. "Give me a few minutes to throw some stuff in a bag."

"Take all the time you need."

THE THREE-HOUR DRIVE TO DC PASSES WITHOUT A moment of silence. We talk about everything, from our favorite movies, *Braveheart* (mine) and *Blade Runner* (Flynn's), to music we like, music we hate, food we love, food we hate. It's like a first date on hyper-drive.

I keep expecting things to get awkward or for some long pause to stretch between us and make me think this was a mistake, but that never happens.

When a song comes on the radio that one of us likes, we turn it up. I sing along while Flynn whistles. And I kinda, sorta love it. We talk about high school, managing to steer clear of saying Blake's name, even though he's woven into almost every memory we resurrect.

I ask Flynn about all the times he came into the store slurping a milkshake, and he confesses that he had been hoping I'd say I wanted one because he'd secretly bought two and had one slowly melting in his car.

"You could've just told me that."

With his eyes trained on the highway, he brings our intertwined hands to his lips. "You were intimidating."

I laugh until I realize he's being serious. "You think *I'm* intimidating?" That's probably the last word I would ever use to describe myself. Flynn Hudson, with his six-foot-two frame, muscles for days, and smile that makes women's legs go weak, had been intimidated by *me*.

"Scariest woman I've ever met," he says.

"I find that hard to believe."

He nods. "It's true. I think—and I know this is going to sound insane—but I think part of me knew that you would've been it for me. At seventeen, that shit was terrifying."

I think you would've been it for me, too, I want to say. I'm not the kind of woman who needs to date a bunch of guys to know when I've found one I want to stay with. But I don't say it because making that kind of statement with everything going on right now doesn't seem fair to either of us. I still don't know what we're doing. Is this what casual dating feels like? It certainly doesn't feel casual to me, but I have zero frame of reference.

We go through a drive-through for dinner, and I make fun of him for taking me for fast food on our first date. He laughs and promises to make up for it on the next one.

Will there be a next one?

God, I hope so.

By the time we pull into his apartment complex, the sky is painted in strips of reds and oranges, and I find myself wondering what sunset would look like from inside the cabin of that tiny airplane. Maybe one day, I'll find out.

The air is even warmer here than in Still Springs and thick as pea soup. Flynn collects my bag from the trunk and carries it up the three flights of stairs to his apartment. While he's unlocking the door, I check my phone for the first time since the airplane. Jade messaged a bunch, asking about my day and if I wanted dinner tonight. The messages gradually got more concerned as the hours passed. Her last one makes me laugh.

I need proof of life ASAP

"Everything okay?" Flynn asks, his brow furrowed as his eyes graze over the handset. He looks genuinely worried, and I realize he probably thinks Blake is the one who's texting me.

"Yeah. Sorry. It's Jade," I tell him, watching his shoulders relax. "She wants to know I'm alive." I tap out a quick text, then throw my phone back into my bag.

Flynn's apartment smells like fresh paint and resembles a posh hotel room. Everything is black and white and glossy. He tosses his keys on the quartz countertop and sets my bag down in front of a door that I assume leads to the bedroom. The place is spotless. Seriously. You could eat off his floor.

Flynn waits in the kitchen, a shoulder propped against the wall, watching me with an unreadable expression as I roam.

I run a finger along the top of a stiff leather couch that screams bachelor. "This doesn't feel very comfortable."

"It's not," he says with a laugh, following me as I meander into the bedroom toward a mammoth king-sized bed without one throw pillow. I can see the ensuite from here and a tub that I will absolutely be using.

I sink onto the end of the bed. "What about this?" I ask, bouncing a little on the springy mattress.

"Much comfier," he says.

"Oh yeah?"

He stops just out of reach, pink climbing his jaw. "Yeah."

I lean back to look up at him. It's hard to tell if he's freaking out. I tell myself not to be crushed if he says this was a mistake.

Hopefully, Jade won't mind driving three hours to pick me up. "What are you thinking right now?" I ask, my stomach flipping.

"Right now? Let's see. Right now, I'm thinking, 'Holy shit, Ruby Quinn is in my bedroom'."

I hook my finger through the belt loop on his shorts and pull him between my knees. "Is that all?"

He shakes his head before bending to capture my mouth in a soft, sweet kiss. Against my lips, he whispers, "I'm also wondering how good you'd look stripped out of those clothes, stretched out beneath me."

"Would you like to find out?" I reach for the hem of my tank top and drag it over my head, feeling bolder than I ever have in my life.

The way his gaze rakes down my body sends a rush of heat pooling between my thighs.

"Hell yeah, Quinn. I wanna find out."

I wake to a *bang* and a curse. A dark shadow huddles next to the nightstand, rubbing its knee. It takes a moment for me to remember where I am and who the shadow is. Familiar flutters grow in my stomach as I watch Flynn continue trying to sneak around, realizing there's nowhere in the world I'd rather be.

"You'd make a terrible burglar," I say through a yawn, stretching my arms toward the headboard.

Flynn straightens. Even in the murky light, I can see he's already in his uniform. "Shit. Sorry for waking you."

"It's fine." I snuggle deeper into sheets that smell like his spicy aftershave. "Did you sleep okay?"

"Best night I've ever had. You?"

"Good. Really good."

He kisses me, slow and thorough. "I'm getting an Uber, so you can use the car while I'm gone."

"You don't have to do that," I say, even though the thought of him being willing to give up his car for me makes my chest squeeze.

"As much as I like the idea of you being stuck here doing nothing but pining for me, I figure you may go a little stir-crazy being cooped up on your own."

"Don't worry about me. I'll be fine." I haven't felt this light in years. There's a bit of guilt there too, but Jade assured me she's handling everything back home, so that helps.

Flynn hesitates in the doorway, tapping his fingers against the frame. "You'll be here when I get back?"

My lips tug up into a smile. "Yeah, Hotshot. I'll be here when you get back."

He's left his keys on the counter beside a fan of takeout menus and some cash with a note that says: *For food. x*

That he thought to leave them out for me makes me grin like an idiot as I open cupboard after cupboard, hunting for the coffee for his fancy coffee machine.

There are four of everything: plates, mugs, spoons, forks, and knives. He owns two pots and two skillets. I find the coffee in the pantry next to a box of Raisin Bran and a tin of spaghetti. The oven doesn't look like it's ever been turned on.

In the fridge, I find a carton of eggs, a stick of butter, and milk. It's kinda sad. I honestly thought Flynn had been living the high life out here, when it looks as if he's barely home. Maybe he's happy with that, though. He's traveled and seen the world. Maybe he loves living out of fancy hotel rooms and never being in the same place for too long.

My stomach sinks at the thought.

But if Flynn is happy, then good for him.

I make myself a cup of coffee and wrap my fingers around the warm mug, inhaling deeply and hoping the caffeine injection clears my head. I sip slowly, managing not to burn my tongue as I head back into the bedroom. Flynn has one dresser. The top drawer is filled with plain black dress socks and boxer briefs. It's a welcome change from Blake's love of colorful boxers with stupid sayings on them. The rest of the drawers contain stacks of T-shirts, shirts, and jeans. His closet holds a couple of suits, some dress shirts, and his pilot uniforms in plastic dry-cleaning bags.

There's no sign of a woman anywhere in this place. It's silly, but the thought that maybe Flynn didn't bring just anyone here makes my heart soar.

With no plans for the next three days, I take a long, luxurious shower, realizing too late that Flynn doesn't own a hair dryer. I let my strands air dry on the little balcony overlooking the community pool, sipping my cup of coffee and reading a book on my phone.

Once I no longer resemble a drowned rat, I take Flynn's car to Target to buy a hair dryer, some cereal I like, a few snacks for later, and the cutest pug coffee mug that I couldn't leave behind because it's Target, and if you don't buy at least one thing you don't need, that's against the rules.

On the way out of the strip mall, I pass a small vet's office with a Now Hiring sign pinned to the window. I stop the car to take a quick picture of the name of the practice, then go back to Flynn's to sit by the pool for the day. Since it's the middle of the week, it's just me and the retirees attending the water aerobics class at noon.

I don't think about the vet's office until I'm in Flynn's bed that night, curled beneath sheets that feel like they're weaved from clouds.

According to the job listing online, the Potomac Animal

Clinic is looking for a veterinary nurse—a position I would've been qualified for *if* I had finished college.

I click through the other jobs within a twenty-mile radius, but everything seems to require at least a four-year degree. An hour later, I have six tabs open: three job sites, two college homepages, and one Chinese takeaway.

There's an animal shelter a bit farther away that's hiring, but the pay is crap—definitely not enough to cover another year of college. That's assuming all my credits would transfer. It probably wouldn't even be enough to cover rent.

I'm not sure why I bothered checking in the first place. It's not as if I'm going to stay here—or that Flynn would even want me to. I honestly don't know what we're doing, if there's a future for us, or if this is how people in the dating world behave. Blake and I didn't have to think about how to date. We just hung out, and eventually, the hanging out turned into making out, and that led to more.

I switch off my phone, irritated at myself for entertaining the idea of moving when I know I'll never abandon my family. I need to get my head out of the clouds and come back to earth. Still Springs is my home, and Flynn's job and life are here. When he's not a million miles away.

We have no future together.

We only have right now.

In a couple of days, I'll be going back home, and Flynn will fly off on his next adventure, leaving me behind.

I tell myself not to be disappointed.

It doesn't work.

FLYNN WILL BE BACK IN A FEW HOURS. I SEND HIM A QUICK text, hoping to catch him before his flight.

> I'm at the grocery store. Do you want something to eat when you get back?

You mean besides you?

> Smooth, Hotshot. Very smooth.

You know it.

Butterflies take over my stomach as I push the cart down the aisles, picking up the ingredients for Mom's famous spaghetti sauce that Jade texted me earlier. I'm not a great cook, but I figure our last dinner together should be something homemade.

Even though he's bringing me back to Still Springs in the morning, I'm so excited to see him again that I can't sit still.

After being here for three days, pulling into his apartment complex feels a bit like coming home. I spend the next hour cooking and straightening up. Once the place is spotless, I sit at the peninsula and stare at the door like a dog waiting for her owner to come back from work. If I had a tail, it would definitely be wagging when the knob finally turns.

I melt a little at the sight of Flynn still in his uniform, his black tie loose at the neck and his hair sticking up a bit at the back, like he's been running his hands through it. I melt a lot at the smile playing on his lips when he sets his black bag down beside the door and drags me in for a hug.

"I missed you so much it scares me," he says, squeezing me tight.

"I missed you too."

He pulls back and glances over my shoulder into the kitchen, inhaling deeply. "Something smells amazing."

"I made dinner."

"You did?"

When he lifts the lid on the smallest pot, I nod, my face heating. "It's only spaghetti."

"Spaghetti cooked by Ruby Quinn," he amends, catching my chin and capturing my lips with his. "Will it keep? There's something I need to do that's been on my mind for the last three days."

I turn the burner off. "Oh yeah? What's that?"

Flynn drags me into the bedroom and practically throws me onto the bed. We tear into each other like the world is ending, which it kinda is. I'm leaving, Flynn's going to disappear back to his busy life, and all this will be over.

When I reach for his boxer briefs, he moves back before I can get them off.

My pout quickly fades as he kisses his way from my breasts down to my navel. The inside of my hipbone. My inner thigh. "Flynn..." I say, a little breathless and already so turned on that my vision has turned hazy. "You don't have to..."

"Don't have to what?" he murmurs, hooking a finger beneath the waistband of my underwear and tugging down.

"You know. Do *that*."

He stops for a moment, glancing up at me from beneath his stupidly thick lashes, my underwear nearly halfway down my thighs. "Do you not want me to?"

"Yes. Maybe? I don't know." *Shut up, Ruby!* "I guess I'm worried about you."

Blake was never that into oral sex.

Actually, let me rephrase that.

Blake was never into *giving* oral sex.

Flynn's forehead drops to my belly button. His heavy sigh tickles my bare skin.

Great. Now he's mad at me. I should've just faked it like I always did to get to the next part, and—

I glance back down, finding a pair of warm brown eyes watching me.

"It's okay to be selfish sometimes, Ruby," Flynn says. "In fact, when our clothes are off, I want you to be completely and totally selfish."

"I'm trying, but I know that if it takes too long, you'll get bored and lose"—I gesture to the undeniable bulge in his boxer briefs—"*that,* and it'll kill the mood and...why are you smiling?"

I'm telling him one of my biggest fears and he's laughing at me.

"Quinn, I know how to get myself off. When it's my turn, I'm going to get a little bit selfish and tell you what I need to get me there. And if I'm being completely honest, I'm being damned selfish right now, too, because I've been thinking about doing this since you wore that denim skirt to Mr. Burn's physics class on the first day of spring our senior year."

My mouth falls open, and a squeaky "Oh" spills out.

"So, if you really, really don't want me to go down on you, I won't. The last thing I want is to make you uncomfortable. But if you're only saying it because you think I'm not going to enjoy it..." His eyes heat up. "Let this be my chance to prove you wrong."

"Okay. Sorry. Yes. I want you to. If you want to, I mean." *Shut up, Ruby. Close your mouth and shut up.*

Flynn's hands still from where they've been idly rubbing my thighs, and he sits back on his haunches. A lock of dark hair falls over his furrowed brow. Suddenly, his smile returns, and he pushes off the bed. "Don't move," he says before disappearing out the door.

My knees instantly fall closed, disappointment replacing desire as I tug my underwear back in place. I've completely ruined the mood—maybe even the night. I press the heels of my hands to my eyes, listening to the banging of cabinets out in the kitchen. A *clink*. A *pop*. A curse. Followed by footsteps growing louder.

"I thought I told you not to move." Disapproval laces Flynn's mock-hard tone. He's standing at the side of the bed with a bottle of champagne in one hand and a single glass in the other. He tips the bottle into the glass, one corner of his mouth pulled up.

"None for you?" I say, desperate to recapture the mood.

He shakes his head. "I can't drink when I'm working." Before I can ask what the heck that means, he sets the bottle on the nightstand and whips something from behind his back, settling his hot-pink pilot's hat on his head. He looks ridiculous —and ridiculously sexy in nothing but black boxer briefs and that hat, and I have the sudden urge to find my phone and take a picture so I can remember this moment forever.

"Ladies and gentlemen," he says, eyes on me, "this is your captain speaking."

Chills break out over my skin. I have to bite my lip to keep from giggling when he hands me the glass.

"I'd like to extend a special welcome to Ms. Ruby Quinn, who's joining us in our first-class cabin."

My laughter bubbles like the champagne as I raise my glass in a salute and take a sip. The tension in my body melts a little more with each fizzy swallow. The mattress dips when Flynn climbs onto the bed at my feet.

"Looks like we have clear skies ahead," he says, slipping off my underwear then catching my knees and dragging me toward him. The glass in my hand bobbles, spilling icy liquid down my bare chest.

"Although you should keep your seatbelts securely fastened in case there are a few unexpected bumps along the way," he murmurs, his voice thickening as he bends his head to catch the drops with his tongue, making a stop at each of my breasts before settling himself between my thighs. "Until you arrive at your destination, Ms. Quinn, I'd like you to sit back..." He slides his mouth up my inner thigh, the press of his lips silky soft compared to the bite of his stubble, "relax..." I squeeze the stem of my glass when his tongue finds my center and the heat from his next words vibrates against my core, "and enjoy the flight."

Turns out, Flynn's hips aren't the only part of him that's dedicated. I melt like ice cream on a hot day, focusing on the steady sweep of his tongue.

"Harder," I whisper, rocking my hips up and into him.

He responds instantly, his fingers contracting where he's gripping my hips.

I find myself holding my breath as my stomach tightens and my thighs clench, knocking his hat askew. This feels so damn good, I never want him to stop. If he wants me to be selfish, then I'll be selfish forever.

He reaches down to stroke himself as he continues to work me over with his tongue. The sight is so hot that I find myself getting closer and closer to the bliss I'm so used to finding on my own. And then I'm there, gasping and panting as my entire body thrums with the most intoxicating wave of pleasure I've ever experienced.

"That's it," he murmurs against my center. "Drown me."

I'm only beginning to come down from my high when Flynn eases back on his heels and drags his forearm across his mouth, his cocky smile well-earned.

He goes to get up, and I manage to think through the rose-tinted haze, my gaze falling to the thick bulge in his boxer briefs.

"Where do you think you're going?" I steal his pink cap, settling it on my head with a smirk. "Looks like I'm the captain now."

His brows quirk toward his disheveled hair. "And that makes me...?"

I grip his hard length, stroking him through the cotton briefs before peeling them down and off. "I guess that makes you my ride." I guide him toward my entrance, still slick and swollen from his mouth.

His chuckle rumbles against my neck when he drops forward, nudging his way inside, filling me until my body cradles his. The noise he makes, somewhere between a moan and a curse...the thought of having this strong, beautiful man at my mercy...I feel like I'm flying again.

Flynn's hips rock, steady and deep. I touch him everywhere. The cut of his arms. The swell of his shoulders. The steady thump of his heart beneath his toned chest.

His eyes squeeze shut, and he winces. It's the same expression he had at the picnic when he'd hurt his neck.

"Does it not feel good?" I ask.

His eyes snap open. "What?"

"This." I gesture to where his body disappears into mine. "You look like you're in pain."

He almost laughs. "No, Quinn, you feel fucking incredible." His head dips and his tongue strokes over my nipple. My back arches off the bed, my whole body longing to connect with his. "I'm just trying to keep it together so I last."

"Don't."

He glances up at me from beneath his lashes, mouth still attached to my breast.

"Don't keep it together," I say. "I want you to lose yourself." To be as lost as me so we can find each other.

The smile he gives me knocks my heart right into my throat. He's moving again. The wet sound of our bodies meeting mixes with our rough breaths and throaty moans. My hands make their way into his hair, tugging and dragging until his lips crush against mine. The steady sweep of his tongue matches each thrust of his hips, filling and receding. He palms my breast, pumping harder.

I'm not sure how my left leg ends up over his shoulder, but it does, and my body feels as if it's going to splinter in two as Flynn slams into me.

My hand slips between us, finding my clit, still swollen from his mouth. "Fuck yes," he whispers, his pupils blown out as he watches me touch myself, both of us panting. "Fly with me, Quinn."

His movements turn frantic, frenzied, a man searching for release.

He falls forward, catching his weight on his elbows, the damp hair at his forehead grazing mine. Feeling him pulsing inside of my body drags out my own orgasm, both of us shuddering, our eyes exchanging words that never find their way to our lips.

Flynn's arm slips beneath me and he rolls onto his back, taking me with him, my head finding its place beneath his chin and my ear pressed to his pounding heart, listening to my new favorite song.

CHAPTER TWENTY-SIX

FLYNN

I'M TRYING NOT TO GLOW LIKE A HEART-EYED FOOL, BUT I'M failing.

My arms and legs are tangled up with Ruby's as we lay facing each other on my bed, the sheets long discarded and bunched up at our feet. But the heat coming off her body isn't the only thing keeping me warm.

It's the way she's staring right into my eyes, robbing me of my breath and turning my legs to water. I can't tell if this thing between us is moving too fast or if it's just right. All I know is that a river of happiness is flowing through me, and I don't want it to stop.

I reach out to tuck a wisp of silky black hair behind her ear. "I keep thinking I'm going to wake up."

Her eyes light up, and she tilts into my hand. "Well, don't wake me up. I'm happy right where I am."

That sends the butterflies in my stomach into overdrive, and she's guiding me onto my back and climbing on top of me, planting soft kisses all over my face. She leaves no spot untouched, and by the time she pulls away to gaze down at me, I'm beaming like an idiot.

She rests her head against my chest and lays over me like the most perfect blanket, and I silently tell my stirring dick to calm the hell down so I can enjoy just being with her like this.

We also can't start something up right now; I promised I'd drive her back to Still Springs this morning, then I need to get back to DC in time for my next shift. *Fuck.* I twist my neck to glance at the clock on the bedside, wincing at the time. I wrap my arms around her and bury my face in her hair. *Just a couple more minutes.* She squeezes me back so tightly—so possessively —that I almost gasp, but I love it.

Something presses my rib cage at the thought that this might be all I ever get. That once Ruby goes home, all the pieces of her life in Still Springs will fall back into place, leaving no room for me. It pushes the words out of my throat.

"I've been thinking," I say quietly, my fingers playing with her hair. "About us."

She tilts her face up to look at me. "Is there an *us*?"

"I hope so."

She doesn't reply, and I swallow tightly. "I know it's a complicated situation, and I'm not trying to push you into anything. But after I drop you off today, I'm going to be away again for a few weeks, and I kind of... I want to take something with me to hold on to."

She blinks up at me, visibly unsure of what I'm trying to say.

"Do you want to keep seeing me?" I ask, a rush of nerves squeezing my throat.

She turns her face into my chest, resting her soft lips against my skin. "No. I've lost all respect for you now. I've got what I wanted, so I'll just take the ride home, thanks. And then you can be on your merry way."

A slightly terrified laugh gathers in my throat. "I really hope you're joking."

Ruby's playful smile fires relief into my bloodstream, and I tease out an angry look then weave my fingers through her hair, using it to jerk her mouth up to mine. We make out for way longer than we have time for, our breaths hot and uneven, and my dick swelling.

I'm always so caught between wanting to eat this girl alive and wanting to talk to her about everything. Like the idea that's begun forming in my head of how this thing between us could possibly work. How it could look like something resembling a relationship. For one, there's a beautiful town about halfway between DC and Still Springs that always gives me a good feeling when I drive through it.

I'm trying hard not to think I'm out of my mind by imagining myself living there with Ruby. It's been less than two months since we first kissed, and she's still legally married to my former best friend.

But it's not like Ruby and I just met. We've known each other for years, and she's already seen me at my worst and forgiven me for my childish bullshit in high school. This connection humming between us feels so natural, so right. To me, at least.

Her fingers gently clasp my neck, and she brings her lips to my forehead. "What's going on in that handsome head of yours?"

I tip my face back until our gazes lock. "I want this to work, Quinn."

Her eyes melt before she drops another kiss on my lips, which must be the thousandth one this morning. "There's a lot to think about," she says softly. "Right now, I'm trying to deal with the fact that I'm not going to see you for three weeks. I'm not used to that."

A rock lodges in my throat. "I know."

Blake's only ever lived a few streets away from Ruby; he works at the restaurant next door to her store.

What the hell do I have to offer? A handful of texts sent from Barbados? A new souvenir T-shirt every time I drop into town for half a day? Twenty-one vacation days a year with the likelihood of being miles away for the rest?

Who in their right mind would ever accept that?

It's not an entirely fair question. Plenty of pilots I work with are married, some with young families. Their partners are understanding enough about their crazy schedules to make it work, but I know it's not easy.

My gaze drifts back to the girl lying on top of me. After only ever dating the guy who was constantly there, would she consider the guy who's almost never there? Could my heart even handle being away from her that much if we were together properly?

I jolt when her phone pings from the bedside with a series of alerts. She groans and rolls off me. "It's probably Jade."

She gathers a sheet around herself and picks up her phone, her brows gathering.

I don't even need to ask, but she tells me anyway.

"It's Blake."

A pit opens in my stomach. She sits on the edge of the bed with her back to me, hunching over the screen as she scrolls through his string of messages. *Fuck, what's he saying?*

After an excruciating minute of silence, Ruby twists to look at me. "Do you mind if we get going?"

The hole in my stomach doubles. "Sure. Of course."

I get up and step into my boxers, turning away from Ruby while I get dressed so that she doesn't have to see my face.

He fucking summoned her, and she's going.

Back to her husband.

My god, I'm the other woman.

An uncomfortable silence elbows its way between us as we get ready to leave, deciding to make a pit stop at the café downstairs for takeaway coffees and muffins. I don't tell Ruby that the last thing I feel like doing before I take her back to Blake is eating. But I gladly toss back the double shot of coffee like it's medicine as I drive us toward the highway out of DC.

We chat quietly about safe topics, like what our weeks ahead will be like and all the stuff she has to do at the store. She mentions something about an animal shelter job she noticed near DC, and my heart trips over itself. But I try not to jump to conclusions, and I don't push the topic. Ruby loves animals; I can't hope too hard that it has something to do with me. When she reaches across to cup my thigh, I lay my palm over the back of her hand, folding the tips of my fingers around hers. It settles my nerves a little.

I'm dying to ask her what Blake said, but it turns out I don't need to.

"Blake asked if we can talk about the divorce today," she eventually volunteers.

I don't know if her tone is so heavy because she doesn't like the idea of getting divorced, or if she doesn't want to see him, but I don't ask. I just stroke my fingers over hers while my other hand stays locked tightly around the steering wheel.

"Does he know you're here with me?" I ask.

She shakes her head. "I don't think so. Jade told me he freaked out when he realized I'd left town, but she didn't tell him where I was."

She sighs, and I give her hand a gentle squeeze. "You haven't done anything wrong."

He had an affair for months and then slept with her hours after you got married, I want to add, but I don't. No point in rubbing that in.

"I know," she says, her free hand tracing the edge of the window frame. "But it's a shit situation, and I want things to be normal again."

My throat bobs. *Normal. As in how it used to be? Ruby and Blake? Forgive and forget?*

A perfect week together in DC doesn't mean she's over the guy she was with for a decade.

The topic falls away for the rest of the drive, and I don't have it in me to press Ruby about it, given there's so much in her head already. But by the time I make a right off the highway and into Still Springs, the contents of my stomach are lining my throat. I have to leave her here soon, and I have no idea whether this is the beginning of a relationship between us or the end of something heartbreakingly beautiful and much too short. I like having all the answers—knowing where I stand—and right now, I'm in no man's land.

The tension inside me boils over when I catch sight of Blake sitting on Ruby's grandma's front porch.

"Fuck," I hiss out.

Ruby's mouth falls open. "He didn't tell me he'd be waiting for me!" She shrinks down in her seat, but it's too late. Blake's gotten to his feet and is holding a hand to his brow to block the sunlight, his gaze fixed on my car, which he'd recognize from the last time he was in DC.

"What do you want to do?" I ask Ruby, the car already slowing. My gut contracts as I wait for her to duck down and hide or tell me to drive to the alley around the back to let her out there.

She exhales a tight breath. "It's okay. You can pull over. He's going to find out about us anyway."

For everything Blake's done, I can't help but feel bad for the guy when Ruby and I pull up together outside her house. We both step out of the car, and I'm bracing myself for Blake Harrington on the rampage.

But instead of flying toward me with his fists, he stands frozen solid, his jaw hanging as his eyes shift between Ruby and me. I don't think he can quite believe that she's capable of wanting anyone other than him. While she and I could make up a story about me having been nothing more than a friend to her this past week, not even Blake is dumb enough to believe it.

"What are you doing here?" Ruby asks him in a flat tone. "I said I'd come down to the restaurant later."

His hand flies to his chest. "What am *I* doing here? What the fuck is *he* doing here?" He shoots me a disgusted scowl like I'm vermin.

"Go inside and we can talk there," Ruby orders him. "I hope you've come here to say that you're ready to sign the divorce papers. But first, I need to say goodbye to Flynn."

Blake lurches forward, and my muscles tighten, ready to block the hit. But it's Ruby he reaches for, wrapping his arms around her.

"Stop it! What are you doing?" she shrieks as he turns his nose into her hair, breathing her in. Jealousy burns through me, and I clench my teeth, half a second away from physically yanking him off her and pulling her into me.

But Ruby's already wrestled out of Blake's grip, her eyes narrowed. "Don't you touch me. If this is how it's going to be, then go away. We can talk another time."

I'm lost as to what to do right now. I want to back Ruby up and tell Blake to piss off, but is it really my place to?

When he makes a grab for her elbow again, I push between them, holding a hand out at Blake. "She told you not to touch her," I say as calmly as I can. *Get your fucking hands off my girl.*

His brows fling up, and he bursts out laughing, but there's no amusement in his face. "Oh, I see. You two are best buds now. After Ruby told me how much she fucking *hates* you."

Ruby lets out a sound of irritation. "Go home, Blake. I don't want to talk anymore." She turns to me, her voice softening. "Do you have time to come inside for a few minutes?"

I keep my eyes off Blake. If he'd been a better partner to her, he wouldn't be in this situation.

I check my watch, my stomach as tight as a fist. Fucking work. "I've only got a couple of minutes."

I cautiously follow Ruby up onto the porch, and Blake jogs up behind us. "Great. We'll all go inside and have a little chat then, shall we?"

I step in front of him, blocking his path. "Not you. She asked you to go home."

"The fuck I will," he spits. "I'm not leaving you alone here with my *wife*."

Ruby huffs. "I'm going inside," she says to me. "I can't deal with him right now."

My eyes stay locked on Blake. "I'll meet you in there."

"Flynn," she protests.

"It's okay. I just want to have a little talk with Blake. I'll be right behind you."

He meets my stare and crosses his arms like he's accepting a challenge, but I'm not offering a fucking duel. It's probably a good thing if Blake and I at least try to talk. Because I sure as shit don't want to leave him on Ruby's doorstep looking like he wants to set fire to the place.

"I'll be right inside," she says warily before the door clicks shut behind her.

For a few tense moments, Blake and I stare each other down. I truly hate that things have gone this way for us, but that's not the main thing on my mind right now.

"I want to make something clear," I say, keeping my voice low. "She may be technically married to you, but she doesn't want this side of you." I wave my hand at his fighting stance and clenched jaw. "So, if you want to talk to her, you're gonna need to calm the fuck down. Or you'll have to deal with me."

His face twists up. "Is that right?"

I just look at him, my expression telling him all he needs to know. *Don't you fucking hurt her.*

Blake's gaze travels down and up my body like he's searching for evidence of something. "So, how long did it take?" he asks, a know-it-all look plastered on his face. "You can tell me. How long did it take for Ruby to open up her legs for you and show you what you've been missing?"

I lunge forward and twist his collar in my fists, turning and shoving him back against the brick wall. "Say that again. Go on. See what happens."

Blake wrestles out of my grip, breathing so loudly that I'm ready for steam to start spouting from his ears.

"I can't fucking believe you," he says, pacing back and forth on the porch. "I can't fucking believe you would do this to me."

I lean my back against the wall, a sick feeling swelling in my stomach. "I didn't mean for it to go this way. I didn't want this situation any more than you."

"Liar!" He turns around and stabs a finger at me. "You've wanted this the whole fucking time. You said it yourself in that pathetic speech."

"Okay, fine, yes—I wanted her. I tried not to, but I can't help the way I feel. But I was prepared to live without her if that meant she was happy with you. I stayed away from you both for eight years. I did nothing, I said nothing."

"And I'm the idiot who brought you back." He shakes his head at himself.

"C'mon, man. Are you really blaming me for your marriage breaking down? You've been seeing another woman behind Ruby's back for months. On your *wedding day*. I honestly didn't come here to screw everything up for you, Blake. You did that all by yourself."

He scrapes a hand through his hair so hard that, for half a second, I consider it. The guy in me who played soccer alongside Blake since I was a kid—who shared a lot of good times with him—considers it. I could walk away right now and not be the one standing in the way of any possible reconciliation between him and Ruby.

But then I think about how I felt when she lay wrapped around me this morning, and the idea blows away like sand particles in the wind. If Ruby wants to be with me, I don't have a hope of pushing her away. And Blake doesn't deserve her after what he did.

He glares at me, looking fed up as fuck. "Okay, Hudson, you've had your fun. Now it's time to shove off, back to your lonely life of planes and pussies, and leave Ruby and me alone. I'm telling you right now: stay the hell away from her."

My fists curl at my sides. "That's not going to happen. Not unless she's the one asking."

"Fuck you," he snaps through his teeth. "Acting like you're any better than me. You're a delusional idiot."

"Excuse me?"

He throws a hand up. "You're not serious about her! I've never heard you talk about any woman for more than one fucking minute."

Because none of them were her.

"You pretend you're better than me," he continues, shoving my chest. "But you're just a fuckboy who's gonna screw around on her the moment you fly out of town and feel like getting your dick wet."

"You're really starting to piss me off." I step forward to meet him until we're practically nose to nose. Fury rises up in my throat at the thought of Blake saying these things to Ruby after I'm gone because it couldn't be further from the truth. I'd never dream of cheating on her.

Blake's thighs press against mine, his eyes flashing. "Oh, I'm pissing *you* off, am I? You mean like your best friend stealing your wife?"

"I didn't steal her." I give his chest a light push as a warning. "She married *you*. She chose *you*. Right from high school. Even though you fucking lied to me about having asked her to the prom when you hadn't, and you're still lying about it." His eyes dart away at the realization that I've figured that one out. "So, congratulations: that little piece of fiction got you the girl," I add. "For almost a lifetime. But then you had to go and screw someone else. That's on you."

His cheeks stain red. "So convenient for you. I bet you were spying on me that whole time at the wedding. Waiting to catch me out like a rat."

"Blake, that doesn't even make any fucking sense. Why would I think you'd cheat on Ruby at your own wedding? It's fucking disgusting."

His lips fall open. "The bonfire night," he suddenly remembers. "Ruby said you had a hug. She apologized for it like it was a..."

"Nothing happened," I finish. "No lines were crossed."

"But you wanted to," he says, seething. "You wanted to fuck her so damn good. Give her a little taste of Hotshot Hudson."

The tight coil inside me snaps. My fingers tighten, but he's already made a swing. His knuckles clock me in the upper cheek, and I fucking lose my shit and shove forward to punch him back.

But Blake's paced backward, yelping in pain as he shakes his hand vigorously. "I think you broke my hand," he gasps, holding up his swelling knuckles. "You broke my hand—you broke my fucking hand!"

Is he serious? Something wet drips down my cheek, and I hiss a little as I press my fingers to the cut on my upper cheek.

The front door swings open, and Ruby bursts through the

gap. The panic in her eyes makes my heart clench, and I push past Blake to go to her, mumbling reassurances and apologies. Right now, I want to fall through the floor and pretend like none of this is happening.

Her soft palm grips the side of my arm, and she shouts at Blake to go away before pulling me inside and slamming the door shut.

Then she's helping me into the kitchen like I'm more injured than I am, but the truth is, my heart is so fucking sore for her. What I said to Blake was true. I didn't want this situation; not like this.

She gently dabs a damp cloth against my cheek, her brow tight. My fingers find those of her free hand gripping the counter, and I drag her into me, wrapping her in my embrace.

"I'm so sorry," I say into her hair.

I'm sorry.

You don't deserve this.

I love you.

The words that have been trapped inside me for so long press against my throat, aching to be let out, but I can't say them. It's too soon. It'll scare her away. It's not the right time.

"Don't be sorry," she says into my shoulder, brushing her nose back and forth over my T-shirt. "I saw him hit you through the window. I'm the one who's sorry. I should've come outside sooner."

I pull back and cradle her face in my palms. "No, I'm glad you didn't."

Her distressed eyes blink into mine. "I'm sure what he said wasn't pretty."

There's no way I'm going to repeat any of Blake's awful words, so instead, I say, "I don't want to leave you here with him."

I don't want to leave you at all.

But fuck, I'm so late, I can't even bring myself to glance at my watch. I'm sure I'll still make the flight, but I'll be putting the pedal to the metal.

"I can handle him," Ruby says, and I fold her back inside the protective warmth of my body, holding her in my arms one more time before I have to force myself from her.

She watches me from the porch as I reluctantly get inside my car. I sit back in my seat and lay my hand over my chest, gazing at her through the open window. When she presses her own palm to her chest and gives me a soft smile, my throat locks up.

A sharp pain clamps around my heart as I drop the car in gear and put my foot on the accelerator, doing what feels completely unnatural and driving away from her.

It's been eight years since I took this same road out of town as a heartbroken teen, knowing I wouldn't come back for a very long time. That moment was far from easy.

But today, watching the turnoff for Still Springs disappear behind me through the rearview mirror feels like the hardest thing I've ever done.

CHAPTER TWENTY-SEVEN

RUBY

PART OF ME WONDERED IF FLYNN WOULD FORGET ME WHEN he drove away three days ago. I imagined him flying off into the sunset the same way he had eight years earlier, never to be heard from again.

But the string of messages I've gotten since have left me feeling just the opposite. Warm and fuzzy. Hopeful. *Seen.*

He'd texted before takeoff. He'd called when he landed. I've talked to him while falling asleep, and every morning when I wake up, there's a text from him as well.

He misses me.

He wants to find a way to make this work if it's what I want.

Am I insane for even considering it? For dragging out my laptop in the middle of the workday and applying to that job at the animal shelter with crappy pay? Maybe I am, but so what? Don't I deserve to be a little crazy after everything that's happened?

Right now, Jade and Dad are signing the final partnership paperwork with Mr. Harrington, securing Quinn Brothers' future.

It's time I do the same for myself. After giving up so much

for my family, I'm ready to find a life that makes *me* happy. The thought is scary and liberating all at once. The world has opened up, full of possibilities and promise.

Once I click send on my resume, I shut my laptop and lean back in the chair, smiling so wide my face hurts.

Then Jade walks in with puffy red eyes, and my smile vanishes. I shoot to my feet, my heart thundering in my chest. "Why are you crying? What happened?"

She dabs at her eyes with a balled-up tissue. "The merger is off. Blake's parents pulled the plug on the whole thing."

My hand flies to my chest. "*What?*"

That doesn't make sense. Blake promised me the merger would go ahead. Then I almost laugh. *Blake promised me.* That should've been a big, fat red flag. Blake is a damn liar. "Why would they do that?" I whisper. This merger wasn't just good for us, it was good for their business as well.

"It doesn't matter," she mutters, squeezing the life out of her tissue.

"Yes, it does. Tell me why, Jade."

Her head drops as if she can't even look at me.

My stomach sinks as realization dawns. "This is my fault, isn't it?" Blake hasn't texted me once since his fight with Flynn. Would he really encourage his family to do something like this out of spite?

What am I thinking? This is *Blake.* Of course he would.

"No," Jade insists, shaking her head. "This is *not* your fault. It's Blake's. His lies have... I don't know. It's like they've poisoned everyone's minds."

My throat tightens. She's right. Blake has been controlling the narrative this entire time. And what's worse, I've let him.

Jade's shoulders straighten, and she gives her cheeks one final swipe before tightening her ponytail. "Screw them. We'll figure this out on our own."

We. She's including me in this scenario. And why wouldn't she? I'd been planning on discussing my plans for the future with Jade and Dad over a celebratory dinner tonight. But now...

"How?" I ask. "Without the Harringtons, you can't afford the building next door."

"I don't know, but we'll find a way."

That word again. *We.*

If there was a way to save the store without taking on an outside partner, Jade and Dad would've tried it by now.

They need the Harringtons.

Maybe it's not too late. Maybe if I explain what really happened, Blake's parents will change their minds. There's no point keeping the secret now that the merger is off. What do I have to lose?

Not a damn thing.

I tell my sister I'll be back and run right out the front door, straight over to the restaurant. The moment I set foot inside Harringtons, silence replaces the buzz of conversation. There are only two free tables in the entire place.

The only person not staring at me is a little girl mesmerized by her tablet.

Blake's mom breezes through the kitchen's swinging door, a tray balanced on her shoulder. When her eyes lock with mine, she comes to a halt. Her expression hardens before she turns away, carrying the two plates of prime rib over to a couple in the corner. The tray slams down, and she practically throws the food at her customers.

Heat creeps up my neck as whispers invade the silence. "Mrs. Harrington? I need a word with you. In private."

"I have nothing to say to you," she says in a voice laced with frost.

That's too bad because I have plenty to say to her.

I take a deep breath. "Blake lied to you about what happened between us. I thought you'd like to know the truth."

Our audience lets out a collective gasp. Mrs. Harrington darts a glance around the restaurant as if she'd forgotten we were surrounded by people.

She motions for me to follow her through the swinging door, into the kitchen.

The cook glances at us from behind the steamy grill. Two servers pause their conversation beside the soda fountain, their eyes bulging. Thankfully, there's no sign of Blake or Tammy.

Mrs. Harrington doesn't stop until she reaches the restaurant's office, and the door falls shut behind us. Instead of taking a seat at the desk, Blake's mom stalks from one side of the room to the next, a lioness in a cage.

"Well?" she snaps. "Go on. Tell me your *truth*."

A shaky breath leaves my lips. "I didn't leave the wedding to run off with someone else."

"Do I look stupid to you? I saw you and *Flynn Hudson* leave together—half the town did!"

"He had a car, and I needed to get away." That's all she needs to know about Flynn.

She stops, her shoulders stiffening as she glowers at me. "And your little romp with him down in DC? Oh, yes. I heard all about that from my son. He's devastated about the separation, and you're off gallivanting with his best friend!"

Guilt churns in my stomach, but I refuse to give in and say I'm sorry. I'm finished apologizing for things that aren't my fault. "Blake has been having an affair with Tammy."

Mrs. Harrington jerks back as if I'd slapped her. "My son would never do such a thing."

"It's the truth. He's been sleeping with her for months. Flynn caught them together hours after we got married."

Her eyes widen for a split second before narrowing. "That's

a little convenient, don't you think? The man you ran off with—"

"Jade was there too." For the first time since we came in here, Blake's mom looks as if she's considering the possibility that her son isn't as perfect as she thinks he is. I wipe my clammy hands against my shorts. "When I confronted Blake at the reception, he admitted to the whole thing."

Mrs. Harrington shakes her head, as if that will stop the truth from reaching her ears.

"*That's* why I left the wedding. And before you ask, I didn't say anything because Blake begged me not to tell anyone so you wouldn't call off the merger."

Her expression darkens.

Here goes nothing.

"I'm asking you to reconsider the partnership with Quinn Brothers. So much work has been put into this from both sides; it would be a shame to see all those hours wasted over what happened between Blake and me. Please, think about this before you pull the plug on something that could be so good for our families, our businesses, and our community."

Although her lips press flat, she mutters a promise to discuss it with her husband.

Figuring it's the best I can hope for, I leave the office and briefly consider slipping out the back door. But I'm finished hiding. I push through the swinging doors, back into the restaurant, and walk straight through the gauntlet of whispering townspeople with my head held high.

CHILI PROBABLY ISN'T THE BEST THING TO COOK WHEN IT'S ninety degrees outside, but it's Dad's favorite, and if I'm going to bring up the possibility of me moving, I want him in a good mood. Which is why I also picked up a gallon of fudge swirl ice cream at the grocery store—Jade's favorite. I won't even consider this if they're not on board. And I need to know they are before I broach the topic with Flynn.

I haven't had a chance to ask him yet whether he sees us as moving toward a long-term thing, but it feels like we're on the same page. After everything that's happened, a fresh start is exactly what I need.

I turn off the burner and start ladling chili into the glass bowl to bring it over to Dad's when someone pounds on the front door, making me jolt. I pull it open to find Blake standing on the other side, scowling.

My soon-to-be ex-husband inhales a deep breath, his gray eyes hard as steel. "You are un-fucking-believable," he spits.

I shut the door in his face.

He sticks his foot in the gap at the last second, letting out a pained howl loud enough to make Bandit start barking.

"Move your foot, Blake." If he doesn't, he's going to lose it.

He catches the edge of the door I'm still trying to close, holding it open using his hand with busted knuckles. "After the shit you pulled, you're talking to me whether you like it or not."

The lace curtains in Mrs. Felton's front room twitch. A moment later, she hobbles out onto her porch, her gray hair rolled in foam curlers and a matching pink robe wrapped around her stooped shoulders.

"Five minutes, Ruby," Blake presses, using my distraction to force the door open a bit wider. "You owe me that much."

"*I* owe *you*?"

"Everything okay, Ruby Quinn?" Mrs. Felton shouts, her voice crackling like dried leaves.

Blake answers before I get a chance. "Everything's fine, Mrs. Felton."

"I wasn't askin' you, Blake Harrington," she snaps. "I was askin' her."

I can't help but smile a little. After my conversation with Mrs. Harrington, the truth had spread like wildfire, thanks to the kitchen staff, who'd evidently been eavesdropping. Things are finally starting to look up. "It's fine, Mrs. Felton. I can handle him."

She tugs the belt around her robe a little tighter before shifting the rocking chair on her front porch so that it faces us and plops right down like she's getting ready to referee a tennis match.

"You couldn't keep your mouth shut for a little bit longer, could you?" Blake grits through his too-bright teeth.

In hindsight, I never should've kept my mouth shut at all. "Your parents pulled out of the merger. What was I supposed to do?"

"I was going to fix it!"

Yeah, right. "How were you going to fix it?" I fold my arms over my chest, waiting for his answer. "Go on, tell me."

Pain flickers across his face as he rakes a hand through his golden mop of hair. "It doesn't matter now, does it? They fired me, Ruby. My own fucking parents fired *me*. They're not giving me the restaurant either. That place was my inheritance, and now they're selling it and leaving me with nothing."

Hold on. Did he just say—"They're selling?" I gasp. "But the merger..."

He rolls his eyes as if I should've known better than to hope. "Dead in the fucking water. Now the waitresses, the cooks, the busboys, Tammy—every single person who worked at Harringtons is out of a job so that my parents can retire to fucking Florida."

I thought things were getting better, that his parents were going to change their minds. Last night, Dad had said Mrs.

Harrington had scheduled another meeting for this afternoon. Was it to break the news about them selling the restaurant? I need to call Jade right away.

"I hope you're happy," Blake snarls, "because this is all your fault."

I glare at him. How could he think any of this makes me happy? That I wanted any of this to happen? It's like Blake is so caught up in his own lies that he completely forgot his role in all this. "You cheated on me, *remember?*"

His mouth twists into a mocking smile. "Yeah, and you ran off with my best friend."

I'm not going there with him. "My relationship with Flynn is none of your business."

"*Relationship?*" Blake cackles. "What relationship? That guy doesn't know the fucking meaning of the word. God, Ruby, how can you be so naïve about everything?"

Maybe Flynn didn't do relationships before, but things are different between us.

Blake shoves his phone in my face. My brain takes a moment to process the photo on the screen: a bare-chested Flynn smiling beside a beautiful woman with glossy, dark-chocolate hair draped over her string bikini. They're sitting at what looks like one of those bars inside a pool.

Maybe it's an old picture.

But from the cut on his cheek, I know it's not. Reluctantly, I take the handset, flicking to the next new photo. Flynn lying on a sun lounger in a pair of navy-blue trunks with little pink palm trees, his abs glistening like a freaking Greek god. The back of Flynn's ruffled hair from where he's sitting in the cockpit of an airplane. Flynn's smiling lips wrapped around the straw of a cocktail. Lips I'd kissed the life out of not that long ago.

My chest burns as I scroll back to the photo of Flynn and the stunning girl leaning closely into his shoulder.

"Do you know what Hotshot Hudson does for a living?" Blake sneers. "He flies and he fucks. He's going to chew you up and spit you out, the same way he does everyone else." He pries the phone from my hand, tucking it back into his pocket. "I hope it was worth it."

Doubt seeps into my mind, tightening my throat.

Who was that woman? Are she and Flynn together? We never agreed to be exclusive, so I have no right to be angry or upset, but there's no stopping the feeling of betrayal burning through my core.

Blake pulls out a rolled-up manilla envelope from his back pocket that I hadn't noticed and waves what I assume are the divorce papers in my face. "You see these right here? I'm not signing them. Every time you fuck him, I want you to remember that you're still my wife."

"Get out." My voice cracks and tears threaten my eyes as I shove him toward the steps. "Get out right now or so help me, I will call the police and have them throw you out."

Blake stumbles down the stairs toward his truck parked in the driveway. I run back into the house, searching for my phone. I grab it and sink to the floor, ignoring the string of messages from Flynn asking about my day as I search for those photos. Doubt and dread twist and curl in my stomach, settling like bad seafood.

The woman's name is Bianca. Of course it is. Beautiful, exotic Bianca.

According to her profile, she's an air hostess. Is she the one Flynn had been seeing? The one he claimed wasn't his girl-friend? She sure as hell looks like his girlfriend with the way she's hanging all over him.

Is he sleeping with her? Is he lying in bed with her right now and texting me at the same time? The thought makes me want to puke. Blake's words seep in like toxic sludge, infecting my brain. He knows Flynn so much better than I do. Until now, the two of them had remained close over the years, despite the distance. He knows what Flynn is like, and all I have is some fantasy version that lives in my head and in my heart. We spent a few days together. Anyone can pretend to be anything for a few days.

Like I pretended to have my shit together, like I didn't have responsibilities back home, like my life wasn't a disaster. Maybe Flynn was pretending to want something more out of some sort of messed-up sense of responsibility for his speech, for what happened after the wedding, or for how he acted in high school.

Maybe I'm so desperate to see the good in people that I'm blind to the bad. Like I was with Blake, missing every clue I should've seen that he'd been two-timing me.

All Flynn and I have are a few stolen days together and a past riddled with misunderstandings. And if I can't leave Still Springs now because of the store, that's all we're ever going to have. Even if Flynn does want to be my boyfriend, I don't want to do long distance. Life would be tough enough with his crazy work schedule. What's the point in being in a relationship with someone you never see?

This is Flynn's life: jet-setting off to exotic locations with beautiful women. Why does he need me when he has the Biancas of the world on his arm?

I can't go down this rabbit hole right now. Not when there are more important things at stake. I close out the app and call my sister. She answers on the first ring with a watery, "Hey."

Tears spring to my eyes. "I'm so sorry, Jade," I say, my own voice breaking.

"What do you have to be sorry for?" she asks between sniffles.

This entire freaking mess. "Maybe if I'd just stayed with Blake—"

"Don't even go there. None of this is your fault. It's Blake's."

"You're right," I agree, even though I find it hard to fully believe that. I've been so naïve in thinking that my new...*relationship? Fling?* I don't even know anymore. But I've been stupid to think that whatever I've been doing with Flynn wouldn't have any consequences. It's one thing for me to be shunned by the town, but for my family to suffer more than they already have? I can't allow it.

"Screw Blake," Jade says, sounding more resolute.

"I have. Would not recommend."

She huffs a half-hearted laugh, but I can't find it in myself to even smile.

"What now?" I'm not just asking her, I'm asking myself. What the heck am I supposed to do about Flynn? How can I leave my sister and my dad with everything about to go under? After the merger was complete, Dad was meant to retire and finally find some peace. Now it'll be the Harringtons who'll be sipping cocktails on a beach in Florida while Dad's stuck here trying to save everything his family's worked so hard for.

"I don't know," Jade says after a few moments. "There has to be some way to make things work. I'll talk to Dad tonight. We can all meet at the store tomorrow morning, say, seven o'clock?"

I inhale a deep breath of chili-laced air, my hands beginning to tremble when I realize what I need to do. "I'll see you tomorrow."

The moment the call ends, I dial Flynn's number.

The call goes straight to voicemail. Hearing his deep voice brings on a fresh wave of pain pinching my chest. "Hey, Hotshot. It's Ruby. I'm so sorry to do this over voicemail. You deserve better, but I don't think I could get through this if you were on the other end." Tears clog my throat, and I have to swallow three times so I can continue. "My life is falling apart," I say. "The store is in trouble. I can't see myself being able to leave any time soon, and it's not fair for me to ask you to wait around. Starting something with you, it...it just isn't going to work." I want to add "right now," but how can I? He's been waiting for me for so long—how can I ask him to wait longer? He deserves to find happiness with someone else, someone who fits into his life like Bianca, even if that thought makes me feel like my chest is being cut open. "I wish... I wish things had happened differently for us, but..."

But what? But nothing. That's it. No amount of wishing is going to change the past ten years.

"I'm sorry, Flynn. Please don't call me because I won't answer." If I answer, I'll waver. I'll make an excuse for this—for us—and I'll end up being hurt all over again. "Just pretend the last few weeks didn't happen." *Because that's possible.* "I'm sorry," I say again, my voice breaking. "But it's time to let me go."

CHAPTER TWENTY-EIGHT

FLYNN

OF COURSE, I CALL HER.

How can I not?

My fingers shake as I press my phone to my ear for the second time today, each call going straight to voicemail and dragging me further back down into that cavity in my stomach that formed the instant I heard Ruby's message.

Three days ago, I was strolling around this luxurious resort in The Bahamas in a lovestruck daze, calling her, texting her, her sweet voice warming my ear and lighting me up inside. Feeling like everything I've ever wanted was finally in front of me.

Then, out of nowhere, *that* message arrived, sending my gut plummeting to the floor.

She asked me not to contact her, and I want so badly to respect her wishes, but how can I back away without another word between us?

"My life is falling apart."

Those words draw my palm to my chest, making me rub the ache that won't let up. What happened while I was gone?

I want to tell her that sometimes things have to fall to pieces to come back together, building something even more beautiful. I want to tell her that I'd do anything for her, anything to make her smile.

I've tried calling her eight times in the seventy-two hours since then, but she's not picking up. I promised myself I wouldn't try more than three times a day because I don't want to come off like I'm fucking desperate, even though I am. I've left a few voicemails and sent text messages asking her to please talk to me, but they've all dropped into a black hole of silence.

I step into the air-conditioned hallway outside my resort hotel room, forcing myself to get my shit together and figure out how to get through another day without losing my mind. All I want to do is go to Still Springs, but I'm trapped in a paradise I don't want, sitting around a luxury resort paid for by the country music star I flew here three days ago.

I'm sure a huge part of why Ruby's pulling back from me is because I'm not there with her—exactly as I feared it playing out when I drove out of Still Springs. From the moment we first kissed, I haven't been in her company for one second in which she's seemed anywhere near as distant and resigned as she sounded in that voice message. Flying in that Cessna, lazing around my apartment—even in those few minutes we had together after my bust-up with Blake—she wouldn't stop touching me, kissing me, gazing at me with those eyes.

She wants me; I *know* it. I feel it.

But in the past few days, something's gotten to her. Broken her spirit. And I bet I fucking know who.

"Flynn!" a husky female voice calls as I wander aimlessly into the pool area clutching a towel and a book, like I have the focus to read.

My gaze snags on Bianca stretched out on a sun lounger, her manicured hand waving me over. She was booked as a flight attendant on this job and keeps insisting that we spend our run of days off together—even though she's not paying nearly as much attention to my co-pilot, Jesse, who's admittedly a sun-fearing loner.

I don't want to be rude, so I draw in a breath and head over to her. Bianca jerks her chin at the lounger beside hers, smiling widely. "I saved you a spot."

I want to be alone so I can wallow in my misery, but I plonk myself beside her, dumping my book onto the teak side table.

"Still in that mood, grumpy-pants?" she teases, smirking at me through her sunglasses.

"Sorry, I haven't been feeling very festive these past few days."

I sigh and flip through the drinks menu for something to do, even though I can't have anything alcoholic because I'm scheduled to fly tomorrow. But that's not going to bring me any closer to Ruby. I have to return the singer and her family to Nashville before picking up another passenger and flying them to Costa Rica. It's the same fucking story: Flynn Hudson ferrying rich people around the world, helping them go about their lives while mine falls apart. I wish I could drown myself in mojitos with extra shots of rum.

Bianca crosses her arms, pushing up her bikini cleavage and making a guy strolling past do a double take. But all I see in front of me is a beautiful woman who isn't my Quinn.

"You gonna tell me what's on your mind?" Bianca asks.

I flop back against the lounger, lacing my fingers behind my head. Fuck, do I tell her? Around six months ago, while we were on a job in Paris, Bianca kissed me outside a whisky bar on the Champs-Élysées and breathed words into my mouth about falling for me. I delicately let her down, hating the crushed look it brought to her face.

Would it upset her if I told her the reason I'm dying inside right now?

She makes the decision for me. "It's a girl, isn't it?" Bianca guesses in a voice braced for pain, and my eyes snap to hers. My expression must tell her that she's hit the bullseye, and there it is again—that same crushed look from Paris. She turns her gaze away, her fingers tightly gripping the edge of the lounger.

"We don't have to talk about it," I say quietly, wondering if I should get up and go. It's not like I'm company worth keeping anyway.

Instead of moving, I fight off a question in my head. *Why?* Why do I have to be so crazy in love with a girl who lives in Still Springs instead of the beautiful brunette lying beside me who looks at me like I'm everything she's ever wanted?

Bianca flops an arm over her head, staring up at the sky. "Wow. I honestly never thought I'd see this day. I *want* to be happy for you, but..." She flattens her palm against her chest. "*Ouch.*"

"I'm sorry," I murmur, even though I'm not entirely sure what I'm apologizing for. "You don't need to be happy for me. Look at me." I point at the heartbroken face I don't have a hope of hiding.

She shifts on her lounger to face me. "Any girl who walks away from you is seriously screwed up."

I give her a half-hearted smile. "Thanks, Bianca."

But I know that's not what's happening here. It's just an incredibly complicated situation, and Ruby's message implied that things aren't going well back home. If there's anything I know about Ruby, it's that she feels like it's her responsibility to fix everything—whatever the cost. And this time, the cost is me.

Please talk to me, Quinn. Let me figure this out with you.

"Now tell me who she is and what happened," Bianca says. "Shit, I should probably put on some bulletproof armor before hearing this, but..." She shrugs one shoulder. "Maybe I can help you."

A weary exhale blows through my lips as I turn my gaze to the aquamarine ripples of the lagoon pool stretched out before us, questioning where to even start.

I go back to the beginning, telling Bianca everything—from high school to the prom—the day I fled Still Springs and spent the next eight years so far away from Ruby that I thought I was finally over her. Then I run her through the wedding and the shit show that followed. How it—unbelievably—transformed into the best few weeks of my life. I try to put into words what it was like to discover that the connection between Ruby and me wasn't just strong, it was extraordinary. Life-changing.

Finally, I share the details of the voicemail that arrived three days ago without warning and punched me in the heart.

When I finish, Bianca's staring at me with her lips slightly parted. "Holy shit. I never stood a chance, did I? Which is strangely healing. Man, you've been spoken for since, like, forever."

That's me. Spoken for. Earmarked. Set apart and claimed—all by someone who won't talk to me.

A part of me wants to be upset with Ruby for leaving a message like that and refusing to take my calls. Perhaps it could help me start to get over her.

But I can't. She's been through so much in these past few months, and I can't blame her for being scared. I didn't mean to come on so strong so soon, but it's where my heart took me.

"Flynn, what the hell are you even doing here?" Bianca scrunches her brow. "It sounds like you've been running from this girl for far too long."

"You know I can't just up and go." I checked my schedule again this morning. It's a fucking nightmare—far worse than Bianca's. Our Challenger jet sitting at the local airport right now can fly all over the world without a flight attendant on board, but it's going nowhere without a pilot.

Still, Bianca's words have dislodged something tight in my chest, and I reach for my phone and thumb through it again, searching for messages that I know won't be there.

Ruby hasn't posted anything on Instagram, either. The last picture in her feed is still the one she snapped from the window of the Cessna plane. *Man,* I'd felt so many emotions that day. I'd thought it'd been me taking Ruby apart for the first time, but she'd nailed me to the wall just as spectacularly. Pushing away the memory that hurts too much to think about, I swipe back through her images until my gaze finds what it wants, eating up the sight of her face like it's medicine.

I haven't checked Facebook for a while, so I tap on that app in case there's something I'm missing. My page opens up, and photos of myself flood the screen. Wait, what? I'm sitting by this same pool in these same swimming shorts, except it was three days ago. I know that because I've still got a smitten-as-hell smile on my face. There are also images of me drinking a cocktail, sitting in the cockpit—

"Why are there photos of me on Facebook?" I blurt.

"Uh, because it's Facebook?" Bianca leans closer to peer at my phone, bringing a waft of coconut-scented sunscreen. "Oh, I took those, doofus. I tagged you in them."

"You posted these pics of me?" I make hurried swipes until I land on a photo of Bianca and me sitting at the swim-up bar on our first afternoon here, her arm stretched over us to snap the selfie. I remember her taking the photo—I just had no idea it'd end up plastered to my Facebook page.

"We look cute in that pic," she says wistfully.

"We look like a *couple*." My stomach flips over itself. Did Ruby see these? Is that why she left that voicemail?

I throw my feet off the lounger and grab my towel and book, an urgent feeling twisting in my stomach.

Bianca sits up. "Flynn, they're just a few harmless photos."

Not to her.

I tell her I have to go, then weave through kids taking running dives into the pool, finding my way down to the beach so that I can think.

Blake cheated on Ruby.

He blindsided her—a man she'd completely trusted for ten years.

You couldn't pay me all the money in the world to make me screw around on Ruby. But after what she's been through, I don't blame her for having trust issues. And the man who caused them has been in her fucking head; I just know it.

If only I was there to reassure her, to hold her against my chest and whisper into her ear the words I've been dying to say for nearly half my life.

I hold my phone to my ear, calling her again.

Voicemail. I grip the handset so tightly it could break and bite away the urge to throw the damn thing into the ocean.

I can't take any more heartache over you, Quinn. I can't fucking take it. But I will. I'll do it for you. Whatever it takes to prove to you that I'm not him.

As pissed as I am that Bianca tagged me in photos that I didn't want Ruby to see without an explanation, she was right. What the hell am I doing here?

I drop my ass onto the sand, drawing my knees up and staring at the foamy waves tossing themselves at the shore. A few yards away, two little girls are playing a game with their dad, where he chases them onto the sand then pretends he's being dragged back into the sea by a giant octopus.

Every square inch of my insides coils up.

I'm so tired of being a quiet observer of other people's lives.

Of being without the one person who makes me feel whole, and safe, and the opposite of alone.

I pull my phone out of my back pocket and swipe open my

emails, scrolling down to the one I received a few days ago but ignored. It was from an industry headhunter, inviting me to apply for a job based out of DC as a pilot for a single, ultra-high-net-worth client. I've been glossing over emails like these because my employer's always been good to me. But the fact is, I'm currently attached to a jet that's rented out every day of the year, putting me in the air for around two hundred days out of three hundred and sixty-five. Working for a single client would mean I'd be flying a plane for that person's private use only. I don't know anyone who flies two hundred days a year—not even presidents. A friend of mine who lives in LA has a gig like that, and while he's paid full-time on a retainer, he's only away a few days a month, on average.

The ache eclipsing my abdomen loosens a little the moment I reply to the email, flagging my interest in the position. There's no guarantee I'll get the job, but if not this one, maybe it'll be the next.

I'm not just doing this for Ruby, and I can't bring myself to hope that vastly reducing my hours in the sky would be enough to bring her back to me. But being with her has confirmed the growing awareness in me that I want something more in my life than airports and hotel rooms.

The email sends, and my palms instantly clam up when I think about my boss and his endless support of me. But I'm sure he'll understand that—while I don't want to give up flying—I do need to take a step back.

Before I put my phone away, I begin typing out another message to Ruby, but everything I want to say comes up short when I see it written as a toneless text message.

I drop my forehead onto my knees, willing my thoughts to reach her, even though I know they can't.

Please don't give up on us yet.

Let me show you how much you mean to me.

Eight years ago, I started running from this—from *her* and how she makes me feel. And now my legs are tired. My soul is tired. My heart is tired.

Stop running.

Go to her, Flynn.

Fight for her. The way you never did in high school because you were always too scared, too shy, too considerate of Blake, who turned out to be a lying prick who hurt the most precious thing in the world.

Instead of slipping my phone back into my pocket, I navigate to another number. My boss has plenty of backup staff available, and a distracted pilot isn't good for anyone, so I know I'm going to get what I want—no questions asked. I'll get the country music star back to Nashville, but after that, I'm going to need some time off. Even though all I really need is one day. One conversation. One girl.

Because Ruby Quinn has spent her entire life putting other people first.

It's time someone else did that for her.

CHAPTER TWENTY-NINE

RUBY

"COME ON, DAD. NO ONE WOULD BUY THAT," JADE GROANS, covering her face with her hands as she leans back in the office chair.

My sister and our dad have been holed up in here all day, poring over ideas to save the store. I've tried to come up with something that will help, but I'm blank. Empty. Useless.

Part of me wants to tell them to cut their losses and put the place up for sale. To let it all go. But this store has been in our family for three generations, and neither of them told me to give up on *my* dream. I did that on my own. So, I stay quiet, drowning in bitterness over what I've sacrificed to stay here, even though I only have myself to blame.

The animal shelter near DC emailed me last night requesting an interview. I still haven't responded. I'm not sure why. Maybe I like punishing myself.

"What do you think, Ruby?" Jade asks.

I glance up to find Dad and my sister both staring at me expectantly. "I'll go along with whatever you think is best."

They exchange frowns, something they've been doing a lot the last couple of days.

Before they can ask me what's wrong, I push to my feet. "I'm going to put out some of those new soaps," I say, grabbing one of the boxes stacked in the corner and carrying it into the front.

Using a box cutter, I slice through the tape holding the box closed and lift the lid. The organic lime and ginger hand soap smells good enough to eat. Jade has been ordering some atypical products to see if we can try and appeal to the sustainable, natural buyers.

She appears in the doorway, her arms folded over her chest, still frowning. "Have you heard from him?"

"I don't want to talk about it," I mutter. I can't handle an actual conversation about Flynn without turning into a sobbing mess.

I imagine Flynn probably would've been pretty upset when he got my message and tried to call. No doubt, he would've been pissed off too. But the truth is, I don't know for sure because I switched off my phone right after I left that voicemail. A voicemail I've regretted since the moment I hung up.

If I hadn't turned off my phone, then I would've driven myself crazy looking at those pictures of him with *Bianca*.

You're not technically together.

That doesn't make it hurt any less.

You don't know if he slept with her.

Rationally, I understand seeing a few photos and jumping straight to the conclusion that he's with someone else isn't fair, but after Blake, that's where my mind goes: Flynn is just another guy who went off with another woman right after being with me.

There's another reason I haven't checked my phone: *Ruby Quinn is a coward.*

Thinking of the sacrifices I was willing to make after only a few days—of how much more it hurts to have lost Flynn than it did to say goodbye to the man I was with for a decade—terrifies me.

I was content with my life in Still Springs before. I just need to find that again.

Trying to ignore the heaviness in my stomach, I head for the aisles just as the bell rings. I dart down the closest aisle, hoping to avoid another "concerned" customer asking how I am after what happened, and stop where Jade has created a cute display of locally sourced organic products. I set down the box and fish out two soaps, placing them one in front of the other until the space is full.

The sound of someone whistling drifts over the hum of two customers chatting at the front of the store. *Wishful thinking*. I go to collect more soap when I hear it again.

This time the whistling is closer, and I can make out a tune: "Be My Baby" by The Ronettes.

Chills break out over my arms as I whirl around.

Flynn is standing behind me in a pair of dark shorts and a white T-shirt, sunlight crowning his dark hair.

But he can't be here because he's supposed to be in Costa Rica and then San Francisco. I'm no geographer, but I know for a fact that Costa Rica is nowhere near Still Springs.

"What are you doing here?" I breathe, clutching the soap to my chest a little tighter to keep from throwing myself into his arms.

Silence stretches between us, his gaze trailing over my face as if he's drinking in my features while I do the same.

His eyes seem to snag on the shelf behind me. The faintest trace of a smile touches the lips that I long to feel against mine.

"If you grab one of those," I say, nodding my chin toward the XXL magnum condoms, "I don't know whether I'll laugh or cry. Probably both at the same time."

Flynn takes a halting step forward, sending me back into the shelf. "Please don't run away from me," he says, his voice huskier than I remember. "I dropped everything to come here, pulled out of all my shifts, because I needed to see you."

He'd done that...for me?

The bell rings again, and his head jerks toward the sound. When he turns back, his brows are pulled together. "Can we go somewhere private to talk? There's some stuff I want to say to you."

I want to go somewhere private, but talking is the last thing on my mind right now because talking leads to questions. Questions I may not want the answers to.

"Does it have anything to do with Bianca?" The question pops out before I can stop it. Bitter and pathetic wasn't the vibe I was going for, but here we are.

Flynn's shoulders sag as he releases a heavy sigh. "I knew if you saw those photos, you'd think the worst. After what happened with Blake, I don't expect you to trust me right away. But I need you to understand something." He shifts closer. The intensity in his gaze keeps me rooted to the spot. "All I think about is *you*," he says. "All I want is *you*. I've dreamed about being with you for ten years—do you think there's any chance in hell I'm going to screw this up? You're *it* for me, Quinn. There isn't a girl in every port. There's only one girl. In one port. Wherever you are."

When he's here, looking at me like this, I almost believe him. But he's not always going to be here. "You came all this way to tell me that, huh?"

"Well, I did try to call," he says with a soft chuckle before shaking his head. "But no. I came all this way to tell you something else. Something I've wanted to say to you for a decade." He steps so close that his shorts brush my bare knees.

His next words steal my breath. "I'm in love with you, Quinn. I love everything about you. I love the way you put everyone else first, even though, to me, there's no one more important in this world than you. I love how your nose crinkles up when you smile, how you make me laugh when we're together, how you tease the hell out of me, and how perfect you feel when you're in my arms. I loved you the day I met you, the day I left, and the day I came back. Because of my mistakes, I feel like I lost ten years that I might have had with you. I don't want to lose ten more. All I'm asking for is a chance to make you happy."

I don't even realize I'm crying until he brushes his thumb across my cheek, wiping away my tears. "How do you know that you can make me happy?"

His shoulders sag a little more. "I don't, okay? Maybe this is all a big mistake waiting to blow up in our faces. But I know I would try every second of every day. And I know that if I was lucky enough to call you mine, I wouldn't even look at anyone else, let alone go off with them."

I want to try, I really do. But this won't be easy like it was with Blake, and I know a huge part of that is because of Blake. Because trust, even if it's broken by someone else, is a difficult thing to repair.

I hope it's not impossible, but I don't know. All I know is how I feel right now.

"It's so hard," I confess. Caring for Flynn—that part is easy. Simple. Inevitable, even. It's the other stuff I'm not sure I can handle.

"Of course, it's hard. What he—" Flynn's voice catches as his thumbs continue grazing my tear-stained cheeks. "What he did to you is entirely unforgivable, and my longest relationship lasted a month, so I have no idea if I'm doing this right. But just because it's hard doesn't mean it's not worth it. Because to me, all the beauty of the world isn't out there," he says, gesturing toward the window and the street beyond, "it's in here." His thumb skims my lower lip as his fingers curl around my jaw. "I know my job scares you, which is why I've started applying for positions that will keep me at home a lot more."

I don't want him giving up his life for me. "Flynn—"

"Don't freak out," he says with a soft chuckle. "It's something I need to do no matter what. And I want you to understand that this trust thing goes both ways, Quinn. Every day I'm away, every time I leave you, I find myself wondering how long it'll take for you to decide I'm not worth the goodbyes. That you want something different. I'm pretty sure I'm never going to check my voicemail again."

"I'm so sorry for that. Gosh, I'm an asshole."

"Such an asshole," he agrees, his smile growing. "It's a good thing I love you."

My heart is pounding, but my mind is screaming, *it's too fast.*

So? Who's to say fast can't mean good? That it can't mean right?

His beautiful eyes burn into mine as he gazes down at me, and I can feel what he wants, what he's asking for. He wants me to stop him from leaving right now. He wants me to tell him that I'm ready to put my fears aside and let him love me.

My chest constricts as a war breaks out within myself. I want to fall into his arms right now and tell him how I feel about him, but this choice isn't just about me. It's about Jade, my dad, this store. It's about giving up what I've always known in favor of a gamble that may not ever pay off.

"I know you're not sure yet, and that's okay," Flynn says softly, but I don't miss the pain in his eyes. "I've become a bit of an expert in waiting for you. I can wait as long as it takes." He presses a kiss to my forehead, whispering against my skin. "Even if it turns into never, I'll still be out there, up in the sky somewhere, waiting for you."

I want to melt against him, but my unsteady legs won't move. He takes a small step back like it physically hurts him to do so, leaving too much distance between us.

But when he turns and walks out the door, I let him.

I drift back toward the register to find tears glistening in Jade's eyes.

"You heard?"

She nods. "If you don't go get that man, then I will."

My heart twists painfully. "I can't."

She's quiet for a moment, her head tilting as she considers me, the mist slowly clearing from her eyes. "It's time, Ruby. Time for you to be selfish. You have given up everything for this store—for us. Dad will be fine. I will be fine. It's time to do something for yourself. Something that makes *you* happy."

Her words circle in my head, searching for somewhere to land. But the answer is already there.

Flynn makes me happy.

Maybe not forever, but I'll never know if I don't take the leap.

I clutch my stomach as it bottoms out with nerves. Can I do this? Can I really leave my family behind to chase what I truly want?

It's time, Ruby.

Time for you to be selfish.

I dart forward and press my cheek to Jade's before I turn and run for the door, the bell screaming when I throw it open. I search up and down the street, my gaze finally landing on Flynn's tall frame as he pulls open the door to his car.

And just like at the wedding, I run.

Only this time, I'm not running away from a man.

I'm running toward one.

CHAPTER THIRTY

FLYNN

IN THE SPLIT SECOND THAT PASSES BEFORE RUBY REACHES me, my heart ruptures. It rips open, and hot, melting, liquid love pours inside as she flings her arms around me like she's scared I'll disappear. She's squeezing me hard like I'm the source of something vital. Like she needs me as much as I need her.

That's when the doubt that lives in my head catches up, shouting at me over the feelings crowding my throat.

This is probably just a hug goodbye.

She cared about you, and this is hard for her too, but that doesn't mean anything's changed.

You can't keep hoping like this: thinking every hug, every look in your direction means she wants you to stay. You saw her face in there; she's not ready.

My eyes water over her head as I drop my chin into her hair, tightening my embrace and breathing her in. Letting the warmth of her, the scent of her, the comfort of her, burrow deep into my bloodstream so that I can never forget how this felt.

For ten years, I've orbited this girl from near and far, watching through the window with my hand pressed to the glass, just wanting *in*. To be let inside, where nothing feels strange and everything makes sense. And for the most perfect moment of my life, I was there. She let me into her heart, her world, and showed me what love looks like in all its breathtaking colors.

But I can't hold on anymore.

I can't keep gazing through that window, aching to be let inside.

It hurts too fucking much.

While I meant everything I said about waiting for her—and I know I'm powerless not to—I can't keep feeling her wrapped up in my arms like this, my heart beating against hers, if this is all I'm going to get.

If I have to wait, I'll wait from afar, like I've always done.

My throat bobs hard as I stick a knife into my own chest and take a step back, delicately untying her arms from my body.

Don't look into her eyes. It'll make it ten times more painful when you say this.

I keep my gaze low, my voice coming out throaty. "Quinn, I have to go."

She shakes her head. "No."

A single word is all it takes to make me drop my forehead helplessly against her shoulder. Her soft palms catch the back of my neck then glide down my shoulders, holding me in place.

"I need to tell you something," she whispers shakily.

Slowly, I lift my head back up and let my eyes find hers and take their fill, that jolt of connection shooting straight into me. "Yeah?" I ask softly, preparing myself for the worst.

Let me have it, Quinn. You want to tell me never to contact you again? Never to step foot back in this town because I loved you so fucking hard that I couldn't wait until longer after your wedding to bang on that window? I'll understand. I'll deserve it.

Those ocean-blue eyes stare right into mine, so many

thoughts swirling through them that I can't make heads or tails of what she's about to say.

She takes a deep breath. "The first day of junior year, when you sat down next to me at that lab table, I tried so hard not to stare, but I couldn't stop. Your hair stuck up at the back like you'd just rolled out of bed. And you sneaked in a stick of spearmint gum, even though it was against the rules. I had such a hopeless crush on you—even when you were being awful. I used to write your name in my diary over and over. And every soccer game, there was only one player on the field I watched."

My brow creases up as she continues, my teeth biting down on my bottom lip.

"In these past few weeks, that crush has turned into something more," Ruby says. "Because the boy you were back then was nothing compared to the man you've become. I love the little pieces of yourself that you've shown me, and I find myself holding my breath as I wait for more. I love your eyes, and the way they carry all your emotions. I love the way you look at me and make me feel seen. I love your smiles—even the cocky ones. Especially the cocky ones. I love how beautifully you whistle along with the radio, and that you call me Quinn like it's something special just for us, and that you seem to know what I need —even before I do, sometimes."

My heart clenches as she gently takes my hand in hers, her gaze falling there.

"I know you love me," she says, squeezing my trembling fingers. "I can feel it. And I want to say those words back to you, but everything's happened so fast, and..."

I sink lower until our faces are level so that I can gaze right into her eyes. "It's okay."

Her soft eyes flicker back and forth between my own. "I'm falling for you. So hard and fast that it scares me. I can already taste those words on the tip of my tongue. There's something building inside me that feels so real, so important somehow, that the thought of being without it terrifies me. Like I was so close to living only half a life when something that fills up every part of me was still out there, waiting for me."

The tear wobbling in the corner of my eye bursts free, rolling down my cheek.

"If you're willing to bear with me through the mess that is my life," Ruby says, "if you can be patient while I pick up the broken pieces and try to put them back together, if you're willing to forgive me for leaving stupid voicemails, then...I'm yours."

The dam inside me breaks, and I drag her against my chest, burying my face in her hair and wrapping her inside my arms. She clings to me like I'm the most precious thing in the world—like it's me who's on the other side of a window that she's been gazing through.

"I love you so much," I whisper into her neck. "I've loved you for so long. I'm never going to stop."

I know she's not going to say those things back to me, but if actions speak louder than words, Ruby tells me how close I am to hearing them when she turns her head and covers my mouth with hers.

My knees buckle as she parts my lips and presses her tongue against mine, a soft moan rumbling out of her throat that ignites a desperate hunger in me. I clutch the back of her neck and spin her around, pinning her against the car with my hips and sweeping our tongues together until she gasps. The universe around us catches fire, and she swallows every moan I make like she's as starved for me as I am for her, her mouth locked to mine, leaving no part of me untouched by the depth of this feeling.

"What now?" I breathe against her lips, which isn't entirely fair because I'm still kissing her so much that she can't answer.

And she's kissing me just as urgently, her fingers dragging in my hair, her body pushed up against mine, as close as she can get.

All right, Still Springs, do we have an audience yet? Are Mr. Chen and his dog sharing a popcorn tub over on that bench? Is Ruby's nosy-ass neighbor recording this whole thing from her porch with a long-range lens? Are we on the front cover of the local newspaper yet?

I couldn't care less about any of it. I look only at Ruby, whose eyes are as dazed as mine, her flushed cheeks lifting like she can't stop smiling. "Take me with you," she says. "Right now. I want to go wherever you're going."

"You want to leave Still Springs?" This girl's given twenty-six years of her life to this town, and I search her face for doubt, but all I find shining in her eyes is hope, relief, and even though she won't say it, a touch of love.

"I'm not letting you leave without me this time," she says, and I almost fall apart.

I cup her precious face in my hands, the feelings that have been bottled up inside me so tightly finally finding air as I take what feels like a full breath for the first time in ten years.

"Then I'll drive, but you have to tell me where *you* want to go," I say into her eyes. "You don't need to put anyone else first anymore. Whatever makes you happy, it's yours. So, you just need to ask yourself, Quinn. What is it you want?"

Her hand slides into mine, her smile lighting up my heart. "You."

EPILOGUE
RUBY

AFTER SIX MONTHS OF DATING FLYNN HUDSON, I'VE learned one thing: every hello is worth every goodbye.

Because each time Flynn comes home, it's a bit like falling in love all over again. Having the chance to miss him makes me appreciate the time we do spend together, which is thankfully a lot more often now that he's working as a corporate pilot for one family based out of DC.

"I've missed you, Quinn," he whispers, tossing the mail beside the fruit bowl and sweeping me off my feet, settling me onto the butcher block counter of our rental that's halfway between DC and Still Springs.

"Missed you too, Hotshot." I catch him by the tie and drag his mouth to mine.

Even though he's usually exhausted when he gets back from a job, he's never too tired to ask about my day at the shelter where I work or kiss me until we're both delirious.

"I love you," I say against his lips, still telling him every chance I get. Each time I do, he gets this goofy, lopsided smile. My new favorite.

His hands slip up my flannel-covered thighs, the lights from our Christmas tree flashing in my peripherals. As interested as I am in where this is going, the thick manilla envelope at the top of the mail pile demands my attention.

"What's that?" I ask.

"You know what it is," Flynn says with a suggestive smirk, nudging my knees apart with his hip.

"Not that." I smack his shoulder. "*That.*"

His brow pinches as his gaze drops to the envelope. My name is printed on the front, but I don't recognize the return address.

Hold on.

Jacksonville, Florida.

There's only one person I know who lives in Jacksonville. I slip a finger beneath the flap and work it open, careful not to damage what's inside, holding my breath when my suspicions are confirmed.

Blake sent the divorce papers.

I flip through the tabbed sections, finding Blake's signature and initials scrawled on every single line. "He signed them," I whisper.

It's only been six months. I never expected him to sign them this soon. I'm still flipping through, dumbfounded, when a folded piece of paper falls out, addressed to Flynn.

We glance at each other before Flynn unfolds the note, his wary eyes scanning the words.

"Well? What does it say?"

He hands me the note and pushes himself off the counter, an unreadable expression on his face as he starts down the hallway.

Be better to her than I was.

Holy crap.

I read those words over and over again, my lips curving upward. *He's happy for me.* I know it shouldn't matter, but it does.

When I think about Blake, part of me still feels sad. Not that we ended. It's clear that our time together had run its course. I'm sad about how we parted ways, with him literally skipping town in the middle of the night—without a word to anyone—and following his parents to Florida.

But that's all that remains. The sharp bitterness that used to settle in my stomach whenever I thought about him has faded.

Flynn returns a moment later and tugs the note from my grasp so he can take both of my hands in his. "I've been thinking," he says, his eyes twinkling as his thumbs graze over my knuckles.

When he doesn't immediately continue, I give his fingers a squeeze. "About what?"

"How I would've asked you to prom."

My eyebrows knit and my cheeks flush as I stare into his deep-brown eyes. For once, Flynn's emotions are locked away. I shift on the counter, butterflies collecting in my stomach.

"I wanted it to be good, you know," he says. "Way better than when Josh got Lara those donuts."

A laugh bursts out of me. I'd completely forgotten about Josh Murphy's pink-iced donuts.

"I looked up so many promposals, but none of them seemed right. Although, there was one that involved puppies."

"I *do* love puppies."

"I know you do." His grin fades into something more serious. "But then I realized that the reason I never got the words out is because I was trying to put on some big, impressive production. And I'm not going to make that mistake again."

I press a hand to my pounding heart. "Hotshot Hudson, are you asking me to be your date to prom?"

He shakes his head. "I'm actually thinking of something a little more permanent." He withdraws something from his pocket. A small, black velvet box.

I gasp as his lips tilt into a smile, a blush coating his cheeks. Flynn sinks to one knee and gazes up at me, love gleaming in his eyes. "I can't wait another minute, Quinn. Ten years took so much out of me. So, what do you say? Have I made up for high school enough that you'll let me stay forever this time?"

Tears spill from my eyes as I slip to the ground next to him and glide both my hands down his cheeks. "Forever isn't long enough. But let's start there."

ACKNOWLEDGMENTS

When we decided to write a romance novel together, we were probably as intimidated as we were excited. How does one even write a book with someone else? Would our writing styles gel together? Would the story become an uncontrollable mess of conflicting ideas? What about the confusion of working across opposing time zones? But when we sat down at opposite ends of the globe to write this book, we discovered almost immediately that this was going to be a wonderful process. Our ideas didn't clash; they complemented each other's. The two time zones turned us into a marvelously efficient 24-hour-a-day operation that made us excited to wake up in the morning and read what the other had written. And what brought us together in the first place was our mutual love for each other's writing as well as our shared taste in books (and book boyfriends), so of course, our writing styles fit together like Ruby and Flynn. Writing Hating the Best Man felt almost bewilderingly easy, and we hope this is just the beginning for us.

There were also more people involved in creating this book that we want to thank!

Firstly, to our amazing editor, Andria Henry: You were the first person in the world to read this story other than us, and your genuine excitement and encouragement inspired us to believe in ourselves and keep going. You are a brilliantly sharp and savvy editor, and we love working with you. Thank you!

A huge hug of appreciation to the super talented Juliette Cross, Alice Duke, N J Gray, and Lyndsey Gallagher for your beautiful words and support, which mean so much to us. Thank you for taking the time out of your busy writing schedules to read this little love story.

We also want to thank our wonderful beta readers for putting up with our early drafts and providing your valuable feedback: Megan Kitzmiller and Kathleen Pasqualini.

To Sam Palencia from Ink and Laurel—we are so in awe of you! Thank you for creating the cover of our dreams and working with us on our favorite part of being an author (covers, of course).

To Gib Dow—champion of the skies and real-life Flynn Hudson: We cannot thank you enough for all the time you spent answering our endless questions about flying and life as a corporate pilot. Asking you point-blank whether it was possible to fly a plane on autopilot and hook up with someone at the same time was, without a doubt, a hysterical highlight of our careers—especially when you gave us the answer we wanted! ;) In all seriousness, though, thank you for being so generous and cool. Without your insights, this book might've crashed before it even took off.

We must shout out our gratitude to all the Bookstagrammers and online friends who've supported us over the years—both separately and together. We couldn't do this without you, and we feel so lucky to be a part of this special community who fall as hard as we do for kissing books.

Finally, a big thank you to our families and friends for accepting us as we are. It turns out that being an incurable romantic is a lifelong condition, but within the love that we immerse ourselves in every day (literally), you are always at the heart of it.

Hugs and HEAs,
Jenny and Natalie x

ALSO BY JENNY FYFE & NATALIE MURRAY

STILL SPRINGS

(*Adult Contemporary Romance*)

Hating the Best Man

Loving the Worst Man (Fall 2023)

ALSO BY NATALIE

THE HEARTS AND CROWNS TRILOGY

(*Young Adult Fantasy Romance*)

Emmie and the Tudor King

Emmie and the Tudor Queen

Emmied and the Tudor Throne

OMNIBUS EDITIONS

(*New Adult Fantasy Romance*)

Emmie and the Tudor King New Adult Omnibus

ABOUT THE AUTHORS

Jenny and Natalie are romance authors living on opposite sides of the globe who found each other through fate and bonded over their mutual love for swoon-worthy fictional men and spicy books with loads of pining. They thought it could be fun to try and write one together, so they did and discovered that the only thing more addictive than writing about hot heroes falling hopelessly in love (with some hilarious high jinks on the side) was doing so with your writing soulmate. Jenny also writes fantasy romance as Jenny Hickman, and Natalie writes solo contemporary romance as Natalie Murray.